A Promise Fulfilled

PATTY DINELLI

abbott press

Abbott Press books may be ordered through booksellers or by contacting:

Abbott Press
1663 Liberty Drive
Bloomington, IN 47403
www.abbottpress.com
Phone: 1 (866) 697-5310

ISBN: 978-1-4582-2312-8 (sc)
ISBN: 978-1-4582-2311-1 (hc)
ISBN: 978-1-4582-2310-4 (e)

Library of Congress Control Number: 2021902385

Print information available on the last page.

Abbott Press rev. date: 02/10/2021

Acknowledgement

"I want to thank my husband Reno Dinelli and my whole family for their patience, understanding and help while I was working on my book. I would especially like to thank my son John, my granddaughter Sophia and my grandson in law Peter. If not for you three I would never have kept my computer working."

I don't know where to begin or if I even can. All that has happened seems like so long ago, and yet it isn't. It all seems like a dream, or like it was happening to someone else and I was just looking on, watching, unable to prevent all that was taking place. It was just outside the town of Baton Rouge, Louisiana, in the bayou, hidden from prying eyes. The air was heavy and sweet smelling inside the small neat cabin. It was hot, and you could hear the droning of the flying insects outside.

A young girl was weathering in pain, trying to hold back the scream she knew was coming, knowing she would not be able to stop it. She was only seventeen, so young to be going through all this, but there was no way to stop what was happening now. Nor did she want to stop.

The young man sitting in the dark corner was beginning to sweat profusely, wanting to help the young girl, to ease her pain, to make it stop, but he could not. Best to leave it to the older woman, bending over the young girl, coaxing her softly to help. Telling her the pain would soon stop and it would all be over and all the pain she was suffering would all be worth it.

"Why did I do this? Marta was right when she told me that all our actions have consequences," young Thomas said very softly, not wanting to draw any attention to himself.

My mind drifted back to January, to the year 1843. That's the year I was told that my father, Sir Phillip Westley Sanduvale the Third, set sail along with his wife, Lady Elizabeth Duncan Sanduvale, to America. My father had been granted twelve hundred acres of land in Baton Rouge, Louisiana, for serving the crown during the rebellion. They would move there to start a new life and raise their children.

It took four and a half months to cross the ocean, as the winter was very harsh and the captain had a hard time keeping the ship on the right course. After some time at sea, they finally docked at the port of Baton Rouge. After disembarking, Phillip went to the livery stable to purchase a two-seater wagon to transport all their luggage and themselves to their new home. The trip to the plantation took almost five hours, but when they did arrive, the place took their breath away. The house was a big two-story building, with a wide porch going all the way around it. All around the bottom of the two-story house were floor-to-ceiling windows, and when they went inside, Elizabeth was pleasantly surprised how light and airy the rooms were. There were six bedrooms upstairs, with a large master bedroom and five smaller bedrooms. The staircase going up to the rooms was wide and made of beautiful polished dark wood. There was a large kitchen with a large pantry adjoining it. There was a spacious family room, a parlor, and an office for Phillip to work out of.

Close to the house was a large barn. Also on the property were twelve cabins used to house the slaves that went along with the plantation. After Phillip checked out the house and barn, he went to the cabins to meet with the slaves. He found eight men and seven women staying in some of the cabins. Phillip was glad that they spoke some English. He asked who was in charge, and one of the men spoke up and said he was. He told Phillip his name was Joseph and that he was the foreman for the previous owner.

Phillip was glad that Joseph spoke English, and he asked Joseph if he would meet him in the morning to show him the property and to pick a couple of women to help his wife in the house. Joseph replied he would and would be outside at daybreak to show his new master around.

The next morning, Phillip and Joseph rode out at daybreak to survey the plantation. It was almost all flat ground, with a few rolling hills. On one of the hills, not too far from the plantation, was the previous owner's graveyard. It had about twenty graves on it. When Phillip asked Joseph if he knew who was buried in the graves, Joseph pointed to them and told him who was there. Three of the graves held the previous owner's wife and two sons. Some were slaves and their families. The rest he did not know, as it was before his time there.

After Phillip explored most of the land, they returned to the plantation. He told Joseph that he would inform him in a few days what they would be planting and where. He then went to tell Elizabeth about their land and that he would take her around to see it. But first, Phillip thought they would go into town and buy more slaves, as he did not think there were enough for what he had planned to plant.

The next morning, bright and early, Phillip with Elizabeth headed for Baton Rouge, taking the two-seated wagon to transport the new slaves back to the plantation. It took only three and a half hours to get there, as they were not as loaded as they were when they first arrived at Baton Rouge. When they arrived, Phillip went straight to the livery stable to board the horse and wagon. He asked the old man in charge to take care of the horse for him until they returned. He helped his wife down from the wagon, looked at his watch, and saw they had time to eat some lunch as the old man told them the auction would not start until one o'clock and it was only eleven thirty. Phillip looked around for a fairly clean looking place where they could enjoy some lunch.

They found a place close to the wharf, where the auction was to be held. They dined on fresh fish and fresh vegetables. When they finished the meal, they had just enough time to get to the auction. As the two hurried along, they passed a young black boy standing on the corner hollering, "Shine, shoeshine," to anyone who passed by him. Hearing that the boy could speak English, Phillip stopped and asked the boy his name.

"Jacob, sir. My name is Jacob."

"Well, young Jacob, tell me the name of your master, and I will purchase you from him."

Standing as straight and tall as he could, Jacob replied, "No, sir."

"What do you mean no?" said Phillip, starting to get irritated. "Do you mean you won't tell me his name or you don't want me to buy you?"

Jacob replied with a slight smile on his face, "I mean no, sir. I can't tell you his name. I is no slave. I is a free man with papers."

"Oh," said Phillip as Elizabeth hid her amusement in a cough. "Well," said Phillip as he turned a slight shade of red, "let me put it another way then. How would you like to come to work for me as my manservant for pay?"

Looking from the man to the women, Jacob thought. *They look like decent folk. It would be a roof over my head and food in my belly.*

"Well," said Phillip, "what do you say, Jacob? Is it a deal?"

Jacob's smile broadened as he stuck out his hand and replied, "Yes, sir, it is."

"Good," said Phillip, shaking Jacob's hand. "Meet me at the stables in a couple of hours."

"Yes, sir," he said as the two walked away.

When Phillip and Elizabeth finally made it to the auction, it had already started. Elizabeth was clearly appalled by all the men and women that were being led up to the platform to be auctioned off. They were shackled in chains with barely any clothes covering their bodies. The stench emitting from them was almost unbearable, as they had been kept in the hole of the ship for the entire trip here from Africa, where they had been captured. Their bodies and clothes were caked in their own feces and urine. You could see the weaker ones were sick as they stumbled along, trying to stay upright. Elizabeth definitely disapproved of all this and said so to her husband. Phillip explained to her that there were no other workers around that would do this type of fieldwork. Therefore, it was necessary for him to purchase the slaves. Elizabeth still did not approve of owning a person, no matter what the reasons were.

Standing in the hot sun, smelling the awful odors, Elizabeth took out a scented handkerchief and placed it over her nose and mouth. She thought she would be sick as she reached over and touched Phillip's arm. Turning his attention to his wife, he saw how pale she was. He took her by the arm and led her away from the crowd to a place beneath a shaded tree, where the wind blew away from the auction. Phillip told her to wait for him there. He would come back for her when he finished his purchases.

Elizabeth sat down on a bench under a tree. After a while, Elizabeth felt better. When Phillip returned to the auction, it was well underway. In order to buy some of the strongest of the lot, Phillip had to pay a higher price, but he was able to purchase ten fairly healthy men and eight able-bodied women to help his wife when she needed help.

Elizabeth was happy to sit and wait, as she did not like watching the men and women's faces as they were being sold off like animals. After a while, Elizabeth, feeling better, got up to return to where her husband was. On her way over, she looked at the platform where the auction was taking place. She stopped as there was a very young black girl still standing there alone. What caught Elizabeth's eye was the tiny baby. The girl held tightly to her breast. She was nude from the waist up, as had been the other slaves. Looking over and seeing his wife standing there, Phillip finished paying the slave master what he owed him, then walked over to where his wife was. Looking in the direction his wife was looking, he spotted the young girl with the baby.

Phillip, knowing his wife all too well, knew exactly what she was thinking, and as he walked over to stand next to her, he gently said, "No."

"What do you mean no?" she replied to him.

"I mean no, I will not buy you this young girl, as I have already bought eight women to help when you need them. And the ones I have purchased are far healthier than this one, and besides, this one has an extra mouth that will need to be fed when it gets older," he replied.

"Really, Phillip, just how much can this tiny thing eat?" she said to him with pleading eyes she knew he could not resist.

Looking the young girl over, Phillip thought to himself, *The girl would not be half bad if she could be rid of the filth she has all over her.*

"I don't know," he said out loud. "Maybe someone has already purchased her."

The slave master, standing close to them and overhearing their conversation, quickly spoke up. "No, no one has bought this one, as no one wants the baby."

"What will happen to her and her child?" Elizabeth asked the man.

"I will send her to another port to try to auction her off again. If you are willing to buy them, I could be persuaded to cut my price on this pair. Besides, she has good teeth," said the man as he pulled her lip up to expose a good set of teeth. Phillip did not like this man—the way he treated the slaves, as if he were bargaining for the price of a horse.

Looking from his wife, with her irresistible pleading eyes, to the greedy slave master, Phillip sighed and gave in. After paying the reduced price for the girl, he told Elizabeth to wait there with the girl while he went after the wagon. When he got to the livery stable, Jacob was sitting by the wagon the old man had pointed out, which belonged to Phillip.

"Good, you're here," said Phillip. "Climb aboard. You can help me load up the slaves I just purchased."

He looked over at Jacob. As he paid the old man for taking care of his horse, he noticed the odd look on Jacob's face.

"Is there a problem?" Phillip asked Jacob.

Making his face go blank, Jacob replied, "No, sir, no problem at all."

When they arrived at the wharf, Phillip and Jacob jumped

down. Phillip helped his wife up into the front seat. He told Jacob to lift the young girl holding the baby and put her in the second seat. Jacob did so while holding his breath and wrinkling up his nose. The two men then proceeded to load the other slaves into the back of the wagon, bound together so they could not escape. When Phillip and Jacob climbed into their seats, Phillip reached under his seat, pulled out a rifle, then handed it to Jacob, telling him that if anyone tried anything, he was to shoot them. Jacob's eyes widened as he took the gun with shaky hands. As it turned out, Phillip needn't have worried. Everyone was so exhausted that escaping was the last thing on anyone's mind.

It was a slow journey back to the plantation. By the time they arrived, it was already getting dark. Phillip pulled up to the front of the house and helped his wife down. Then he helped the girl and her baby get off the wagon. Climbing back on board the wagon, he told his wife he would be up later, as he wanted to get the slaves unloaded and in their cabins for the night. Phillip pulled up to one cabin, got down, and was met by Joseph. Together, the three men unloaded the ten men into the cabin. As Joseph was from the same vicinity in Africa as some of the men, Phillip had Joseph tell them in their strange language to lie down, cover themselves with the blankets provided to them and get some rest. The ones who understood Joseph did as he said. The ones who did not understand him just followed the others, as they were just too tired to care.

Phillip looked them over and saw all but two had lain down. One of the two men who was still standing had a silly look on his face, as if he did not comprehend what was going on around him. Phillip motioned for him to lie down, but the man just grinned at him and stood there. Irritated, Phillip reached down, grabbed the rope tied to the man's ankle, and jerked on it, sending the bewildered man sprawling to the floor. The man still had that silly grin on his face, as Phillip threw him the blanket. Phillip turned his attention to the other man. Looking up into the big man's eyes, Phillip took a few steps backward. The look was so intimidating, it made Phillip afraid for a second. Looking again into those eyes, Phillip saw the triumph the man felt and knew he had made a mistake retreating from him. Phillip reached down, picked up the bullwhip he had brought with him, and showed it to the big man. Upon seeing this, the man, with a look of murder in his eyes, lay down. *Good*, thought Phillip, *he knows the bullwhip*. Phillip looked the man over once again, taking in all the tattoos on his arms, chest, and face, which made him look very sinister.

Phillip shut the cabin door and had a lock put on it. He then had Joseph take the women slaves to another clean cabin and tell them to lie down and cover themselves with the blanket. Without any trouble from them, he had Joseph stand guard on the cabins for the night. Phillip had Jacob follow him to the big house and showed him to a spacious, clean room on the bottom floor of the house, behind the kitchen. He told Jacob it was his room. The room had a nice soft bed with a desk and chair. It also contained a wardrobe to hang his clothes in, when he got some. Phillip told Jacob goodnight, and that he would see him in the morning with instructions on what his job would entail.

When Phillip went upstairs to his and Elizabeth's bedchamber, he found Elizabeth sound asleep. Phillip quickly undressed and donned his nightshirt. Getting into bed, he reached over and pulled his wife close to him. Not quite waking up, Elizabeth snuggled up to her husband. Touching his cold feet, she came wide awake. "Oh, good. You're awake," Phillip said, smiling to himself.

"I am now," she replied, a little annoyed. Turning toward him, she asked if everything was all right.

Phillip told Elizabeth about the two men, saying he felt he had gotten cheated and thought he should return them both to the slave master and get his money back. "Are you sure you can't work with them? Maybe, in time, they will learn to do what you want," Elizabeth said.

"I don't think so. The one that acts so simple may be taught and does not seem like he would hurt anyone. But the big one I am not so sure of. I think he could become a problem. But enough about them. I have a problem of my own, and I think you might be able to help me with it," Phillip said as he pulled his wife close and kissed her deeply.

The next morning, Elizabeth was up early. She had breakfast, then went outside to begin what she knew was going to be a long day. Phillip met her in the courtyard not far from the cabins and asked what she would need. Elizabeth asked her husband if he could spare a few of his strongest men for her to use today to help her with her chore. Phillip replied that he could, as he was only going to map out the fields he would be planting. He kissed his wife goodbye, then told Joseph to get two of the strongest of the old slaves and send them to his wife. Then Joseph and the others were to go with him.

After Phillip and the others left, the two slaves came over to Elizabeth. She had them start a big fire in the courtyard, then go to the barn and bring the big washtub next to the fire. When the fire burned down to mere embers, she had them place the tub on the coals. Elizabeth then had them bring buckets of water and fill the tub to the brim. When she thought the water was ready, the two men went and brought out one of the slaves. She had the men strip the loincloth off him, and with a terrific battle, they put him in the tub. Keeping the man in the tub was hard, as he thought he was going to be cooked and eaten. Scrubbing him with the scrub brush and soap was almost impossible. When Elizabeth thought the man was clean enough, she had him rinsed with clean water, hauled out of the tub, and wrapped with a clean blanket. He was then taken to a clean cabin, where he was given clothes and was shown how to put them on, which resulted in another battle. Afterward, the exhausted man was given something to eat and left to rest.

This went on all through the morning until all the men were clean, clothed, and fed—all except the tattooed man. He had to be tied to a tree, with water and soap heated in a bucket, which was then thrown on him until he appeared clean enough. He was then rinsed, dried, and taken to a cabin by himself. He was given clothes but tore them up, all except the pants. He tore the legs almost off of them but left enough to cover his most private parts. After all that, the big man was worn out, so he was left some food and locked in his cabin.

Then the real battle started as Elizabeth and three of the strongest women attempted the same routine with the new women slaves. They fought like wild animals, kicking, clawing, and biting. When it was all done, Elizabeth hobbled back to the house, rubbing her bruised arms. She was exhausted but knew she wasn't finished yet. Elizabeth had the woman slave, named Anna, who worked in the house, prepare a bath of hot water, not for herself but for the young girl with the baby, and she was not looking forward to the encounter.

Anna had set up the tub in the room that had been given to the girl to sleep in the night before. When Elizabeth and Anna entered the room, the girl was not in the bed. In fact, the bed had not been slept in at all. Elizabeth looked around the room and found the girl behind the bed, holding her baby tightly to her body. Speaking in a soft voice, in the same strange language Joseph had spoken to the men the night before, Anna told the girl to come out, but she would not move from where she was at. Her eyes were big pools of black, and Elizabeth could see she was frightened, but no matter how hard they tried, she would not budge.

Getting irritated, Anna went behind the bed, grabbed the baby away from the young girl, and started to go to the other side of the room, but before she made it around the bed, the young girl jumped up and onto the bed, then onto poor Anna's back. She was screaming like a wild animal while Anna was screeching like a wild woman. The young girl was pulling Anna's hair and biting her neck.

Not knowing how to defuse the situation, Elizabeth quickly took the baby from Anna, who was by now hysterical. Elizabeth held the baby by one leg over the tub of water. Seeing this, the young girl climbed off Anna's back and moved forward toward her baby. She was whimpering softly to herself, and her eyes were pleading with Elizabeth not to hurt her child. Anna, now very mad, struck with full force. Grabbing the girl from behind in a strong bear hug, she lifted her off the floor and flung her into the water headfirst without removing her bottom cloth. Elizabeth hurriedly laid the now screaming baby on the bed and went to help Anna with the choir at hand before Anna could drown the sputtering girl.

Between the two women, they scrubbed the girl clean. All the dirt and grime was gone, along with perhaps some skin. Her hair shone, as did her whole body. They lifted her out of the tub and wrapped a blanket around her. Wrapping a towel around her hair, Elizabeth motioned for Anna to put the girl on the bed while she quickly picked up the baby to bathe it also. As Elizabeth put the tiny little boy, as she discovered that was what it was, close to the water. All the girl did was watch as she was too exhausted to do anything else. After getting the baby bathed, dried, and wrapped in a warm cloth, Elizabeth handed the baby to the girl, who immediately put it to her small breasts, where the baby latched on and quieted down to eat.

After Elizabeth and Anna cleaned up the room, they left the two alone to rest. The two women made their way to the kitchen, where they ate a little fruit, cheese, and bread, as they were too exhausted to fix anything else to eat and it was close to the evening meal. While the two women ate, Elizabeth asked Anna how she had gotten her name. Anna explained that all the slaves were given names like hers by the previous owners. She told Elizabeth that their real names were too hard for the white people to pronounce.

When Phillip came home that evening, he seemed happy with all that he and Joseph had accomplished. As he was explaining to Elizabeth about the crops and what he was going to plant, he noticed that Elizabeth was hardly listening to him. In fact, she looked as if she was about to fall asleep in her soup.

"Elizabeth, am I boring you?" he asked her.

"What? I'm sorry. I guess I didn't hear you. I had a very exhausting day," she replied.

"Oh, do tell me what has exhausted you so that you can hardly stay awake," Phillip said.

At the tone of his voice, she answered her husband sarcastically, "I am sure you would find it rather dull compared to your day." At that, she got up, excused herself, and went upstairs to bed.

The next morning, Phillip had Joseph gather all the new slaves in the courtyard, and with the help of Joseph, he explained what he expected of them. "If you do what is expected of you, you will be treated well, get plenty to eat, and have a good place to live in." He went on, "If not, you will be punished. As I point to you, you will step forward, and you will be given a new name, as your names are too hard to pronounce."

One by one, they all stepped forward and received their new names, all except the slow-witted one and the big tattooed man. He decided to let his wife try her hand with the slow one as she had asked to be able to try. The big man refused to step forward. After the third time, Phillip lost patience with him. He reached down and picked his gun up from off the ground. As a chicken scurried across the courtyard, Phillip took aim and fired his gun. The chicken flew into the air, feathers flying everywhere, then dropped to the ground, dead.

There was a loud "awww" coming from the slaves as they retreated from Phillip. Most of them remembered the gun from some of their relatives being shot while being captured from their villages in Africa. *So they do know what a gun is. Good,* thought Phillip as the big man came forward to hear his new name but would not acknowledge it. He would only respond to his African name, Man-te-nee-wa. When Elizabeth heard the shot, she ran outside to see what had happened. She ran over to where Phillip was holding his gun up to the group of workers. She refused to call them slaves.

"What happened?" she asked her husband.

"Nothing. I was just demonstrating how my gun works," Phillip replied as he motioned for them to move forward and follow Joseph. He kissed her goodbye, told her he would be back around dusk, then added, "Oh, by the way, I am leaving you another one to teach. No name yet. Thought you would like to name this one yourself." He then turned and joined the workers.

As Elizabeth turned, she came face to face with the one her husband called slow-witted. At first, she was startled, but as she looked him in the eye, she could see he would not harm her or anyone, for that matter. He stood there looking Elizabeth over with a wide grin on his face. He looked so silly, she started to grin also. When he saw that, he jumped up and clapped his hands, frightening Elizabeth, making her take a step back. As she did, he did as well. Seeing he thought Elizabeth was playing a game, she stood very still with her hands at her side. He did the same, still with the silly grin on his face. Elizabeth raised her hand, gently touched her finger to his chest, and said to him, "Sam, your name will be Sam."

Sam poked his finger into Elizabeth's shoulder, almost knocking her down, but said nothing. Elizabeth realized that Sam could or would not talk. She groaned out loud and said, "Now what? What am I supposed to do with you now, Sam?" He just stood there, grinning. Elizabeth turned to go to the garden, where the other's she had to teach to speak English was waiting for her. As she started to walk, Sam also started to walk, so close, he was almost walking on her. She stopped, and so did Sam. Using her hands, she finally made Sam understand that he must walk beside her, not behind her.

Using the hand technique, over the next few months, and with the help of Anna and a few of the other older slave women, they were able to teach the new women to speak English, at least enough to communicate with Elizabeth and Phillip. Sam would mimic everything Elizabeth or the others did, and when he did it right, everyone would clap their hands, along with Sam. Elizabeth took the young girl and her baby under her wing and took extra care with teaching her everything. She found out the girl's name was Mar-ta-nee-tra, but because it was so hard to pronounce, Elizabeth shortened it to Marta. She also named Marta's baby Eli. The men all learned English while working in the fields with the older slaves.

Everything went along smoothly. Phillip got all the crops in, in time for the spring rains, so everything flourished. The house was in perfect condition for them to have their neighbors over and get acquainted; all the workers got along and worked well together, except for the one called Man-te-nee-wa. Every Sunday, the local preacher would stop by after the Sunday service to help teach the workers. They learned new songs and loved singing them out in the courtyard. A few of the workers chose partners, and the preacher would insist that he marry them so they didn't live in sin in the eyes of the Lord. Man-te-nee-wa was the only one to cause trouble and be punished for it, and for this, his hatred for Phillip and Elizabeth grew worse every day. Many times, Phillip wanted to sell him again at auction, but Elizabeth would talk him out of it, saying even Man-te-nee-wa deserved second chances.

One morning, Elizabeth didn't come down for breakfast, so Marta was on her way up the stairs with a tray containing eggs, bacon, and toast, with jam and a cup of hot coffee. While climbing the stairs, Phillip was on his way down when the two passed each other. Phillip, seeing how well Marta had filled out in the last several months, reached over and caressed her cheek. Surprised, Marta moved past him in a hurry and entered Elizabeth's bedchamber, she noticed the room was still dark and Elizabeth was on the side of the bed holding the chamber pot. Marta sat the tray down and went to the window and threw open the curtains to let some light in.

When she saw Elizabeth, she could see she was very sick. Marta went over and took the chamber pot from her and put her back into bed. She then took the tray of food and placed it in front of Elizabeth, telling her to eat a bite and she would probably feel better. When Elizabeth looked at the food in front of her and caught a whiff of it she threw up her hands and scrambled out of bed reaching for the chamber pot all in one motion. When she threw her hands into the air, it knocked the tray of food also into the air. When Elizabeth finished being sick, she looked up and started laughing. She laughed so hard, tears ran down her cheeks. When the tray flew up, the food landed on Marta. The eggs landed on her head with a piece of bacon, and a piece of toast with jam was stuck on the side of her face.

"What's so funny,?" Marta asked, getting a little perturbed. All Elizabeth could do was hold her sides to keep them from hurting from laughing so hard.

Marta reached up to remove the egg from her hair, and when she did, she broke the egg yolk. It ran down off her hair and into one eye and dripped onto her shoulder. Seeing this made Elizabeth sick all over again. Grabbing the chamber pot, she began groaning and throwing up. Marta cleaned up the mess that was made while Elizabeth climbed into bed and held real still. Heading for the door, Marta said under her breath, "Serves you right for laughing at me."

Elizabeth groaned.

"I heard that." Going out the door, Marta replied, "Sure you did. How could you not with those big ears of yours?"

Marta went downstairs, cleaned herself up, then made another tray for Elizabeth and went back upstairs to her room. Elizabeth was still lying in bed, not moving for fear of getting sick again. Looking at the pale women, Marta had a pang of regret, but it quickly passed as she moved to the side of the bed, holding the tray away from Elizabeth. Opening her eyes, Elizabeth groaned, saying, "Please, Marta, no more."

It was Marta's turn to laugh. "This will make you feel better, I promise you. Now sit up while I put this pillow behind you." Elizabeth carefully did as she was told. Marta handed Elizabeth a hot cup of tea with some peppermint in it, along with some salty crackers. Elizabeth sipped on tea and nibbled on the crackers while Marta sat on the side of the bed, very still.

After a while Elizabeth felt a little better. "How do you know all this?" Elizabeth asked the girl. "And where is Eli's father?"

With a fierce look on her face and her jaw clenched, Marta said, "I don't know the father of my boy."

"How could you not know who his father is?" Elizabeth insisted. Marta blurted out the story to Elizabeth. "It was on the ship where we were kept, down in the hole at the bottom. We were put there, all of us altogether. We were shackled hands and feet. We could hardly move without rolling on top of one another. One night, while I was asleep on the floor, I was suddenly picked up, turned, and thrown on the floor onto my stomach. My loincloth was pushed up, and I was mounted from behind by a strong man. He then plunged into me and raped me violently. Because we made so many stops along the way to auction off some of us, it took a long time to travel. Nine months later, two weeks before arriving here, I gave birth."

"I am so sorry," Elizabeth said. "I wish I could change everything back for all of you and make things better."

"No worry. I am all right here. I have a nice room for me and Eli. We have food, and I don't have to work hard in the fields."

"I am so happy you feel that way. I think you and I can become very good friends," said Elizabeth. "Well, if you feel we are friends, then, as your friend, I must tell you something."

"Yes, then what must you tell me," replied Elizabeth. "You are going to have a baby of your own."

"What? How can that be? How can you be so sure?" asked Elizabeth, trying to think back to when her last cycle was.

When Elizabeth realized she had missed a cycle, her face showed her excitement. It made Marta clap her hands together and laugh out loud. The two women hugged each other. "That is why I am so nauseated at the smell of food," she said, looking at Marta for confirmation as Marta slowly shook her head yes. Marta told her that some women get sick and some women don't. Some are sick for only a few months and some longer. "I can't wait for Phillip to get home so I can tell him the wonderful news," Elizabeth said excitedly. Elizabeth stayed in bed, lying quietly so as not to get sick again. She sipped on tea and nibbled on the crackers Marta kept her supplied with.

When the day started to turn to dusk, Elizabeth got up and got dressed, she brushed her long hair until it shined, then she proceeded to go downstairs to greet her husband when he arrived home. When Phillip and the workers came home, Phillip noticed his wife sitting on the porch. He also noticed she looked a little pale. Phillip dismounted from his horse and asked Jacob to take it to the stable and tend to it. After Jacob took the reins, he started toward the barn. Phillip hurried to the porch, taking the stairs two at a time. He was beside Elizabeth in an instant, getting down on his knees to be eye level with his wife. At the same time, Elizabeth rose to hug her husband. They came together, knocking Elizabeth back down to sit on the bench again and toppling Phillip over.

Elizabeth cried out, "Oooh, no," her face turning red from embarrassment.

As she went to stand to assist her husband, Phillip, putting his hand up to stop her, said, "Please stay seated, Elizabeth. I will come to you."

After Phillip got to his feet, he sat down on the bench beside his wife, who now had her hands over her face, shielding the grin, trying not to laugh out loud. "Are you all right?" Phillip asked Elizabeth.

"Yes, yes, I am just fine," she replied.

"Then what are you doing sitting out here on the front porch, and what do you find so amusing, Elizabeth?" Phillip asked.

"First, I am so sorry. It's just, you looked so startled when I knocked you over."

"Yes, and second?" he said, starting to get irritated.

"Well, you see ..."

She suddenly felt very shy. Maybe he wouldn't be pleased with her news. The tears just came. They weren't there a minute ago.

"For God's sake, Elizabeth, what is it?" he said, raising his voice in exasperation.

He doesn't have to shout, Elizabeth thought, now with a case of the hiccups.

"Please, tell me what's wrong," Phillip pleaded.

As Elizabeth turned to tell him her big news, with tears running down her cheeks and snot running from her nose, she looked pathetic. In between hiccups, she blurted out, "You ... hic ... are ... hic ... going ... hic ... to become a father."

The look on Phillip's face was one of disbelief. It turned to pure joy, and the wide grin Phillip got on his face told Elizabeth she need not worry, for he was elated over her news.

That night when they were in bed, Phillip asked how she knew she was going to have their child. She related the whole story from the beginning of her day to when he came home. They laughed together at the morning antics with the eggs. Then Phillip rolled over and gave her a very passionate kiss, and when he thought they were both ready and was about to mount her, Elizabeth suddenly rolled over, jumped from the bed, and reached for the chamber pot. On hearing his wife being sick, Phillip groaned, rolled over, and covered his head with his pillow.

Unfortunately for Phillip, Elizabeth was one of those women who would be sick with every little movement of the bed and any smell of food. After trying for one week to share a bed with her husband, Elizabeth decided to move into the room next to their room so her husband could get some sleep. One evening, Elizabeth retired early, as she was exhausted and wanted to get in a few hours of sleep before she was hit again with a bout of nausea. When Phillip went up to bed, he stopped at his wife's door and listened. When he heard no noise, he reached for the doorknob and was about to enter her room, thinking maybe tonight he would get lucky. But before he opened the door, he heard the familiar sound of his wife getting sick. Phillip turned and headed down stairs to his office for a drink of good old whiskey. When he stepped off the stairs, he noticed a light still burning in the kitchen. He went to investigate, and what he saw stopped him in his tracks.

In the soft light stood Marta, wearing a shift made from thin material, showing off the curves of her body. Her hair was not covered with the usual colored bandana that she wore. Marta was softly humming to herself while reaching up to put away the dishes on the shelf when Phillip came up behind her, placing both hands on her shoulders. He began kissing her ear, then her neck, and then her shoulders. Phillip turned her around. At first, Marta was surprised. Then she looked into Phillip's eyes and saw the lust she was all too familiar with. He leaned down and softly kissed her on the lips. Then he intensified the kiss by running his tongue over her tongue. He heard the small groan in her throat and knew she would give in to him.

Phillip picked the girl up and headed for the stairs, still kissing her deeply. When he got to the top, he went past his wife's bedchamber and stopped at the door to listen. Not hearing any movement, he continued to his bedchamber, went in, and gently laid Marta on the bed. Then he undid her shift and pulled it off her shoulders. At first, Marta began to panic, as she loved Elizabeth like a sister and did not want to betray her, but as Phillip assaulted her with kisses, her reserve started to fade from her mind, and she thought to herself, *I want to be loved. No, I need to be loved.* Marta was so caught up in the sensation that she was feeling, she began to kiss him back. Before that, Phillip had guilty feelings about what he was doing, but Marta's reaction surprised him and pleased him, as Elizabeth did not react to his lovemaking at all.

With Marta such a willing partner, Phillip quickly finished undressing the girl. Then he undressed himself. He got back on the bed and pulled her close to him, all the time caressing her breasts, her back, and her buttocks. When Marta started to do the same to Phillip, he almost lost control. Gently he laid her on her back, and she rolled onto her stomach. He rolled her back, and when she started to roll back onto her stomach, Phillip held her on her back. He kissed her eyes and her cheeks, down to her neck and then her breasts. She started to moan softly and thrash about, wanting to turn over so he could enter her, but to her surprise, he entered her gently from the front, moving slowly in and out of her. The sensations were building to a peak inside her, and she thought she would explode. Phillip, sensing she was nearing her climax, plunged deeper into her, and within seconds, they reached their climax together.

Marta started to cry out. Phillip kissed her to silence her and pulled the covers up over them. He pulled her to him and felt the wetness on her cheeks. He asked if he had hurt her. She replied, "Oh no. It was wonderful. I have never had such pleasure."

"But you have a baby. Surely you experienced that pleasure then?"

"No, no, the man who fathered my child took me by force, from behind, as that is the way it is done in Africa, as the animals do it." Now Phillip understood why she kept wanting to flip onto her stomach. They fell asleep, and when Phillip woke up, the sun was beginning to rise. He rolled over and saw Marta rolled into a ball sleeping as close to him as she could get. He was amazed at how responsive this girl was. Unable to stop himself, he bent down and kissed her, waking her up. At first, she didn't remember where she was, but as the realization set in, she sat straight up, staring at Phillip with a frightened look on her face.

Phillip put his finger to his lips and silently motioned for her to be quiet. He then got up and started to dress, motioning for her to do the same. Whispering to her, Phillip told her he was going downstairs; she should wait a few minutes, then follow him down if the coast was clear. She nodded, and he left. Marta felt so bad when she remembered last night but could not tell herself she did not enjoy it. Waiting for a while, she opened the door and started to make her way down the stairs silently. When she just got past Elizabeth's room, the door opened, and Elizabeth emerged from her room. Marta jumped, turning to face Elizabeth, who, in turn, jumped backward. Marta put her hand over her mouth to quell the scream and said, "Good Lord, you gave me such a start, missy."

With a knowing look on her face, Elizabeth replied, "Did I now?" Marta turned a deep red and thought to herself, *She knows.* Interrupting Marta's thought, Elizabeth, with a small smile on her face, swept past Marta and proceeded down the stairs. Once downstairs, Elizabeth swept into the kitchen, greeting her husband warmly, bending down to kiss his cheek. Expecting it to be Marta,

Phillip, caught off guard, choked on the coffee he was drinking. Patting him on the back, Elizabeth sweetly asked him if he was all right.

"Yes, yes, quite all right. It's just that I didn't expect you down this morning, as sick as you were last night."

"Oh, yes. Well, you see, I got over being sick and was waiting for you to come and tell me goodnight, but when you didn't, I just lay there listening to strange noises. I guess it must have been the wind blowing outside. Wouldn't you agree, dear?"

"Yes, of course, that must have been what you heard. What else could it have been?" he replied.

"Yes, indeed. What else could it have been?" Elizabeth said with a smile on her face.

Marta hurried into the kitchen after going to her own room to change her clothes and to put her kerchief on her head to cover her uncombed hair. As she was leaving her room, she encountered Jacob on his way to the kitchen also.

He stopped and said, "Good morning, Marta."

She noticed he had a funny look on his face. Jacob said, "I was on my way to the kitchen last night for a late snack when I saw two people going up the dark stairs. A man carrying a woman—must have been Master Phillip carrying his wife to bed." Turning a bright red, Marta did not reply but pushed past him and headed to the kitchen, saying to herself, *Good Lord, does everybody on this plantation know what I did last night?*

Entering the kitchen, Marta did not look at the two people sitting at the table having a polite conversation. She went straight to the stove and started to fix breakfast. Looking under her eyelashes at Elizabeth, who still had a sweet smile on her face, Marta, grinning to herself, took some bacon and slapped it on the hot stove. Within minutes, the room was filled with the smell of hot greasy bacon. As Jacob entered the room, Elizabeth was running out, almost knocking him down. "What the ... what's got into Missy Elizabeth?" he asked no one in particular. Marta, looking from Jacob to Phillip, just shrugged her shoulders, turned, and finished cooking breakfast for the two men with a smile on her face.

Twice a week, Marta would visit Phillip in his bedchamber. It was with an unspoken agreement between Elizabeth and Marta. Elizabeth was happy to let Marta take care of that part of her marriage to Phillip, as she did not care for it very much. Marta, on the other hand, liked it very much. The two women got along very well under this agreement, as Phillip was satisfied and happy, which made everyone else happy. Elizabeth was very confident that Phillip loved her very much and knew nothing would ever change that.

A few months went by, and Elizabeth's nausea improved, but she kept up the ruse for a few more months. She knew once she was over being sick, Phillip would want her back in his bed. She told herself she was doing it for Phillip, as she could not bring herself to please him like Marta could, surmising this from the sounds made coming from his room. Maybe, she thought, she would ask Marta to tell her how to please Phillip someday, but not now. But Phillip had other ideas and decided he wanted his wife back in his bed. It had been five months since he held her. He missed the conversations they had while lying together in bed. He felt he could forgo the lovemaking for the next few months until after the baby was born. The truth be told, the guilt he felt was beginning to bother him, so that night, he made love to Marta for the last time and told her he was sorry. He had enjoyed their time together, but it was time to end it. Marta was sorry, as she too enjoyed the lovemaking, but she understood what he was saying as she also felt guilty. She did not spend the night with Phillip but left when they were through.

On a warm day in the late fall, Elizabeth, feeling much better, being back in her husband's arms at night, decided to sit in the garden and soak up some sun. She sat there admiring the garden and daydreaming of the birth of her baby, due within a couple of weeks. While sitting there half asleep from the warm sun, she heard a noise. She turned to see who was there. It was Sam. He always seemed to find her whenever she was outside. He had picked some flowers from the garden and brought them to her as he had a big surprise for her. When she saw it was Sam, she got a big grin on her face, as Sam always brightened up her day. He offered her the straggly bouquet, and when she thanked him, she asked if he could find a vase to put them in with some water until she went into the house. Sam shook his head yes and hurried off to do Elizabeth's bidding.

Elizabeth turned back around, facing the sun once more while she waited for Sam to return with the vase. A few minutes later, she thought she heard Sam's footsteps returning, and when she went to turn around, she was grabbed from behind and brought up against a hard body. Knocking the chair over, unable to move or breathe, she started to panic, and when she went to scream for help, a large, dirty hand covered her mouth. She was held so tight, she thought she would pass out, so she tried to wiggle and kick but to no avail. Then everything went black as a big hand hit her on her jaw and she was knocked unconscious.

When she regained consciousness, she was being dragged through a sugar cane field, where she could see she was surrounded on all sides by the tall sugar cane stalks. Realizing she had woken up, her captor let go of the arm he had been dragging her by and let it fall beside her. She felt as though her arm had been pulled out of the socket and had no feeling in it.

Her captor came around and stood over the top of her. To her horror, she saw it was Man-te-nee-wa. She started to scream, but he kicked her in her side, making the scream die in her throat. He reached down and tore her thin dress and shift down to her waist, exposing her swollen white breasts. Reaching down, he squeezed them hard, making Elizabeth catch her breath and cry out. She then started to fight with all she had as she knew what would come next. Man-te-nee-wa hit her again, this time, a glancing blow to her head. Dazed, she held still. As her head cleared somewhat, she realized there was no use in fighting. She thought if she lay still, he would do what he wanted, then leave her and run away.

Unbeknownst to either one of them, Sam had come back and

seen what had taken place in the garden. He hid, as he was afraid of Man-ta-nee-wa. He followed them to the sugar cane field and hid a few rows away from them. Sitting on the ground with his arms around his knees, he rocked back and forth, silently crying for his beloved Elizabeth. As the violence continued against his Elizabeth, he started to emit sounds like an animal, making Man-ta-nee-wa stop and listen as the sounds raised the hair on the back of his neck. When he didn't hear any more, he looked back down at his captive.

When he saw she would not fight him anymore, he turned her on her stomach, tore her dress down the back, and violently raped her. She lay still, hoping that was the end, but it was not. He turned her over, and she saw in his crazed eyes all the hatred and loathing he had for her. She started to fear for her life and that of her unborn child. Elizabeth started to scream, but the blow stopped it, and the next one broke her nose and split her lip open. As she opened her eyes and looked into his, she knew she was going to die.

She put her arms around her stomach, trying to protect her precious little baby, but to no avail. The next blow came from the machete he carried with him. It sliced through Elizabeth's shoulder, across her breast, and down to her stomach. The sound that came from just beyond where Man-te-nee-wa was standing sent chills down his spine. He had never heard a sound like it before, not from any creature or man. Frightened beyond words, Man-te-nee-wa dropped the machete and ran for his life.

When Elizabeth came to and opened her eyes, Man-te-nee-wa was gone and sitting on the ground, holding her head in his lap, was Sam, dear, lovable Sam. Tears were streaming down his face, and he was trying to wipe away all the blood, but there was way too much. Elizabeth reached up with her good arm and patted him on the cheek.

"Shhhh," she whispered to him, trying to console him.

"Missy Lizzy," Sam said in a shaky almost, inaudible voice. That was the big surprise he wanted to give her that afternoon in the garden. He had been working for weeks to say it and finally was able to say it, so he went to the garden to say it to her. Elizabeth was very surprised and very pleased when she heard what he said and tried to give him a big smile. Not knowing how to help Elizabeth or to stop the bleeding, Sam tried to pull the flesh together, and that's how Phillip and the workers found them.

Phillip had arrived home with Joseph and the others just before dusk. When he rode into the courtyard, he got a funny feeling in the pit of his stomach. He dismounted and asked Joseph to care for his horse. After Joseph took the horse and headed for the barn, Phillip started up the stairs. When Marta came around the corner, Phillip asked her where Elizabeth was. Marta replied that she didn't know, as she was looking for her as well. She told Phillip the last time she had seen her, she was in the garden, talking to Sam. Phillip descended the stairs and headed for the garden with Marta following behind him. When they got to the garden, no one was there. Phillip took in the scene and knew something had happened. With the chair overturned, the strewn flowers on the ground, he started to get a chill.

"Maybe they went to the shed for something," Marta said, hoping she was right. When they got to the shed, there was no one there, either. Starting to panic, Phillip went to the barn and rang the emergency bell. When everyone heard the sound of the bell clanging. They hurried out to the courtyard to see what had happened. Phillip explained what was wrong, that he could not find Missy Elizabeth as they all called her. He told them that she was last seen in the garden with Sam and he wanted everyone to fan out to search around the whole grounds. Marta and Anna went back into the house to search it thoroughly but turned up nothing.

When everyone met back at the courtyard and reported they had found nothing, Phillip and Jacob went back to the garden to see if anything had been missed. Jacob called Phillip over to show him the drag marks and some blood on the ground. Phillip got a huge knot in the pit of his stomach. He told Jacob to go to the barn with Joseph, get all the torches there were, hand them out to everyone, and then meet him in the courtyard. He told another one of the slaves to go get the hounds to track his wife and Sam, then went to get his gun. When he got to the courtyard, all the torches were lit. He told everyone to spread out and follow him. They were to search every inch of ground until his wife was found. Jacob and Joseph led the way, holding their torches close to the ground to follow the drag marks. It was slow going as the search party looked in every shadow and behind every tree. They found one of her slippers. A few yards away, they found the other one. Phillip was so afraid for his wife, his heart was beating loudly in his ears from the blood rushing to his head. He could only think that Sam had finally gone off the deep end and had kidnapped his wife to do her harm.

When they got close to where the two people were, they could hear the awful moaning of an injured animal, but when they came upon the gruesome scene, they found it wasn't from an animal. It was Sam, rocking back and forth with Elizabeth in his lap. When Jacob and Joseph moved aside so Phillip could get through to his wife, they had tears running down their faces. The scene Phillip came upon was so gruesome that he almost threw up.

Swallowing back the bile in his throat, Phillip screamed, "Noooo," and rushed forward. "You bastard. Get away from her. What have you done?" Seeing Phillip rushing toward him, Sam started to panic as he looked into Phillip's crazed eyes.

As Jacob and Joseph came forward to help Phillip get Sam away from Elizabeth, moving past her mutilated bloody form, they crossed themselves as they knew something evil happened here. The two men held Sam as Phillip gently lifted Elizabeth's head off Sam's lap. Then Jacob and Joseph kicked and beat Sam almost unconscious for what they thought he had done to their beloved mistress. Phillip sat down beside his injured wife and gently lifted her up onto his lap. With tears streaming down his face, he lowered his head to her ear. He told her how much he loved her and for her to please hang on, that he could not live without her.

Elizabeth opened her eyes and looked up at her grieving

26

husband. She then, with all the strength she had left, lifted his hand and placed it on her stomach. With her eyes pleading, she looked from his eyes to her stomach. At first, Phillip did not know what she wanted him to do. Then, with a horrified look on his face, he shook his head no. "Please, don't ask me to do it," he softly said to her. "I can't do it. It would risk your life. I couldn't live with that." Looking at him again, pleading, he relented. Phillip gently laid his wife on the ground. He told all that were gathered there to come forward, make a circle around them, and hold their torches up high to give him all the light he would need for what he was about to do.

There was a lot of moaning and groaning among the gathering, but Phillip ignored them. He bent down and took out the knife he always carried with him. He looked at his wife once again, and when she smiled at him, he mouthed the words, "I love you." She closed her eyes. He cut just below her rib cage and opened up her stomach to expose the baby. He then motioned for Marta to come forward and lift the infant out while he cut the cord. Marta wrapped the baby in her apron and cleaned out its mouth. A few seconds later, the baby started to cry, a small, frail sound but loud enough to be heard. A loud cheer went through the crowd, and the women wept for their mistress, who had been so good, so kind to them all.

Marta tried to hand the baby over to Phillip, but he would not take his son. He was so consumed with despair over what had happened to his wife, he was unable to rationalize what was going on around him. Exasperated by Phillip's actions, Marta pushed him aside and bent down close to Elizabeth's chest. She heard the faintest breathing, getting close to Elizabeth's ear. Marta softly said, "Open your eyes and look at your tiny son." When Marta got no response, she said it louder. "Elizabeth, open your eyes now. Do you hear me?" Panic starting to set in, Marta shouted, "Elizabeth, wake up now."

Slowly opening her eyes, Elizabeth, looking dazed from Marta to Phillip, who had bent down beside Marta, said, "Very low. You don't have to shout."

Marta, now crying, held the baby up close to Elizabeth's face.

The smile that slanted across Elizabeth's face at seeing her son was more than the group gathered there could take. Tears ran down all their faces, even the most hardened men.

Marta stood up and left the babe lying on his mother's chest. She moved back to give Phillip and Elizabeth time together. Elizabeth looked into her husband's eyes as he looked into hers. Without saying a word, they each conveyed their love for one another. Taking hold of her hand, he kissed it gently. When he looked back at her, he saw she was gone. It took Phillip about twenty minutes to gain control of himself and stand up. When he did, he turned to look at Sam, still being held by Jacob and Joseph. The look on Phillip's face made everyone step backward and cross themselves.

Not trusting himself from grabbing Sam and choking the life out of him with his bare hands, he told two men to take him to the plantation to lock him in a cabin until he got there. As the two men did as they were told, the other men joined them. Jacob and Joseph took hold of the hounds on their leash and tried to get them to return to the way of the plantation, but they just kept barking in the other direction and pulling on their leash, wanting to track something moving toward the river. Then, one of the hounds broke loose and took off. Jacob told Joseph to release his hound. When he did, the hound took off after his partner. Jacob and Joseph took off after the dogs.

Phillip, wrapping his wife's body in his coat, bent down, carefully lifted her up into his arms, and started the long journey home with the women following him, softly crying and humming a hymn as they walked. When they finally reached the plantation, all the men were mulling around the courtyard, waiting for Phillip to return with his wife's body. Phillip asked Anna and one other woman to take his wife's body upstairs to their room, clean her up, dress her, and leave her on the bed. Anna and one of the stronger slave women did as Phillip asked. When he could no longer see his wife's body, he turned his eyes in the direction of the cabins. When the group of people looked at him, they all crossed themselves once again. There was no sign of reason in Phillip's eyes, only hatred at what that bastard had done to his beloved wife.

Phillip told two men to go get Sam, to bring him out to the courtyard. While the men did as Phillip instructed, Phillip went to the barn, got a rope and crate, brought it out to the courtyard, and threw the rope over a tree limb. He then placed the crate under the limb. When the men brought Sam out, he was unrecognizable. He had been beaten about his face and body by all the men for what they thought he had done to their mistress. When he was taken over to Phillip and looked into Phillip's eyes, with his one eye that would open, Sam became very frightened and tried to break free, but Phillip motioned for the men to tie the rope around Sam's neck and place him on the crate. They did, then stepped back away from him.

Marta, seeing what Phillip was about to do, ran forward, taking hold of Phillip's arm. She screamed, "Nooo, please don't do this. Sam could not have done this awful thing. He loved Elizabeth, as we all did."

On hearing Marta's voice, Sam tried to turn his head in her direction but could not. With tears rolling down his face, Sam said, "Missy Lizzy." Hearing Sam utter his wife's name enraged Phillip even more. With his arm raised, he brought it back hard against Marta, knocking her backward to the ground. In the same instance, he kicked the crate out from under Sam's feet. Dazed, all Marta could do was watch as Sam jerked and twitched on the rope. It was over in seconds as the weight of Sam's body broke his neck.

The slaves did not know what to do. They felt bad. They did remember how Elizabeth had taken Sam under her wing and taught him how to do things for himself and how he loved her for it. They remembered how Missy Elizabeth had treated Sam with the utmost respect and kindness. She would rebuke anyone who teased Sam or did him harm. They also remembered the little things Sam would make for Missy Elizabeth and his stupid grin when she praised him for it. Now, most were beginning to have doubts as to whether or not Sam did this terrible deed, but they said, "Who else would have done it?" as they looked at each other.

Not long after the hanging, Jacob and Joseph came running into the courtyard with the hounds still barking and jumping on Jacob, trying to reach something he was carrying. As they approached Phillip, Jacob saw Marta still lying on the ground, silently crying. He went to her and knelt down beside her. Lifting her up, he asked what had happened. Marta pointed to the tree, and when Jacob saw what had been done, he felt he had failed. Phillip came over to the two men. He asked them where they had been. Jacob said that when the dogs got loose, they had picked up another scent and followed it to the river.

"When we got to the river, we found this." He unrolled a blood-smeared shawl belonging to Phillip's wife, and out rolled a bloody arm. "What the hell is that?" asked Phillip as everybody crowded around for a closer look at the object on the ground. "If you look closer in the light, you will see it is Man-ta-nee-wa's arm."

Holding a torch close, Phillip did indeed see the tattooed arm of Man-ta-nee-wa. "What happened to him?" Phllip askied.

"We think it was Man-ta-nee-wa that took your wife, not Sam."

There was a loud gasp from the slaves as they stepped back and again crossed themselves. Phillip motioned for them all to be quiet and told Joseph to go on. "We think Sam saw him take her and followed them to the surar cane field. Being afraid of Man-ta-nee-wa, Sam hid, watching what was happening to his beloved Elizabeth, not being able to stop him. We think when Man-ta-nee-wa saw us coming. He got afraid, killed Elizabeth, and ran off toward the river. He probably thought he was safe, so he sat or laid down to rest. When he did, the gators smelled the blood on him, attacked him, and ate all but the arm we found."

Phillip, overwhelmed at what he had done to poor Sam in his fit of rage, backed away and headed for the house. He went straight to his office and took a bottle of whisky, poured a glass full, and drank it. He didn't know if he was going to be sick to his stomach or not as the realization of all that had happened tonight began to sink in. He drank almost the whole bottle before he passed out.

Jacob helped Marta up, and between the two of them, they managed to cut Sam down, drag him to his cabin, and get him on the bed, where they cleaned him up. They left him there for three days. During those three days, Phillip stayed drunk, trying to forget what had happened to Elizabeth, what he had done to Sam. Phillip listened to the drums the slaves beat on, day and night, wondering when they would stop. The slaves lit a fire and danced around it for three days, dancing and chanting. On the second day, they picked up Manta-nee-wa's arm and threw it in the fire, raising their arms to the sparks caused by the arm to chase away the evil. On the third day, they stopped, all coming together in the courtyard. Some went to Sam's cabin, wrapped his body in a clean white cloth, and brought it out to the courtyard. Some of the women, including Marta and Anna, went into the house. They wrapped Elizabeth's body as well in a clean white cloth. They then carried her down the stairs, where they were stopped by Phillip. "Where are you going with my wife?" asked Phillip.

Marta stepped forward and gently said, "It is time for them to be buried. As you know, in this heat, the bodies will not last any longer."

"Yes, yes, of course. Please give me a few minutes to clean myself up."

"We will be in the courtyard, where we will place the bodies in coffins that the men made," replied Marta, not looking at Phillip as they went on outside. When Phillip finally made it outside, he saw they were all ready to go. Six slaves were on each side of the coffins, ready to carry them to the gravesite on a hill close to the house. They waited for Phillip to lead the way, and when he stepped to the front of them, they started off, singing softly a song Elizabeth loved for them to sing. They had sent for the preacher, telling him only that Elizabeth had died giving birth and that Sam had died from a poisonous snake bite while picking flowers from the garden to put on her grave.

When they got to the top of the hill, the preacher was already there. He took Phillip's hand and led him over to the spot that had been dug for the graves. The preacher saw how his wife's death had affected Phillip, and his heart went out to the man. His sermon was based on how the deaths were no one's fault and no one should shoulder the blame or feel guilty, for it was God's will to take these two souls to heaven. Needless to say, there was a lot of squirming going on during the service. After the service, while the preacher was there, Marta asked the preacher if he would please baptize the newborn baby. He replied, "Yes," and everyone gathered around while this was being done. All except Phillip; he had gone back to his office and began drinking again. At the end of the week, Phillip emerged from the house. He was cleaned up and freshly shaven. Everything returned to normal—or as normal as could be. Phillip was not the same person. He was withdrawn and unfriendly, hardly speaking to anyone, especially to Marta, as he still felt guilty and vowed to stay away from her.

As I, Thomas Wesley Sanduval, got older, I began to ask more questions about my mother and father. I was told that Lady Elizabeth had died at childbirth, nothing more. I was told how my parents came to be here in Baton Rouge, Louisiana, where I was born. I was raised by a young slave named Marta, who was our cook and housekeeper, and by Jacob, my father's manservant, among other things, both of whom I love very much. Marta was more like the mother I never knew than a servant. Her young son, Eli, was like my brother and my best friend, along with Jacob.

Jacob kept me in line; he taught me manners, the way of life, keeping me out of trouble and out of the way of my father's wrath. When I asked Marta why my father did not have time for me, she would only reply, "Because your father is a very busy man, running this large plantation to keep a roof over all our heads." Marta also said, "I believe he still grieves for his wife even after all this time."

Hearing that made me feel guilty, as if it were my fault she died. Don't get me wrong—my father had me raised right. He made sure I had a good education, made sure I could raise the right crops and that I could run the plantation. But he never took any time just to talk to me, like a father and son. To be honest, after a while, I stopped wanting his attention. I started to notice that when we were in the same room, he could not look at me, and when he did, he would quickly look away.

The year of 1856, I turned twelve and Eli turned thirteen. We did everything together. Closer than two peas in a pod—that's what Marta always said. When we weren't working the plantation, we would be exploring all around the area. On one of those days, while out on one of our adventures, we discovered a large pond not far from the large river that ran along the border of our land.

The pond was overgrown with trees, some of which fell and landed in the water, making a perfect place for jumping off and into the pond. Now, neither Eli nor I knew how to swim, but we were determined to learn.

When we told Marta and Jacob about the pond, they said to be careful as it might have alligators wandering over from the nearby river. So, Eli and I got long poles, and when we went there before swimming, we would poke the water all the way around the pond and all the way to the bottom and all around the fallen trees. We never encountered any gators, so we would jump off the dead trees into the water. We learned to swim. We spent all our free time there.

Later that spring, we got new neighbors on the Nelsons' old rundown plantation that had been abandoned for several years. Mr. Nelson had been a gambler and had lost his plantation during a horse race to a Mr. Pierce. Mr. Pierce, along with his wife Caroline; his son, Jason; and their daughter, Jennifer, moved into the old house. My father and I went to make their acquaintance to see if my father could be of service to them. As it turned out, Mr. Pierce did need use of some of our slaves to help fix up the house, clear some land,

and get some crops in the ground until he could buy some slaves of his own.

My father agreed to loan him some of our slaves, and when his crop came in, Mr. Pierce would give my father a percentage of the crop to pay for the use of our men. I liked the Pierces; they were down-to-earth people, not like some of the snobbish neighbors we had. Mr. Pierce was a portly man in his midforties, with gray in his brown hair. He had friendly brown eyes and was of medium height. His wife, Caroline, appeared to be younger. She was a short, chubby woman with light brown hair and laughing blue eyes. Their son, Jason, was around five feet, eight inches tall, tall for a lad of thirteen. He had sandy brown hair and soft brown eyes with golden eyelashes. I guess, for a boy of those years, you could say he was sort of nice looking.

Their daughter, Jennifer, was a gangling young girl at the age of ten. She was skinny with long legs and arms. Jennifer had long blonde hair and light blue eyes, like her mother's, with spiked long black eyelashes. At first impression, she came off as a tease and a tomboy. Jennifer loved her brother Jason. She tried to tag along wherever he went, and Jason didn't seem to mind too much. When Jason, Eli, and I all became best friends, we had to include Jenny, as we all called her, into our group.

Eli, some of our slaves, and I spent most of that spring clearing land, plowing the ground, and planting crops for Mr. Pierce while some of the slaves helped Mrs. Pierce fix the house so it was liveable. That harvest season, Mr. Pierce had a bumper crop of sugar beets and cotton. He was able to pay my father the percentage they agreed on and had money left over to purchase his own slaves. He even had enough to get them by until the next harvest season.

When harvest season came, everyone was busy harvesting their crops, but when the season ended, work on the plantations slowed down for a while until it was time to begin again. At the very end of harvest season, everybody would get together at one person's house to celebrate. This year the gathering will be held at our plantation.

All the preparations were done. All the food was prepared, now all we needed was for the people to show up. When they did arrive, everyone had brought food and drinks to share with everybody. After everyone's bellies were full, there was music played by some of the local men that had brought instruments with them. Anyone that wanted to dance did.

It was a great time, with lots of laughter and lots of stories to tell. Later in the evening, the men all gathered together to have a good cigar, a good glass of bourbon to drink, and a discussion about the crops that would be best to plant in the coming year. All the women would also get together to see who had a new baby or to talk about the latest fashions they saw in the catalogs they received every few months. They shared receipts and talked about what vegetables they would can for the winter.

Most of the younger children would play hide-and-seek or tag, under the watchful eyes of their mothers. The older ones might pair up and go for a stroll also under the watchful eyes of their mothers. The girls who didn't would gather in a group and talk about which one of the boys had gotten cuter since the last gathering they attended. The boys would also get in a group and do the same, laughing amongst themselves, afraid to look in the direction of the girls.

This year Jason, Eli, and I snuck over to the slave cabins to watch and see how they celebrated the end of their hard-working season. The music they played was very different from the music we were used to hearing. It was primitive and sensual sounding. We watched from a distance, hidden behind some wagons as it was taboo for us to even be there. Some of the men sat on the ground, beating on small drums, while others played flute-like instruments.

The women were swaying back and forth to the music, slowly at first, but when the tempo of the music picked up, the women began dancing faster, swaying, turning, and jumping into the air. Faster and faster they went, until it almost turned into a frenzy. The women's dresses would dip low on their shoulders, and their skirts would rise up, showing most of their legs.

Preparation started dripping down their necks and onto their almost exposed breasts, making their clothes stick to them, showing off the curves of their bodies. In the moonlight, their skin shimmered, making them look almost unreal. It mesmerized all three of us. We could not take our eyes off of the women. A funny feeling started to creep down from my belly to some lower parts of my body, a warm strange sensation making me want more, but more of what? I didn't know. I just knew I wanted it to go on until I found out what it was.

All of a sudden, we heard Jenny's voice behind us. "What's you boys watching? Can I see?" she said with laughter in her voice. All three of us jumped and turned around at the same time, yelling no. Jenny, with a big smile on her face, said, "It don't matter no how. Momma wants you, Jason. We're ready to go home." Jason groaned, looked at his sister, then at us, defeated, and said goodnight. Eli, shrugging his shoulders and looking over at me, said, "I had better go to before I gets into trouble too." After they all left, I turned back to listen to the music and watch them dance, but by now, they were all breaking up into pairs and going off disappearing into the darkness. The only woman left was still dancing by herself even though the music had stopped. When I got a good look at her, I was surprised to see it was Marta, still swaying to the nonexistent music.

She was a fine-looking woman. Fairly tall for a woman and slender with curves where they should be. She had nice features. Her nose wasn't flat like most of the other slave women. Her eyes were large black pools, with long black eyelashes. Her mouth was full, almost too full, but all in all, she was a fine woman to look at. I felt myself blush at thinking those thoughts about Marta, when suddenly I felt myself being lifted off of the ground, shaken, and turned around to come face to face with an angry Jacob.

His face clearly showed his disapproval. "What you doing here, boy? Why aren't you in your bed, where you belong?" Before I could answer, Jacob looked past me and saw Marta. His face softened for a minute, but then his face turned red, and he really scowled. "I ought to tan your hide, young Thomas," he said. I tried to explain that we were just watching and not doing anything bad, but as he looked me over, the evidence showed plainly in my tight pants.

"Best you had better get to the house and to your bed." As I turned to go, he slapped me on the back of my head. "That's for all them evil thoughts you be having. Now, get and no more thoughts, you hear?" I ran all the way to the house and up the stairs, to my bedroom. Confused as to what thoughts I was supposed to be thinking about, *Maybe I will ask Jacob in the morning*, I thought as I drifted off to sleep.

When morning came, I went down to the kitchen for breakfast. When I saw Marta, she didn't look anything like I thought she did last night. She wore a bright-colored scarf on her head and a dress tied at her neck that hung loosely from her body, covering any curves she might have had. I am not sure what happened last night. It must have been the music and the moonlight playing tricks on me.

I ate my breakfast and did my morning chores. I told Marta I was going to meet up with Jason and Eli and would be back in the afternoon. Marta handed me a cloth bag, saying it contained some fresh-baked bread and some apples. "I know how you children like to eat, so when you get hungry, you will have something to get you through till you get home." I thanked her and headed for the door, but Marta pulled me back to her and gave me a big hug and a kiss on the cheek, as she always did. "You're not too old yet for me to hug you, are you?" she said.

I must have turned red, as I thought of the night before. I stammered, "Uh ... uh," and ran out the door, almost knocking Jacob down as he came in.

"What in the world?" Jacob said as he snorted and helped himself to a cup of coffee.

I met up with Eli in the courtyard just as he was finishing up his chores and we headed for the pond, where we would meet with Jason and Jenny. It was already getting hot, and it would feel good to get in the cool water. It was a long walk to the pond, and by the time we got there, we were both sweating, making our shirts soaked with preparation. Eli hurriedly took off his clothes, down to his cutoff long johns, which we used to swim in. We were talking and laughing about the night before, about the lecture I got from Jacob. Before I could get my pants off, Eli ran out to the edge of the tree that had fallen into the water. Looking back at me, he jumped into the water and began to swim and splash around.

I hollered to tell him we hadn't checked the water with our poles, for him to get out. He didn't hear me. I ran out onto the dead tree to get his attention, and that's when I saw them: the sinister-looking yellow eyes, barely visible above the water. I screamed, but it was too late. The next occurrence happened so fast, I could not react quickly enough. I heard Eli's piercing scream, then saw all the blood bubbling up surrounding him. I tried to grab his hand to try to pull him up, but the gator was too strong and started pulling him under to the bottom of the pond.

I was sick, as I could not help my best friend. I stood there almost in shock when, all of a sudden, someone ran past me and dove into the water. It was Jason. He and Jenny had ridden up in their wagon and heard Eli's piercing. Scream. More blood. It was too quiet. Nothing was moving, so I got down on my hands and knees and put my face close to the water to see if anything was moving. Suddenly, Eli's face was almost touching mine. Afraid it was the gator coming back up, I threw myself backward, almost into the water. When I realized it was Eli, I grabbed hold and tried to pull him up out of the water while Jason pushed him from below. Before I knew it, Jenny was beside me, and between the three of us, we managed to get Eli out of the water and onto the bank.

After we got Eli out, Jenny and I helped Jason climb onto the bank. When Jason caught his breath, we went over to Eli. Jason put his ear to Eli's chest but could not hear him breathing. He turned Eli over on his side and started to hit him on the back. Nothing. He pounded on his back and said, "Come on, Eli breathe." Nothing, so Jason laid him on his back and started pushing Eli on his chest. Jenny started to panic, telling Jason, "Do something, or he's going to die." At about that time, water bubbled up out of Eli's mouth, and he started to choke. Jason quickly turned him on his side again and let the water run out. He took a deep breath and opened his eyes, but Eli did not focus on any of us.

He began to shake uncontrollably. Jason said he was probably going into shock. He told Jenny to run to the wagon, get the blanket they had brought with them, and cover Eli up. While Jenny did that, Jason and I looked Eli over to see where he had been bitten. He seemed all right, until we looked down at his left foot and saw it had been bitten clean off just above the ankle and was still bleeding. Jenny came back with the blanket and started to cover Eli up when she saw his foot was missing. Now Jenny is not one to cry over most things. She is the bravest ten-year-old I think I ever met, but when she saw what had happened to Eli, she began to weep and couldn't stop. Jason told his sister to go get the wagon and back it up over here so we could get Eli in it to take him home. Jenny was glad to do something, anything, to get away from the awful sight of her friend's missing foot.

Jason tore the bottom of his shirt off and tied it around Eli's leg just above where his foot should have been to help control the bleeding as he had lost a lot of blood already. When Jenny had managed to get the horse to back the wagon up to where we were, Jason and I lifted Eli gently up into the back of it, covered him with the blanket, gathered up all our stuff, and started for the house.

When we arrived at the plantation, Marta was in the courtyard, hanging out the washing on the line to dry. When she looked up and saw the wagon pulled to a stop, she knew something was wrong by the look on our three faces. Marta looked from me to Jenny, then at Jason, and when she saw that we were all covered in blood, she began to panic as she looked around. She couldn't see Eli lying in the back of the wagon. Marta hurried forward, shouting, "Eli, Thomas, where is Eli? Where is he?" As she got closer, I pointed to the back of the wagon, and she hurried over, fearing the worst.

When Marta got around to the back of the buggy and saw Eli all pale and bloody. She started to feel him all over to see where he was hurt, and when she lifted the blanket off of him and saw his missing foot, the scream she let out was so piercing. It made Jacob and some of the others come running. Jacob reached Marta just in time to keep her from falling to the ground as she had fainted at the site of her son's injury. Jacob looked over at Eli and saw how pale he was. Then he saw Eli's foot was missing.

Jacob fought back the nausea that was rising up in his throat and asked the two women that had rushed over, to take Marta to her cabin. He then asked the men to help him lift Eli out of the wagon and get him to the cabin. Jacob sent a young boy to town to fetch the doctor as quickly as possible. Meanwhile, I didn't know what to do. I felt sick to my stomach, and I felt guilty for not being able to help my best friend when he needed me. I should have seen the gator sooner and warned Eli before he went into the water. I should have jumped in to try to save him. I should have done something, just anything, but I didn't. Instead, I froze. I thank the Lord that Jason and Jenny came when they did. I just hope the Lord sees fit to save Eli's life.

When I turned to look at Jason. I saw he was comforting Jenny, who was silently sobbing on her brother's shoulder. I asked Jason how he had gotten Eli away from the gator. Jason said that when they pulled up close to the pond, they heard me scream to Eli and saw all the blood coming up to the surface and knew it could only mean a gator attacked him. So, he grabbed the knife he always carried with him on our adventures and dove into the water without thinking. He could not see, as the water was so churned up and murky from all the thrashing of the gator's tail on the silt from the bottom of the pond.

Jason said he dove down until he found the gator and grabbed hold of it. He then felt his way toward the head, and when he reached the soft part of the gator's neck just above its shoulder, he stabbed his knife in as far as he could. The gator thrashed about, then let go of Eli and sank to the bottom of the pond. He said that's when he grabbed hold of Eli and started pushing him to the top of the pond, and not a minute too soon, as he was running out of air. I didn't know that the gator had already bitten off Eli's foot.

I told Jason I thanked God for him and Jenny coming when they did, as I could never have forgiven myself if Eli had died in that pond. Jason said, "It was nothing. Eli is my friend too."

Jenny chimed in, saying, "And mine too."

I looked at Jason as a person would look at a hero, and I looked at Jenny in a different way too. I no longer saw her as a small pest of a girl. I saw a strong, determined young girl who would grow up to make some man a strong partner.

About that time, my father rode into the courtyard. Seeing all the commotion going on around us, he rode over to the wagon to see what was going on. When he saw the three of us covered in mud and dried blood, he dismounted his horse. He grabbed me to see if I was all right. For the first time in my life, I saw concern for me on his face. When he saw that I was all right, the concern he showed was gone as quickly as it had come.

After he heard what had happened, he thanked Jason for all that he did, then told us to go into the house and get cleaned up. After we climbed down from the wagon and went inside, Phillip headed over to Martha's cabin to see how Eli was doing. When Jacob came in, I asked him how Eli was doing and whether we could go see him. He said it was best we didn't go over for a while; it would be better for everyone just to wait for the doctor to come and check him out. When Jason heard what Jacob said, he told Jenny they had best head home, so the two of them said their goodbyes, climbed aboard the wagon, and headed out.

The doctor came and left, and I still had not heard how Eli was doing. I asked Jacob again if he thought it was all right to see Eli. Again, he said it was best I did not go over there for a while. Since when did I ever listen when I was told not to do something? One night soon after, when it was dark, I snuck out as quietly as I could and made my way over to Marta's cabin to see Eli.

When I got to the cabin, I couldn't bring myself to knock on the door. The image of Eli's missing foot kept coming into my mind, and I chickened out. I went to the side of the cabin and peeked into the window. There was a small fire burning from the fireplace that made a soft flicker of light in the room. I could make out Marta sitting in a rocking chair next to a cot, which Eli was lying on.

Marta was softly mumbling something and moving what looked like a chicken claw over the top of Eli. Eli moved and started to groan. Marta laid the object on her son's chest, then reached for a bowl near her and began to spoon something into Eli's mouth. A few seconds later, the boy calmed down and rested more easily.

I made my way back to the house. *So far, so good*, I thought. Just as I was about to sneak back into the house, I was grabbed by the back of my neck and turned around once again to face an angry Jacob. Now, I know that I had grown to be five foot nine inches tall, and Jacob was a few inches shorter than that, but he was still a very strong man. The look he gave me made me shrink down to his eye level.

Jacob asked, "What the devil are you doing out here in the dark, sneaking around like a thief?"

I stammered out that I wanted to see how Eli was doing and quickly told Jacob what I had seen, trying to take his mind off me. I told him how weird it all seemed to me. Jacob let go of me, and I quickly stepped back, sighing with relief. Jacob laughed and said, "Marta was probably keeping the flying insects away from her boy and giving him some water with some pain medication in it to keep him calm while he heals. Give him a few days, then go see him. I know you two have a bond like brothers and that you are worried about him, but the best thing right now for Eli is time."

"I guess you're right, Jacob, "I said, and I turned to go into the house.

That's when Jacob reached up and slapped me on the back of my head, saying, "That's for sneaking out."

I guess I have probably been hit on the back of my head about a thousand times. You'd think I would have learned by now and been more careful. I didn't try to see Eli the rest of that week, but I kept up on his progress through Marta, Jacob, and the workers.

Finally, Marta sent word for me to come see Eli. I ran all the way, but once I got to their door, I started to tremble and thought about the previous time I had seen him, with his foot eaten off by the gator, all covered in blood. I was afraid he would not forgive me for being such a chicken, for not jumping in to help him. I almost chickened out again. I finally knocked on the door, and when Marta opened it, she had a big smile on her face. She told me to come in.

As I moved past Marta, her hand brushed across my face in a motherly touch. I could see in her eyes that Eli was going to be all right. As I looked past Marta, I could see Eli sitting up in the rocking chair with a blanket covering his legs. When Eli saw me, his face broke out in a wide grin. He waved for me to come on over and sit on the cot close to him. I sat down and asked him how he was doing. He said it had been rough going for a while, but the pain was kept down by a potion his mother gave him.

He lifted the blanket covering his legs and feet. My eyes widened as his foot—or should I say lack thereof—was exposed. The end of his leg was all covered, I thought, with some kind of red mud. Eli explained that it was a medicine poultice to keep infection away. The end where his foot use to be was all black. Eli explained to me that the black flesh was where they had to burn it to stop the bleeding, but the doctor assured me that when it was thoroughly healed, the flesh would be normal, with a certain amount of scarring.

Eli put his hand on my shoulder and said, "Don't look so sad, Tommy. Look at it this way. When the teacher has us do one of her pirate plays, I will be perfect for the lead pirate." Then he broke out laughing. It was contagious, and I started to laugh along with him. Marta, hearing the sound of our laughter, came in to see what it was all about. When Eli explained about the pirate, she also laughed with us. Then Marta said more seriously, "It's healing up nicely. No smell of gangrene, so there's none present, which is a very good sign. That means my boy is going to be all right." Then she leaned over and kissed Eli on the cheek.

While Marta went about doing her chores in the other room, Eli talked about what happened. I told Eli how sorry I was that I hadn't seen the damn gator sooner so he could have gotten out and would have been all right.

"Not your fault, Tommy. I can only blame myself. You tried to tell me we didn't check the pond first, so don't blame yourself." Then Eli got real serious and leaned closer to me. He talked low as he said he was afraid that he wouldn't get to meet his maker when the time came.

I asked him, "Why not?"

He said, "Because I'm missing my foot. I'm not whole any longer. How can I walk through those pearly gates on one foot?"

After another hour of visiting together, Eli got tired, so I said goodbye, and as usual, as I was leaving, Marta gave me a big hug. I bent down so she could kiss the top of my head. Marta thanked me for coming and said, "You're good medicine for Eli, and he will heal faster with you around to bug him. After all, you know he thinks of you as his brother. You should come again soon."

I said I would and left for home.

As I walked back to the house, I could not stop thinking about what Eli had said about not going to heaven on account of his missing foot. It made me feel even guiltier. That night, I tossed and turned, dreaming about Eli's foot. In my dream, I was standing near the pond, looking down into the water. Everything was quiet and very peaceful. As I stood there looking deep into the clear water, it began to ripple, and the color got darker. Something was moving deep down on the bottom. The object started to move and started rising to the surface. Fascinated, I couldn't take my eyes off of it. The water turned bright red, but I could still see the object coming closer and closer. I started to toss and turn in my bed, wanting to wake up. I turned to run, to get away, but my feet were sinking in the mud on the ground. Just as I got my feet free, the object shot up and out of the water, floating just above my head. It was a giant foot, Eli's giant foot. I started to run, and as I was running, the foot was trying to step on me.

Just as the foot was about to smash down on me, I woke myself up with my feet running in the bed. I sat up, sweat was running down my face. I took the dream as a sign of what I had to do.

The next morning, I got up early, ate breakfast, did my chores, and then headed out to meet up with Jason and Jenny. We met at the gravesite by the hill, as we were going to catch lizards today. I told Jason and Jenny about what Eli had told me of his fear of not going to heaven because of his missing foot. After thinking about it for a whole five minutes, the three of us devised a plan to retrieve Eli's foot. Two days later, Jason, Jenny and I headed over to the dreadful pond to carry out our plan.

In the back of Jason's wagon, we bought a rope, an axe, and a clean white empty flour sack, along with a big machete. As we neared the pond, Jenny started to panic. Jason told her not to worry; she was staying in the wagon working the horse. We pulled the wagon as close as we could to the big tree lying in the water. We threw the rope, axe, and machete on the ground. Jason and I jumped down off the wagon while Jenny tended the horse. We went over and picked up the two long poles and started to poke all around the pond. We poked among the fallen trees in the water and all along the bottom. When we were sure there were no gators in the pond, we threw down the poles.

Jason and I picked up the rope and moved to the edge of the pond, looking at each other. Jason nodded, and we both took a big gulp of air into our lungs, jumped into the water, and swam to the bottom. It was hard to see in the murky water, so we carefully felt our way along the bottom until we came to the gator, still lying on the bottom.

When I touched it, it was slimy. A piece of it came off in my hand, and I almost opened my mouth to yell. When we moved up to the head, we tied a rope around its neck, then swam to the surface, where we once again took in big gulps of air. After catching our breath, we got out of the water, took the loose end of the rope, and tied it to the wagon. Jason had Jenny move the horse slowly forward. As she did, we could see the gator slowly rise to the top of the water.

As the gator was being pulled out of the pond. The smell was so bad that Jason and I both had to throw up. After we emptied our stomachs, we turned back to the task at hand. Jenny stopped the horse on Jason's signal and turned to look at the big gator. Jenny turned pale but did not throw up. She had thought ahead and had brought along one of her mother's lilac-scented handkerchiefs, which she had placed over her nose and mouth. Jason and I got back to our task at hand.

Jason took the axe and started to chop at the gator's stomach. It took a while, as the skin was still very tough, and every so often, he had to stop and step away to get fresh air into his nose and lungs. I took over when he stopped but had to take a break every once in a while to breathe in some fresh air as well. When we did finally finish getting through the skin and into the stomach, we found fish remains, along with bones of a large bird that had unwisely landed in the pond. At last, we came across Eli's foot—or what was left of it.

There was enough skin and flesh on it to keep it together, but it would not have been so in another couple of days. The foot was not that beautiful black color but a sickly gray color. *No help for that*, I thought. Jason looked at me, and I looked back at him to see which one of us was going to pick the foot up and put it in the sack. After about ten minutes of staring at one another, Jenny jumped down off the wagon, picked up Eli's foot, and carefully put it in the sack. Jason and I just looked at Jenny with our mouths open in awe.

Then Jenny said as we just stood there staring at her, "It's not alive. It can't kick you or do anything to hurt you. Jeez, boys are supposed to be brave, not little scaredy cats."

Red-faced and without a word, we took the bag, helped Jenny

climb upon the wagon, and after picking up the rope and axe, climbed on behind her. We rode back to Eli's cabin in silence. When we got there, Marta was picking vegetables from her garden. As we climbed down, we told Marta we had something special for Eli, so she took us into the cabin to see him.

Eli was standing on his one foot with crutches under both arms. He was surprised to see us but was also very pleased. "What's you all doing here on a day like today? I thought that you would all be out on an adventure."

"We were," Jenny piped up as Jason hit her in the ribs with his elbow. I explained what we had done, leaving out the part about Jason and I throwing up and not picking up his foot, but Jenny was happy to fill Eli in on all of it. Jenny then handed Eli the sack as I said, "Now you can meet your maker when the time comes because you now have your foot to take with you."

Eli opened the sack and looked inside while holding his nose. Eli started to shake and turned away from us. We felt good because we had done something good for Eli. When Marta came into the room, she asked, "What in God's name is that awful smell?" She looked over and saw Eli's shoulders shaking. She asked again what was going on. Marta was stunned when Eli handed her the bag, and when she looked inside it, she nearly fainted and shouted at Eli, "What in tarnation is going on here? Is that really your foot, Eli?"

When Eli turned around, he was laughing so hard, he had tears streaming down his face. "I am sorry, Mama. It's just when I told Tommy about not going to heaven because I was missing my foot, I really didn't think he would go and get it, let alone get Jason and Jenny involved in helping him get it."

As Marta scolded all of us, we looked at each other and busted out laughing. As Marta began to get over being mad at the foolish thing we had done, she saw the humor in it and began to laugh along with us. As she looked from Tommy to Eli, she murmured to herself, "Just like two peas in a pod."

When word got back to Jenny's mother about the foolish stunt we had pulled, Jenny wasn't allowed to go with us anymore. Mrs. Pierce put her foot down and told her daughter she would be enrolled into finishing school to become a lady. No matter how much we apologize or pleaded or swore to never pull another thing like that again, we could not sway Mrs. Pierce to change her mind. That September, Jenny left for Miss Jenkins Finishing School for Ladies in Massachusetts, and she would be gone three long years.

Between school and working on the plantation, all three of us boys were kept busy so we didn't have much time for just hanging around and going on adventures. With Eli not able to keep up, he stopped going. With Jenny not here, it just wasn't the same anyhow, Jason missed his little sister a lot, and truth be told, so did I. I missed her laugh and her crazy antics and the silly things she said. We missed Eli as well, as he kept us all in stitches and on our toes with scary ghost stories.

As Eli could no longer work in the field or stables, my father made him a bookkeeper. With Jacob's help, he learned quickly and was very efficient. Jason was also kept busy working with his father on their plantation, as was I, so the three of us saw very little of each other after that. When I thought about all that the four of us had been through together in the last few years, I couldn't wait for all of us to get together again.

When we three boys did get together again, we caught up on all the news. Eli was seeing a girl a few cabins down from his own. Jason was also seeing a girl from the general store in town. He had met her while running errands with his father. Me, I wasn't seeing anyone. I couldn't get away from Jacob or Marta long enough to get with one. Oh, yes, I tried. It was one night, during the end of another harvest celebration given at our plantation, as it was our turn again. When everyone arrived, I looked around for Annabelle Guitz, a pretty German girl who lived on the other side of the Pierces' property. She had long brown hair, pretty brown eyes, and very large, plump breasts. After everyone was finished eating and broke up into groups, I sauntered over to the group of girls that Annabelle was talking to.

I noticed that when I looked her way that she had been giving me the eye, so it didn't take much prompting from Eli and Jason to go over to her. Although, if I told the truth, I was shaking like a leaf.

When the girls saw me coming, they poked their elbows into poor Annabelle's sides, making her blush. When I reached Annabelle's side, I could hear all the girls beginning to giggle, and I almost chickened out. Annabelle said in a low, sultry, accented voice, "Allo, Tommy. How are you this evening?"

I managed to stammer back, "Fine. Would you like to take a walk with me?"

She nearly jumped on top of me and said a little too loudly, "Jes, I would."

I offered her my arm, and we started to walk and talk. When we got out of sight of everyone, Annabelle pulled me behind some bushes. I lost my footing and fell backward, landing on Marta's flower garden.

Before I knew what was happening, Annabelle lunged and landed right on top of me, knocking the air out of my lungs. She started kissing my face and pulling on my hair. As soon as I caught my breath, I grabbed her hands to keep her from making me completely bald. Annabelle was stunned and asked, "Vhat is the matter? You do not like me?"

"Yes, yes, but let's take it a little easier and enjoy it, okay?"

She rolled off of me and we sat up, not saying anything, just facing each other. We leaned in and kissed lightly, but not before bumping our foreheads together. Then Annabelle grabbed my hand and placed it on her large, plump breast. The kiss deepened, and I started shaking with desire.

I was about to push Annabelle back down on the ground when I was suddenly lifted off the ground. Groaning, I turned to see that all too familiar face of Jacob's. He didn't say a word, just helped Annabelle to her feet and pointed to the house where people were beginning to say their goodbyes and leave for home. In the moonlight, I could see Annabelle's face turn a shade of red, as I suspected mine did as well. Annabelle picked up her skirt and ran, calling over her shoulder, "Call on me soon, Thomas."

I looked at Jacob, and he pointed toward the house, so I turned to go and felt the slap to the back of my head before it even landed. That night, I thought of how close I came to being with a girl. Then I really tossed and turned.

The next morning, Jacob was the only one at the kitchen table when I came down. I didn't look at him, as I was still a little upset over what had happened last night. He told me to sit down. Then he began the "talk." When he was through, I didn't know if I was burning up with a fever or from being so embarrassed. Did Jacob really think I was that naive or just plain ignorant in these matters?

After all, I have watched our animals breed and snuck peeks at our workers mating. I wasn't stupid or naive, just inexperienced in the matter. How was I going to get experience if Jacob kept popping up and stopping me from getting some experience? And just how much brain damage was I going to get with each slap on the back of my head, I wondered.

Life went on, as did work, and time passed. It had been almost three years since I had last seen Jenny. This year the harvest celebration would be at the Pierces' plantation, and Jenny would be home from finishing school. I was excited to see her again. I don't know why. She had always been such a pest, but the truth is, I missed her a lot.

The night of the celebration came, and I rode over to see Jason, or so I told myself. I was pleasantly surprised when I walked into Pierce's house and saw what a beautiful young lady Jenny had turned into. She still had the tiny freckles on the bridge of her small straight nose, and her eyes were still that beautiful mischievous blue when she smiled at you. Her lips were full and sinuous. She had not grown much taller, as the top of her head came just to my shoulders. I had grown to six feet four inches. I guessed that I was about a foot taller than her, so that would make her about five feet, four inches.

What caught my eye the most was her figure. She had filled out in all the right places. Her hips were slightly rounded, and her breasts were creamy white, spilling out over the top of her dark blue dress just enough to entice a man. I frowned at that thought, which caught me off guard. All in all, she was a vision to behold.

Jenny was surrounded by several young men, all vying for her attention. When she looked up and saw me, her face lit up; it was the same expression she got when we went on one of our adventures. Her eyes turned a deeper blue and obtained that mischievous, teasing look. As she came toward me, she held out her arms, and when we came together, she gave me a big hug. I put my hand under her chin and lifted her face up to mine, and without hesitating, I leaned down and kissed her full on her mouth.

Jenny stepped back a little to see my face better. I noticed her face had turned a shade of red with embarrassment. What the heck was the matter with me? I made my features go blank so they would not betray how the kiss had affected me. To break the awkward silence between us, Jenny said in a slightly shaky voice, "You look well, Thomas."

"As you do too," I replied. Several of the young men who had followed Jenny over when she came to see me cleared their throats to get her attention back to them.

"Oh," she said as she looked at them, then back to me. "Thomas, you remember Charles, Steven, and Jack?"

"Yes, I do," I replied as I looked over their heads and saw Jason dancing with Emily Cox, the girl he had met at the store in town a few years back. "Now, if you'll excuse me," I said to Jenny, "I see your brother and would like a word with him."

"Yes, of course," Jenny said with disappointment in her voice. "Will I see you later?" she asked.

"Maybe," I said, and I walked away from the group.

As I neared Jason, I couldn't help but notice how tall Emily was. She came all the way up to eye level with Jason. She was tall for a girl, as Jason was now six feet, two inches tall. Emily had curly strawberry-blonde hair with big brown eyes that twinkled. Her features were plain except for her heart-shaped lips and the dimple in her cheeks. Her legs were long, and her shape was nice, albeit a little on the plump side. Her personality was so bubbly, it was contagious.

Around Emily, everyone was relaxed. She had a way of removing tension from the room and putting everyone in a good mood. I was happy that Jason had found someone like Emily. They suited each other perfectly. When Jason saw me, he beamed with pleasure. He took hold of Emily's hand and headed toward me. As they passed the table with the punch on it, Emily told Jason she was thirsty and would get something to drink and would join us in a few minutes. Jason told her all right, but don't take too long, as he kissed her hand and left her there.

The two of us went outside for some fresh air and a place to be without any interruptions. Jason and I caught up on everything that had gone on in our lives since we last saw each other. I told Jason how Eli was doing and how things were going on the plantation. Then Jason asked me what I thought about his sister, Jenny—if I had seen her yet and what I thought about the way she had changed. Careful not to disclose how I reacted to Jenny, I simply replied, "I think she is growing into a fine young lady and will someday make a great wife for some lucky man."

"Really," said Jason.

As he was about to ask me just who I thought that lucky man might be, some of the people started to come out for fresh air. I took that opportunity to tell Jason, "I ought to be getting home as I have a lot to do in the morning." I asked Jason to say my goodbyes to his parents, to his sister, and also to Emily. Jason made me promise to visit again soon.

As I rode home on my horse, I rounded the bend and nearly ran down a young girl walking on the dirt road. I recognized her as one of our slaves who worked on our plantation, one whom I had grown up with and was in the group of kids I played games with. I reined in my horse and stopped in front of her. I asked the girl, whose name was Roslyn, why she was out here walking alone and not with someone.

Roslyn replied that she had come to the celebration with a group of others but that they had all left earlier without her. She said she saw it was getting late and decided to start for home. I could make out her face in the bright moonlight and could see it was tearstained. I also noticed that her blouse had been torn. I asked Roslyn what had happened to her. She started to sob and turned to walk away. I steered my horse in front of her again and, in a harsh tone, demanded to know what had happened.

Roslyn told me that she had been dancing just outside in the courtyard with some of the other girls when they all paired up with some of the boys and took off. She stayed back and kept on dancing to the music by herself alone. As she talked, my mind drifted back to the night I spied on Marta dancing alone. My mind abruptly came back to what Roslyn was saying when I heard her say, "And he tried to have his way with me." I asked her in a calm voice what had been done to her.

She didn't want to tell me, saying it was all right; nothing had happened, and she had managed to get away. No matter how I asked or how many times I asked her, she would not say who he was. I told Roslyn to get up on the horse and I would take her home, as it was too far for her to walk this late at night. When she hesitated, I told her that the person who had done this to her might come this way, running into her. On hearing that, she did not hesitate again but put her foot in the stirrup and let me pull her up to sit in front of me.

We rode along in silence, and when we arrived in front of her cabin, I helped Roslyn down. About that time, my father, who had left the Pierces' a little after me, rode past the cabin and saw me standing beside Roslyn with her tearstained face and torn blouse. His face became contorted and red with anger.

Phillip told the girl to get in her cabin and to keep her mouth shut about what had happened tonight and to not say anything to anyone. Roslyn was so afraid of Phillip, she just shook her head yes and hurried into her cabin. Then my father turned to me and, in a cold voice, said, "Thomas, I will not tolerate you sleeping with the slave girls. Do you understand?" I was taken back at the venomous tone of his voice. When I tried to explain what took place, he was too angry to listen to me.

Better to tell him in the morning when he has calmed down, I thought, so I turned away from him and took my horse to the stable, where the young stable boy would remove the saddle, rub the horse down, and feed it before retiring for the night.

In the morning, it wasn't better. My father had already left, and Jacob was waiting for me to have breakfast. While I ate my breakfast, Jacob drank his coffee. He told me that my father wanted me to go with him into town to the docks to see when the ship would be loaded with our cargo and what time it would be leaving port.

I said okay and finished eating my breakfast. On our way out, Marta came in. When she saw me, she looked away. Jacob had gone ahead and brought the buggy around and said it was time to leave. Marta came over and gave me a big hug that I thought lasted a little too long, so I bent down for her to kiss the top of my head, and when I looked into her eyes, I could see the pain and sadness in them. Before I could ask her what was wrong, Eli entered the room, came over, and shook my hand, then grabbed me and hugged me tightly.

Before I could ask Eli what the heck was going on, Jacob grabbed hold of my shoulder and pulled me out the door. We climbed aboard the wagon and headed for the docks in Baton Rouge. When I asked Jacob why we took the wagon instead of riding the horses, which would have been faster, he shrugged his shoulders and replied, "I have to bring back some supplies."

Jacob hardly spoke a word until we got to the ship. Then he told me to go ahead, go aboard the ship and find out from the captain if everything had been loaded and what time the ship would be departing. I asked Jacob, "Why me? Don't you usually take care of that part of the business?"

Jacob answered back rather curtly, "Because your father wants you to learn this end of the business. Now get going."

I ran up the gangplank, thinking how strange everyone was

behaving this morning, but I supposed it was because I had turned seventeen and figured my father was teaching me a lesson for the night before and how I had behaved toward him. As I reached the top of the gangplank, I turned toward Jacob. I saw him uncover what appeared to be two trunks in the back of the wagon. I saw two burly men lift them out of the wagon and head for the gangplank.

As they neared the top of the gangplank, I felt a sense of dread wash over my entire body. They were my trunks. I looked back at Jacob just as he was riding away. I yelled and started to run down the gangplank but was stopped by the two men carrying my trunks. I told them to get out of my way, but they blocked my path going down. I couldn't budge them to move; all I could do was watch until Jacob was out of my sight. Then I really started to panic and began to fight the two men, to no avail.

I heard a calm voice behind me, telling me it would do no good to fight this, as we were already preparing to leave port. I watched as the gangplank was being hauled up. The calm voice said, "The vessel has already caught the tide, and there is no turning back. It would be best if you just accept it and do not fight what you cannot win. It is what your father wanted."

My father, I thought as I turned toward the voice behind me. *Why?* I thought. Was it because he thought I'd had my way with the slave girl? Why didn't he let me explain, and where was he sending me?

The calm voice cut into my thoughts and brought me back to the man the voice belonged to. As he held out his hand, he said, "I am Captain Richards, and this is my ship. Your father paid me good money for your passage to England. And In two years, your passage will be paid for me to bring you back to Baton Rouge. In the meantime, I advise you to make the best of it and enjoy the voyage, for all our sakes." The Captain's voice was stern to get his point across. I looked over at the ship's railing and saw the dock was too far away for me to go overboard and try to swim back. Also, the sea had gotten too rough even to attempt it.

I looked at the captain, and he read the defeat on my face as I nodded my head yes. The captain signaled for the two men to release me, and they let me go and went about their duties.

"Mr. Gage," the captain said to an older man who had appeared at his side, "please show young Master Sanduval to his cabin." The captain then nodded his head at the older man. "Mr. Gage will give you directions on how to get there." After that brief statement, the captain turned and walked away.

Mr. Gage, a short, plump man with white hair and bright blue eyes with a twinkle in them, was curiously looking at me. He may have been short, but was very muscular from all the work he did on this vessel. He bent down and, with no effort, picked up one of my trunks and motioned for me to pick up the other one as he inclined his head for me to follow him.

We walked down a narrow hallway, then down a flight of stairs to a lower deck. When we came to a door, Mr. Gage stopped, opened the door, and stood aside so I could enter the room. Once inside the dark room, Mr. Gage, following just behind me, put down the trunk and lit a lamp swinging just above his head. He then went further into the room over by a bed and lit another lamp sitting on a small table next to the bed.

As the lamp's flames grew brighter, I could see it was a fairly large, clean room. Besides the bed and a small table, the room contained a larger table with two chairs in the middle of the room. By one wall was a small desk and chair. There also was a wardrobe in which to put my clothes, in when I unpacked. In one corner was a screen, and behind the screen was a basin with a pitcher of water sitting on a small table and a chamber pot.

Mr. Gage spoke up. "The chamber pot will be emptied once in the morning and once in the evening. If you need anything, just pull the cord by the bed, and someone will come and assist you. You are below deck, so you shouldn't be disturbed by the noises coming from above. If you get where you need fresh air, you can go above and walk the deck. We have two other passengers traveling with us.

You will probably meet them when we serve the noon meal," Mr. Gage informed me. He then told me how to get to the dining room. Then, turning to leave, he said, "If there is nothing else I can do for you, I will be off to do my chores."

I thanked him, saying, "No." He turned and left the room, closing the door behind him. I turned my thoughts to my father and what had just transpired, trying to control my anger. I opened my trunk to put away whatever was in them. On top of the clothes were two envelopes addressed to me, one in my father's handwriting and the other in Marta's.

I read my father's first. The letter started off,

> Dear Thomas,
>
> If you are reading this letter, you are now aboard a vessel headed for England. I want to explain my actions. I want you to know you did nothing to bring about this change of events. I talked to the slave girl. She told me the story. There is talk of unrest coming to our Southern states, but never mind that. This was an opportune time for you to better yourself and your education. I thought it also time you learned to be a gentleman, as you are getting older. You need to know how to carry yourself and become a better man.
>
> When these two short years are up and you return to the plantation, you will be ready to take charge of running everything, with a minimum amount of help from me.
>
> Signed,
>
> Your father, Phillip Thomas Sanduval the Third

Short, simple, and to the point. No "I miss you" or "I love you," just him being him. I tossed aside his letter and picked up the one from Marta.

I walked over to the bed, lay down, opened the letter, and began to read it.

> My dearest Tommy,
>
> I am so sorry your father did this to you, but he thinks he is doing what's best for you.

At that statement, I snorted and said out loud, "You mean what's best for him." I continued to read,

> He also thinks it's best for the plantation. I am also sorry we did not get to properly say goodbye to each other, but it is not forever. Please remember, Jacob was just following orders.

Another snort from me.

> He hopes you forgive him. He loves you like a son, as I do. Eli's better. The pain is almost gone, and he gets around good on his crutches, so no need to worry about the place. Please take care of yourself, and be careful until you get back home. It will be hard, but I will write to you again. Love from all.
>
> Signed,
>
> Marta

Reading Marta's letter and feeling the love in it made me homesick already.

"How will I ever make it two years?" I said out loud. Then I shook myself to snap out of myself pity and vowed to make the best of a bad situation, to prove to my father I was already a man. I had never been further than Baton Rouge, so I would make this my own big adventure, I told myself.

I folded the letter and carefully put it in the trunk. I began to put away the clothes packed in the trunk. They were all new, so that told me my father had planned this some time ago. I began to get mad all over again. I berated myself for this and went back to hanging up the clothes. I had never seen clothes like these. They were certainly different from the clothes I wore.

The coats were made from fine silk material with velvet collars, and some had leather patches on the elbows of the sleeves. They all looked to be form-fitting. There were five altogether in different colors. Two in black, one in brown, one in gray, and one in dark green. There were five white shirts. Three had ruffles at the collar and on the sleeves, and two were plain except for the pleats on each side of the pearl buttons down the front of them.

The breeches that came with the clothes looked like they were too small to fit me. As I held them up to my lower body, I saw they only came down to my knees. There were also five of them, and they also came in different colors. Two black, two brown, and one gray. There were six pairs of long white stockings and three pairs of shoes with slight heels on the bottom of them. The shoes were all shiny black, two plain and one with large buckles on the front of them. Then there were two weird-looking hats.

I laughed out loud at the thought of me wearing those ridiculous-looking clothes. What a dandy I would look like. I thought of how Jason and Eli would laugh and make fun of me. When I looked for regular clothes like I was wearing now, I found only one pair of breeches and one plaid shirt. Now, how was I going to get by on those for two years?

I looked through the trunk again but found nothing more except for a packet in the bottom of one of the trunks.

I opened the packet and saw it contained a bank account voucher for a bank in England. Thank goodness. I thought I would have to go to work as soon as I stepped foot off the ship. It also contained papers showing that I had been enrolled in a school of business. Well, it seems my father had taken care of everything except for where I would be staying. But then a piece of paper dropped out from between the papers for the school. It was a letter introducing me to a Mr. Shelby Markham, a longtime friend of my father's. Apparently, I would be staying with him and his family for the duration of my stay in England.

I walked over to the bed and fell on it, groaning. I asked myself, *Why me?* I don't know how long I lay there feeling sorry for myself—I guess until my stomach started to growl and I realized I was getting hungry. Being a growing boy, the thought of food always cheers me up. Besides, there was nothing I could do about it now, so no sense in starving myself.

I rose, went over to the basin, poured some water into it, and splashed water on my face and on my hair. I dried off my face and smoothed back my hair. I then relieved myself in the chamber pot. I went to the door, opened it, stepped into the dimly lit hallway, shut the door, and started walking. I made my way to the upper deck and all the way to the dining hall on very shaky sea legs.

The smell of the food at first made me a little queasy, but after I sat down, I felt a little better. There were two other passengers sitting at the table, talking to Captain Richards and Mr. Gage. Captain Richards pointed to the two others and introduced them to me. The first one was an older man with close beady eyes. He said his name was Rafael Marcus and that he was on his way to France to settle his grand-mère's estate, as she had recently passed away. I told him I was sorry to hear that. He waved the sentiment away with his hand.

The other passenger was a young man about my age. He had curly auburn, almost-red hair with laughing green eyes. He said his name was Sean O'Leary and that he was Irish. When he talked, he had a strong Irish accent. He was on his way to England to attend school, but first, he would go to Ireland to visit some relatives.

I introduced myself to them. I told them I had business in England and that I would also be attending school there. I looked up at Captain Richards to see if he was going to say anything about that, but he did not, so I sat back and relaxed. A young boy came to the table and began serving lunch to all of us. I was careful not to eat too much, as I still felt a little queasy and did not want to become sick.

After everyone had finished eating, Captain Richards offered everyone coffee and a good cigar. I declined, as did Sean. We got up, saying we were going to stroll around the deck and get the feel of the ship under our feet. Mr. Marcus accepted his offer and stayed to talk longer with the captain and Mr. Gage.

As Sean and I walked, we talked about where we came from. Sean said he was originally from Ireland, but his parents had moved to America as they wanted a better life for their family. He told me he was one of five children. I told him he was lucky, as I had no siblings, only a father, as I was told my mother had died giving birth. But I did have a lot of friends back home, I added.

I explained to Sean about all the slaves we had to work on our plantation. I told him how I had worked alongside them, how we had all grown up and played together. Sean thought it was sad that people were held against their will, made to work for others even if they didn't want to. I had never thought about it that way. I had always thought of them as friends and family. Heck, weren't Eli and I like brothers? I would have to think about what Sean had said.

I learned that Sean had three older brothers and a younger sister. The more we talked, the more we learned about each other, and the more I liked Sean. I knew that, traveling to England with Sean, this trip would go by a lot quicker, with him to talk to every day. He was funny, quick-witted, and full of stories keeping me entertained.

Every day after the noon meal, the two of us would walk around the deck, talking about our lives and our families. I told Sean all about the adventures Eli, Jason, Jenny, and I had. He would laugh and thought everything was funny except for the part about Eli and the alligator. Sean told me about all the things he and his family did together. I envied Sean very much. Sean and I became very good friends, and time did go by faster.

The ship docked at several different ports along the way so the crew could unload some of the cargo it carried and load other cargo bound for America when it returned. Usually, when we were in port, Sean and I would go ashore to look around for a few hours. Sean bought a few items for his family, and I bought a bright, colorful scarf for Marta and a few trinkets for Eli, Jason, Jacob, and Jenny.

All in all, the time flew by. Before we knew it, we were docking at Cardiff, a port near South East Wales, on the Irish Sea. As we sailed by Ireland, Sean pointed out Dublin, where he and his family were from. Of course, we could not see it as we were too far away. When we got close to docking in Liverpool, England, Sean and I went to our cabins to prepare to disembark from the ship.

I packed all my things into the two trunks after dressing in one of the new outfits I was supplied with. I also donned one of the new hats. When I looked down at myself, I became very self-conscious. I thought I looked ridiculous. Two men came and took my two trunks away, or I swear, I would have changed back into my old clothes.

My new clothes were cut very form-fitting and left little to the imagination. Well, like it or not, I could not stay in this cabin forever. I opened the door and peeked into the hallway. The coast was clear. I ambled out, shut the door quietly, and started down the hall, doing what I thought a million-dollar strut would look like, especially in shoes with two-inch heels.

I didn't get very far before I heard what sounded like choking coming from behind me. As I slowly turned around, I saw Sean holding his hand over his mouth to conceal the laughter bubbling up inside him. I felt my face flush and turn red. Looking him over, I realized Sean was dressed almost identically to me. I must have looked at him the same way he had looked at me, as he no longer held back his laughter. His laughter was so contagious that I couldn't help myself. I began to laugh along with him.

We laughed so hard our sides were hurting, and tears were running down our faces. Finally, when we stopped, we took hold of each other's arms, strutting up the stairs like two young male peacocks, laughing all the way up. When we reached the ship's railing, we looked around and saw Captain Richards standing alongside Mr. Gage and Mr. Marcus. We sobered up fast. Captain Richards came over and shook our hands, complimenting us on how fine we looked. He told us it has been a pleasure to have us aboard his vessel. Then he turned to me and said, "I will see you in two years." We then shook hands with Mr. Gaga and Mr. Marcus. As we started down the gangplank, arm in arm, I could swear I could hear the men trying to control their laughter. When we reached the bottom of the gangplank, we turned to wave goodbye and saw the big grins on all the men's faces. I turned red all over again.

Sean's coach was already there. His trunks were already loaded onto the back of the coach, so we said our goodbyes, promised to stay in touch with each other, and slapped each other on the back. Sean climbed inside, waved his hand out the window, and they were off. I was sorry to see him go. All of a sudden, I felt very homesick and very alone. I shook myself and looked around at my surroundings. I saw so many people moving about. It was so crowded, they were bumping into one another.

I noticed the air was not fresh smelling, like back home. It was full of soot and had a bad smell to it. The docks and the town looked dirty, as did the dock workers. Just as I was about to turn around and run back up the gangplank to beg the captain to take me home, a big coach, being pulled by four horses, pulled up alongside me and stopped. It was so luxurious, I could not help but stand and stare at it with my mouth open.

The driver, looking down his nose at me, asked with a snobbish, bored voice, "Are you Master Sanduvale?" All I could do was stand there and nod my head yes. I felt so intimidated by this man. A footman standing on the back of the coach jumped down, picked up my trunks, and placed them on a rack on the back of the coach.

After securing them, he came around and, without saying a word to me, opened the door to the coach and motioned for me to enter.

Before I had sat all the way down, the footman nodded to the driver to start off. The driver whipped at the horses, and they took off at full gallop, throwing me back against the seat. As the coach passed, the footman grabbed hold of the straps on the back of the coach, hoisted himself up onto a ledge where he would ride all the way to where we were going.

As I sat on the plush seat, I noticed how soft and comfortable it was. I sat back and relaxed while starting to enjoy the ride. I watched as we passed the docks and the ships. Soon, we were going through the town of Liverpool, passing houses, shops, and stables. The air smelled of burning coal, rotting fish, and sewage. You could see the sewage running in ditches down the sides of the dirt roads.

I was thankful I wasn't staying here and hoped the place I would be staying at for the next two years was a lot better. The coach traveled along a bumpy dirt road for quite some time. As I watched the scenery go by, I could see we had left the town behind us and was now traveling in open country. The sky was very blue, and there were many green trees and bushes in the landscape now. The ground was covered with green grass, with small colorful flowers throughout it. The day was warm, and with the swaying of the coach going back and forth, I began to get drowsy and dozed off.

I awoke sometime later, when the coach came to an abrupt stop, throwing me somewhat off of the seat. My hat sat crooked on my head, and my clothes were slightly rumpled. The door to the coach was swung open by the footman, who stood there with an amused look on his face. Looking just past the footman, I could see a tall elderly man about my father's age, standing on the top step of the porch.

He was dressed as I was but far more elaborately. His frock was orange, with white lace at the neck and sleeves. His black velvet breeches were just to the knees, making the white stockings he wore appear even whiter than they were. He wore his graying hair tied back into a queue.

Beside the man stood a petite woman, younger than the man. She was very pretty, with light brown hair and smoky blue eyes. She was also dressed elaborately. Her dress of rich silk was deep blue. It was low cut, with lace at the top of her bosom and on the sleeves at the wrist. From the waist down, her dress flared out, making her stand away from the gentleman. I thought she must be the man's wife.

What caught my attention next was standing just behind the couple. She was unbelievably stunning. She had dark shining hair, swept up on top of her head. Her face was heart-shaped, with a small straight nose and pouty lips. Her skin was smooth and lustrous white, like the sheen of a fine pearl. Her neck was long and graceful, and her perfectly shaped breasts showed just above her red silk dress.

When I looked into her eyes, I saw a hint of amusement in them. *Is she laughing at me?* I thought as I became self-conscious and started to turn red. As I turned away from her, I caught a glimpse of my reflection in the window of the open door of the coach. My hat sat very crooked on my head. My hair was sticking out from under it, going in all directions from where it had come loose from the ribbon it had been tied with.

One side of the collar of my shirt had come undone and was sticking straight out, and my jacket was hanging crooked on me. Upon seeing this and again looking at all their faces, I turned an even deeper red and thought I must look like an idiot. I tried to smooth my hair back down at the same time I straightened my hat, but the darn curly stuff just didn't want to cooperate, so I fixed my collar and smoothed out my clothes as best I could and stood tall and straight, albeit red-faced.

At last, the older man came down the stairs. He extended his hand to me and spoke in an amused tone. "Welcome to Larkspur Manor, young Master Sanduvale. My name is Sir Selby Markham."

I reached out, grasped his hand, and shook it in the manliest handshake I could muster. His handshake was very firm and hard. I liked him right away. As Jacob always said, you could tell about a man by the way he shook hands with you.

Sir Markham then introduced me to his wife after she made her way down to us.

"This is my wife, Lady Margaret Markham."

I did my best bow, took her soft limp hand, brought it to my lips, and softly kissed it, saying how delighted I was to meet her. I then turned my attention to their daughter, who had not joined us, but I stayed on the top step. Sir Markham, pointing in the direction of the young girl, said, "And that spoiled child is my charming daughter, Melissa Markham."

Still, she did not move or acknowledge her father. Mrs. Markham began to fidget, wring her hands together.

"Missy," her father called her, "this is Thomas Sanduval, my good friend Phillip's son, whom I told you about."

Still nothing. When I looked up at her, I saw the yawn, along with the bored look on her face. Then I heard a slight gasp come from her mother. Starting to get annoyed at this chit of a girl with no manners, I bounded up the steps two at a time. When I reached her, she was startled and turned to go into the house, but before she could move, I reached over, grabbed her hand, turned it palm up, and planted a lingering kiss on it.

Bowing low, I whispered in a mocking voice, "At your service, my lady." Melissa jerked her hand away, gave me a murderous look, turned, and ran into the house. By this time, the Markhams had made their way up the stairs and were apologizing for the rudeness of their daughter, saying they didn't know what had gotten into her lately. I chuckled to myself as I thought of the look she gave me as I followed the two into their home.

Going through the big wooden door, I looked around and was awestruck by all the riches that surrounded me. The walls were all painted off-white. Some were covered with rich wood paneling. All the walls had fine paintings of art hanging on them. Every room had large windows with coverings made of rich silk brocade hanging on them to keep out the cold. In almost every room, there was a large fireplace, all with carved wood mantels.

From the ceilings hung large chandeliers that sparkled like diamonds, giving off light. Each room had beautiful oriental rugs full of bright colors, all except one. It was a large room with bare wood floors that were polished until they shone, occupied with only six chairs. Lady Markham explained that this room was called the music room and was used for recitals and for dancing when they entertained. She said the chairs were for the musicians to sit on while they played their instruments.

The second floor contained all the bedrooms, where the family and their guests stayed. On the third floor were the servants' quarters. In every bedroom, there was a large fireplace, a desk with a chair, a large four-poster bed, and a large wardrobe for clothes to hang in. On the far side of the room was a large screen, and behind the screen was a big porcelain tub. Alongside the tub was a funny shaped seat, called a toilet. Sir Markham said it was new and all the rage from France. Instead of a chamber pot, you sat down on the seat and did your business, and when you were finished, you pulled a chain hanging above the seat, and it would wash everything down a pipe into a ditch outside to run down the side of the street.

I was shown to my room and told my clothes had already been pressed and hung in the wardrobe and that my toiletry had been placed behind the screen, ready for me to freshen up before dinner. I thanked all three of them for showing me around their beautiful home and told them I would freshen up and join them later, then shut the door. Glad to be by myself, I went over and sat on the chair to process everything I had seen today. I got up and looked in the wardrobe and saw that all my clothes had indeed been pressed and hung up.

Next, I went over and laid on the bed to see how comfortable it was going to be. I sank down and was surrounded by warmth and comfort and felt I would get a good night's sleep. But what I really wanted right now was to try out the new chamber pot chair, as I would call it. I got up, went behind the screen, undid my breeches, and let them fall down past my knees. Cautiously, I sat down. It was comfortable and sturdy, so I sat and did my business, but when I finished and started to rise, a stream of water hit me on my bottom and scared me somewhat. I stepped forward and tripped on my breeches, falling to the floor with a thud. Cursing, I got to my feet and pulled up my breeches over my wet bottom. I reached up, pulled the chain, and watched in fascination as everything disappeared.

I washed my hands and face, combed my hair and tied it back with a ribbon. Looking at my reflection in the mirror hanging above the basin, I thought I looked a little more presentable than when I first arrived here. I sat in a chair by the window and looked out at the grounds around the house. They were kept up immaculately. All the bushes were trimmed to the same height, and all the roses were in bloom. I started to think of home and how all the magnolias would be blooming and how the air would smell sweet and clean.

I shook my head to clear it of any thoughts of home and brought my mind back to the present. I thought about Melissa and what a beautiful girl she was, although somewhat snobbish. I knew I would get along with Sir Markham. All I had to do was agree with the man, and all would be fine. Lady Markham would be easy. A little flattery and she would be putty in my hand.

Melissa, on the other hand, could give me trouble. She was a spoiled, uppity, rebellious young girl. I could see in her eyes she could be a handful. I would have to be on my guard around her and at the top of my game. Again my mind wandered back to the plantation, and I found myself thinking about Eli and how he was doing. I thought about Marta and Jacob and what they were doing. Heck, I was so homesick, I found myself missing my father.

I shook my head again and silently scolded myself. I was determined to make the best of my situation if I wanted these two years to pass by quickly so I could return to my old way of life. As I sat there, I noticed the light starting to fade from the window I had been staring out of. There was a light rap on the door.

"Yes, come in, please," I said. A manservant opened the door and announced that dinner would be served shortly. I nodded my head and told him I would be right down.

After the servant left, I put on my jacket, ran my hand over my hair to make sure it was still in place. I then stepped out of the room, shut the door, and headed for the stairs. A few steps down, I heard another door open and close. It was Lady Markham and her daughter, Melissa. Coming down the hall toward the staircase, I overheard what the young girl said to her mother.

"I don't care, Mother. I don't like him, so why do I have to treat him nice. He is like a backwoodsman."

"Because," replied Lady Markham, "he is the son of a very dear friend of your father's. You will honor your father by treating young Thomas with respect, or you know your father will make you pay."

"All right. I will be civil to him, but I will be glad when these two years are up."

After listening to the two women's conversation, I slowed my step and waited for them to catch up to me. As they approached me, I turned and gave them my best smile and then extended my arms to the two women to escort them both down the stairs into the dining room. Lady Markham was delighted by my actions, but her daughter shot daggers at me, which only made me laugh to myself.

The next morning, after breakfast, Sir Markham took me to the school my father wanted me to be enrolled in for the next two years. He introduced me to the scholars that would be teaching the classes I would be attending, for all my father wanted me to learn. When that was done, Sir Markham introduced me to some of the young men who would also be enrolling in this school, as their families were acquainted with the Markhams. One of the young men's names was Devon Brown. He was from London and was a year older than me. Another young man by the name of Clyde Smyth, who was from Birmingham, was also a year older than me. He was amiable and somewhat of a prankster, not like Devon, who was more reserved but also liked a good joke.

I liked the two right away and was glad to be associated with them. I was also surprised and delighted to see my friend Sean O'Leary, from the voyage, here. He said he would also be attending this school. I introduced Sean to Clyde and Devon, and from that day on, the four of us were inseparable. We did everything together whenever we could.

As I settled into a routine of going to school, doing tasks for the Markhams, and enjoying nightlife out with my friends, time seemed to fly by. Melissa and I even made a pact to get along so things between us were tolerable. In fact, we even became somewhat friends and attended some outings together.

Over some time, I began to notice Sean was not going out with the three of us as much as he used to. In fact, we hardly saw much of him. When I asked Sean about it at school one day, he brushed it off as being too busy between studying and working. He said he just didn't have the time. But as he was explaining it to me, I noticed he would not look me directly in the eye. I didn't think too much about it, as I had suddenly become busy myself.

A year went by before I knew it, and then six more months flew by. Just six more months and I would be graduating and would be heading home. In the year and a half that I had been here, I had received only a few letters from home. They were all from Marta and all contained the same contents. Everyone at home was fine. Eli was doing well, Jacob was fine, and everything on the plantation was going smoothly. When I read them and reread them, I got a strange feeling that she was leaving things out. There was talk in England that things in America were brewing, but because it was just talk, I didn't pay much attention.

Devon, Clyde, and I decided to celebrate with a big night out on the town, as there would be no school the next day. We decided to go to a different club, one with more adventure to it. The club we chose to go to was in the seedier part of London, which made us a little apprehensive and daring. When we arrived at the club and went inside, it was dimly lit, and the clientele was a bunch of riffraff, most of whom appeared to be dock workers.

It was filled with women looking for a good time and someone to buy them a drink. *Well,* I thought, *this is different and should be interesting.* The three of us found a table to sit at. It looked as if it hadn't been cleaned for months. We looked around and spotted a man serving drinks to customers, so we got his attention and ordered our drinks. We sat, talked, drank, and tried our best to pick up three young ladies who kept looking in our direction.

All of a sudden, there was a commotion coming from the other side of the room. Voices were raised, and threats were made. I recognized one voice as belonging to my friend Sean and said as much to Clyde and Devin. The two men inclined their heads to hear better in the crowded, noisy room. Devin spoke up and said, "I think you're right. That does sound like Sean, and he definitely sounds upset."

We rose from our table just as the three young ladies were heading our way. Clyde sighed and mouthed the words, "I'm sorry," shrugged his shoulders, and followed Devin and me to the other side of the club. We made our way over to Sean just as an older gentleman struck Sean across the face with a glove and challenged him to a duel. The older man then reached down, grabbed a young lady sitting next to Sean, pulled her to her feet, and almost dragged her out of the club.

When Sean looked up and saw us, his face was red with anger, along with the red mark left by the man's glove. I asked him what had just happened. Had he just gotten caught with that man's daughter? And I laughed. There was no humor in Sean's face or voice as he shrugged his shoulders and told us to sit down. Sean then asked the waiter to bring a round of drinks to the table.

After Sean finished his drink and calmed down, I asked him again just what had transpired here tonight. As Sean tried to tell us what had taken place, he was so excited that his Irish accent became so thick that none of us could understand him.

"Whoa, take a deep breath and slow down," I calmly said to him. He took another sip of his drink and started to tell us the whole story, more slowly this time.

Sean told us he had been seeing this young girl, whose name was Maude, for over a year now, which explained why he quit hanging around us almost a year earlier. The three of us presumed the young lady being dragged out of here was indeed Maude and that the older man doing the dragging was her father.

Sean abruptly corrected us, telling us that she was the old man's wife. On hearing this, we all gasped but said nothing else and said for him to continue. "As I was saying, I have been seeing Maude for almost a year now. About six months ago, she told me that she was married and was very unhappy." By this time, Sean said that he had fallen madly in love with the girl. Then, two months ago, she told him she was with child and that the child was his, as her husband could have no children.

Sean said they had met here tonight to make plans to run away together, but somehow, the old man had found out and had come to confront Sean, which he did by challenging Sean to a duel. At that point, we all had another drink while processing what we were just told. Finally, Sean asked me if I would be his second and if Devin and Clyde would be his witnesses.

As the duel was to take place the next day, at dawn, we all agreed and said we would meet at the appointed site before dawn to go over everything. Early that morning, when everyone arrived, I took Sean aside and asked him to apologize to the man and try to work things out. Sean refused, reassuring me that he was an excellent shot, that he would only wound the old man. Then he would take Maude away with him.

But just in case something did go wrong, Sean gave me an envelope addressed to his family and asked me to be sure they got it. I assured him I would and added, "But you can give it to them yourself."

We shook hands, then grabbed each other and hugged one another. Sean stepped back and, looking me in the eyes, said, "You're a good friend, Thomas, and I am glad we got to meet." Then he turned and walked away.

The sun was just coming up when a fancy carriage rode up and stopped. The old man and Maude got out. The gentleman in charge of the duel motioned for Sean and the man to come forward. He then instructed the two men on the rules of dueling and on fair play.

They would each take their place, standing back to back, and when they heard the firing of his pistol in the air, they were both to walk ten paces forward, turn, and fire their weapons at each other. The first man to go down was to stay down, and the man standing would be declared the winner. If neither man was hit, their seconds would bring them another loaded pistol. They would take aim and fire again until someone went down.

As the two men took their places, I looked at Sean. The look on his face was one of disbelief. I looked over to where Sean was looking. What I saw made my blood run cold. Maude was clapping her hands, and her face had a look of madness mixed with glee. The shot rang out, and the two men counted out the paces, turned, and fired their weapons. Both men stood, but as the smoke from their pistols cleared, I saw the look on Sean's face as the blood began to seep out of his forehead. He fell face forward to the ground before I could get to him.

I turned him over and could see he was gone. His eyes stared up at me with no life left in him. The physician that was to attend the wounded came rushing over. Bending down, he closed Sean's eyes and checked his breathing by putting a looking glass up to his nose and mouth. There was no breath coming from him. The physician turned and said, "I am sorry, but your friend is gone."

I couldn't believe Sean was gone. As I stood up, I turned and looked in the direction of Maude. She was hugging the old man and kissing his cheek. With a look of disgust and sadness on his face, he put her away from him, climbed into the carriage, and sat down. Maude climbed in behind him and sat down. As their carriage sped away, you could hear Maude laughing and the old man telling her to shut up.

After the undertaker declared Sean dead, two men came over, lifted Sean's body, and carried it over and placed it in the hearse. As I watched the hearse disappear around the drive, I was stunned and could hardly control my legs to stand on them. Devon and Clyde came over and stood behind me, saying how sorry they were about Sean.

Devon said he had been talking to the undertaker after the duel and was told that this was the third time he has had to bury a young man that was shot by the old man. Devon said it seemed as though the young girl, Maude, made a game out of tricking her husband into dueling over her with younger men. He said Maude was probably never carrying Sean's child.

When I asked the undertaker why the old man put up with his wife's madness, he replied, "He is an old man with a beautiful young wife, but someday, she will go too far and get what is coming to her."

I took the letter that Sean had given me and put it in my inside jacket pocket, to take it to his family later. The next day, I took the ferry across the Irish Sea. When I got across, I hired a hack to take me to Dublin. I found Sean's grandparents, along with some uncles, aunts, and cousins. I explained what had taken place with Sean and how he had died. I told them how much he loved them and how he talked about them all the time.

The look of sadness and grief was etched on all their faces, but there was no sign of surprise. Sean's grandfather explained to me that Sean was a very impetuous young boy, always doing things without thinking things through, always doing things to upset the applecart, so to speak.

As I thought of some of the things Sean had told me about when we were aboard the ship, I came to see that he did do things without thinking. His grandparents invited me to attend Sean's funeral, which would be held in about a week, giving them time to retrieve the body and prepare for the wake. I said I would be there.

A week later, I was back in Dublin to join the festivities and say goodbye to my friend. His body lay in state in his grandparents' living room so all his relatives and friends could pass by and view his body before being buried.

I was glad I had come to pay my last respects, as it was more of a celebration of Sean's life than a mourning of his death. Everyone drank to his living, danced to his memory, and shared stories relating to his life growing up. When I felt it was time for me to leave, I thanked everyone for including me in this memorable event and left. I caught the ferry back to Liverpool.

When I disembarked from the ferry, I looked around for a hack to take me home. I was surprised to see Markham's coach there. I walked over and was even more surprised but also pleased to see Melissa sitting inside. When she saw me, she said in a soft voice, "Please get in, Thomas." As I entered the coach, she said in that same soft voice, "I am so sorry for the loss of your friend."

I asked her, "What are you doing here, Melissa?"

She shrugged her shoulders and said, "I thought you would need a ride home and maybe some company."

After our truce, I didn't see Melissa as much, to my regret. On the ride to the Markhams' manor, we struck up a conversation on what we wanted out of life. I said, "After Sean's death, I realized that I needed a purpose in my life, and I think that is what my father was trying to tell me."

Melissa asked, "What kind of purpose are you looking for?"

I replied, "I don't know yet, but will know when I find that purpose. But right now, I just want to get back to Louisiana, back to the plantation and to my old life."

"You really miss it, don't you?" she asked, and I replied yes without hesitation. "No chance of you staying here, is there?" she said.

"No, no chance at all," I replied. Then I asked Melissa what she was looking for in her life.

She answered in a kind of a bitter voice, "I thought I had found what I was looking for, but then I found out it wasn't. It was just a fluke." I asked her what she meant by that, but she just turned and looked at me.

She laid her hand ever so softly on my thigh and started to move slowly toward me. As she got closer, I could feel her warm breath on my face. The sweet smell of her was intoxicating to my senses. I leaned in, and without thinking, I brushed my lips lightly across her lips.

She sighed and put her arms around my neck. When we came together, it was like an explosion going off. Melissa was soft and warm in my arms, moaning and pulling at my jacket. I reached up and undid her dress. It fell away from her creamy white shoulders. I undid her chemise, and it slid down past her breast. I kissed her neck, her shoulders, and finally her breasts.

Taking one of the rigid pink nipples into my mouth, I began to suck gently on it. Then I did the same to the other one, bringing Melissa to a height just above insanity. She was pulling at my hair, and I could feel myself losing control, but between Sean's tragic death and all the drink I had had at his wake, I didn't care.

I gently laid her back on the seat, slid up her dress, kissed her thighs all while releasing my manhood from my breeches. I got on top of her and tried to ease inside her moist velvet sheath, which was no easy feat with the coach bouncing and bobbing up and down as it sped down the rough road. She was moving and bucking against me so hard, I was about to lose all my restraint. I jammed down hard and began to move at a steady pace, all the while trying hard not to fall off the seat.

I felt Melissa tense, moan softly, and a minute later, relax. I knew she had found her release, so I moved faster and an instant later found my own release. We laid there still for a while until our breathing slowed and returned to normal, when all of a sudden, reality sank in. I sat up abruptly and did up my breeches. Then Melissa sat up, and I helped her get dressed.

When we finished smoothing out our clothes and hair, I began to apologize to Melissa for losing my control. Melissa let out a sigh and said, "Don't be sorry, Thomas. It was as much my fault as it was yours. I wanted to cheer you up but chose the wrong way to do it. Besides, it was some of the best lovemaking I have had in a while."

Her words caught me by surprise even though I knew she was no virgin. As her maidenhead was not intact. I was about to comment on that when the coach pulled to an abrupt stop. We had arrived at the manor. The door to the coach was pulled open by the footman, who gave me a knowing look with a wink. I scowled back at him and jumped out to help Melissa down. After stepping down, she turned toward me and pressed her hand on my cheek, smiled a sad smile, and said, "I am sorry, Thomas." She then turned and ran up the stairs and into the house.

As I entered the house, I found everyone had retired, as the hour was late. Instead of going straight to my room, I found my way to the study, poured myself a drink, and sat down. I began to ponder all that had happened today. As I thought about the ride home that night, my mind lingered on our lovemaking and how I had enjoyed it and knew Melissa had as well, so why had she said she was sorry? I finished my drink and went up to bed.

After that night, Melissa and I seemed to avoid each other—or was it just a coincidence that we each had things to do when we happened to be in the same room? Oh, we talked if we ran into one another in the presence of someone else or at the dinner table, but we didn't seek each other out.

It would be only one month before I would be going back home when Sir Markham called me into his study. He told me to take a seat as he closed the door to the study and poured himself a drink, but he did not offer me one. In fact, he was not very cordial at all. Sir Markham sat down, took a big sip of his drink, and looked me directly in the eye.

After studying me and making me uncomfortable to the point where I began to squirm in my seat, Sir Markham said, "Melissa came to me crying, saying she was with child."

After the shock wore off, I asked her who the father was. "At first," he said, "she did not want to tell me, but after much persuasion, she broke down and confessed that you were the father, that you had subdued her the night she had gone and picked you up after your friend's funeral. Is this true, Thomas?"

Caught off guard, I sat there staring at him in disbelief. He asked me again if it was true. I stammered, "No, not exactly."

He pounded his fist on his desk and yelled, "What do you mean, not exactly? Either you did or you didn't, Thomas."

"I can explain, sir, "I said.

He sneered at me, "Then do so," he replied.

"Yes, Melissa did come and pick me up that night, but it was Melissa that put herself out there for me. I was in a pretty low state of mind and had been drinking and admit I did not need much coaxing."

I could tell Sir Markham was thinking about what I had just said as he sat there quietly drumming his fingers on his desk. He knew his daughter, knew her to be a high-spirited young girl and had cautioned her many times to be careful around young men. After a few minutes, Sir Markham said in a stern voice, "I don't care who initiated the whole affair. You will do the right thing toward my daughter, do you understand?"

I sat there, stunned, trying to think of a way out of the mess I had gotten myself into. Where was Jacob when I needed him? A good slap on my head wouldn't hurt about now. I nodded my head yes, that I understood, until I could figure a way out of this.

"Good," I heard Sir Markham say. "We will all discuss the details at dinner this evening, when we are all together and everyone is calm."

At that statement, Sir Markham got up, walked over, and opened the door. With a wave of his hand, he dismissed me, and I left.

I went to school, as it was my last day and I would be receiving my degree in business. It should have been a great day for me, but I went through the motions of the ceremony like a robot. Thankfully, the day ended. I went back to the manor, looking for Melissa, but apparently, she was avoiding me—and doing a great job of it, as I could not find her anywhere.

By the time dinner rolled around, I had regained my wits and was thinking straight again. I was calm on the outside but boiling mad on the inside. I was the first to arrive at the dinner table. I took my seat and waited for the Markhams to show up. When they arrived, Sir Markham started the conversation, not missing a beat. He looked from me to Melissa and back to me.

Sir Markham began by saying that he and I had a talk this afternoon, and after our talk, I had asked for Melissa's hand in marriage and that he had given his consent along with his blessings. I held my composure, to my surprise. Melissa never looked up from her plate, and her mother kept dabbing at her eyes with her handkerchief while Sir Markham kept sighing throughout the whole dinner.

The whole affair was a disaster, but we all managed to get through it in a very civilized manner, as English people do. After dinner, Melissa excused herself and hurried out of the room before I could stop her. I waited for what I thought was an appropriate amount of time, then excused myself and said goodnight. I left the Markhams staring at each other. The look on Lady Markham's face said she was as unhappy about the situation as I was. Well, maybe not quite as much as me, but close.

I ran up the stairs two at a time to get to the second floor. When I reached my room, I passed it by and went straight to Melissa's room. I listened at the door but heard nothing. I knew she was awake as a light was coming from beneath the door. I turned the knob and opened the door without knocking. When I entered the room, I saw Melissa sitting at her vanity staring into a large round mirror. I caught my breath at the sight she made in the mirror.

Looking at the image of her made me realize just how beautiful she really was. Her eyes grew big at the sight of me, you could see how very dark blue they were, fringed in long black lashes. She had been brushing her long dark hair, which hung down her back in shiny waves. Her neck was slender and silky white, like ivory, as were her breasts, protruding just above her thin nightgown.

I walked over, picked up the brush, and began to brush her silky mane of hair. I didn't say a word, just stood there staring at her reflection in the mirror. Melissa leaned back against me, and when our eyes met in the mirror, I could see her tears forming and slipping down her cheeks. She said very softly, "I am so sorry, Thomas—I truly am—but I did not know what else to do." She continued, "I will be showing soon, and you would have been gone. I would have shamed my parents as well as myself."

I stayed calm and asked in a low voice, "Who is the real father?"

With a surprised look, she turned to face me. "How did you know?" she asked. I could see the sadness in her eyes. I wiped the tears from off her cheeks and replied, "Melissa, I was brought up on a plantation where we raised and bred animals. We had workers that got pregnant. Even for a backwoodsman, I knew it was too early for you to tell you were with child after us being together. So, I'll ask you again," I said a little too gruffly, "who is the real father of this child?"

Melissa said, "I have been seeing a young man who is a friend of our family. His name is Gregory Wainfield the Third. He is the son of Sir Henry Wainfield of Wainfield and Trenton, a very large law firm in London. You may have heard of them."

"Yes," I said, "I heard of the name. It has been brought up often as an example in class on how to become successful in business."

Melissa went on to say, "We have been seeing each other for over six months now, with the approval of both of our parents. But we had also been seeing each other on the sly. Three months ago," she said, "I told my parents that I was going with a friend to go shopping, but instead, Gregory and I met at his parents' summer home just outside London. Gregory was very charming and loving. One thing led to another, and we ended up in bed. I knew then that I loved Gregory and had thought he loved me too."

Continuing, Melissa said, "A few days later, when I tried to reach him, I couldn't. I sent him messages, but they were returned to me. After a month of trying to reach him, I stopped trying. I had to do something quick. I became desperate and didn't know what to do. I knew I would be showing soon."

"So," I said, "that's when you decided to subdue me and place the blame on me." Melissa nodded her head yes but would not look at me. "Why didn't you just tell your father the truth of who the real father was?" I asked her.

"Because I didn't want Father to force Gregory to marry me if he doesn't love me. I could not bear that humiliation," she replied.

"So you would force me into marriage and make both our lives miserable," I said.

She looked hurt and said, "Would that have been so terrible." Before I could answer her, she said in a low whisper, "I honestly did not think you would agree to marry me, that you would have protested, then slip away and make arrangements to return to America."

"You think so little of my character that I would do something like that?" I said angrily.

"No, no," Melissa quickly assured me, "deep down, I knew you would do the right thing. I only hoped you would prove me wrong."

"Well, for now, we will go along with your father's wishes until I can figure out a plan that will help us both out of this mess," I told her. Melissa reluctantly agreed with me. As I turned to leave, I stopped and told Melissa not to worry, it would all work out. I added that I thought her Gregory was a big fool if he did not want her. She smiled and thanked me.

I returned to my own room and thought about the mess I was in and just how I was going to get out of it. I could do what Melissa hoped I would do and sneak away. Then I thought of Jacob and all he had taught me to do, to be a man and face my problems head-on. I was determined to fix this the right way, for all our sakes.

My thoughts then turned to my stay in England for the last two years. I had made new friends. I had learned a lot about life and the different ways of living it. I found I enjoyed my stay in England. I enjoyed the nightlife very much as well as the lovely ladies who taught me the likes and dislikes of women, which I became an expert at—or so I thought.

Then I thought about my friend Sean and knew I wanted more from life than that. I knew I wanted more than anything to return home. I was determined more than ever to find a way out of all this.

In the morning, after a restless night's sleep, I got out of bed, dressed and had my breakfast, and left the manor before anyone else had risen. I sent a message to my friend Devon, who had gotten a job in a small law firm after finishing school. The firm was in London. I asked him to meet with me for lunch at a small eatery around the corner from where he worked.

When I arrived, Devon was already there waiting for me. After we exchanged pleasantries, I got down to the reason why I was really there. I told Devon what had occurred between Melissa and me and about the fix I was in. I asked him if he knew Gregory Wainfield. Devon nodded his head yes and whistled through his front teeth.

"You know," Devon said, "you will be going up against a very powerful family."

"Yes," I replied, "but I see no other way out of this, so will you help me?"

"Yes, of course I will help you, but you know there's another alternative to this situation," he said.

"Yes, and what would that alternative be?" I asked him.

"You can always book out of here and skip back to America, old chap."

"I could—Melissa suggested the same thing—but that wouldn't be very cricket of me, now, would it? Besides, it would still leave Melissa on her own, and I think this Gregory should own up to what he did. All I need is for you to arrange it so I can meet face to face with the blackguard. I will do the rest," I told Devon. He thought about it while we ate our lunch, and halfway through, he looked up with a smile on his face and said, "I can arrange the meet. I will send word to you when and where it will take place."

"What can I do to help you," Devon asked me.

"I don't want you to get involved," I said.

Two days later, I received a message and a card from Devon. The message said to meet him at the Gentlemen's Club on Whipple Place. "Bring the card with you. It will allow you entrance to get into the club," the message read. The meet was set at eight o'clock that evening. I went about my daily routine, and when it was time for dinner, I ate in a hurry, explaining I was to meet Devon for a night on the town. I said goodnight to the Markhams, and as I left, I winked at Melissa, making her blush.

Sir Markham had given me permission to take the small carriage for the evening, so I had the driver, Jenkins, bring it around to the front of the house. I got in and settled myself down. Before Jenkins started off, he opened the hatch and asked me where I wanted to be taken this evening. I told him to take me to the Gentlemen's Club at Whipple Place. He looked at me and said, "Are you sure, sir?" I answered yes. He closed the hatch, and we were off.

An hour and a half later, the carriage pulled to a stop. I looked out the window and could see we were near a green meadow and that there were no other houses around. The club was a vast mansion, painted pristine white with immaculately kept grounds all around it. It was well lit up and very welcoming. As I stepped out of the carriage, I told Jenkin's to wait for me, as I shouldn't be very long. "As you wish," he said as he snuggled down lower in his seat to stay warm.

I got out of the carriage and ran across the road and up to the big mansion. I stood and admired the place for a few seconds, then continued up the wide staircase to the big wooden double doors. The doors were magnificent, made out of solid oak with a tiny door at about eye level built into one side of them.

I picked up the door knocker, which was shaped like a lion's head, and let it fall against the door. A few seconds later, the small door opened, and a gruff voice asked, "May I help you?" I held up the card that Devon had sent along with his note to me. The door opened, and I stepped inside. I was greeted by a large, burly looking servant. He asked if he could take my coat and hat. As I handed them to him, I looked around and was caught by surprise. I was standing in a very large, brightly lit room. There were overstuffed chairs and sofas throughout the room. The floors were covered with brightly colored rugs. Beautiful chandeliers hung from the ceilings. On each side of the big room were smaller rooms. But what really caught my attention wasn't the number of men sitting or walking about but the beautiful women accompanying them. Then it dawned on me just exactly what kind of gentleman's club this was.

I looked around and saw Devon sitting on one of the sofas with a pretty young lady and a stuffy looking gentleman. Devon had been watching me, and I could tell by the grin on his face he was amused by my surprise that this wasn't just a place for men to come, have a drink, a good cigar, and some intelligent conversation with each other.

I managed to get the stupid look off of my face and replace it with a bland look of boredom, which made Devon laugh out loud. He excused himself, came over, and slapped me on the back, then led me over to the sofa.

Devon introduced me to the young lady, whose name was Gigi. I bowed low and gently kissed the small hand she extended to me. She murmured low, in a husky voice, "My pleasure, Master Thomas."

"The pleasure is all mine, madame, "I said, "and please call me Thomas."

"Only if you call me Gigi and not madame," she replied with a laugh. Our attention turned to the man sitting there, looking very bored.

"Thomas, I would like you to meet George Wanfield," Devon

said. He did not stand or look up as I extended my hand to him. Getting irritated, I said a little gruffly, "Nice to meet you, George." At that, he did look up. He had sandy brown hair, tied neatly back in a queue, a straight nose, and a square jaw. His green eyes were veiled. I could see how Melissa could fall for this jerk if he lost that attitude.

Devon whispered something to Gigi. She stood up, kissed him on the cheek, and then said goodnight to Gregory and me. She then turned and walked to one of the side rooms. Devon turned to me and asked if I needed anything else. I shook my head no. Devon said, "Then, if you two gentlemen will excuse me, I have more important things to attend to." At that, he turned and walked to the door Gigi had gone through.

As I watched Devon disappear through the door, I hoped that Gregory would get off his high horse so I could talk to him. I turned to face him and said, "In case you are wondering why I asked for this meeting with you tonight, I wanted to talk to you about Melissa." At the mention of Melissa's name, Gregory's head snapped up. I now had his full attention.

Gone was the bored look on his face. It was replaced with one of interest and concern. I told Gregory that Melissa and I were to be married in the next few weeks. He went pale, and then his face turned red, and he clenched his fists. When he stood up, I could see he was a few inches shorter than I was but solidly built. I hoped this conversation would not resort to blows before he let me explain.

All of a sudden, Gregory looked like the wind had been knocked out of him as he sat back down with a defeated look on his face. In a low voice, he said, "Why? Why would she do this to me? She knows I love her, so why would she marry someone else?"

On hearing this confession from Gregory, I relaxed, sat down beside him, and began to slowly tell him all that had happened to bring about the events that led up to tonight's meeting. Of course, I left out the part of what took place in the coach that night. That would be up to Melissa to tell him or not.

Gregory sat there for a while, contemplating what I had just told him. I had grabbed a drink from a passing servant and was sipping on it when Gregory finally told me that he had never received any messages from Melissa and the ones he had sent to her had been returned to him unopened. He said he thought she was mad at him for taking advantage of her that night in his family's summer home. Gregory said he thought Melissa was just mad and was punishing him by not wanting to see him for a while.

I assured Gregory that Melissa had not received his messages either and that the ones she had sent to him had also been returned to her unopened. Gregory suddenly stood up, shook my hand, and thanked me for enlightening him on this very important matter. As he headed for the door, he abruptly stopped, turned around, and said, "No matter what, do not go through with the wedding. I will get to the bottom of this. Please promise me."

Almost laughing, I assured him that I had no intention of going through with the wedding. "Good," he shouted over his shoulder as he went out through the door. "Tell Melissa and her parents I will call upon her in the next few days, after I get to the bottom of all this." Then he was gone.

I sat there, relieved, and finished my drink. As I was about to take my leave, a very pretty young lady approached me and asked if I would like to join her in one of the other rooms. Not one to turn down an invitation of this kind, I obliged the young lady. I had only a slight bit of guilt for poor Jenkins and hoped he had sense enough to get inside the coach.

The next morning I rose early and left for the docks. On my way, I stopped by the lawyer's office and told them to close all accounts in the next two days that my father had set up for me while I was in England. I was informed that it was already in the process of being done. I thanked them and continued on to docks. When I arrived there, I went straight to the dockmaster and made arrangements to board the ship sailing to America and on to Louisiana and finally to my home. I was informed that passage was already booked for me and I would be sailing on the same ship that had brought me here two years earlier. I went about getting ready to leave here before the end of the week. I could hardly contain my excitement, and I kept busy so time would pass more quickly.

The Markham household was not the best place to be right now. It contained an air of unhappiness and despair. Sir Markham was busy making plans for Melissa and his soon-to-be son-in-law, me. Lady Markham would break out weeping every time I came into her view, and Melissa sat about wringing her hands, sighing in despair. I did not inform Melissa about my talk with Gregory, as I did not want to raise her hopes if he did not come through.

Truth be told, I was starting to get worried about myself and began to make a plan B just in case this one did not work out. It was just after noon the next day when one of the servants came into the dining room and announced the arrival of a guest. I stood up quickly and replied it would be for me and left the room with the servant.

Standing in the foyer was Gregory, looking like the cat that had eaten the canary. We shook hands, and I must say, I was very relieved to see that he had most definitely showed up. We headed for the dining room just as the Markhams were all coming out. I stood back and watched how each one of their faces reacted as they saw Gregory standing there.

I could see the great regard they all had for him. Sir Markham's smile widened as he walked toward Gregory. When he reached him, he slapped him hard on his back and almost shook his hand off, saying how good it was to see him again. Lady Markham was like a young schoolgirl, giggling nervously while telling him how delighted she was to see him as Gregory bowed and kissed her hand.

When I looked at Melissa and our eyes met, it was like looking into a thunderstorm. Her features were set in a grimace, and her stance suggested she was about to take flight. As Gregory turned to Melissa, he took a step back away from her. The fire in her blue eyes felt like it burned right through him. Then Melissa found her voice, and all hell broke loose. Her voice became shrill as she looked at Gregory and said, "What are you doing here? Go away." She then turned to me, took hold of my arm, and tried to guide me toward the hallway close to the stairs, where I guessed she would bolt for the stairs and flee to her room above.

I stopped her in her tracks, took hold of her chin, and lifted her face so she would be looking directly into my eyes. I could see the hurt and mistrust in them as she looked up at me. I also saw the tears that were starting to fill them. Hugging her close to me, in a calm voice, I whispered in her ear, "Give Gregory a chance and listen to what he has to say."

Melissa looked at me for what seemed like a very long time, but after a few minutes, she agreed. I let out the breath that I had been holding, as did everyone else. I let loose of her chin, and Melissa turned. Without looking at anyone, she walked back into the dining room and sat down. I motioned for Gregory to follow her. He hesitated for a second, then hastened after her.

When her parents started to follow the two, I suggested they give them time to themselves. I then told the Markhams that if they followed me to the parlor, I would tell them what was going on.

Inside the dining room, Gregory was explaining how his father had found out about the two of them seeing each other, so his father had all the servants and drivers spy on him. When one of them at our summer home saw us there, he reported back to his father of the affair. Gregory's father had all the messages retrieved and returned before they could be delivered to each party.

His father then sent him to Edinburgh to see a client of theirs. It took a week with the client, and he kept sending messages but never heard back. He said, "I now know why, as you never received them."

"Melissa, darling, I swear I did not know," Gregory said. "I thought you hated me for taking advantage of you and not telling you how much I love you. I was going to tell you the next day and ask you to marry me, but then all this happened. If Thomas had not come to see me, I would have never known."

Melissa sat there dumbfounded, trying to process all that he just told her, "Please, Melissa. I do love you. Please, say you will marry me." Melissa started to cry and threw herself into Gregory's arms. They then shared a very passionate kiss.

After I explained everything to Melissa's parents, I assured them that Gregory wanted to marry their daughter. The look of relief and happiness on their face almost made me laugh out loud again. When Melissa and Gregory opened the door, I stood back while everyone hugged and congratulated each other. Melissa came over and gave me a big hug, thanked me, and whispered in my ear, "You really would have been my second choice for a husband." I chuckled and congratulated her and Gregory, and silently myself, for getting out of a very sticky situation.

The next week flew by, with the wedding taking place and all the goodbyes I had to say to all the friends I had made. I was a little sad to say goodbye to Devon and Clyde, as we had become very close these last two years, but we promised we would write to each other to keep in touch. I thanked the Markhams for all their kindness of putting up with me. They assured me it was their pleasure.

As I stood on the deck of the ship, watching the docks, buildings, and people grow smaller as the ship caught the tide and the wind blew out the sails, we picked up speed, and I began to feel the excitement growing inside me. I couldn't believe I was actually on my way home.

"Hard to believe time went by so fast, isn't it?" Captain Richards asked as he held his hand out to me.

I shook his hand and said, "It's good to see you again, sir."

"Likewise," he replied. We stood on the deck and talked a while until Captain Richards said he had to get back to running the ship. He turned to go but stopped, reached in his jacket pocket, and pulled out a worn letter. "I almost forgot to give this to you," he said as he handed it to me. "I am sorry. It's at least a year old Thomas, but I could not deliver it any sooner because of the war going on back in the States."

War? I thought. Yes, there was mention of some kind of war, but it was so far from here, where I was, I really did not pay much attention to the talk, as I they to be mere rumors. I thanked the captain and went below to my cabin. I still had to unpack, but first, I wanted to read the letter I had been given. I sat down, opened the letter, and began to read it with shaky hands. It had been so long since I had heard from home. It began,

My dear Tommy,

I hope you are well. We all miss you terribly and will be real glad when you are home again. You probably have heard there is a war going on here between our South and the North.

Things are starting to get real bad, Tommy, real bad. We is getting low on supplies, and there is a lot of grumbling amongst the slaves on the plantations. Most all the young men, and all the young boys that is old enough has been called to go fight in the war. Eli could not go because of his missing foot, thank the Lord.

Most of the others did join because they promised them their freedom if they joined. Your friend Jason could not join either, as his father had a heart attack and they were no one to run their plantation. But miss Jenny's fiancé did join, and she is worried sick about him. I thank the Lord again that your daddy had since enough to send you away, or knowing you, you would be in the thick of things. I will try to write to you again. Your daddy is doing fine, as is Jacob.

As always,

Marta

After reading Marta's letter a second time, I felt sick to my stomach and guilty for not being there and doing my part instead of gallivanting around England like a pompous ass, having a good time with a war going on back home. I hurried and put my things away, then changed into my old clothes I had worn over here. Although I had filled out quite a lot and grown taller, the clothes, albeit a little tighter and a little shorter, fit me well enough for the trip home. It felt great getting out of the European clothes.

I went above deck and saw Mr. Gage. I stopped and said hello, then continued to the dining room for some lunch. The only one there was Captain Richards. He nodded for me to come sit and have some lunch, so I took the chair next to him and sat down. He handed me a bowl of piping hot stew and a piece of freshly baked bread. I took it and thanked him. After a few bites, Captain Richards asked if I had gotten settled in all right. I answered yes, I had, and thanked him. Then I asked him to tell me about the war going on back home.

Captain Richards took a deep breath, then slowly let it out. He said, "It's not something I like to talk about, but I will tell you what I know. If you recall, there was trouble brewing between the North and the South for quite some time, but it really started to escalate in 1861, the year your father sent you to England. Things really took a turn for the worse when the North pushed their way South. It got real bad from then on.

"It got even worse the year of 1826, when President Lincoln was trying to abolish slavery, among other things. General Grant took the upper hand over General Lee. Although the war did not start in Louisiana, it did make its way through there. The input of the war played havoc on the people of that state, as well as all the other Southern states, as supplies were cut off going there and thousands of lives were lost or ruined."

Captain Richards rubbed his hand over his face, as if trying to erase the memories, I noticed how worn and tired he looked. He went on to tell me how bad it really was. "Most of the slaves had either ran off or rioted, starting fires in the cane fields or burning down barns and homes—even killing folks they worked for for years and slaying their livestock." Upon hearing this last bit of information, I must have turned pale, as the captain asked if I was all right. I nodded my head yes, as I was unable to speak.

A young steward came and asked if we were through with our lunch. The captain nodded his head that he was through, and I shook my head yes, as I couldn't choke down another bite after listening to what the captain had just told me. The young steward cleared the table and left.

Captain Richards turned to look me directly in the eyes and said, "Your father knew what was coming. That's why he sent you away when he did. There was nothing you could do to prevent this war. You should not blame yourself or feel guilty or blame your father. He only did what he thought was right for you."

I sat there looking at the captain for a minute, letting what he said sink in. Then I nodded my head that I understood. I got up and excused myself and went below. I lay down on the bed and thought about everything, from Captain Richard's explanation to Marta's letter, they basically said the same thing, but that didn't change the way I was feeling.

I turned over and tried to clear my mind of everything, but it kept coming back to Marta's letter. I sat up like a bolt of lightning. I grabbed her letter and read through it fast, until I came to the part about Jenny's fiancé joining the fight against the North. When did Jenny get engaged? I thought she was too young, but then I realized she would be going on seventeen years old now. A pang of jealousy hit me like a ton of bricks. Then I said to myself, *Get a hold of yourself, man. She's like your sister. You should be happy for her.*

It was the middle of the year. It would take at least two months to get back home, weather permitting. I sighed, got up, and poured myself a glass of water and drank it, trying to ease the throbbing that was beginning in the back of my head. The more I stayed in my room, the more my mind wandered. Finally, I decided it would do no good to wallow away the time in my room.

When I reached the deck above, I took in several gulps of fresh air to clear my head. I began to walk the deck like Sean and I had on our way over to England. I thought about all that had taken place in my short life. I was now nineteen years old. When I got home, I vowed to myself to make a better life for all the people I loved.

On the trip home, I did everything I could to make the time pass by faster. When I woke up in the morning, I would get up, get dressed, and eat my breakfast with Captain Richard's and Mr. Gage. After breakfast, I would help Mr. Gage with whatever chores he had to do that day. Some days after the noon meal, if there were no chores to do, Captain Richards and I would partake in a game of chess for a couple of hours. Afterward, I would retire to my room below deck and read one of the books the captain had loaned to me.

When it was time for dinner, I would always eat with either the captain or Mr. Gage or sometimes both of them. We would talk for a while after dinner, and before I would retire for the night, I would take a stroll once around the deck

The closer we got to America, the more careful we became. Some nights, if another vessel was spotted in the distance, our ship would slow to a stop and all the lights would be extinguished. Everyone aboard would be very still and not make a sound until we heard the sound of the other vessel pass by. Everyone held their breath until we were sure it was far away from us. During the day, if one was spotted in the distance, we would veer off course until it could no longer be seen. Because this procedure was making it take longer to get home, I asked why we did this. Mr. Gage replied, "Because under cover of darkness, we can't be seen by the enemy, and during the day, we get out of their way." He went on to explain that there were still blockades up around some of the ports. "Any ships caught bringing in supplies to the enemy will be charged with treason, imprisoned, or hanged."

The ships that passed by were likely to be ships patrolling these waters from the North, equipped with canyons capable of blowing a ship like this out of the water. We were fortunate that we only had two close calls. On the ninth week of sailing, we sighted the Louisiana coastline in the distance. All I could think of was that in a few days, the Lord willing, I would be home at last.

After gathering all my things and packing them up, I went topside and stood by the rail. The excitement of being this close to home bubbled up inside me. Not knowing what I was about to encounter made me a little apprehensive. All sorts of questions popped into my mind, like how were the people I cared about doing? How was my home, and how had everything changed?

As we came closer to the docks, I could start to see some of the destruction. The docks alongside the one we were about to tie up to were totally destroyed. Most of the other docks were empty. What had once been a thriving port of call was now a dismal burnt out port. My heart sank at the sight I encountered. There was no cargo waiting to be loaded onto any ships and no passengers waiting to go aboard them. It was deathly quiet.

As I looked past the docks, I saw very few people on the streets and only a few skinny stray dogs sniffing for food. It gave me an eerie feeling. We pulled alongside one of the few docks that were intact and safe enough to use. No one was there to meet me. *How could they?* I thought. *No one knows your home.* But that knowledge didn't keep my stomach from tying itself into knots.

When all my things were unloaded, I said my goodbyes to Captain Richards and Mr. Gage once again and thanked them for the safe trip home. Captain Richards said, "Take care of yourself, young Thomas. I probably will not see you again, God willing. I will be retiring after this trip. Now we have to shove off, as it isn't safe to stay in port any longer than necessary."

I shook his hand and said, "Godspeed," turned, and ran down the gangplank to where my two trunks had been placed. As I turned to wave goodbye, I saw the anchor was already being hoisted up and the ropes untied from the dock.

I watched as the ship drifted along with the tide and the sails caught the wind. I turned my attention to the almost empty street.

There were two old men sitting in front of a rundown store. I caught myself thinking out loud, "How could this have happened in the two short years I was gone? Was the town always this run down and I just didn't notice because it was always filled with all kinds of activity going on?"

As I looked up and down the street, I saw old man Williams' stable. It was too far to carry my trunks, but I could walk there and maybe rent a horse and wagon. As I got nearer the stable, I saw how dilapidated the place was. I stepped inside the dark building and waited until my eyes adjusted to the dimness. I looked around, and all I saw were two old horses and one pretty shabby wagon.

I called out, "Hello, anyone here?" From behind me, a small voice said hello back, but I could not see anyone in the dim light. I said hello again. A few seconds later, a small towheaded lad about six years old came slowly out from behind the old wagon. From a small patch of light shining through a broken board on one wall, I could see the apprehensiveness on his small dirty face. I could sense that at any minute, he would try to dart around me and bolt through the open door.

I slowly bent down to eye level with the young boy and said in a soft voice so as not to scare him any more than he already was, "Are these your horses and wagon?" He slowly nodded his head yes. "I would like to rent them from you, if that is okay." Again, he just shook his head yes. "Where is your father?" I asked him.

With a squaring up of his shoulders and an angry look on his little features, he spat out, "He's dead, kilt in the war."

"I am so sorry," I replied. "Who takes care of you?"

"I do," said an old man entering the building from a side door, holding a very large shotgun under one arm. "I am Andrew Williams, and who might you be?" he asked.

"Andy, is that you?" I asked as I stuck out my hand and said, "It's me, "Tommy Sanduval."

"Well, I be darned. It really is you, ain't it, Tommy?" Andy said as he lowered his gun. The two shook hands and slapped each other on their backs.

Andy then introduced me to the young boy, who was now hanging onto Andy's leg. "This here's my grandson James, Robert's son. You remember my son Robert?"

"Yes, yes, I do, and I am so sorry for your loss," I replied as I thought about the young boy with blond hair with whom I had gone to school. Looking at his grandson, I could see the resemblance to Robert.

Andy and I talked for a while. He told me how the war had affected the whole South. He said that a lot of the young men had been killed or maimed. Then Andy said, "As bad as the war was, the rebels running around looting and killing in the name of the South is far worse." This last part he spoke with bitterness in his voice. He said, "It makes all the men and boys kilt in the cursed war all for nothing. What about you, Tommy? I heard you had gone off to England. What brings you back here?"

"I did go to England—before the war broke out," I said defensively. "It was my father's wishes, and I am sorry I was not here to help."

"No matter. One more boy would not have made a difference in this war. It would have taken thousands more men and artillery," Andy replied, brushing off my statement with a swipe of his hand. "Now, what can I do for you, Tommy?" he said.

"I would like to rent a horse and wagon to take my things to the plantation," I told him.

"You can use them and bring them back when you come to town again, free of charge," Andy said. He helped me hitch up the wagon to one of the better horses he had left after the army had confiscated all the others. I climbed aboard and sat on the loose seat. *God,* I thought, *I hope I make it home.* As I started out of the stable, I flipped Andy the last coin I had in my breeches.

"Bless you," he said. "Keep an eye out on your way home."

"I will," I called back as I led the horse over to the dock where

I had left my trunks. When I got there, I loaded them up, climbed back up, settled myself down, and set out for the long ride home.

As I rode past all the shops, houses, and businesses, I could see the destruction caused by the war. Windows were broken out. Doors were hanging by their hinges. Some were burnt, and some were just sitting empty. Of the few people I saw on the streets, I could see the pain of despair etched on their faces and the utter defeat in the way they moved about.

Most were women and very young children or very old men. Once again, I felt that heavy pang of guilt in the pit of my stomach for not being here and doing my part, whatever that might have been. As I made my way out of town, I saw much more destruction in burnt-out barns, homes, and crops all along the way.

Hours later, I reached the outskirts of our property. I turned onto the road that led to our house, and along the way, I saw several fields of our sugar cane burnt to the ground, along with some of the outbuildings. As I got nearer to the cabins, I saw some of them had also burned, but they looked repairable. When I turned into the view of the house, I saw it was all intact except for the storage shed attached to the back of the house. I let out the breath that I had been holding, along with a sigh of relief.

I pulled in front of the house and reined in the horse that had pulled the wagon. The poor thing looked almost dead and was glad to stop. I jumped down from the wagon and started up the steps of the house. I heard my name being called from behind me. I turned around and saw Marta standing a few steps below me. The basket she had been holding dropped to the ground, and with outstretched arms, we ran to each other.

"Lord be praised," Marta said with tears in her eyes. When I reached her, I swept her up in my arms. Holding her tightly, I twirled her around in a circle. She was laughing and crying at the same time. About that time, Jacob and Eli came rushing out to see what all the commotion was. When Jacob saw me, he went down the stairs, two at a time. He grabbed my hand and shook my arm so hard, I thought it would fall off. I gently put Marta down. Then we grabbed each other and hugged one another, and when we parted, Jacob had tears in his eyes. To make light of the situation, I smiled and said, "Still allergy season, huh?" He just grunted and made as if he was going to slap my head.

I looked past Jacob and up the stairs, where Eli was standing, taking everything in. He stood on one leg with a crutch holding him up, and he had that silly grin on his face, like he always got when he bested me at something, like the time we got in a fight over Lily Mae when we were younger. He liked her and, she was flirting with me. Eli got mad and asked her what she was doing with this pretty boy. I said, "Who you calling pretty?"

He replied, "You. The only way you could be any prettier was if'n you were black."

I shot back at him, "Well ... well ..." and couldn't come up with anything to say.

I took the stairs in long strides and reached Eli in seconds. We stood for what seemed like an eternity, just looking at each other. Then, suddenly, we were slapping each other's backs and hugging and talking at the same time. I stopped and Eli said, still grinning at me, "It's about time you were getting yourself home. Things were getting pretty rough around here."

"I know," I replied. "I would have been here long before now, but your mom's letter was delayed almost a year. I got her letter when I boarded the ship for home."

"Don't matter none, your home now, "Eli said. I turned and motioned for Marta and Jacob to join us. As I watched the two climb the stairs, I noticed how they had aged in the two short years I had been away.

Once again, the guilt washed over me, and I silently vowed to make things better. I didn't know how, but I would. When we all got to the kitchen, Marta made coffee and brought out a freshly made pie. As she cut the pie, she said she was sorry if it didn't taste right, but they were low on supplies and didn't have all the right ingredients that went into making the pie.

The pie smelled great and made my mouth water. I hadn't realized how hungry I was, as I hadn't eaten since I'd left the ship that morning. I ate three pieces of pie and drank two cups of coffee. Marta sat down beside me and watched as I ate with a big grin on her face. When I looked around, they were all watching me eat, and then Jacob blurted out, "Christ, didn't they feed you on the way home?" and everyone started laughing. God, it was great being home.

As we sat there drinking our coffee, we exchanged stories of all that had happened to each of us in the previous two years. Then Marta asked me why I had not asked about my father or Jenny. I stopped drinking and looked her in her eyes, and then I said, "I should have been here, not sent away to England. My place was here with my family." Looking right back at me, Marta informed me that my father had not come out of his room since the plantation had been set on fire. I really did not know how to respond to that. Right now, I was still angry at my father. I still loved him and hated to hear this about him. I had always thought about my father as needing no one, a very strong person detached from feeling any emotion.

"What about Jenny?" I asked to change the subject. Marta sighed a deep sigh, then said, "Jenny is engaged to be married."

Keeping myself from showing any emotion, I said, "I know. You wrote me that in your letter. I'm happy for her."

I excused myself from the table, squeezed Marta's hand, and told them I would see them all later this evening, as I had some unpacking to tend to. I went upstairs, and when I got to my father's room, I stopped, tapped on the door, and opened it. As I entered the room, it was dark and smelled musty. I went over to the window and drew open the heavy curtains.

As the light came in across his bed, I saw my father lying there. I stared in shock at his appearance. He had grown old in the time I had been gone. What had been a strong-looking man when I left was now white headed, with lines crisscrossing his face. He had lost weight and looked like a broken man. My father looked twenty years older than his sixty-some years.

I felt a pang of pity for him as I walked over to the bed. I reached out and gently shook his shoulder. Phillip stirred and opened his eyes, blinked a few times, then settled on me. "Thomas, is that you?" he said. "Is it really you?"

"Yes," I replied. "It's really me. I am home now." While still looking at his eyes, I could see the former spark was no longer there. I saw how the war had affected him, and I was hit with remorse at how angry I had gotten at him when all he wanted was to protect me.

"Please, sit here on the bed with me and tell me how our crops are coming along. Will we be getting a bumper crop this year?" my father asked me. I was taken aback as I realized his mind was working as if nothing had happened and that I had never gone away.

I replied, "Yes, the crops will yield a high quantity this year."

"I am sorry I cannot help in the field today, but maybe tomorrow," he said and sighed. I patted his hand and told him it was all right, just for him to rest and get better. "Thank you, son," he said, then shut his eyes. I left the room and shut the door. I then went back downstairs, where only Marta was waiting for me. She told me that Eli had gone to finish the books so he could tally up the supplies we had left and Jacob had gone to fetch the workers from the fields.

"I am sorry I did not tell you about your father earlier. I wrote you about him almost six months ago, but now I know you did not receive the letter." Marta went on to say, "I know how overwhelming this must be for you, as this all falls on your shoulders now that you are home. Eli, Jacob, and I will do all we can to help you, as will all the rest of the slaves that are still here."

"How many are still here?" I asked Marta.

"Near all of them. A few of the younger boys ran off, and we ain't heard from them since, so don't know if they is all right or not," she replied.

"About my father, just how bad he is. Will he get better?" I asked.

"The doctor said his mind snapped when he saw all the looting, the burning of all the buildings, and the killing of his livestock that took place on the plantation," she answered, then added, "not from any of our own but slaves from the other farms and from the rebels that came through here. Your father could not stop what was happening here. It's like his heart and mind broke and he can't be mended."

"But did the doc say if he would get better?" I said.

"The doctor didn't know. He said only time will tell," Marta replied with a sigh and a shrug of her shoulders.

"Thank you, Marta," I said, "for all you, Eli, and Jacob did while I was gone. You could have left too. Why didn't you?"

"Where would we have gone, Tommy? This is our home, the only one some of us has ever had."

I went over and put my arms around her and kissed the top of her head. She hugged me tightly, and when she let go, I headed for the door, saying, "I am going to inspect the lay of the land and assess the damage."

On my way out, I called over my shoulder, "I will be back soon. When I return, I would like to talk to Eli."

Marta nodded her head and told me to be careful, then added, "Take your rifle with you, as there are still rebels scouring the land around here." I did as she suggested and picked up the rifle on my way out.

I went to the barn and saddled a horse and rode out. On my way, I rode past the slave cabins. I counted two cabins burnt clear down and one that had some damage but could be restored. I made notes as to what we would need to rebuild and repair them. Next I rode to the fields. I saw firsthand what my father saw. Two large sugar cane fields were completely destroyed by burning them to the ground, but two fields had been left in fairly good condition. *Good*, I thought, *we can salvage these so not a complete loss, and maybe we can survive till the next planting.* I got sick to my stomach when I came upon all the animal carcasses, where they had been slaughtered. What a waste.

I made more notes on everything that would have to be replaced and replanted. I really did not know how I would go about doing all this, but I vowed I would somehow find a way to do it, as there were too many people depending on it. By the time I returned to the house, it was already dusk.

I left my horse at the stable and went in search of Eli to go over the books and view the list of supplies we had left. When I knocked on the door to Eli's cabin, a young slave girl answered it. She looked familiar to me. Then it dawned on me as to who it was. It was the same girl I had brought home from Pierce's party that night two years ago.

"Roslyn, isn't it?" I asked.

"Yes" the girl answered, not looking me directly in my eyes."

"Is Eli here?" I asked her.

"No, but he will be shortly," she replied.

"Do you live here now?" I asked, thinking maybe she was here cleaning Eli's cabin or maybe she was one of the ones that their cabin burned down and her family was sharing Eli's.

"Yes," she said, and about that time, a baby started to cry in the other room.

"Excuse me," Roslyn said, and she disappeared to the other room. When she reappeared, she held a newborn baby in her arms. "This is Josie," she said.

"Oh, so you are married?" I asked her.

"Yes, I am married. This is mine and Eli's daughter," she replied.

I was taken aback by that statement. *Eli married and with a daughter? Why didn't he tell me?* I wondered. Just then, the door opened and Eli stepped inside, holding the hand of a small girl, about the age of two. At first glance at me, Eli could tell I was surprised, as I still had a dumbfounded look on my face.

"Ah, I see you have met my wife and daughter. This is our other daughter, Joy," Eli said with a big grin on his face.

"Yes, I have," I replied. "Why didn't you tell me you were married with a family?"

"And miss the look on your face just now." He laughed. Then he got serious and said, "I was going to tell you earlier, but you already had a lot to process with your father, the plantation, and all the destruction. I figured my news could wait a day or two."

"Well, congratulations, "I said as I shook his hand. "When did all this happen?"

"Just after you left, Roslyn helped my mother with some small chores that had to be done with me and we fell in love and married, and you seen what else came along. Roslyn got pregnant right off but she lost it a month later. ""I am sorry," I said, not knowing what else to say. "It's all right. God works miracles, as you can see," Eli said.

"Praise the Lord," Roslyn chimed in.

After that, Eli and I got down to the matter at hand. We went over the books and made a list of the supplies we had on hand. We found we had neither enough money nor supplies on hand to rebuild the two cabins or repair the one cabin partly burnt, along with the damage done to the back of the house. The supplies we had left to take care of all of us, food-wise, was also in short demand. There was probably only enough to get us through the summer. I told Eli, if the remaining crops yielded a bountiful crop and we could sell them for a good price, we could make it through the winter if we were careful.

As the hour was growing late, I told Eli we would figure it all out in the morning after we got a good night's sleep. I said goodnight to Roslyn and Eli, congratulated them again, and went to the house. When I got there, everyone had retired, but Marta had left some food on the stove for me. I sat down and ate, then went upstairs to check on my father. He looked worse, I thought. I would send for the doctor in the morning.

I tossed and turned all during the night, until I finally came to a conclusion on what I had to do to help the plantation survive this ordeal. That morning I got up, dressed, and went downstairs. I went to one of the cabins and asked one of the young boys to go fetch the doctor. As I watched the boy ride out, I went back to the house to wait for Eli and Jacob to come in.

When Marta got here, she started the coffee and then made

breakfast. Within a few minutes, the two men joined me. Over a cup of coffee, I told everyone what I had planned. I explained that I would go to the large bank in New Orleans and borrow the money needed to repair everything and to get the supplies we needed.

"But don't you need collateral to borrow money from a bank?" Asked Eli.

"Yes," I replied, "I will use the remaining crops we have left, and I will put the plantation up for the collateral as well. When we rebuild and replant the crops, we will be able to make the payments on the loan. I know it will be rough the first few years, but we will survive and save the plantation." They all agreed, it sounded like a solid plan that would help them get back on their feet.

Marta came over and patted my shoulder, gave me a big hug, and said it sure is good to have my boy back home. As always, Marta had a way of lifting my spirits up. After we finished eating and having our coffee, we all went about our morning routines. Jacob went to check on the workers in the fields, Eli went to the office to make a copy of the books to take to the bank, Marta fixed something for my father to eat, then went to try to get him to eat it and I ended up helping the stable boy clean out the stables while I waited for the doctor.

We only had the four horses left, but that would give me two horses to pull the wagon I would need for the supplies I would be getting from New Orleans. The doctor arrived late that afternoon. I accompanied him upstairs while he examined my father. When he was through, he motioned for me to leave the room. A few minutes later, he came out, and I asked him how my father was doing. He replied, "Not good, I'm afraid. His mind is not functioning right." The doctor continued, "We don't know why this happens, but we do know that a person usually gets worse until they have lost all memory of who they are and all those around them."

The doctor went on to say that it was being studied in the larger hospitals to find a cure if possible, but for now, all we could do was keep the person comfortable.

"Oh, one more thing," the doctor said. "Your father could become violent and may try to hurt someone or hurt himself. I am sorry, Tommy. I wish I could do more, but I can't. I will come and check on him in about a month." He then went downstairs to talk to Marta.

I went into his room and saw my father awake, staring up at the ceiling. I walked over to his bed, and he shifted his eyes over to me. "Thomas," he said, "is everything all right?"

"Yes," I replied, "everything is fine. Now get some rest, and I will send Marta up with something for you to eat."

"No," he shouted. "It isn't proper. Do not send that young slave in here to me." I was astonished at how quickly his mood changed from serene to menacing.

"No, I won't," I assured him, and he calmed down.

I left the room and hurried downstairs. When I entered the kitchen, the doctor was just leaving. "I gave Marta some pills for your father. They will help keep him calm," the doctor told me.

I thanked him and he left, saying, "I will see you in about a month." Marta came over and stood by me, her eyes filled with tears as she said, "I am so sorry, Tommy. I have known your father for a long time. He is a good man."

I thanked her and said, "Send Moses up to take care of my father, Marta, at least for a while, until we see how this is all going to play out."

"Moses is a big, strapping young man with lots of patience and a big heart. I know he can handle my father without hurting him if he gets out of hand. I don't want to put you in harm's way." She looked up at me with sad eyes. I knew that at one point, my father, Elizabeth, and Marta had all been very close, from some of the things she told me when I was little.

A few days later, I rose early and informed everyone I was ready to go to New Orleans. I sent one of the young boys to hitch up the horses to the wagon. I ate a bite of breakfast and started to leave when Marta stopped me and handed me a sack of food for the road.

When Jacob came in, he informed me that he would be riding along with me, saying he had business to attend to in New Orleans.

Because everything had slowed down on the plantation, I agreed. Besides, I would welcome the company and a man to handle a gun and watch my back wouldn't hunt none either.

When we were finally ready to go, I asked Eli if he would be in charge until we got back. He agreed he would and said he would take care of the place as if it were his own. Marta gave me a big hug and kissed my forehead when I bent down, telling us to be careful and keep an eye out for rebels. We waved goodbye and started off.

Luck was with us as we made it to Baton Rouge, where we caught a flatboat to take us by water to New Orleans without encountering any trouble. We arrived in New Orleans later that evening. When we got the horses and wagon taken care of at the livery stable, we headed to the nearest hotel, where I got two rooms. Then we had some dinner in the kitchen, as Jacob wasn't allowed to eat in the dining room. When we retired to our rooms, mine was on the second floor, while Jacob's was out back. When I started to protest, Jacob stopped me, saying it was all right, as we wouldn't be here that long and he didn't want no trouble. I didn't agree but let it go for now.

The next morning, we met for coffee and some pastries. In the kitchen again, after eating, we made our way downtown to the bank so we would be there when it opened. There were a lot of soldiers hanging around, and as we walked, we overheard a lot of talk about General Grant marching closer to Shiloh and a lot of grumbling about General Lee possibly surrendering to the North. There were a lot of angry comments and a lot of disappointment among our soldiers. I told Jacob that I hoped we could conduct our business quickly and head back home.

Just before we reached the bank, we encountered a couple of drunken soldiers. As we walked past them, one of them, while looking at Jacob, said in a jeering voice, "You best go home and chain up your slave, boy, or he will probably run off or soon be freed by Lincoln." Then the drunk spat at Jacob's feet. I froze in anger, and with closed fists, I started toward the man. Before I could grab the man, Jacob stopped me, saying in a calm voice, "No, Master Thomas. The man don't mean no harm. He's just smarting from the beating they all took," and he turned and winked at me. I stopped as I realized Jacob was being sarcastic. The soldiers gave us a glare but moved on, grumbling to each other.

When we entered the bank, I asked to see the manager. Jacob said he would wait for me there at the front while I took care of business. When the manager came, we shook hands and he introduced himself to me as Mr. Samuels. I shook his hand and told him my name. He asked, "What can I do for you, Mr. Sanduvale?"

I explained the damage to the plantation and how much I figured I had to borrow to get supplies and rebuild. Then I showed him the books and said how I could put the plantation along with the remaining crops up for collateral. Before he even said it, I could read the answer on his face. When Mr. Samuels spoke, I could hear the despair in his voice. "I am so sorry, Mr. Sanduvale, but under the circumstances, I cannot loan you the money."

He continued, "Your plantation is in bad need of repairs and has no value to the bank. With so many in your position, we already have too many plantations as collateral. If things don't get better, the banks will be in trouble. I just can't loan you the money without more solid collateral. Again, I am sorry."

With a sick feeling in the pit of my stomach, I rose and shook his hand, then, with defeat written all over my face, turned and walked to where Jacob was waiting.

Seeing the slump to my shoulders, Jacob came toward me and said, "It's gonna be all right, Tommy. Yes, sir. It's gonna be just fine."

Then Jacob walked over to the manager and held out his hand. To my surprise, Mr. Samuels took his hand and shook it. Then he said to Jacob, "I didn't see you standing there, Jacob. How have you been?"

"Just fine, Mr. Samuels," Jacob replied.

"What can I do for you today? Are you here to make a deposit?"

"No, sir, a withdrawal," Jacob said.

"Oh, I see," said Mr. Samuels.

The two men walked over to his desk and sat down. "Now, just how much would you like to withdraw?" Mr. Samuels asked Jacob.

"All of it," he replied.

"Are you sure you want to do that in these trying times," he said to Jacob.

"Yes, I am sure. It's for a good cause," Jacob answered. I just stood there with my mouth open as they conducted their business. When all the transactions were done, Mr. Samuels stood, as did Jacob. The two men again shook hands and said goodbye.

As Jacob walked past me, he had a big grin on his face. He said, "Shut your mouth, young Thomas. The girls are all looking at you." I turned red, shut my mouth, and followed Jacob out the door. As we walked back to the hotel, I bombarded Jacob with questions. He chuckled and told me in a matter-of-fact way that he had been depositing money in this bank for years—a nest egg, you might call it. All I could reply to him was, "Oh."

We arrived back at the hotel shortly before noon, so we grabbed a bite to eat in the kitchen. After eating, we went to our rooms and packed up to leave. After settling our bill, we headed for the livery stables to get our horses and wagon. Jacob said for me to go ahead and get the wagon and then head to the general store and he would meet me there. As I climbed aboard the wagon, I flipped the man a coin, then headed over to the general store to meet Jacob.

When I arrived at the store, there were stacks of supplies sitting out front. Two young boys came out of the store and started loading the supplies into our wagon. There was flour, sugar, coffee, salt, beans, and a lot more being loaded. When everything had been loaded, they covered everything with a large canvas. Jacob came out of the store, followed by the storekeeper. The man shook Jacob's hand and thanked him for his business.

Jacob climbed aboard the wagon and sat beside me. Then he threw each of the boys a penny and thanked them for their service.

The two boys yelled thanks and ran into the store. We watched them head for the jars of candy. "Well, Tomas, ain't you gonna get this wagon movin'? We won't get home 'til next year if'n you don't," Jacob said.

I got the horses moving, then said with a big lump in my throat, "Jacob, I don't know when I will be able to pay you back, but I swear, I will repay you all your money."

"I have lived a long time at the plantation," Jacob replied. "It's the only home I really belonged to. I hope I can contribute something to help fix it back up. Now, can we please start for home."

"Yes," I said with a big grin on my face and determination in my voice, "but I will pay you back." Then I slapped at the horses with the reins.

It was a long, slow trip heading home. Jacob and I took turns with the horses while one or the other of us slept, only stopping to rest, feed, and water the horses. We made good time, as we didn't encounter any trouble from any renegades, rebels, or runaway slaves.

After almost five days of being gone, we finally arrived back at the plantation. It was almost dark when we pulled up to the front porch of the house. I jumped down off the wagon as Jacob climbed down from the other side, both of us plum tuckered out from the long ride home. Several slaves came out of their cabins, all carrying rifles, to see who had ridden in this late.

When they saw it was Jacob and I with all the supplies, they started shouting, "Hallelujah," bringing more people out of their cabins. I instructed the men to take the wagon around back and unload it into one of the sheds that was still intact, then take the horses and tend to them. I then informed everyone the supplies would be divided up among everyone in the morning.

Jacob said he was plumb worn out and was heading for his soft bed. As he turned to leave, he said to me, "I almost forgot: a load of lumber will be delivered here in the next few weeks."

"What? When did you order the lumber?" I stammered.

"I ordered the lumber before I went to the store, while you

were getting the wagon. No more questions. Now, goodnight. I'll see you in the morning." At that, he slowly climbed the stairs and disappeared into the house before I could thank him again.

Marta came out and informed me that there was hot coffee and she would warm some food for me. I said I would take the coffee but no food—I was too tired to eat anything. After everything was seen to, I went inside and sat down at the table, where Marta handed me a cup of coffee. I told Marta how I was unable to get the loan. She asked, "But the supplies, how did you manage to get them without the loan?"

I told her about Jacob and about the account he had at the bank. I told her how he had withdrawn all his money so we could get what we needed to keep the plantation running.

Marta replied, "I don't believe it."

"Believe it or not, it's true. That old man had a savings account in New Orleans. In fact, he was quite well known there."

"I can believe that," Marta then explained. "The old rascal takes off every two or three months and goes someplace for days at a time, never telling anyone where he is going or what he is doing. He's been doing it for years, right after he gets paid."

"Right after he gets paid," I said, taken by surprise. "What do you mean, he gets paid? I didn't know my father paid his slaves."

Marta laughed and said, "He don't, Thomas. Let me tell you a little story. You see, Thomas, Jacob is no slave. He be a free man, not like the rest of us." I started to ask her what she meant by that, but Marta held up her hand and stopped me, then went on talking.

"Jacob came to work for your father with papers. The man who owned Jacob and his family gave them to him. Jacob's father saved the man's only son from drowning in the river they lived near. The man said he would give him anything he wanted, he was so grateful. Jacob's father asked for his only son's freedom, so the man gave Jacob his papers." Marta continued, "Jacob stayed working for the man until his mother died in childbirth and his father was killed in a slave uprising a year later."

"I am so sorry, I didn't know. I always just assumed that Jacob was a slave too," I replied. That night, I slept restlessly. I couldn't stop thinking about Jacob and what Marta had told me and what my friend Sean had said on the ship to England—that no man should be a slave to another man.

That morning, I rose early and went downstairs. Marta had the coffee made, so while I waited for Eli and Jacob, I had a cup. When the men arrived, the four of us sat down and had a long talk and made some decisions on a matter important to me.

A week later, Eli and Jacob had all the slaves assemble in the front of the house. Marta, Eli, Jacob, and I stood on the steps of the porch, and when everyone settled down, I looked out at the sea of black faces, all very familiar, as I had known them my whole life. Some shuffled their feet, while others fidgeted with their hands, waiting to see what I had to say.

"As you all know by now from the few soldiers that straggle through here once in a while, the war is ending and President Lincoln is preparing a bill to free all slaves," I said. At that statement, a loud cheer went up. I waited until it got quiet again, then continued, "I do not know how long it will take for the bill to go through, but I am not going to wait to see." A low murmur went through the crowd. "I am giving all of you your freedom, starting today." There were several gasps. Some of them questioned what I was saying, not quite understanding, not daring to hope they heard right.

"Starting today," I said again, "you are all free. Those of you who want to stay on and work for me will earn a wage and a place to stay. Those of you who want to leave are free to do so, although I am hoping you all stay, as I have never thought of any of you as slaves but as part of my family."

After a few seconds of quiet, a large cheer went through the crowd. People were hugging and laughing and crying. Then a low chant started up and grew louder: "Tommy, Tommy, Tommy." I went down the steps and walked through the crowd, shaking their hands and congratulating them on their freedom.

Afterward, Eli explained to all of them what they had to do. Eli had worked on all the papers all last week. He told them to come by his cabin. He would have them make their mark in a ledger, and they could then pick up their paper showing they had been given their freedom.

As I turned to walk back up the steps, where Eli, Marta, and Jacob were waiting, I saw them standing there with wide grins on their faces. Their white teeth sparkled in the sun, and their eyes lit up with joy. As I climbed the steps and stood by Marta, she reached up and kissed my cheek. With tears in her eyes, she said how proud she was of me, then she turned, patted Eli on the arm, and went into the house, with Jacob following her.

I turned and looked at Eli, still standing there with that silly grin on his face. "What?" I said.

He reached over and hugged me, saying in my ear, "This is the nicest thing you ever done—except for getting my foot back for me." At that, we both broke out laughing.

The next day, Eli handed out papers for each person. By that evening, it was all done. Everyone, except for five young boys, wanted to stay and work for me on the plantation. The five boys received their papers, as well as some money, and they were told that if things didn't work out for them, they were welcome to come back here. This would always be their home. They agreed.

Everything went along as if nothing had changed. Before we knew it, it was August. The crops were all growing in abundance. The repairs to the house and cabins were all made. Everything was in order at last.

I was preparing to meet Jason on the main road to take a trip to New Orleans to celebrate his birthday. I dressed in my finer clothes, packed a small bag for the trip, and was off after putting Eli and Jacob in charge. I rode my horse slow and admired my surroundings. It had been a long, hard year, but everything was good now. Jenny and Gregory had set a date to be married right after harvest season was done, at the end of October. Things seemed good for Jenny.

Gregory had stopped drinking, I was told, and had started keeping the books for Mr. Pierce. He seemed to be doing well and not letting the past clog his mind.

When I reached the main road, Jason was already there, waiting for me. "I thought you might be riding one of your old plow horses to get here," Jason said as he laughed.

"No, sorry. I guess I was riding slowly, as I was daydreaming, but I am here now, so let's get going," I said as I kicked my horse's flanks and shot forward. We rode like two young schoolboys instead of young men in our twenties.

It took us a while, but we made it to Baton Rouge, where we took the flatboat to New Orleans. It didn't take any time by water, and we arrived in New Orleans early that evening. After disembarking from the flatboat, we took our horses to the livery stable and had them boarded, telling the young lad in charge to be sure to wipe them down, feed them, and water them. He nodded his head yes and led the horses inside. After leaving the stable, we walked the short distance to a hotel, but they were booked up. The clerk told us there was another hotel closer to the docks where we had just come from. He said they might have rooms available for us.

We thanked him, then picked up our bags and headed back toward the docks. As we neared the hotel, we noticed how seedy this part of the town was, but when we entered the hotel lobby, it looked clean and quiet enough, so we booked our rooms. After checking in, we both went to our room to wash the dust off and clean up a bit. After that, we met downstairs in the dining area for a bite to eat. We had a delicious meal of baked chicken, okra, and freshly baked cornbread, all washed down with strong black coffee.

After we finished our meal, we headed for the nearest saloon to have a drink, play some cards, and maybe meet a couple of ladies. We found one close by, and when we walked in, we saw that there were indeed several young ladies present. Jason walked over to the bar, and I sat down at a table. Jason joined me after ordering our drinks. Soon, we were knee-deep in a card game, but after several hours with no luck, we decided to take our leave.

As we started to go, two of the young ladies that had been giving us the eye walked over to us. One of them said, "Care to buy a couple of ladies a drink?"

Jason, not one to be backward, said, "Sure, let's get a table, and we'll order some drinks."

One of them, with red hair, sat in the chair next to me. She wasn't beautiful, but she was easy to look at. I guess her hair was more auburn than real red. She wore it up, showing off her white neck and shoulders. She was a little plump but had a nice shape, with very ample breasts showing white above her low-cut green velvet dress, which matched the color of her eyes.

She was about a head shorter than me and had a soft, smoky voice when she spoke. The other young lady who latched onto Jason was thinner and a little taller than her friend. She had long blonde curls, hanging down her back and pale blue eyes. She had a clear voice, albeit a little nervous. She also had a great figure.

Looking at the girls, I thought, *Not bad. Besides, beggars can't be choosy.* I hadn't been with a girl since I left England, so I was starting to chomp at the bit delete. Thinking of England brought back memories of all the beautiful young ladies I had bedded. It also brought back painful memories of my friend Sean.

I shook my head to clear it and quickly put those memories away. I was here to celebrate Jason's birthday and have a good time, and by God, I was going to, I vowed. I lifted my glass and said, "To you two ladies and to having a very pleasant evening." At that, we all raised our glasses and drank to the toast.

I don't remember how many toasts we drank, but when I woke the next morning, I opened one eye, then closed it again. My mouth was dry, and I had a splitting headache, bad enough that I didn't want to raise my head up. I slowly turned and caught a glimpse of a white arse sticking out from under the covers.

I raised my eyelids and saw the redhead lying on her stomach, her red hair willy-nilly all over the pillow and covering her face, where the pins had popped out during the night. I raised my hand and gently lifted the hair from her face. In sleep, she had a much softer appearance to her features. She stirred and opened one bloodshot green eye, groaned, and shut it again. I carefully inched my way up, swinging my legs over the bed, and slowly sat up, holding my head.

After a few minutes, I stood up, slowly walked to the washbasin, and splashed water on my face and head, then dried off. Looking in the mirror, I looked awful. Still feeling the effects of drinking, I reached for my clothes and managed to get dressed. I went around the bed and shook the redhead's fanny, lowered my head, and whispered in her ear, "Thanks. I had a great time last night, but have to go now."

"Me too," she whispered back and drifted off to sleep.

I left some money on the nightstand next to the bed. I really had enjoyed myself. I quickly let myself out of the room and walked down the hallway just as Jason was leaving his room. When Jason saw me, he started to smile and said, "Now that's what I call a real celebration," and laughed.

"Well," I replied, "it's not every day a friend turns twenty-two."

We went downstairs and had breakfast. While eating fried catfish, grits, fresh fruit, and strong black coffee, we compared our night with the two ladies and decided we both made out fine. After we ate, we walked to the livery stable and got our horses. We wanted to ride to the other side of New Orleans and see what adventures awaited us there.

The man at the stables told us that there were a lot of stores, businesses, saloons, and fancy houses on the other side of town. "More population in that direction," he said. "It is a richer part of New Orleans, with classier people living there."

We thanked him, got on our horses and rode away.

We soon found the man was right: even though it was crowded at the docks, the streets here were lined with people, walking up and down the walkways lining the streets. Some talking to each other, some entering stores to shop. There were a lot of fancy carriages lining the streets, filled with families taking an early-morning ride.

As we rode on, we saw the houses were also very impressive, with large white pillars lining the front porch, and the grounds around the houses were immaculately kept. As we neared the center of town, we came to a lot of places to eat. On every corner, there were men of color playing all kinds of instruments and singing lively songs that made you want to tap your feet. We got caught up in the excitement and decided to stop and eat lunch.

After eating a spicy lunch, we visited some of the stores where Jason bought some material for his mother and Jenny to make dresses for themselves. I bought a hat for Marta. It had feathers on it, and she could wear it to church, I thought.

After several hours of seeing this part of New Orleans, we decided to ride on farther out of town. As we rode on, we passed a tannery and tallow factory. The smell was very strong, we decided to turn back and head for the hotel. As we rode along, we saw a large white mansion at the end of a long road. Planted all along both sides of the road were large lilac bushes in full bloom, with large purple flowers amongst the dark green leaves. The road was paved with white crushed seashells. The grounds around the house was covered in green grass, green shrubbery, and lilac bushes. There were all colors of flowers in bloom everywhere.

We turned to ride down to the large house when we saw a sign that read, "Lilac Lane, No Trespassing, Private Property." Now, being the adventurous types that we were, we ignored the sign and rode down the lane to the big white house. We could smell the sweet scent of lilacs all around us. It was very intoxicating. As we got close to the house, we could make out the balconies on the front of each of the three stories of the house. And when we were right in front, we saw the most beautiful women we thought we had ever seen.

We reined in our horses and stopped to gape at the women. They stood like goddess, fanning themselves, dressed in sheer gowns, in all colors of pastels. Their hair was done up with a few ringlets hanging to one side of their head, cascading down onto their creamy light brown skin.

Jason sucked in his breath, as did I. We moved the horses to the rail by the large front porch and started to dismount, but before our feet even touched the ground, a black man, dressed in a black suit and white shirt, appeared on the front porch. He asked in a polite tone as to our business here. We explained that we were sightseeing around New Orleans and had come upon this place on the main road. We were curious and came to investigate it. The man said in his polite tone, "I am sorry, but it is by invitation only, and only a very few are given invitations. You will have to get back on your horses and ride away if you do not have an invite."

We stood for a second and then took a step up on the porch. That's when we heard the click of the half dozen or more rifles. When we looked up, we saw the glint of sun bouncing off the rifle barrels poking through the double doors—behind some of the women, who by the way, didn't look the least bit disturbed. They just went on fanning themselves.

We backed down the steps, turned, got on our horses, turned them around, and rode back to the main road.

"Now, what in tarnation was that all about?" I said to Jason, sitting on his horse.

"I really don't know," he replied, rubbing his forehead. We rode back in silence, each of us in our own thoughts about the big white house.

On our way back, we stopped at a tavern to quench our thirst, as our mouths were very dry. We sat down at a table. The man behind the bar came over and asked us what we would like to drink. We ordered a pint of ale. When the man returned with our ale, Jason asked him about the house on Lilac Lane—what the deal was.

He looked around and quietly said, "It is a house for gentlemen callers—very rich gentlemen callers." When asked about the women there, he lowered his voice even more and said, "The young women who reside there were born from a white man and a black woman or vice versa. They are neither white nor black. They are known as Mulattoes, and they are some of the most beautiful women in New Orleans, if not the world," he said proudly.

He then informed us you could only visit one of them if you had an invite, which was given out by the madam who ran the place, and you only got one if you were very—very rich—or if you had a high-up position in high-up places. "Oh," said Jason and I at the same time. We paid the man for our ale and headed out for the long ride to our hotel.

When we arrived back, it was almost dinnertime, so we dropped the horses off at the livery stable to be taken care of. We were a little tired and very dusty from all the riding we did today, so we decided to treat ourselves to a bath at the bathhouse and get a shave while we were there. On our way to the bathhouse, we heard two female voices calling out to us. I turned around to see the lovely redhead and her blonde friend waving at us. As they walked toward us, Jason whispered, "Maybe we will get lucky again tonight," then poked me in the ribs with his elbow.

The redhead asked in her low, smoky voice, "Where are you to gents off to?" All the while, the blonde was rubbing Jason's shoulder. I informed them what we had planned, then asked if they were free for dinner tonight. Both girls answered yes at the same time and then began to giggle.

"Good," Jason replied. "We will see you both around seven o'clock in the dining room of the hotel." As the girls left, giggling to themselves, we headed for the bathhouse, with grins on our faces.

The water was hot and as I sank into the tub up to my neck, I could feel the tension leaving my muscles. "I think, all in all, our trip so far has been fun if not enlightening, don't you agree?" Jason asked me as he smoked a cigar while soaking in his tub.

"Uh-huh," I murmured as I began to soap myself up and wash the grime from my hair and body. It felt good to get the dust off of me.

After rinsing off, I relaxed a while longer, enjoying the warm comfort of the water. Jason did the same, not talking, just relaxing and thinking. My mind wandered to the big white house. I truly thought I had never seen more beautiful girls than the ones at that house. Jason must have been thinking the same, as he stood up to grab a towel and began drying himself off. He said, "I wonder what it would be like to bed one of those girls from Lilac Lane."

I opened my eyes and looked at him. Then I began to laugh. "What?" he said.

"Oh, nothing," I replied. "It's just that I was thinking the same thing, and we will probably never know." I stood up, reached for my towel, and began to dry myself.

"You're probably right. I don't see us getting an invite to a place like that," Jason said, laughing.

The man who ran the bathhouse came in with our clothes. He had them dusted off and pressed. After dressing, we went into another room, where we were shaved. We asked the barber who was shaving us if he had heard of the house on Lilac Lane. He replied, "Yes, the house is very famous. It's known all over Louisiana."

We finished up just in time to get to the hotel to meet the two young ladies in the dining room. We had a great dinner of chicken in a spicy creole sauce with browned potatoes and carrots with freshly baked bread and butter, served with white wine. After we finished, we decided to take a stroll around the docks.

We walked slowly, with the redhead holding onto my arm. I broke the silence by asking her, "By the way, what is your name?" She said it was Annabelle but people called her Anne or Red. She added that she was born in Jackson, Mississippi, but had come here to New Orleans with the promise of a job. The job offer fell through because of the war, but she added, "Then I met Lucille, whom I call Lucy. Lucy was born in New Orleans and knew jobs here for women were scarce, so we became escorts for gentlemen in order to survive."

Anne told me that the manager of the hotel gave them a room, and in return, they gave the manager two-thirds of the money they made. I told Anne I was sorry that she and Lucy had to make their living that way. She just laughed and said, "It's all right. It really isn't a bad way to earn money, just a little rough sometimes."

By the time we finished our stroll, it was after ten o'clock, so we headed back to the hotel and to our rooms. I told Jason I would meet him around six in the morning. We would grab a bite to eat then catch the ferry for Baton Rouge. He agreed, said good night, and then he and Lucy disappeared into his room.

I opened the door to my room and stood back as Anne entered the room. I closed the door behind me as Anne lit the lamp. It made a soft glow around the room. I took off my coat and threw it on a chair. I walked over to Anne and undid the pins from her hair. It fell down in a mass of red fire across her white shoulders. I reached back and undid her dress. It fell to the floor. Then I undid her chemise and petticoat and watched as they drifted to the floor. She stepped out of them, and I caught my breath.

Even though she was plump, it didn't take away the beauty of her creamy white breasts and hips or of her well-shaped legs. Anne slowly reached over and undid my shirt and slid it off my shoulders. As the shirt fell to the floor, I kicked off my shoes and pulled off my stockings. Anne then reached over and undid my breeches and pulled them to the floor. When I stepped out of them, we came together. I bent down and kissed her lightly on her lips, then the hollow of her neck, just below her ear. She groaned loudly in her throat. I picked her up and carried her to the bed, where I laid her down gently.

I kissed her neck all the way down to her full, plump breasts. I took one of her pink nipples into my mouth and slowly sucked on it until it stood erect. Then I did the same to the other one. Anne was moaning and tugging at my hair. I moved back up to kiss her mouth, which was slightly parted. I plunged my tongue in and moved it over the soft recess of her mouth. Without hesitation, her tongue thrust back at mine.

I slowly moved my hand down her soft stomach onto her thighs and down until I found her secret place. I rubbed the mound beneath the soft, downy curls until she started to buck and thrash about, wanting more. I lifted my body on top of hers and entered her slowly. She let out a sigh of pleasure as I moved slowly in and out until I could no longer control myself. Anne was reaching her peak. I pushed all the way, entering her fully.

She arched upward and dug her nails into my back. That was my cue. I moved faster and faster until we both achieved our pleasure together. I held her close, still inside her as we drifted off to sleep. We made love again in the early morning hours. I told Anne I enjoyed the time I spent with her but would soon have to leave for my home.

She was drowsy and content. She raised up on one elbow and kissed me long and slow. When she pulled away, she said she wished I could stay as I had treated her like a lady and not a prostitute. She said she liked how I cared about satisfying her pleasure, not just my own. Then she thanked me for it.

Anne bit her bottom lip and told me that when we left the hotel, we should leave before dawn and we should leave by the back door, not the front one. When I asked her why, she looked down at her hands and said, "Because if you don't, you will be mugged by two very bad, very big men, who will then rob you. I know this because I have seen it happen before."

"Oh, I see, do you notify them or does someone else," I said, starting to get angry.

"No, no, not me," Anne protested. "The hotel manager lets the men know when you check out. Then they do the rest," Anne said, looking me straight in the eye. Getting over my anger, I kissed her and said not to worry, for her to go back to sleep.

"We'll talk later," I said.

Anne lay back down, and before long, she was asleep. I waited a long while to make sure she was sleeping. When I was sure, I quickly and quietly got up, dressed, threw my things into my bag, and left some money on the dresser for Anne. I left the room and slowly made my way down the dimly lit hall to Jason's room. When I got there, I very softly rapped on the door. Within seconds, Jason answered and asked what was wrong. I told him we had to leave earlier than planned and briefly explained why. He said to give him a minute to dress and he would be right out.

A few minutes later, we were headed down the stairs. When we heard the manager talking to a gruff-sounding man, we stopped on the stairs and listened. The manager was telling the man that we would be checking out around six and for him and his partner to be ready. The gruff man finished by saying, "All right. We'll wait out by the horse trough and follow them to the livery stable, where we will jump them." Then the two men went outside, and the manager went into the back room. We waited, making sure the coast was clear. Then Jason and I hurried down the stairs, where I went over to the counter and put the money for our rooms. We quickly made our way to the kitchen in the back of the hotel, where we exited through the back door into an alleyway leading to the main street. We made our way to the end of the alley. We looked out into the darkness and were just able to make out the forms of the two men by the water trough.

We quickly and quietly made our way across the street to the other side. This side of the street was lined with trees, so in the dark, we made our way from tree to tree away from the hotel to the livery stable. Once there, we saddled our horses, woke the boy sleeping in the hay, and paid him.

Leaving the stable, we walked our horses until we were sure we wouldn't be heard or seen. When we thought we were far enough away, we mounted our horses and rode to the wharf, where we would catch the ferry to Baton Rouge. We made it to the docks without any incidents and dismounted. We walked our horses up the gangplank onto the ferry and tied them to the railing.

We talked to the captain in charge and asked how long before we got underway. He told us when the sun came up, we would be on our way. In the meantime, we could grab a cup of coffee in the wheelhouse. We thanked him and made our way to the wheelhouse and coffee. After getting our coffee, we stood at the rail and watched as more people boarded the ferry.

Just as dawn was breaking, the ferry pilot announced we were getting underway. As we stood and watched the docks grow smaller, we noticed two burly men standing on the wharf, watching the ferry drift farther away. Jason and I looked at each other, shook hands, and agreed it was a close call.

Later that morning, we landed in Baton Rouge. We untied our horses and led them across the gangplank to dry land. We took in the sights and sounds around us, and we both agreed it was good to be back. After making sure our travel bags were securely hooked to our saddle horns, we mounted the horses and started off for home.

A few hours later, we came to Myers Inn, where we decided to stop and get something to eat and drink, as we hadn't eaten since the night before. After tying the horses to the rail, we dusted ourselves off, climbed the stairs, and went inside the place. It was crowded, with loud, drunken dock workers. The place smelled like sour wine, sweat, and piss. We stood in the doorway, adjusting our eyes to the dimly lit interior of the place. I looked around the room for a fairly clean place to sit and order a drink and some food. As my eyes scanned the room, they fell on the most exquisite-looking girl I had ever seen, even more beautiful than the ones on Lilac Lane, I thought.

She was young, maybe seventeen, small in stature, with a riot of golden curls cascading down her back to just below her waist. Her skin was light brownish gold, which made me want to reach out and caress her all over. I couldn't see her whole face, but from her side view, I could tell she was exceptional.

The girl was carrying a heavy tray, laden with drinks, to a table with three drunken sots setting at it. Just as the girl was setting the heavy tray down, I noticed one of the men. I will call him Ox, as he was built like one. His head was huge, with dirty, greasy brown hair. Sweat was running down his grimy face. His bloodshot eyes were close together, and his nose was large and crooked from being broken. His mouth was big, with thick lips, and his crooked teeth were stained yellow and rotten. *I can almost smell his foul breath from here*, I thought.

Ox reached a big beefy hand and placed it on the young girl's arse, causing her nearly to drop the heavy tray. She yelped and tried to take a step back, but Ox held her in place with his big, beefy hand. She looked up, then around as if trying to find a quick exit from the man. When she looked in my direction, I sucked in my breath. *Those eyes—a man could drown in them*, I thought. I had never seen eyes that color before. Were they deep blue or a deep purple, depending on which way the light hit them.

Nevertheless, they were like deep pools of water, surrounded by long golden eyelashes and perfectly arched darker gold eyebrows. I took several steps toward her, then felt a hand on my shoulder. Jason stopped me and said almost in a whisper, "What are you doing?"

"I am going to that girl's aid," I replied nonchalantly.

"And what, get yourself killed in the process?"

"I am not planning on it," I said.

"Have you thought this through?" Jason replied.

"No, but I think I can handle the big one if you can distract the smaller man sitting next to him," I answered him.

"Oh, and what about the other one?" asked Jason tartly.

"I thought you might handle him also, my friend," I rejoined as I pulled free from his grasp on my shoulder and moved quickly forward. I heard Jason groan, then curse, as he followed behind me. When I reached the table, I said very politely to the man I call Ox, "I think the young lady would like for you to remove your big, dirty paw from her lovely arse," smiling as I looked over at her. She immediately turned red and looked at Ox.

As Ox looked up at me, his ugly face turned bright red, and I could almost see smoke coming out of his large flared nostrils. Then he bellowed, looking in my direction, "Oh, she would, would she?" I can honestly say, as I waved a hand in front of my nose, I could smell his foul breath.

I simply answered him, "Yes." Ox rose to his feet, and I had to look up at him, as he was a good two inches taller than me and a good hundred pounds heavier.

Looking down at me, he roared, "And just who do you think you are? Are you going to make me?"

With my best smile, I said, "Allow me to introduce myself. My name is Thomas Wesley Sanduvale, and I don't want any trouble, so if you would kindly keep your hands off this young lady's, umm, backside, I would be grateful."

"You would, would you?" he said, laughing out loud, with the other two men and the rest of the clientele joining in. At this point, Jason tensed, ready for action.

"And if I don't, Thomas Wesley Sanduvale," Ox spat out, "what are you going to do about it?"

I turned to look at Jason, who had a bad look on his face, and gave him a wink, which made him groan out loud. Then I turned to look at the young girl, who looked at me as if I were deranged and motioned for her to step back.

After she retreated far enough back, I returned my gaze, which had turned hard and angry at this point, back to Ox. With all my might, I swung my right fist into his large, flabby gut. For all my effort, all I got was a very small grunt from Ox, a loud groan from Jason, and a very weak "Look out" from the girl.

When I woke up, my head was throbbing, and my left eye was swollen shut. Jason was sitting next to the bed. I was lying in a room I did not recognize. Jason was eating food off a table placed next to him. When I tried to move to sit up, I let out a low groan of pain.

"Ah, coming around, are we?" Jason said. "And how do we feel?"

I looked at him out of the eye that wasn't swollen and asked from a cracked lip, "What happened?"

Jason explained that after I so gallantly tried to save the fair damsel in distress, I was beaten to a pulp with just one blow by the big man's big fist. "After you were laid out cold on the floor, your helpless fair damsel gave the big ogre a piece of her mind. So much so, he sat back down and left her alone, with the whole room laughing at him. The owner came over and had a couple of men carry you up here to recuperate. Meanwhile, the young lady brought up some food and drink for us to eat, and as you can see, that's what I am doing."

In between bites, Jason said he was told the young girl in question was the owner's niece. "He was grateful for your attempt at chivalry. He also sent you up a raw piece of meat for your eye." At that, Jason picked up the raw piece of meat and slapped it on my eye.

"Oww," I said. "What was that for?"

"Really, Thomas, for being so pigheaded and not waiting to see what would have transpired between Goliath and the girl," said Jason. "I am sure this is not her first encounter and it won't be her last. She seemed very capable of just how to handle the situation before you butted in and embarrassed her and yourself."

"I guess," I agreed. I sat up and started to eat something as my stomach began to growl. "But," I said with a mouthful of food, "you have to admit, she is one beautiful young girl."

"Yes, yes, she is," Jason admitted.

In the morning, after a restless night's sleep for me, as Jason slept like a baby, I got up, got dressed, washed my face, and smoothed and tied my wild hair back. I surveyed my black eye and considered it not too bad, thanks to the raw meat I kept on it all night. My lip was split and bruised, but all in all, I decided I would live. Jason had gotten up before me and had gone downstairs. I was about to join him when he entered the room, followed by the young girl for whom I had suffered the black eye.

She was carrying a tray full of food that made my nose twitch with appreciation and hunger. Jason motioned for her to set the tray on the table. She did and moved back without looking up at me. Jason was having fun at my expense. I could see the laughter in his eyes as I looked from him to the girl. *Damn him*, I thought. He knew how uncomfortable I was.

After a few minutes of dreadful silence, Jason finally said, "Oh yes, Thomas, this is Celine, your damsel in distress. Celine, this is Thomas, your knight in shining armor." Celine and I both turned red. To hide my embarrassment, I started to bow. At the same time, Celine did a low curtsey, and our heads collided. I turned an even deeper red, as did the girl. We heard Jason burst out laughing, as he could no longer contain himself. Jason laughed so hard, he doubled over with tears rolling down his cheeks, and his sides began to ache. Celine, totally mortified, backed to the door, looking at Jason, then back to me. I saw she was about to bolt through the door, so without thinking, I charged at her to try to stop her from doing so.

When Jason was able to look up, he saw the startled look on Celine's face, as if she were a deer caught in a trap. He saw Celine had brought her knee up and caught me off guard as her knee made contact with my crotch. I stopped dead still, grabbed at my crotch, doubled over in pain, and fell forward. Celine groaned and ran through the open door way before she could be stopped.

As I rolled on the floor, moaning and trying to catch my breath, Jason came just out of range of me. Still laughing, he replied, "I think that went well, don't you, Thomas?" I kicked at him, not making contact. When I was able to get up, Jason helped me to my feet. After the cursing, laughter, and ribbing, we sat down and ate our breakfast.

After eating, we headed downstairs. I surveyed the room, but the young girl was nowhere to be seen. I was disappointed, as I would have liked to have apologized for my behavior the previous night and this morning. Jason went over to the owner of the establishment to pay for whatever we owed him.

As I walked over to join them, I heard the man say he was Celine's uncle and that she was here with him because she had lost both her parents at a very young age, just as Jason had told me the night before. Jason paid the man for the food we had eaten this morning, then went outside to get the horses and pay the boy who had taken care of them last night.

I waited until Jason left, then asked Celine's uncle if I could talk to him. He shook his head yes, so I stepped forward and offered him my hand, introducing myself to him. The man shook hands with me and said, "My name is James Gustersen." After talking a while, I asked Mr. Gustersen if I could call on his niece, Celine. After studying me for some time, he finally replied, "I would think that would be up to my niece, don't you agree?"

"Oh, yes of course, but I don't see her anywhere around this morning to ask her."

"No, and you won't for a few days. She went into town with one of the women and one of the men that work here. They are picking up supplies for the inn and running some errands for me and won't be back until the middle of the week."

With disappointment in my voice, I replied, "Oh, uh, all right, uh, thank you for your hospitality. I will be seeing you soon." Then I turned and left the inn with Mr. Gustersen staring after me and shaking his head in amusement.

Jason was waiting for me with the horses. I hurried over and threw my travel bag over the horn of my saddle, then mounted my horse and rode toward the main road with Jason right behind me. We rode along in silence for about an hour when Jason said with humor in his voice, "Well, aren't you going to talk about your behavior last night."

"Not really," I replied, "not much to talk about. Only, I am going to marry that girl, come hell or high water. Yes, sir, I am." Then I kicked my horse's side and galloped away, leaving Jason behind with his mouth wide open.

After riding for some time, we finally came to the fork in the road that took me to the plantation, while Jason had to ride a while longer to get to his. Jason reined in beside me, and we shook hands. He thanked me for a most memorable birthday. Then he said, "Seriously, Tommy, think about what you said. Don't go falling in love with the first girl you meet and ask her to marry you. All I'm saying is think on it." Then he slapped his horse on its rear and galloped down the road, waving goodbye with his hand in the air. I yelled after him, "I am going to marry Celine," and rode on.

When I got home, I jumped off my mount and yelled for Marta and Jacob to come hear my good news. Marta was the first to appear on the front porch, wiping her hands on her apron. She asked, "What in the world are you yelling about, Tommy?"

"Where is Jacob?" I asked excitedly.

"I am right here," Jacob said as he appeared in the doorway. "What is all this racket about?" I ran up the stairs two at a time, took hold of Marta, lifted her off the ground, and swung her around.

"Put me down, young man. Have you lost your mind?" she asked.

"Tell us what's got you so all fired up," Marta said as I gently let her down. "I am going to get married," I blurted out.

Both Marta and Jacob said at the same time, "You're what? And just who is this girl?"

"Let's all go inside and I will tell you all about her," I replied. As we stepped inside the light of the kitchen, Jacob saw the condition of my face and asked, "Did you get caught with some man's daughter and get beaten up? Is that why you are getting married?"

As I reached up and felt my split lip, I laughed and said, "No, no, it's nothing like that." Then I told them the whole story. While relating my story to them, none of us noticed my father standing in the alcove just outside the kitchen. Hearing the commotion coming from outside his window when I rode up, my father got up and made his way downstairs and hid in the alcove to hear what was going on. That's when he heard me telling Marta and Jacob about Celine. I noticed when I mentioned Celine by name the look that passed between Marta and Jacob. They knew of her. So I said, "Well, what do you think?"

Marta stammered, "Don't you think you should get to know this girl before you ask her to marry you?"

"Yeah," Jacob chimed in, "you don't go around marrying total strangers. You got to know them first."

"Yes, I intend to get to know Celine, and then, I am going to marry her," I said in a voice that brooked no argument from either of them.

With that, I got up, said goodnight, and went upstairs to bed, leaving Marta and Jacob staring after me, whispering to each other. My father had quietly gone back to his room after listening to our conversation. The next morning, I headed out to the fields to check on the crops. Marta had gone up to take Phillip his breakfast. She tapped on his door, then pushed it open. Expecting to find him in bed, she was taken aback when she saw him sitting at his desk instead.

"What on earth?" she said. Phillip turned around and looked at Marta. When he looked at her, it was with admiration. It took Marta back, and she almost dropped the tray, as she had not seen that look for many years. She caught herself and said, "You must be feeling better if you are able to get up now?"

Phillip replied, "Yes, I do feel better. The medicine the doctor gave me seems to help me."

He motioned for her to come forward and put the tray on his desk. Marta hesitated for a moment, then stepped forward and set the tray down in front of Phillip. As Marta went to take a step back, Phillip reached out and grabbed her wrist. Marta froze in her tracks, and a soft yelp came from her throat.

"Marta," Phillip said in a quiet toned voice, "I am not going to hurt you. I need your help, all right?" Phillip let her go and continued, "I overheard Thomas talking to you and Jacob last night."

Interrupting him, Marta asked, "How, how could you hear him? You couldn't unless you were downstairs yourself."

"Never mind all that," he replied, starting to sound annoyed. Marta took a couple of steps back toward the open door." Waving his hand, Phillip went on, "As I was saying, I overheard your conversations with my son, and I need to find out about this girl without Thomas knowing about it."

"But why?" asked Marta, already knowing the answer.

"Because if it is who I think it is, Thomas must not get involved with her. Now, get out and send Jacob up to me right away. And Marta, I am warning you, do not say anything about this to Thomas, do you understand?"

Looking into Phillip's eye's, Marta could see the deranged look back in them. The medicine might have been working, but she thought his mind was still off. "If you and your son, Eli, want to continue living here, and you want to see Thomas, you will do what I say without question." Marta shook her head yes and quickly left the room.

On her way down, Marta ran into Jacob, just coming in. "The old man wants you upstairs right away." She then quickly told Jacob what had transpired between her and Phillip a few minutes earlier. Jacob reminded her that the doctor had warned them that he could regain some of his memory and lose it again. He just didn't know what happened with this kind of sickness.

Shaking his head, Jacob went on up the stairs and into Phillip's room. Marta waited nervously for Jacob to come down, and when he did, he did not look happy. Jacob explained to Marta what Phillip wanted him to do. Phillip wanted to have one of the field hands to spy on Thomas whenever Thomas left the plantation. Then the field hand was to report back to Phillip all that was going on.

"And if they don't, then what?" Marta asked.

"Then," Jacob replied, "he would find himself without a home along with his family."

Marta asked, "What did you tell him?"

"What could I tell him? I agreed to do what he said."

Jacob then walked out of the house with his shoulders drooping down in utter disgust at the spot he was put in. He loved Thomas like his own son. His mind drifted back to when Thomas was a boy. It brought a smile to his face.

I worked the plantation from sunup to sundown the next few days, hoping it would make the time go by faster so I could go back to the inn and see Celine. I couldn't get her off my mind, no matter what. All I could think about were those eyes and how a man could drown in those violet-blue pools. I had never seen a person with eyes that color.

Not only her eyes, but her perfectly shaped lips, so soft and lush looking. I could almost feel them on my own lips. They looked as if they were meant to be kissed over and over. Her skin was the color of dark honey. Her breasts rose just above the cut of her blouse, round and firm-looking, just waiting to be caressed and kissed until the nipples became hard and stood erect.

I shook my head to erase the image in my mind but could not get rid of it. I decided I would ride to the inn in the morning and see if she had returned yet; otherwise, I would never get any work done. After making that decision, I got back to what I was doing.

When I finished my work, I rode over to Eli's to see what he was up to. I hadn't seen him for a while, as both of us had been busy. I knew from Marta that he and Roslyn were expecting again any day now. I rode up to the cabin, and as I got off my horse, the door opened, and Eli came out to greet me. We shook hands and hugged each other. Eli said, "Keeping yourself busy these days, huh?"

"Yeah," I answered. "Trying to get the rest of the planting done before the rains come."

"It should start soon," replied Eli.

"How's the family doing these days?" I asked him.

"Real good. Should have number three any day now," he replied.

"Number three, huh? I asked.

"Yeah, hoping for a boy this time, as I am starting to feel outnumbered with all these women under my roof." At that, we laughed.

"I hear you," I said. "Three women against one man. I don't know. Those are some bad odds."

"What about you, Tommy? You got any girl in mind that you can start calling on?" Eli asked.

"Maybe I have one in mind," I said. "Matter of fact, I'm thinking of calling on her tomorrow."

"Really," Eli replied. "Now, this is getting interesting. Tell me about her. Do I know her?"

"Whoa, slow down. One question at a time," I said, laughing. "First off, no, I don't think you know her. I met her at Myers Crossing. She works and lives at the inn there. Her name is Celine, she looks like an angel, and I am going to marry her."

"This sounds serious. Does she know this?" Eli asked me. "And when do we get to meet this angel?"

"Not for a while. I have to get to know her myself. Our first meeting didn't go very well," I told him.

"What do you mean, it didn't go well?" he asked.

I told Eli about the attempt to rescue Celine from the man I called Ox, then went on to tell him of the introduction to her by Jason. Eli could not contain his laughter, and tears rolled down his face. Starting to get offended, I said, "I don't think it was that funny. Anyway, now you know why I have to get to know her. Mostly, I want her to get to know me, so she won't think I'm a clumsy baboon."

"Amen to that," Eli said.

"I am going to ride over tomorrow and ask if I can call on her."

"Well, good luck, and stay away from any Oxen you might encounter," Eli said, laughing as he opened the door. "Let me know how you make out."

He went inside, and I stepped off the porch, grabbed my horse's reins, and headed over to the stable, still hearing the laughter coming from the open window in Eli's cabin. I had to smile myself. It really was funny when you thought about it.

The next morning, I was up bright and early. I poured myself a cup of coffee, cut a piece of fresh homemade bread, and put some homemade jam on it. After eating, I went outside and informed the workers what had to be done for the day. If anything went wrong, they were to tell Jacob or Eli, and they would tend to the problem.

I went back to the house for my coat and hat, and about that time, Marta came into the kitchen. I told her where I was going and that I would be back by evening. I kissed her on the cheek, then left to get my horse from the stable.

As I rode toward the inn, I was so preoccupied, planning on what to say and how to approach Celine so as not to scare her away. I didn't notice the lone rider trailing always behind me. If I had, I would have recognized the young black boy, whose name was Lester, riding one of our horses.

When I reached the inn, I dismounted and tied my horse to the hitching post in front of the inn. I looked around, but there wasn't a soul in sight. I bounded up the steps but stopped at the door, telling myself to slow down and not to look so anxious and make a fool out of myself again. I opened the door and went inside, standing there for a minute to let my eyes adjust to the dim light.

As I looked around the room, I noticed it wasn't as crowded as it had been the last time I was in the place. I chose a table in the corner of the room, with my back to a wall and a good view of the whole room. I did not want to be taken by surprise if Ox happened to be here. I glanced around again. Luck was with me—no Ox—so I breathed a sigh of relief.

I scanned the room for the young Celine. When I didn't see her there, I began to get disappointed. *Maybe she isn't back yet*, I thought. Then I heard a light laugh coming from the area where the kitchen was. I looked over and there she was, coming through the doorway. I caught my breath at the sight of her, and my heart started to race so fast, I thought it was going to beat right out of my chest.

Celine's uncle told her a customer had just come in and sat down and that she should go out and take his order. Celine nodded and headed toward the corner table. When she was near enough to make out it was me sitting there, she hesitated, and I could tell by the look on her face that she recognized me. She put her chin up and continued forward.

As she stood in front of me, all I could do was stare up at her. I could not believe the total perfection standing in front of me.

"May I get you something to eat or drink?" she asked in a voice she hoped sounded like she was bored. But to her own ears, her voice sounded like she was begging to be kissed by this total stranger, sitting in front of her.

Celine thought he looked like an Adonis or one of the gallant knights she read about in one of the books she borrowed from her friend Rebecca. From the black curly hair that stuck out from beneath his hat to the perfectly shaped eyebrows just above eyes that were almost black, except for a tinge of dark blue and was surrounded by long black lashes. Celine thought his eyes were so alive with expression that she could almost hear him laughing at her.

Wait, she said to herself. *He is laughing at me.* Then she said out loud, "What the?" and stamped her foot in anger.

I could not help myself. She was looking at me like I was a big bowl of pudding that she would like to take a big bite of. I know this because that's exactly how I pictured myself looking at her. Celine turned her back on me and started to walk away.

I got myself under control, reached out, and lightly took her wrist, and at that movement, I felt as if I had been struck with lightning, as did Celine just from touching each other. I immediately apologized to her. "I am so sorry," I said. "I don't know what came over me." Breaking into my best English accent, I said, "I do sometimes get a little carried away. Please do forgive me."

Celine thought he sounded very sincere, so she turned to face him and said in her very best English accent, "That's quite all right. I do forgive you." At that, we both broke out in a fit of laughter. "Now, what can I bring you to eat and drink?" Celine asked me. I ordered a beef plate and a tankard of ale. I asked if she could join me. She looked around and noticed the place was beginning to fill up, as it was close to the noon hour. "No, I am sorry," Celine said. "I can't."

"Oh, all right, then. What time do you finish your shift? Perhaps we can have dinner," I replied.

Looking over to where her uncle stood, she answered, "Maybe, but I really do have to go now." Celine turned and headed toward the kitchen. I watched as she waited on other customers as I slowly drank my ale. My eyes followed her every move, and I couldn't help noticing how very precisely she did everything.

She was so graceful in the way she moved her body and so expressive when she moved her hands and tilted her head while talking to people. The sound of her voice when it drifted over in my direction was like beautiful music. Everything about Celine made me want to pick her up and take her upstairs to one of the rooms. I wanted to make mad, passionate love to her until she felt the same way about me.

I couldn't get over how this one young girl had taken over my heart and soul so completely in such a very short amount of time. All I could think was, *What if she doesn't feel the same way about me? What if she doesn't want anything to do with me? What then?* I looked down at my plate and realized I hadn't eaten a bite.

"What the hell?" I murmured to myself. "Get a hold of yourself, man. You're not a young schoolboy with a crush on someone. You know the ropes. You will make her want you just as bad as you want her." Determination setting in, I told myself I would make a plan, but in the meantime, I would eat my meal. While chewing on a piece of roast, I asked myself, *What has come over me? I have never felt this way about any other girl. Well, maybe a little like this with Jenny, but well, we're more like brother and sister, aren't we?*

I sat in the corner all afternoon, sipping on ale and watching Celine moving from one table to another, only moving to relieve myself and checking on my horse. Close to five o'clock that evening, I went outside and took my horse to the stable and had him fed and watered. I flipped the young stable boy a coin, telling him I would return for my horse in a few hours.

I turned to go back inside when I looked up and saw Celine standing on the porch out front. I hurried over and asked, "Are you free for the evening?"

She replied yes, so I asked, "Would you like to get something to eat?"

She replied, "No, if it is all right with you, I would just like to stay outside in the fresh air and maybe go for a walk."

I told her it was all right with me, as the place was full of people by now and was becoming increasingly loud. Besides, I needed to stretch my legs. I held out my arm to her. She took it, and we began to walk away from the inn. Celine was not very tall. She barely came up to my shoulders. We walked in silence for a while. Then we both began to say something at the same time.

I laughed and told her to please go first. Celine asked where I lived and about my family. I answered her first by telling her about the plantation where I lived, that it was only a short distance away from here. I then told her about my father and how, because of the war, his mind stopped working right, and it wandered at times from one thing to another. I told her I did not know my mother, as she had passed away when I was born.

I told her about Marta, Eli, and Jacob and how I loved them like my own family. After walking and talking for over an hour about myself, I said, "Enough about me. What about you? Where do you live? Tell me about your family." When Celine started to talk, I could hear the sadness in her voice, but because it had gotten dark by this time, I could not see her expression.

Celine told me that she did not know her father, he had been killed while working on the roof of a barn. He had lost his footing and fall into his death. There was nothing they could do to save him. She had been very young and did not remember anything about him, only what her mother, Leann Jenkins, had told her before she died a few years later. Celine had come to live with her mother's brother, her uncle, here at the inn. She had been here ever since.

"I am so sorry about your parents," I told her.

"As I am about yours," she replied.

We walked and talked some more, just enjoying each other's company, not seeing or hearing the young black boy following them a little distance behind them, out of sight but within hearing distance.

Soon, the young couple came to a river and a grove of trees. As Celine led me through a grove of trees, by moonlight, I could just make out the shape of a small cabin in the middle of the grove. Celine led me over to the cabin and opened the door. She told me to wait there as she entered the room. A minute later, I saw the room light up and saw Celine standing in the middle of it, holding the lantern she had just lit.

She motioned for me to come inside and close the door. As I stepped inside and pushed the door close behind me, I surveyed the small, neatly kept room. In one corner was a neatly made bed. Next to the bed was a small table upon which Celine placed the lantern. In the middle was a table and two chairs. On one wall was a small fireplace, and in the corner, next to it, sat an overstuffed chair. In the other corner stood a screen. I presumed it had a commode and washbasin behind it.

Celine watched as I examined the room. Then she asked, "Well, what do you think?"

I answered her, "Very nice, but who lives here?"

"I do—sometimes, that is," she replied. "I found this place while I was exploring the area when I first came to live here with my uncle. No one ever came to clean it, so after a few months, I started to clean it up, and when I want to be alone, I come here."

"I see," I replied. "It's a very nice place if you want to be alone."

I looked over at Celine, and my heart nearly burst with the feelings I had for her. I started to go to her and take her in my arms, to kiss her passionately, to tell her how I felt about her. But then I remembered the look on her face the last time I tried to touch her.

No, I thought, *take it slow and easy, or you will scare her off again*. Celine stood there watching the emotions play across Thomas's face. She saw the lust in his eyes. She felt the sensations start at her breast and work their way down her body, to the very core of her being. Her breathing quickened, and she ached for something but did not know what.

She waited for him to come to her but saw him hesitate. Then he turned toward the door, opened it, and said to her in a gruff voice, "We had better get back. It's getting late."

I saw the hurt look on her face but took it as a look of relief. Celine blew out the lantern, went out, and closed the door behind her with a loud bang, so loud it scared the young boy that was spying on them.

Lester felt all over his chest to see if he had been shot. Seeing that he hadn't been, he let out a loud sigh of relief.

"What was that?" Celine asked me.

"Probably just an animal forging around for food," I answered her. We walked back to the inn not saying much to each other, both in our own thoughts.

When we reached the inn, Celine asked, "Are you hungry?"

I replied, "No, it's getting late, and I think I had best be going, but if you don't mind, I will come early Sunday morning with my buggy, and we could ride into Baton Rouge—that is, if it would be all right with your uncle."

Celine smiled up at me and said, "I would love to." Looking down at her, she looked as if I had just told her it was Christmas.

I could not help myself. I took hold of her chin, bent down, and ever so lightly kissed her lips. A jolt of lightning ran through both of us, and we both took a step back from each other. Celine hurriedly said goodnight, turned, and ran up the steps and into the inn. I stood very still for a minute, then turned and walked to the stables.

The next morning, Marta was listening to Lester as he related all that he saw last night. Then she went upstairs and reported it all to Phillip. I worked hard all that week to be able to take Sunday off. All I thought about, day and night, was to be with Celine again. When Sunday finally arrived, I woke up early, dressed in my Sunday best, went down, and had the stable boy ready the buggy. I went back to the house for a quick breakfast, or so I thought.

When I entered the kitchen, Marta was just setting a big plate of eggs, bacon, grits, and toast beside a hot cup of black coffee on the table for me.

"I really don't have time for all this, this morning," I told Marta.

"Sure you do, young man," she replied.

"No, no, I don't. I want to be off and at the inn right away," I answered.

"Listen, young man. Anything getting is worth waiting for. Do you understand what I am telling you, Thomas?" Marta said.

I looked straight into Marta's unnerving stare. I knew there was no sense in arguing with this woman. She was more stubborn than any mule on the place. I replied, "Yes, I think I do, Marta, but—"

"No buts," she countered. "The girl will still be there if you take time to eat a good breakfast." *And give Lester time to get around*, Marta thought to herself. "If I am right, she will wait for you," she finished saying.

I started to eat fast but then slowed down as I found I was hungry after all. On slowing down, I started to relax. Marta smiled to herself. She couldn't help but love this boy. After finishing my meal, I got up, gave Marta a big hug, lifted her off the floor, and twirled her around. Marta squealed, "Put me down. What's got into you, you young fool?"

I just laughed and put her down, gave her a wink and a big smile, then simply said, "Love, Marta. I am in love."

"Oh, pooh," Marta answered me back. Then she pushed me toward the door. "Try not to be too late. Lots to do tomorrow," she finished.

"I won't," I said as I left the house, whistling to myself as I went down the steps and got into the buggy, unloosened the reins, and was off.

Marta stood and watched him ride away. She was happy for Thomas but was sad for what lay ahead for him. As Thomas passed by the cabin, he waved at Eli, who was just going to the big house to check the worklist for next week's work schedule. Eli waved back at me and hollered, "Good luck."

My, my, Eli thought to himself, *that boy must be in love*. That's the only thing that would get him up at the crack of dawn on a Sunday morning. Eli saw his mother standing on the porch, watching Thomas ride away. He noticed then his mother motioned to Lester, who was partially hidden in the shadows of the house. Seeing Marta wave her hand, the young boy rode out of the shadows and down the road a distance behind Thomas.

Eli, with the help of his crutches, hobbled over to the porch and up the ramp built on the side of the stairs, making it easier for Eli to get to the top of the porch. When he reached his mother's side, he gave her a kiss on her cheek and said, "Good morning. May I ask what that was all about?"

Marta looked up at Eli blankly, then smiled and said, "That is Thomas going to the inn to visit the girl he thinks he is in love with."

"No, I mean Lester," Eli replied.

"Oh," Marta said, "he is off doing an errand for Mr. Sanduvale," then went inside with Eli following behind her.

As I rode along, I was humming to myself and thought how green the trees were and how some of the leaves were starting to change their colors from green to orange, yellow, and red. I noticed the small blue flowers all along the roadway and how blue the sky was now that the sun had risen. I laughed out loud and thought how everything around me was so alive, things I had never noticed before or just taken for granted.

I laughed again and shouted, "I am in love," and whipped the hoses to a full gallop but not so fast as to tire them out. I was anxious to get to the inn and see Celine. I couldn't stop thinking of her, the way it felt when I kissed her, and I wanted to feel that way again. I was no novice when it came to women—I'd had my share—but none of them ever made me feel like Celine did.

When I was near her or just in sight of her, I grew weak in the knees, and it was hard to catch my breath just looking at her. I couldn't help but wonder what it would be like to be intimate with her. Just thinking about it made me dizzy, and I almost lost control of the buggy going around a curve. I regained control of the buggy and slowed the horses down, trying to think of anything but Celine.

Finally, after a couple of hours, I arrived at the inn. I pulled the horse and buggy to a stop in front of the inn and the young stable boy, whom I got to know as Zack, came over to tend the horses and buggy.

"Morning, Mr. Thomas. Water, feed, and rub them down today?"

"No, not today, Zack," I replied as I threw him the reins and jumped down from the buggy.

I looked around, and there, standing on the porch, was Celine. She had her hair pulled back so that the riot of curls cascading down her back to her waist was like a golden waterfall glistening in the sun. A few short curls framed her face. I couldn't take my eyes off of her face and away from her lips, and when I finally did, I looked into her eyes; it was like looking into the gates of heaven, I thought.

I held her gaze for what seemed like an eternity, and when I finally looked away, my eyes traveled down to her beautiful white shoulders, which were barely covered with a deep burgundy colored dress that brought out the deep violet of her eyes. The dress made her small perfect breasts push up to where the nipples almost showed. My eyes traveled down to her small, narrow waist. Just looking at her made me want to push her down and have my way with her.

When I looked back up into her eyes again, it was like looking into dark blue pools of water with no bottom. Her pupils were dilated, and her breathing was fast and shallow. I started to reach over and take her in my arms when the door to the inn flew open and a couple of early dock workers strolled out, looking at us. One of the men chuckled and said, "Mate, you two ought to get a room." Then the two left the porch, laughing.

I turned to Celine and saw she was blushing, a pink tinge upon her cheeks. "I am so sorry. Shall we get in the buggy now and go to Baton Rouge?" I asked her before she could change her mind. Without looking at me, Celine nodded her head yes, and we walked down the steps to the buggy. Young Zack had just finished wiping the horses down. I tossed him a coin and told him thank you. Then

I helped Celine into the buggy, climbed in after her, and we were on our way.

At first, we rode in silence, but after a while, we were knee-deep in conversation. We found it was easy to talk to one another and started telling each other about ourselves. We began to relax and enjoy each other's company. By the time we reached Baton Rouge, we were laughing, and I felt as if I had known Celine all my life.

Celine had a rough life, and it still wasn't the best life for a young girl, but she didn't complain or act like she deserved more. She just accepted the way things were and made the best of it. I thought to myself that I would change all that for her.

We arrived in Baton Rouge around lunchtime, so we boarded the horses and buggy, then headed out to find a good place to eat. We found a small place on the wharf, so we went inside. It was dimly lit but was clean and comfortable looking. We sat down and ordered something to eat. We dined on fresh cod, cooked in a spicy creole sauce, with sautéed fresh greens, freshly baked bread with creamy butter, and a glass of white wine. For dessert, we shared a bowl of fresh sliced peaches with clotted cream.

After eating, we strolled through town, looking in all the stores. I watched as Celine looked over everything, taking in all the details of everything she saw. It was like watching a small child looking through the window of a candy store. The last store we went to was a dressmaker's shop, which also sold fine material. We went inside, just to look around, when I noticed a piece of material that caught Celine's attention.

I watched as Celine fingered a beautiful piece of material the color of iridescent blue or purple. I wasn't sure, as it depended on which way the light hit it. I asked her if she would like to have it. She said she couldn't afford it. I called the dressmaker over and asked how much material it would take to make this young lady a dress. She looked Celine over, turned her around and around again, and then tapped her finger on her cheek and said, "Approximately two yards."

"Fine," I said, "I will take two yards. Please cut it and wrap it up to go." The lady said she would be delighted to do so and went about cutting and wrapping the material as Celine and I looked around the store. I noticed Celine looked a little ill at ease, so I asked her if she was all right.

Turning a little red, she spoke in a very low voice and said, "I did not mean for you to buy me that material. I am embarrassed for you to have done so."

"I am sorry if I caused you any embarrassment. That was not my intention, Celine. I saw you liked the material, and I wanted you to have it, nothing more, no strings attached. It was just a gift for you for giving me this wonderful day."

"Oh, no. I did not think there was any evil intent on your part. I am sorry, Thomas. It's just no one has ever given me such a gift as this. I really do appreciate it," she said. I paid the lady for the material, and we walked back to the stable for the long trip back to the inn.

We traveled in silence for more than half the trip, until once again, we both started to say something at the same time. "You go first," Celine said to me. "I just wanted to tell you how much I enjoyed spending the day with you, and if it's all right with you, I would like to see you again. I really like you and I think you like me too. What do you say? Can I call on you again?" I said all in one breath.

She looked at me with skepticism. I held my breath as I waited for her to answer my question. Finally, Celine said, "Yes, I would like to see you again," but there was no "I like you too" in her answer, making me a little disappointed. The rest of the way, we talked about the scenery, the weather, things we had seen and done today, but nothing about our feelings.

When we arrived back at the inn, I stopped the horses at the stairs, secured the reins, and then jumped down and went around to help Celine down from the buggy. As I handed her her package, all of a sudden, she was in my arms with her arms around my neck.

When I bent down to look at her, her lips meet mine. She kissed me hard and deep.

I felt like I was drowning. Her kiss was not an experienced kiss, but nonetheless, it aroused me. I removed her arms from around my neck and stepped back. Celine looked up at me dumbfounded and confused, then said, "I'm sorry. I shouldn't have done that. I am not experienced in these matters, and I hope it wasn't that bad."

I moaned to myself and replied, "No, no, it wasn't bad, not bad at all, but you test a man's restraint." She continued to look at me confused, I told her, "Go on inside. Don't worry. I will see you soon." She did, and as I watched her go, I gave myself a few minutes before climbing into the buggy, as I didn't want the ride home to be uncomfortable. On the ride home, I felt as if someone was following behind me, but every time I looked, there was no one in sight.

A few months went by, and the two of us became good friends. I went to the inn every two weeks. We hadn't gone to the cabin since Celine first showed it to me. We went for long walks or buggy rides and had picnics by the river, just enjoying being together. Then, one Sunday, we went down to the river to have a picnic and just relax.

Celine had packed a lunch for us, and I had brought a bottle of wine to drink and a blanket to sit on. When we arrived at the river, we spread out the blanket, sat down, not saying anything, just enjoying the beauty of our surroundings. After awhile we became hungry so we unpacked our lunch and ate it. .

Celine sat on the blanket with her legs under her. I lay down and put my head on her soft lap. I was so content and so consumed with love with this beautiful young girl that had come into my life. We stayed that way for quite some time. Celine watched the clouds roll in, and she would tell me what she thought they looked like. She would say, "Oh, look, that one looks like a rabbit."

Every now and then, I would open one eye, look at the cloud, and laugh at what she thought it looked like. I closed my eyes and listened to Celine describe what she saw. We stayed that way for some time when I noticed Celine had become quiet. I opened my eyes to see Celine staring down at me with the same look of desire I knew was in mine. Looking at her, I reached up and ran my hand lightly over her cheek, then down her lovely white throat and down to the tops of her breasts.

She didn't move, just sat and looked into my eyes. As I caressed her breasts, Celine softly began to moan, bent down, and kissed me long and deep. All of a sudden, the sky opened up, and the rain poured down on us. I jumped quickly to my feet as Celine squealed in surprise, then started to laugh as she quickly got to her feet.

We picked everything up and threw it all into the blanket, then began to run for cover. Before we knew it, we had made our way to the cabin. Celine opened the door and ran inside with me right behind her. I shut the door while Celine made her way over to the lantern and lit it. It flared into a warm glow, casting shadows of us on the walls. Laughing, I looked over at Celine. She was soaked through to the skin, as I was.

I caught my breath at the sight of her standing there, laughing. Her hair had come loose from the pins that held it on top of her head. It tumbled down her back like strands of gold in the lamplight. Her dress was molded to her body, showing every curve of it and outlining her breasts with the nipples erect from the cold, wet material stuck to them.

I groaned and moved forward, taking Celine into my arms, and turning her around, I undid the buttons down the back of her dress with shaking fingers. Her dress fell to the floor in a wet puddle around her feet, and she stepped out of it. I turned her back around to face me, and I saw the desire once again come alive, in eyes that had now turned a dark shade of purple.

I quickly took hold of the ties of her shift and undone them. The flimsy material slipped off and fell to her waist. I bent down and kissed each breast, then took one of her nipples in my mouth and gently tugged on it. Celine moaned and wound her fingers in my hair.

I undid her petticoat and shift and pulled them down. She

stepped out of them and kicked them over to her dress. Celine started to tremble. I didn't know if it was from desire or from being cold, so I hurried and removed my jacket and shirt and pulled them off one inside the other at the same time, with Celine helping me. I kicked off my shoes and pulled off my stockings. I tore open my breeches and kicked them off. I was going mad with desire but held myself in check, as I did not want to scare Celine.

I wanted this to be an unforgettable pleasure for her as well as for me. I lifted her up, and while kissing her, I walked to the bed and gently laid her on it. Laying down beside her, I gently kissed her and parted her lips with my tongue, then entered the soft recess of her mouth and pillaged it with my tongue until she returned every thrust with her own.

I took my time and let her desire build to a frenzy. Then I continued my assault on her breasts, down her flat stomach, and proceeded down to her thighs, when all of a sudden, Celine stilled and tried to move away from me. I took hold of her hips and pulled her toward me, where I attached my mouth gently to her sweet neither parts.

I heard her cry out my name and try to move away from me, but I held her tightly and started to assault her again with my tongue. Celine lay still and thought to herself, If Thomas does not stop this torture, I will surely die. But she soon found what she thought as torture quickly turned to pleasure. The pleasure she was having was bursting all over her body and was so intense, she could not hold back the scream.

Meanwhile, poor Lester, who was trying to stay dry as he huddled up next to the cabin wall, heard the scream. He jumped up from off the ground and looked into the window. He caught his breath at what he saw through the window in the lamplight.

"Oooh, Lord, I did not see that. I swear, Lord, I did not see that," Lester said as he pulled his soaked hat down over his eyes and ears and slid back down the cabin wall, rocking back and forth on his heels.

I knew Celine was ready for me as I made my way back up to her lips. I climbed on top of her, spread her legs apart, and gently slid my swollen manhood a little ways inside of her warm, moist sheath. I lay still, letting her get used to the feel of me. As I moved a little further in, I felt the barrier keeping me from entering her all the way. I lifted myself up on my arms, told her to look at me, and when she did, I pushed down hard to break the membrane and slid all the way inside of her. Celine gasped but kept her eyes on mine.

I could see her pupils were dilated with desire and knew mine would be too. I started to move slowly inside her, then a little faster. Celine just lay there at first, but then she got caught up in the tempo and started to move with me. We moved together as one, faster and faster, until I felt her nails digging into my back and heard the sounds coming from her throat as she arched her back.

I knew she had reached her climax. I drove deeper until I reached my own pinnacle. Then it happened, and when it did, it was like millions of stars bursting all around me, and I wanted it to go on forever. It was pure perfection, something I had never felt before with any other woman, and I knew I never wanted to, only with Celine.

After our breathing slowed down, I reached over, gathered Celine into my arms, and pulled a blanket over our sweaty bodies. A few minutes later, I heard Celine softly crying.

"Did I hurt you?" I asked her.

"No," she replied.

"Then why are you crying?" I asked.

"Because that was the most beautiful thing I think I have ever experienced. Can we do it again?" she asked as she wiped her nose on the blanket.

"Not right away," I said, laughing as I kissed her deeply.

I got up to put some wood into the fireplace to start a fire. When the fire caught hold and started to burn brightly, I moved the two chairs close to it. Then I hung our clothes over the chairs for them to dry. I returned to the bed, pulled Celine close to me for warmth, and held her in my arms. Celine's breathing had become shallow, so I knew she had fallen asleep. After a short amount of time, I too fell asleep.

A few hours later, I woke up thinking I heard something outside. I quietly got up, looked over, and saw Celine was still sleeping, so I went to the window. I saw nothing and decided it must have been the soft sounds that Celine was making while she slept that woke me, or perhaps it was the crackling of the wood burning in the fireplace.

Outside, Lester was chilled to the bone. He wished Missy Marta would find someone else to spy on Master Thomas. He just didn't feel right about what he was doing. Lester decided he would take off and ride on home before he caught his death from a cold. He quietly got up, walked to where he had tied up his horse in a grove of trees, swung up onto the saddle, and slowly rode toward the main road, muttering to himself, "Yes, sir, it's going to be a long, cold ride home. Yes, sir, it surely is."

Thomas lay there, watching Celine sleep, until she stirred and opened her eyes. As she looked up at me, I saw desire flare up into her eyes again. I was amazed and delighted all at the same time.

"Again," Celine said in a husky voice filled with the new desire she had discovered in making love.

I laughed and replied, "Who am I to refuse such a wanton minx like you?"

We made love slowly, making it last as long as we could, but all too soon, we both experienced those glorious, exorbitant feelings we had shared earlier that had left us both breathless. We lay there for a while, basking in these new feelings we had discovered, but as I looked out the window, I saw the rain had stopped and the sun was beginning to go down.

I looked over and saw the fire had almost burnt completely out. I said to Celine, "I think our clothes should be dry by now. We should probably get up and get dressed and head back to the inn, as it is getting late." Looking out the window, she agreed with me, so reluctantly, we got up and lit the lantern.

I helped Celine into her shift and petticoats, then slid her dress over her head and arms. I did up the buttons on the back of her dress while she tried to smooth out the curls hanging down her back. She then proceeded to help me with the buttons on my shirt. After pulling on my breeches, she started to button them up while caressing my crouch. Moaning, I quickly removed her hands, saying, "Young lady, you will be the death of me yet, but if I must die, I can't think of a better way to go." I continued, "But for now, we really must go." Celine faked a hurt expression on her face that made me laugh out loud. "There will be a lot more of this, I promise, a lot more," I said. I finished dressing, and when I had finished, we made the bed and straightened up the room. I made sure the fire was out. Then we picked up the blanket with all the picnic debris in it and headed out the door.

"Oh, wait," Celine said, "I forgot to put out the lantern." So she did.

We walked at a brisk pace back to the main road, where I discovered you could see the cabin from this point. Celine said, "Yes, it is somewhat visible from this area, but when you come from the riverside, it is well hidden." As we walked, the sun began to sink, and it began to get dark and was growing colder. Our clothes still had a damp feeling to them.

When we arrived at the inn, I took Celine around to the side door, where she could go upstairs without being seen. I kissed her long and deep. She kissed me back the same way. I told her I would come again next Sunday if everything went all right at the plantation. Celine replied, "All right," then kissed me lightly on the lips and went inside.

I picked up the horse and buggy and started for home. On the ride home, I smiled so much that when I arrived there, my jaws were hurting something fierce. The next morning, a very sick Lester repeated what he had seen, but in a very polite way, between coughing and sneezing to Marta, who stood a little away from Lester, standing outside the barn.

Marta told Lester to go to bed and stay there. She would bring him some chicken soup along with a cold remedy that would help make him feel better soon. I went outside and across to the barn, where I encountered Marta and Lester talking. I walked up and said good morning to both of them. Marta cheerfully said good morning back. Lester just grunted, turned, and walked away.

"What the heck was that all about?" I asked Marta. "What's got into Lester?"

Marta just shook her shoulders and replied, "Oh, nothing to worry about. He's just come down with a cold and doesn't feel well after being out in the rain. I am going to fix him some nice hot chicken soup. It'll fix him right up."

"I am sorry to hear that, "I replied. "He should know better than to get in the rain, but maybe that will teach him to stay out of the rain from now on."

"Humph," Marta replied, and she started for the house.

"What's that? I didn't quite catch what you said."

Marta did not stop walking, just waved me off with her hand.

When Marta got inside, she went straight upstairs to report to Phillip all the details Lester had told her. Well, almost all, omitting what had taken place in the cabin. Phillip asked Marta if she thought Thomas was getting too serious with this girl. Marta replied, "Maybe, maybe not. Maybe he is just sowing his wild oats."

"Bull," he said, and he motioned for her to leave.

Most every Sunday for the next several months, I made my way to see Celine. We shared every minute we could in the cabin, making love. It seemed we just couldn't get enough of each other. Marta told Lester to stop spying on Thomas, so he did, and he was happy to do so—that is, until Phillip caught on to what was going on. He sent for Lester and told him to go back to following Thomas, but this time, he was to report only to Phillip.

Four months after the first time they made love, Celine woke up very nauseated. She jumped out of bed and just made it to the chamber pot and threw up in it. After some time of emptying the contents of her stomach, she felt better. She washed her face, rinsed her mouth, got dressed, and then went downstairs to start her work day.

When she entered the kitchen, the smell of the greasy food, along with all the other smells of the inn, hit Celine like a ton of bricks. She made it outside the back door just in time to lean over the porch rail as the nausea returned. She wiped her mouth on her sleeve and took in big gulps of fresh air, which seemed to help calm her stomach. She went back inside but made several trips out back before her shift was over.

Celine slowly climbed the stairs to her room, went inside, and laid down on her bed. She rolled over and moaned as she got sick again, lucky that she had moved the chamber pot closer to the bed after she emptied it. Celine thought she must have eaten something bad and had poisoned her stomach, as this went on all week.

At the end of the week, on Saturday, she stepped out on the back porch to get some fresh air. One of the older women stepped out back to get some fresh air also. When she saw Celine standing there all pale and sick, the woman spoke up. "That happened to me too when I got pregnant with my first one." At that statement, Celine's head snapped up in the direction of the woman.

Wide eyed, Celine replied, "What are you talking about? I just ate something bad that has disagreed with my stomach."

"Suit yourself, girly, but they are the same symptoms, no doubt about it. Yes, sir," the older woman said as she turned and went back inside. Celine stood stock still, trying to remember when she'd had her last cycle. *Was it last month?* she thought. She groaned. "It has to be at least one or two months now," she thought out loud. "No, no, it can't be, but what if it is? What will I do?"

The question kept going around in her head, like a bad dream from which she couldn't awaken. She heard her uncle calling her from inside, so she stepped back inside and said, "Here I am, Uncle. What is it?"

"Are you feeling all right, Celine?" her uncle asked her. He had noticed Celine's absence from work lately, and he'd also noticed how pale she was.

"Yes, I am quite all right. I just stepped out for some fresh air. You know how stuffy it gets in here at times, Uncle, but I am ready to get back to work now," she said, smiling at him. She made it through her shift again without any incident.

After her shift was finished, she went upstairs to retire for the night. She passed the older woman to whom she had spoken the other day. It was the older woman's job to clean the rooms upstairs where the guests stayed overnight. As Celine passed by the woman, the woman quietly said to Celine, "Peppermint tea," then hurried on down the hall.

Celine stopped and stared at the woman's retreating back. Celine wasn't sure, but it sounded as if the old woman had said, "Peppermint tea." When she got to her room and went inside, she lay down, as she felt exhausted. No sooner had she lain down than she was hit was another bout of nausea. She lay very still until the sickness passed.

She slowly got up, went downstairs, and walked out back to the garden, where she picked some fresh peppermint leaves and went back inside to the kitchen. Celine boiled some water and dropped the leaves into the hot water to let them steep. She got some salty crackers, poured the hot peppermint mixture into a jar, and went back upstairs. When she got inside her room, she sat in a chair, ate some crackers, and sipped on some of the tea.

After eating some of the crackers and drinking some of the tea, she went over and carefully lay down on her bed. She waited for the nausea to come, but to her surprise, it didn't. She drifted off to sleep. When she awoke some time later, she lay there and thought about her situation. Was she going to tell Thomas? Would he be happy or would he stop seeing her? Celine did not want Thomas to think she was trying to trap him into a marriage.

After fretting over everything for several hours, Celine finally fell asleep. When she woke up, it was morning already—Sunday morning, to be exact, the day Thomas would be coming to see her. Without thinking, Celine jumped up and immediately felt her stomach lurch, she reached for the chamber pot. When her stomach settled down, she drank some of the peppermint tea and ate a few salty crackers.

When she felt up to it, she went to the basin, poured some water into it and washed her face, then her body. When she thought she was clean enough, she dried, put on her shift and a petticoat, and then reached for the beautiful dress she had made out of the material Thomas had bought for her.

This would be the first time she had worn it, but she wanted to look her best if she was going to break the news of her pregnancy to Thomas. Celine had made the dress form fitting all the way to her narrow waist. Then it flared out in a beautiful blue cloud. She had made the dress with long sleeves, which was good, as the weather was turning colder.

When Celine stepped into the dress, she found it a little loose in the waist and shoulders. Had she lost weight, perhaps from not being able to keep any food down? She thought, when she went to do up the buttons and her fingers brushed across her breasts, that they were noticeably more sensitive to the touch. When she finished buttoning the dress, she also noticed her bust was almost spilling over the top of her bodice.

She went to her mirror to see her reflection. The color of the iridescent material brought out the purple-blue color of her eyes. Her best feature, she thought, with the long, dark lashes and perfectly arched eyebrows. She thought her cheeks were a little pale looking, so she pinched them to put some color into them. Her lips were full and pouty looking, and she didn't like the looks of them.

Celine noticed there were dark circles under her eyes and she looked tired. *Well,* she thought, *no help for that.* But she found she felt like crying. *What's the matter with me? Get a hold of yourself. Are you going daft?* she scolded herself. With that, she turned away from the mirror, walked over, and drank a cold cup of tea.

Celine poured another cup of tea and sipped on it. *Thank goodness for this tea. It is helping me overcome being sick.* After drinking the tea, Celine went back to the mirror and swept the gold mass of curls up into a bun and pinned it in place. She then left the room and went downstairs and sat outside on the porch in the cool, fresh air to wait for Thomas.

While sitting there, she thought of how she would tell Thomas the news. *I will just say,* she thought, *"Guess what, you are going to be a father." No, that won't do. I'll say, "How do you feel about children?" Oh,* she groaned in frustration, *I'm beginning to feel a headache coming on.*

Half an hour later, Thomas arrived at the inn. The young stable boy took his horse to the stables to care for it like he always did. Celine watched as Thomas walked toward her, anticipation growing in the pit of her stomach. She thought, *How can I be so lucky to have him want me? He is so handsome. What will I do if he rejects me and the baby? I can't lose him. I, I love him,* she admitted to herself.

As I got nearer to Celine, I could see the distress on her face. I hurried over to her and sat down beside her. Taking hold of her hand, I asked her if anything was wrong. Giving me her most engaging smile, Celine answered, "Why, nothing. What on earth could be wrong on such a beautiful day, especially now that you are here?" Then she raised her hand and caressed my cheek.

Looking into the depths of her eyes, I took Celine's hand and kissed each of her fingertips, thinking I had read her face wrong and that everything was indeed all right. I asked Celine what she would like to do today.

"Let's walk down by the river, where the water comes inland and makes a little pond. We can have a picnic, and when it gets warmer, we can wade our feet in the pond," she said.

She laughed like a little girl. I laughed along with her and said, "Sounds like a good plan."

I took a bottle of wine with two glasses and put them in the basket, along with the food Celine had gathered together. She had gotten us cold sliced ham, cheese, bread, and some freshly baked apple pastries. Celine then added a bottle of her tea and some salty crackers to the basket. I picked up the basket and a blanket, and we started out on our adventure.

After slowly walking for over an hour, we finally came to the place Celine was talking about. It was a little inlet that did indeed make a small pond, with trees all around it. There was a grassy clearance in the middle of it, so we spread our blanket there, and I lay down. Celine filled a plate for me of ham, bread, and cheese. I sat up and poured a glass of wine and handed it to Celine. She said she didn't want any right then, that she had brought some tea for herself.

Thinking nothing of it, I ate some ham and cheese on the bread and drank some wine. I watched as Celine nibbled on some crackers and slowly sipped her tea. "Don't you want a piece of ham?" I asked her.

"Not right now. I had a large breakfast," she lied, as the thought of eating ham made her stomach lurch, so she drank more tea.

After eating, we put away the food and drink. Turning to Celine, I took her in my arms and kissed her deeply. My tongue probed open her mouth and raked across her small white teeth. Celine opened her mouth a little wider, and her tongue fenced with mine. I groaned and pulled her closer until she could feel my rising passion. I cupped one of her breasts with my hand and moved my thumb across the tight soft material covering the nipple.

Celine felt them harden and softly cried out as she pulled away from me. I was stunned and asked her, "Are you sure you're all right? Did I hurt you?"

"No, you didn't, but we have to talk, Thomas," she replied. Celine went over and sat down on the blanket, patting the spot next to her, and motioned for me to come sit by her. After I sat down, she handed me a pastry and took one for herself. After taking a few small bites and a sip of tea, she started to speak.

Afraid she was about to break it off between us, I put my finger over her lips and asked, "We're good, aren't we, Celine? I mean, everything is all right between us, isn't it?"

"Yes, oh, yes," she replied, "but I need to know what is going on between us. Are we going to get married, settle down, and raise children?"

The last question took me by surprise, coming out of the blue like that. I sat for a minute, then answered her. "Yes, I do want to get married, settle down, and have children with you, but now is not a good time," I explained. "With my father the way he is and the plantation just getting back to normal and a dozen other things going on. Now is just not the right time. You understand, don't you, my love?"

I looked at her with pleading eyes, willing her to please understand. I waited, not breathing, for her to answer me, to know that she did understand. Celine looked at Thomas, her face not showing the emotions running rampant in her mind.

She thought, *Not now.* No, it wasn't a good time to tell him about the baby. *Maybe later, but how long can I wait?*

Finally, Celine smiled at me and said, "Yes, I do understand, Thomas."

I let out my breath and pulled her close to me. My heart was pounding against my chest at the thought that I might lose her. I could not—no, would not—accept that. *She is my soulmate and I am hers. I love this girl with all my heart.*

I pushed her back down on the blanket and started kissing her face, her neck, and the tops of her breasts. I undid the top few buttons of her dress and let her beautiful white globes spill out over her dress. I took a nipple and gently tugged on it until it became a hard peak. Celine groaned at the painful sensation it was causing her. I then did the same to the other nipple. When Celine thought she could stand no more, I lifted her dress and caressed her silky neither part, spreading her legs and making love to her with my finger.

Celine tried to move away, but the sensations she was feeling held her there. All of a sudden, Celine felt like she was melting into oblivion. She thrashed about and cried out my name as she arched her back and burst into a million hot coals as the spasms came one right after another. I quickly undid my breeches, releasing my throbbing manhood, and plunged into her hot molten body, all the time watching Celine's face, seeing the pleasure she was obtaining.

Within minutes, I reached my climax, and together, we soared higher than ever before. When it was over, Celine lay slack, like a broken doll, not wanting to move and lose the pleasure she had achieved. I held her tightly and whispered in her ear, "You are mine, Celine, and always will be. Say it, Celine. Tell me you will always be mine, no matter what."

Celine did say it, over and over.

Lester had learned a while back that when Thomas and Celine started to make love. It was his cue to leave, so he would not have to report to Phillip what he had seen. Usually, he would find a hidden place, away from sight and sound and sleep, until he thought they were through.

After we lay there a while, I undid the rest of Celine's buttons on her dress and slipped it off of her, then discarded her shift and petticoat. When she was laying there naked, I ran my hands down her flat stomach, then down over her rounded hips, along her long legs, and then I kissed her small feet.

I jumped up and undid my clothes and let them fall to the blanket. As I stood there watching Celine's face, she lay there, taking Thomas all in—his broad shoulders, smooth chest, flat stomach, and well-proportioned long legs. Then she looked at my manhood, then back up to my eyes, where I saw the love for me in her eyes.

I went to her, reached down and picked her up, carried her to the pond, and walked into the water. I gently put her down into the water, which had been warmed by the sun. I washed her all over, as she did me. We splashed each other and played like kids, laughing and having fun. After, I carried Celine over to the warm blanket and dried her off with part of it, then dried myself.

We lay down, and I pulled Celine close to me to keep her warm, and as we lay there warmed by the sun, we drifted off to sleep.

After a few hours, Lester woke and returned to the spot he had first been watching the couple. When he got settled behind a bush among the trees. Lester peeked out, and when he saw the two naked bodies lying in the sun entwined in each other's arms, he almost fainted.

He drew back into his hidden shelter, rocking back and forth on his heels, and said, almost out loud, "Dear Lord, don't he ever stop. I want Master Thomas's stamina when I finds me a woman." Lester sat back down, pulled his hat low over his eyes, and went back to sleep. A little while later, the couple woke up, got dressed, gathered up all their things, and started walking back to the inn, leaving behind a sleeping Lester hidden in the bushes among the trees.

We walked slowly back to the inn, holding hands to prolong our time of parting. I told Celine how pretty she looked and what a great job she did on her dress. She blushed and thanked me. I thought to myself that I would hurry things along, then we would marry and stay together forever.

Celine was thinking that she wished she had told Thomas about the pregnancy, but she would wait a little while longer and find a better time to tell him, whenever that might be. *Oh well*, she thought, *maybe next Sunday will be the right time*, and she sighed.

The next Saturday, I sent word to Celine that something had come up and I would not be able to see her Sunday as planned but would come the following Sunday. I worked hard all that week and the next to get everything done on the plantation. The next Sunday, I went to visit Celine, but because I had worked from sunup to sundown for the past two weeks, I was exhausted and could hardly stay awake.

We walked to the cabin, and when we entered, I asked Celine not to light the lantern, just to come in and lay on the bed with me for a while. As we lay together, quietly talking, I drifted off to sleep. Seeing how tired I was, Celine didn't wake me until later that afternoon.

Celine watched Thomas sleep and thought how handsome he was. She bent down and kissed him on his lips, lightly running her tongue over his lips. Then she lightly kissed his eyelids, bringing him awake.

"Sorry," she whispered, "but it's getting late, and soon you will have to leave."

I reached up and slowly brought her head down and kissed her lips, which were so inviting. It was a slow, seductive kiss that flared both our passion into awareness. I undressed Celine slowly, and when I was through, I marveled at how truly beautiful she was. As I scanned every inch of her, I thought how she was maturing from a beautiful young girl into a beautiful young woman right before my eyes.

Her breasts had grown into two beautiful globes that made me want to kiss them forever. I noticed her tiny waist had filled out some, along with her marvelous rounded buttocks. I looked down the whole length of her, all the way down to her dainty feet. I kissed each toe and worked my way up to her lips. When Celine could not stand to wait any longer, she reached for me to come to her. I stood up and removed my jacket and my shirt slowly.

I watched Celine's eyes turn from a purple-blue to a dark deep blue, and when I undid my breeches and let them fall to the floor, my manhood spring to life, and I ached for her also. Thomas slowly moved on top of her, and she put her arms around his neck and wound her legs around his buttocks, pulling him close to her, as she loved the feeling of his hot flesh next to hers.

When I entered the silky moist core of her, I almost lost control, but I held myself in check so Celine could ride the wave of pleasure with me. I moved slowly at first, then began to pick up the pace. I could hear and feel Celine climb higher and higher, reaching the pinnacle of her pleasure. I gave one last plunge into the valley of heaven, and we both cried out as we reached our climax together.

I rolled off of Celine and brushed the damp curls away from her face. She lay still, and her breathing was heavy from the pleasure she had just achieved. I reached over and covered her with a blanket, then got up and walked over behind the screen, where I poured water from a picture onto a cloth. I washed myself off, rinsed out the cloth, and poured clean water onto it. I went over and washed the evidence of our lovemaking off of Celine. When I was through, I helped her dress and then dressed myself. We cleaned up and closed the cabin door. Then we walked slowly back to the inn.

I told Celine I was working hard on the plantation and also on a surprise for her. She looked up at me with a big smile on her face and asked excitedly what the surprise was. I told her she would have to wait a few more months to find out, and I assured her it would be worth the wait. The smile faded from her face, as she had thought the surprise was going to be a proposal of marriage. Then she said to me, "A couple of months."

Her mind started to panic, as she thought, *I will be showing by then. It will be hard to hide the fact that I am carrying his child.* She would have to tell him and soon. Celine wasn't listening to what Thomas was saying, so caught up was she in her own thoughts.

"Celine, Celine, did you hear me?" I asked her.

"I am sorry, Thomas. I did not hear what you were saying," Celine answered me.

I repeated, "I do not think I will be coming for a while, but I'll come as soon as I can. I want to get through with things as quickly as possible."

"Oh, all right" she said, caught off guard by his statement. "When you do come again, there is something I must talk to you about."

"What is it?" I asked her.

"Not now. The boy is here with your horse. It can wait until you return to me, "Celine said.

Smiling up at me, I bent down, drew her into my arms, and kissed her deeply, then mounted my horse and rode away. Celine watched as Thomas rode out of sight. She stood a minute longer, until a cold breeze blew around her, giving her a chill. She shook her head, feeling a dread feeling wash over her.

Celine felt it was a sign of something bad about to happen. *Nonsense*, she said to herself, and she hurried into the inn.

I rode along, thinking how lucky I was. I had a beautiful woman who wanted to marry me and have my babies. I thought about the house I was building for Celine, the house my family and I would eventually have.

I had picked out five acres of prime land on the plantation, not far from the main house. I was building it with five bedrooms upstairs. One of the bedrooms would be big, with a fireplace, a big closet to hold all the clothes I intended to buy Celine, and a small room that would have a washbasin with running water and a toilet like the one at the Markhams' manor in England. The bottom part of the house would have a large kitchen at the back, a dining room, a parlor, and a large family room. A large staircase would connect the two sections. There would also be a servants' quarter on the side to house the people who would help out Celine. There would be a large screened porch extending all the way around the house, for us to sit out on during the warm summer evenings. And a big backyard for all our children to play in.

Just thinking about the house and Celine made my heart soar. Soon, I would be able to show it to Celine and ask her to marry me. Thinking about all this made the journey home seem less arduous, and I couldn't wait to share the news with the rest of the people I loved.

Time flew by as I was busy getting ready for the harvest in a few months, and with the building of the house, it left little time for me to be with Celine. It was getting darker earlier, so there was less light in which I could work. When I did ride to the inn to see her, I was so exhausted, all I wanted to do was to sleep next to her. I was too tired to do anything else.

Sometimes we would walk to our private place down by the river, lay on a blanket and fall asleep.

Celine did not mind this, as she too was exhausted, as she was now almost five months along, carrying his baby and still had not told him. Each time she tried to tell him, she would chicken out and tell herself, *Next time.*

Celine no longer waited on customers at the inn, as she and the older woman, whose name Celine found out was Beth, had become friends and had changed positions. Celine helped out in the kitchen and cleaned the rooms upstairs while Beth took over waiting tables and putting up with the rowdy bunch that dined at the inn. Beth told Celine she didn't mind, as she could handle the men. Celine was very grateful she didn't have to cinch her corset so tightly, as she was out of sight most of the time.

Nearing her seventh month, Celine still had not told Thomas but made up her mind to tell him when he arrived this Sunday. She felt relieved to have finally made up her mind. It was like a big weight had been lifted off her shoulders, however Thomas might take the news. She had been grateful that Thomas had not been able to come as often, being busy and all. When they were together and made love, they did so without undressing. Thomas, being exhausted, would just pull up her dress and petticoats and do the deed, then fall asleep beside her.

I was so excited. The house was almost finished. A few more weeks, and I could bring Celine home to show her the surprise and celebrate the end of the harvest season. Thomas thought, *And then I will announce our engagement to everyone.* I rode faster than usual to get to the inn. I could not wait to tell Celine of her surprise.

When I finally did get to the inn, as always, Celine was waiting on the front porch for me. I thought she was looking very anxious and distraught. *Something is wrong,* I thought as I slid off my horse, tied it to the hitching post, and hurried over to her. "Celine, what is the matter? What's wrong?" I asked her.

"There is nothing the matter. Why do you ask?" she replied.

"Everything is fine, I just have to talk to you about something, and it can't wait."

"All right," I said as I sat down on a bench and motioned for her to sit beside me.

"No" she said, fidgeting with her hands, "not here. Let's walk to the cabin," she replied.

"All right," I said, growing uneasy.

We started out for the cabin, and as we passed the stables, I asked the boy to tend to my horse while I was gone.

We walked slowly, both of us in silence as we both thought of what we had to say to one another. I was thrilled about the news. I wanted to share with Celine and could hardly contain myself from blurting it out right then and there. Celine, on the other hand, was worried about how I would take the news.

When we reached the cabin, we went inside, and I went to light the lantern. Celine asked me not to light it. She wanted to tell me first what she had to say. She then went over and sat on the edge of the bed. I walked over and sat beside her. I said, laughing nervously, "This sounds very serious."

"It is," she replied. I took her in my arms and kissed her forehead, then her cheek. Then I reached her mouth and kissed her deeply.

"What is it you need to tell me?" I asked her, still kissing her neck lightly, making her moan.

The passion for Celine took hold of me upon hearing her moan, as I realized we hadn't been with each other for quite some time now. God, we hadn't made love—I mean, really made love, without hurrying, I thought. I moved slowly down to her breasts and released them from the confinement of her dress. I kissed one, then the other, making Celine's passion flare up like a wildfire burning hot, making her forget about talking to Thomas.

She held me to her breast, willing me to continue, to bring her to whatever height she was seeking, unable to think or feel anything but the pleasure she knew he alone could give her. I laid her down on the bed, with my mouth still on her breast, I continued my assault on her with my mouth and tongue. I lifted her dress and spread her thighs and began to prove the very core of her with my tongue.

It started low and began to build with such intensity, traveling from her neither part up to her breasts. Celine began to move, to arch her back, but before she could reach her desired release, I sat up, undid my pants releasing my throbbing manhood, and plunged into her. Celine groaned with pleasure at feeling me inside her. I moved slowly and methodically, savoring each thrust until I myself needed that glorious release. I moved faster, and Celine moved with me, as if we were one, climbing higher and higher until together we reached that feeling of no return.

Celine cried out, clinging to me, her hair damp from our lovemaking. I held her until our breathing became normal once again. We lay still, holding each other. Celine was so content, she forgot to tell Thomas about the baby once again, until he reached over and slid his hand over her protruding stomach. Celine froze. I jerked up, scrambled for the lantern, fumbled for the matches, and tried to light it with trembling fingers.

I redid my pants as the lantern flared bright. I turned to look at Celine as she tried to set up. I held the lantern close and saw the bulging stomach glistening with sweat. I said rather harshly, "When were you going to tell me, Celine?"

The look on her face was pure fright. She replied in a low, soft voice, not looking at me, "Today, Thomas. I was going to tell you today," and without stopping, she rushed on. "I tried to tell you several times. Remember when I asked if you wanted children. You said yes, someday, but not now. That's when I found out, and I thought you would be angry if you knew I was carrying your child now and you wouldn't want me or the child. Honest, I did try to tell you." She started to sob and finished by saying, in between sobbing and hiccupping, "And you are mad."

I pulled her into my arms and held her close to me, rubbing her back and softly telling her everything was going to be all right. In my mind, I thought back to the day she asked me about marriage and having children. I remembered telling her yes but not now—someday. I groaned and pulled her closer to me.

I whispered in her ear, "I am not mad, just stunned, because I had no clue, and I should have, as I know your body like I know the back of my hand, and I should have known. And I would have if I were not such a rutting pig."

Celine laughed as she pictured that in her mind.

I continued, "I just can't seem to get enough of you, Celine. I love you so much."

"And I you," Celine replied. "So you aren't mad? You are happy about the baby?"

"Yes, yes, I am very happy about becoming a father. In fact, I am delighted," I told Celine and kissed her soundly.

"Are you, Thomas? Are you really?" she asked me.

I assured her I was very happy and asked, "By the way, how far along are you?"

"Almost eight months," she answered me.

I swallowed hard and repeated, "Eight months. That doesn't give us much time, my love."

I bent down and kissed her stomach. Celine was thrilled beyond words that I was happy about their baby. I stood her up and helped her straighten her dress up. "You should not be wearing such a tight garment, should you?" I asked her. "I mean, it won't harm the baby, will it?"

"No," Celine answered.

On the way back to the inn, we talked about posting the required marriage band, as it would take a while, and time was something we did not have the luxury of. I told Celine I would be back as soon as I could, and then we would ride to Baton Rouge, sign the papers for the bands, and get things started, and while we were there, we would have a wedding dress made for her.

When we arrived back at the inn, I told Celine how happy she made me and how much I loved her. I kissed her goodbye and said I would see her soon. Then I watched as she went inside through the back door and was out of sight. I waited a few minutes and got my courage up before climbing the stairs and entering the inn through the front door. After adjusting my eyes to the dim light, I looked around and saw Celine's uncle sitting at a table in the corner, working on the books. I walked up and said hello to Celine's uncle, who looked up and acknowledged me with a nod of his head.

"What brings you here, Thomas? Are you here to see Celine?" he asked.

"No," I said, "I am here to see you."

With that statement, he put down his pen and motioned for me to sit down. Folding his large arms over his broad chest, looking me right in the eye, he waited for me to begin. "I am here about Celine," I said, unwavering. "I would like your permission to marry her."

The only thing that moved on his face was one eyebrow, which shot up.

"I see," he said, still staring me in the eye. "Kind of sudden, ain't it?" he asked.

I looked him right in his eyes and told him the whole story, finishing with "I love her, and she loves me. I swear to you, I will treat her and the babe right, always."

Celine's uncle just sat there looking at me for what seemed like an eternity. Then he said, "It took guts for you to come tell me face to face. It took a good man to do that, so, yes, I will give you my blessing after I talk to Celine and see how she feels about all this." He then held out his hand, and we shook hands.

Celine felt like she was floating on a cloud—she was so happy. She could not wait to tell someone about how she felt. She hurried up the steps and found Beth just coming down. She stopped the woman on the steps and hugged her, then told her what had transpired today. Beth congratulated Celine and hugged her back and told her how happy she was for her.

The next Sunday, I took the buggy and rode to the inn to pick up Celine. We slowly rode to Baton Rouge, as the road was bumpy and I didn't want to jiggle Celine around anymore than was necessary. I told her I wanted her to move to the plantation right away to meet everyone and be there to celebrate the end of the harvest season with everyone. After the celebration, we would announce our engagement and our plans to wed the following week.

I also told her I was very close to finishing the surprise for her and that it would be her wedding gift to her from me. She clapped her hands and said she could not wait to see what it was. When we arrived in Baton Rouge, we went straight to the registrar's office and posted our bands and signed the necessary papers. Next, we went to see the clergy to make arrangements for him to come to the plantation two Sundays from today to perform the wedding.

We found a place to eat lunch close by. After eating, we made our way to the shop, where we had purchased the material for Celine seven and a half months earlier. The same woman that waited on us then waited on us now. The woman asked, "How can I help you today?" I told her we had bought material here before from her. She replied, yes, she remembered us, and looked over to Celine, then back to me.

"We would like for you to show us material for making a wedding dress," I said.

She led us to some fine material, where Celine picked out a beautiful silk material the color of light spun gold. Almost the color of her hair, It was embroidered with dark gold flowers all throughout it. I told the woman I wanted enough to make a wedding dress for the young lady here. She said, "Yes, of course" and went to get her measuring tape. When she returned, she had Celine remove her cape so she could measure how much material it would take. Celine turned red as she watched the woman's eyes get big on seeing her condition. Seeing this, I told the woman if she could get it made in two weeks, there would be extra money in it for her own pocket.

Looking up at me, the woman nodded her head in understanding. She turned to Celine and with a smile said, "You will make a beautiful bride." After that, Celine relaxed.

With everything taken care of, we headed back to the inn as

Celine was getting tired and it would be a long, slow ride back. We talked about the baby, whether it would be a girl or a boy and what names we might choose for it. When we finally arrived at the inn, both of us were elated and exhausted. I helped Celine down, helped her upstairs to the back door, kissed her goodnight, and told her I would be back in two days for her and all her stuff.

When I finally got to the plantation, I dropped the horse and buggy off at the stable, as it was late. I had the stable hand take care of them. I went to the house, climbed the stairs, and went inside. I saw the light was still burning in the kitchen. I went in and found Marta and Jacob having a late-night cup of coffee and was talking. As I entered the kitchen, Jacob asked me what was going on. I asked him what he meant as I poured myself a cup of coffee and sat down with them.

Jacob replied, "Because you look like the fox that has gotten into the hen house is what I meant."

I laughed and said, "It's that obvious, huh?" Jacob shook his head yes. "Promise not to hit me on the head, either of you, and I'll tell you."

We all laughed. Then I became serious and told them about Celine, about how much I loved her and about the house I was building. Then I told them about the baby and how happy I was.

I didn't notice the look that passed between Marta and Jacob. I was so happy and so exhausted, I really didn't notice much of anything right then. Marta spoke up and said, "I am very happy for you, Tommy, but are you sure this is the right thing for you right now?"

I replied, "Yes, I am sure, Marta. I love Celine, and I want her to be my wife."

"All right," Marta said, "then it's settled: we will plan a celebration and a wedding." Marta got up, walked over, and kissed me on my forehead.

Then Jacob came over and shook my hand and said, "Looks like congratulations are in order, young man."

After they were sure I had gone upstairs, Jacob turned to Marta and said, "What's we going to do about Phillip? He ain't never going to allow this to happen."

Marta thought for a minute, then said, "We will plan the wedding as we plan the end of the harvest celebration. What he doesn't know, he can't stop from happening."

What neither Marta nor Jacob knew was that Phillip had heard me come home and once again came down and hid in the alcove and listened to their conversation.

When Marta left and went back to her cabin and Jacob had retired to his room, Phillip went over to one of the workers' cabin and knocked on the door. When Lester answered, Phillip told him he had an errand for him to run first thing in the morning. Lester nodded, and Phillip went back to the house and went to bed.

The next couple of days were a flurry of activity as preparations were being made not only for the harvest celebration but also for my and Celine's wedding day. Everybody worked hard and quietly so Master Phillip would not find out. Some of Phillips' workers were sent over to Pierce's plantation to help them finish their harvesting in time. One worker told Jason about the upcoming wedding of Thomas and Celine. Jason said out loud, "Well, I'll be damned. It's about time. Wait 'til I tell Jenny the news."

When Jason finished up his chores, he washed up and went inside for dinner. Jenny was just setting the table with the help of her mother when Jason told them the news of Tommy getting married. Caroline stopped what she was doing, looked at Jason, and said, "It's about time someone snagged that boy." When Caroline looked over at Jenny, who had also stopped what she was doing, to see if she agreed, she saw the sad look on her daughter's face.

She knew that Jenny loved Tommy and had since they were kids. Caroline had always thought that Tommy and Jenny would wed, but Tommy had always treated Jenny like his kid sister, and when Tommy was sent away to England, Jenny had met Jeremy. Jenny caught herself and said in as cheerful a voice as she could, "How wonderful for Tommy."

Just about the time Jason broke the news about Tommy, Jeremy was coming down the stairs, carrying a drink in his hand. He stopped midway down and watched the emotions play over his wife's face. He had known Jenny was in love with Thomas Sanduvale—hadn't she thrown it in his face enough times that she wished he were more like her friend Tommy.

Their marriage was in shambles, and the only thing that kept it together was the baby he and Jenny were expecting any day now. Jeremy swallowed the drink he had been bringing down with him. He went over to the liquor cabinet to pour himself another drink when Jason came up behind him and put his hand on Jeremy's shoulder, telling him it was time to eat. Jeremy nodded his head, poured his drink and went over to the table, and sat down by Jason. Mr. Pierce came in and sat at the head of the table, with Caroline sitting next to him. Jenny rang the dinner bell, then sat down next to her husband. A few minutes later, a couple of young servant girls came in and served each of them baked ham, sweet potato, greens, and freshly baked bread.

Everyone ate and talked, all except for Jeremy; he sipped his drink and barely touched his meal. When Jenny glanced his way, he would glare at her until she turned away. Jenny managed to keep the topic of Tommy's upcoming marriage mostly out of their conversation, as she did not want to upset her husband.

After the meal was finished, Jenny excused herself and said she was tired and thought she would retire to bed early. Everyone bid her goodnight. She kissed her mother and father on their foreheads and started for the stairs. Halfway up the stairs, she heard Jeremy bid everyone a goodnight also. Jenny hurried to get to her room as she and Jeremy no longer shared a room together.

She entered her room and shut the door, locking it after her. She leaned against the door, listening to Jeremy climb the stairs and then approach her door. She heard him stop and try the knob, then continue on to his room across the hall. When she heard his door open and close, only then did she let out the breath she was holding.

Jenny went over to the bed, sat down, and started to undress. Unbuttoning her dress, she stood up and let it fall to the floor. Untying her shift, she let it fall on top of her dress, along with her petticoat. When fully naked, Jenny turned to her mirror and assessed the fading bruises on her shoulders, arms, and legs that were still visible, where Jeremy had hit her while trying to rape her. She was large with his child and had tried to prevent him from doing it, but he was drunk as usual, and even though he had only one arm, he was still very strong. She had stopped fighting him and had lain still, intent on letting him have his way with her so her unborn baby would not get hurt. But when she stopped fighting and lay still and did not respond to him, he stopped, rolled off of her, got up, looked disgustedly at her, and left the room.

This all occurred three weeks ago. The next morning, Jenny had told Jeremy to move out of their room. She did not want him there any longer unless he quit drinking altogether. Jeremy tried to apologize and vowed to never do anything like that again. He said it was the drink that had caused him to do it. She told him she didn't care. Jeremy promised he would try to quit drinking if she would only take him back and forgive him. Jenny replied that maybe she could forgive him in time, but not now, so they kept separate rooms.

Jeremy tried to stop drinking, but too many things haunted him when he was sober. The war was the worst for him to get over, worse than losing his arm, and now his insane jealousy of Jenny and her feelings for Thomas. Oh yes, he had seen how Jenny acted when he came around for a visit, how she would perk up and her eyes would shine just looking at him. He knew this because she used to look at him that way when they first met. Jenny tried to assure him there was nothing between Thomas and her, but he didn't believe her.

The more Jeremy drank, the more he believed there was. Jeremy was glad when Thomas had stopped coming around as often as he had been, but Jeremy had seen the look on his wife's face when she heard the news of his marriage.

It was sometime late in the middle of the night when Jenny heard a muffled sound, almost like a firecracker going off, which woke her. She shook herself wide awake and sat up.

Jenny heard footsteps running down the hall and a loud cracking sound as a door was being busted open. She heard when her mother asked, "What's going on?"

"What's happened?"

She heard Jason respond, "Don't come in," then hollered for his father to get help. Jenny slowly got up and walked to her door, pulled it open, and went out into the hall. So much excitement going on in Jeremy's room. She ran to the open doorway and could see Jason holding a towel on someone's head. She could see the towel soaked with blood. Then she heard a blood-curdling scream coming from somewhere. She realized it was her screaming. She had looked beyond Jason and saw Jeremy lying in his bed, but it couldn't be Jeremy, as half his head was missing. She saw the pistol lying on the ground. Then all she saw were tiny little stars floating in and around her eyes and then just a black void.

Jenny awoke to severe cramping in her midsection. She was lying in her bed, and her mother was sitting beside her, trying to comfort her. "What, what happened?" Jenny asked.

"Oh, my dear, you're awake. Please, lie still. We have sent for the doctor," her mother said. "He should be here shortly.

"Why?" asked Jenny, and then a sharp pain hit her in her lower stomach, and she cried out.

"Please, Jenny dear, try not to move. Everything will be all right," said Caroline.

Just then, Jason entered the room and went to his sister's side.

Caroline said, "Oh, good, Jason, you are here. I will be back shortly. I have to check on your father and make sure he is all right. Please stay with your sister while I am gone." Jason replied that he would, and Caroline left to go see her husband.

After her mother left the room, Jenny took hold of her brother's hand and asked him to tell her what happened. Jason sat down in the chair next to Jenny's bed. He held tight to his sister's hand and said, "I am so sorry, Jenny."

Jason told Jenny that her husband had left a note. He said he would give it to her, but she had to promise not to blame herself.

"Why would I?" replied Jenny.

"You don't remember two nights ago?" Jason asked her.

"Remember what?" she answered with a sense of dread.

"About Jeremy," said Jason.

Jenny looked at Jason and screamed, "Oh my God, Jason. Jeremy, all that blood, his head. Is he all right?"

"I am so sorry Jenny, but Jeremy is gone."

"*No.*" She sobbed. After Jason calmed his sister down some, he told her what had happened.

He said, "We had all retired for the night. Sometime in the middle of the night, I heard a gunshot that came from Jeremy's room. When I got there, the door was locked and I broke it in. I found Jeremy in his bed. He was dead from a gunshot wound to his head, and the gun was in his hand. There was nothing anyone could do for him. When you entered the room, you fainted. You have been out until now. That was two days ago."

"We brought you back to your room and sent for the doctor," Jason continued. "The doctor arrived just before dawn that morning. He examined Jeremy and his room. He confirmed that Jeremy did die from a self-inflicted gunshot. After the good doctor examined you, and he told us that the shock of what you saw made you go into labor, but a very early stage of labor. The doctor was on his way to see another patient when the young boy we sent to fetch him ran into him on the road. He also said he had to go see this patient but would stop back here on his way home."

Jason told his sister not to worry, as the doctor said she had plenty of time before the baby would be born. Jenny turned her head to the wall and placed her hands on her stomach. The tears would not stop coming. Jason, not knowing how to comfort her, said, "I am truly sorry, sister. If there is anything, anything at all, I can do, please tell me. Would you like me to read the letter Jeremy left for you or just leave it on your nightstand to read later? I have another errand to take care of when mother comes back."

Without turning to look at her brother, Jenny said, "Thank you, Jason. You're a good brother. I don't know what I would have done without you."

About that time, Caroline returned carrying a tray of food and drink for her daughter, and behind her was a young black girl carrying a small pail of hot water. When Jason saw her, he took his leave so the women could tend to his sister. He bent down and kissed Jenny on her cheek, leaving the letter on the stand, and told her he would be back.

Jason went downstairs and outside to the stable and saddled his horse. He swung up into the saddle and rode as fast as he could to the Sanduvale plantation to ask Marta to come help Jenny with the birthing until the doctor could return. Meanwhile, Caroline had washed her daughter's face and hands and then tried to get her to drink some tea and have a bit of hot broth to eat, but to no avail. Caroline then sat in the chair next to her daughter and tried to comfort her.

Jenny rolled over and laid her head next to her mother's chest. "Oh, Momma, what am I going to do?" she cried.

"There, there. Everything is going to be all right—you will see," said Caroline to her daughter. "First thing we have to do is keep your strength up. You have a baby that wants to be born, and it's not going to take no for an answer. Do you understand, my dear?"

The very strength of her mother made Jenny feel better.

"Now, if I put these pillows under your back, do you think you could sit up some and drink some of this warm broth and drink some tea?" asked Caroline.

"I will try. Thank you, Momma, for being here for me," Jenny told her mother.

"All right, now, move up a little," Caroline said as she settled her daughter on the pillows. "Good, now, let's eat a little," Caroline said as she spooned a little broth into Jenny's mouth. After Jenny ate and drank some, she grabbed her mother's hand and squeezed it tightly as another sharp pain tore through her body.

Jason rode as fast as he could and made good time getting to the Sanduvale plantation. When he arrived, he pulled his horse to a stop in front of the house, threw down his horse's reins, and took the stairs two at a time and pounded on the door. Within seconds, Marta opened the door. Seeing Jason standing there looking like the devil himself was chasing the boy, she asked, "Jason, what is it? What's wrong?"

"It's the baby, Jenny's baby. It's coming, and I don't think the doctor will make it in time. Can you please come and help her until the doctor arrives?"

"Why, yes, of course I can. Just let me get my bag and a cloak," said Marta as she turned and went into the house.

I was in the stable when Jason rode up, I walked over to the porch, and heard their conversation, so I went back inside, hitched up the horse to the buggy, and brought it out to the porch. When Jason saw me, he nodded his head hello. "So, you are about to become an uncle," I said to him.

Looking very somber, Jason replied, "Yes, but not under very good circumstances, I'm afraid."

"Oh, and why is that? Jenny's all right, isn't she?" I asked, getting very concerned.

"Yes, she is. I will explain later, but right now, I must get back to her. Will you bring Marta to our place?" Jason asked me. He jumped on his horse, turned, and rode away. When Marta emerged from the house, I went up the steps and grabbed her bag. When we got to the bottom of the steps, I helped Marta into the buggy.

I rolled my sleeves down and climbed in beside Marta and started for Pierce's place.

"What's going on?" Marta asked me.

"I don't rightly know," I replied, "but we'll soon find out."

We made good time as I didn't spare the horse and went as fast as the buggy would allow us. When we arrived at the place, we saw Jason's horse tied up out front. I said, "That's funny—Jason would never leave his horse unattended. I can't imagine what's going on here." About that time, the door opened and Jason ran down the steps and helped Marta out of the buggy, then pushed her toward the stairs.

In the meantime, Caroline had gotten Jenny to drink some more tea and sat with her until Jenny had drifted off to sleep. While Jenny slept, Caroline took the time to check on her husband again, as this whole incident had upset her husband very much and she needed to stretch her legs. Jenny woke up as a severe pain ripped across her stomach and settled in her back. She groaned and turned over onto her side. After a while, the pain stopped. She looked around the room for her mother, but saw she was alone.

Jenny glanced at the nightstand and saw the piece of paper Jason had left there for her. She reached over, picked the paper up, and unfolded it with trembling fingers. At first, she could not read it as the tears that began to form in her eyes made the words blurry. Jenny brushed away the tears and wiped her eyes on the sleeve of her nightgown to clear them. When her vision cleared, she began to read the last words her husband would write.

> My dearest Jenny,
>
> I am so sorry to end our life together in this cowardly way, but I can't go on living a lie any longer. You have to know the truth of what kind of man that you married. I was shot and lost my arm not because I was a hero but because I was a coward. I got scared when I saw all the men dropping like flies all around me. I was shot while running away from the battle while all the other true heroes were

177

running toward the battle. I didn't tell you because I just wanted you to look at me the way you looked at Thomas, but knew if I told you, you would never look at me that way. Also, I could not live with the fact that someday my child might find out and look at me with contempt. Again, Jenny, I am so sorry. Please forgive me, I couldn't face myself or you another day. Please forgive me for treating you the way I did.

Signed, your husband,

Jeremy

Jenny held the letter close to her heart while the tears streamed down her cheeks. Then in a fit of anger, she crumpled the letter up and threw it across the room. Jenny was hit with another bad pain but thought nothing could ever hurt worse than Jeremy's letter. She thought he should have told her. She would have understood.

When Marta and I arrived at the Pierces', we were rushed upstairs to Jenny's room by Jason. When we got to the door to her room, Marta stopped, turned, placed her hands on each of the men's chests, and said, "This is as far as you're going. You two wait downstairs. I will keep you informed as to how things are progressing."

We nodded our heads yes and stepped back. I handed Marta her bag, and she turned and entered the room, shutting the door behind her. The room was dark, so Marta did not see Caroline sleeping in the chair next to the wall.

After Marta's eyes adjusted to the dark room, she made her way to the window, where she pulled open the drapes to let what little light that was left of the day come into the room. Then she went over and lit the lantern that sat on Jenny's nightstand. Marta needed more light to examine Jenny. Caroline woke from the sound of the lantern being lit, startling her. She jumped up from the chair she had been dozing in and said, "Oh, Marta, I am so glad you have come. I don't think I could handle this all by myself."

"I am sorry that I woke you, Caroline. I did not see you there when I came in."

Marta said, "No, no, it's quite all right. It's just that it has been a rough few days around here. Now, what can I do to help you?"

Caroline said, "We have to get some hot water up here and some clean nightgowns. We will also need fresh linen for the bed and some clean clothes. Oh, yes, some more lanterns too."

"Yes, I can get all that," Caroline replied and she immediately left the room to tend to it, but before she got out the door, Caroline said once again, "Thank you so much. How can I ever repay your kindness?"

"No need," said Marta, and she shooed Caroline out the door.

Meanwhile, downstairs in the parlor, Jason and I sat in silence. As I looked around, it dawned on me that I hadn't seen Jeremy. He was nowhere in sight. I looked over at Jason, who was deep in thought, and asked, "Shouldn't Jeremy be here?" Jason looked at me, then got up, went to the liquor cabinet, and poured two drinks. He came over and handed one to me. Then he sat back down, took a big gulp of his drink, and began to tell me the whole horrible story of Jeremy's demise.

I caught myself holding my breath as he related the story to me. I exhaled as I shook my head in disbelief. I took a big swallow of my drink and whistled through my teeth. "God, Jason, Jenny must be beside herself with grief and now starting labor in the process."

"That's the least you can say. I think she is still in shock, "Jason replied.

"What will she do now? "I said to no one in particular.

"First, she must get through the ordeal of the birthing. Then, we will worry about everything else afterward, "Jason replied.

A little while later, Jason's father joined us in the parlor. I couldn't help but notice, when he entered the room, how old-looking Mr. Pierce had gotten. His face was etched in deep lines, his eyes had lost their sparkle and were sunken in his head. His shoulders were slumped, and he walked in a very defeated way. I stood up and walked toward him, holding out my hand to him. We shook hands, and then I walked him over to a chair, where he sat down and took the drink Jason offered to him.

"It's good to see you, Tommy, even under these bad circumstances," Mr. Pierce said to me.

"I am so sorry for your loss," I replied.

"Yes, yes, these are very bad times," Mr. Pierce said almost to himself.

Upstairs, Marta had gone over to examine Jenny but found she was in a light sleep at the moment. *Good*, thought Marta, and she gently lifted the covers from her. Marta could see the poor thing was wringing wet with sweat. She hurriedly lifted the wet nightgown, then gently and quickly lifted her legs and parted them. Marta could see blood and fluid seeping out from the opening in Jenny's body. She checked but could see the baby was nowhere near ready to be born.

Unfortunately, Marta thought, it was quite a ways off. Jenny stirred and tried to pull the covers back over her when another pain struck her, and she moaned and tried to roll into a fetal potion. Marta took hold of her and held her from doing so. She told her just to breathe, in short pants, until the pain passed on.

Hearing Marta's voice, Jenny grabbed Marta's hand and sobbed out loud, "Oh, Marta, how much more must I endure?"

Not knowing that Jenny was talking about her husband's death, Marta replied, "Everything in its due time. God sees to that." At that, Jenny gave a short, bitter laugh, turned her head, and softly began to sob. "There, there, child. It will all be over before you know it," Marta assured her.

"It will never be over," Jenny answered bitterly between sobs. Marta was about to ask Jenny what she was talking about—surely not about her baby—when Caroline entered the room.

She was followed by a couple of young girls, carrying two pails of hot water, some clean linen, clean blankets, and a couple of clean nightgowns. "Ah, good," said Marta. "Just what we need to make our girl feel better." Marta instructed the girls to put the hot water next to the basin of cold water and wait for her instructions, so the girls moved aside, out of the way.

Marta told Caroline to mix the hot and cold water together so it was warm, and then they would bathe Jenny. After the water was mixed, Caroline set about removing her daughter's wet gown, then set about washing her daughter's face, hands, and upper body, removing the sweat. Marta bathed her lower body, removing the blood and sticky fluid from her. After she was dried, they put a fresh, warm gown on her. Marta instructed the two girls to remove the bedding as they rolled Jenny over. The two girls worked quickly and removed the sweat-dampened sheets and covers from the bed and replaced them with fresh ones. Jenny was then rolled over the other way, and the same was done to that side of the bed.

When that was finished, the two girls gathered up the soiled bedding and left the room. Marta put a clean cloth under Jenny and between her legs, keeping her somewhat dry and clean. Jenny had to admit, she did feel better—until she was hit with another pain. This went on for about eight hours, until Jenny didn't think she could stand much more.

Caroline was becoming a nervous wreck, watching her daughter going through so much pain. Marta finally told her to take a break, get something to eat, and see about the men eating. Caroline thought she would do as Marta suggested. She was getting hungry and knew the men would be too. She told Jenny she would go tend to things and be right back. She would bring back something to eat and drink for them too.

After Caroline left, Marta checked Jenny again and saw the baby was in position. It would not be long now. She told Jenny she would have to start helping, as it was getting close. Jenny was so exhausted she did not know if she would have the strength to do anything.

When the pain began to be very close together, Marta told Jenny to push hard.

The men downstairs waited apprehensively, trying not to listen to Jenny's cries of distress, when Mr. Pierce spoke up and said, "This is the worst part, you know." Both men looked at him. "I mean, waiting for the baby to get here. I remember waiting for days for you to be born, Jason," Mr. Pierce explained. "Sometimes they pop right out, and other times, they can be very stubborn and take their sweet time."

The two men laughed, cutting the tension in the room. "I suppose so. They probably have minds of their own, even that early in their little lives," replied Jason. I sat quietly thinking of Celine and prayed she would have an easy time of it.

Mrs. Pierce entered the room, and we all stood up. "Please, sit back down. I just wanted to tell all of you it will be a little while yet, so if you are hungry and would like something to eat, please follow me to the dining room, where there is food prepared for us. Marta will keep us informed if there is any change."

While they ate, Jenny's pains grew closer and closer together, and when the next big pain came, Marta told Jenny to push with all her might. Jenny grabbed the top of the bed when the pain came, and she did as Marta instructed her to do. When the pain subsided, Jenny told Marta she couldn't do this anymore. Marta replied, "I am sorry, my dear, but you have no choice in the matter."

When the next pain came, Marta yelled, "Push, Jenny, push hard once more."

Jenny screamed and pushed as hard as she could, and out came her newborn babe. Caroline entered the room in time to hear Marta tell Jenny she had a beautiful tiny son. Caroline rushed to her daughter's side and wiped the tears from Jenny's face. Then Marta handed Caroline the scissors and told Caroline to cut her new grandson's umbilical cord. Marta wrapped the tiny bundle in a blanket and handed him to Jenny.

At first, Jenny did not want to take her newborn son, but when the baby started to whimper, she brought him close to her breast, and tears of joy ran down her cheeks as she kissed his tiny head. Marta pushed on Jenny's stomach to make sure everything else was expelled from her womb, then cleaned her up and made her comfortable as the two young girls came again with fresh linens and a clean nightgown. After removing the soiled bedding and putting on clean bedding, the girls cleaned the room and left.

Marta washed and dried the crying baby and wrapped him in a clean blanket and then gave him to Jenny. Marta instructed Jenny on how to nurse her son. After several attempts, the baby latched on to his mother's breast and suckled contentedly. Marta and Caroline left the room, telling Jenny to rest while she could.

When the two women entered the dining room, the three men jumped up and rushed forward, eager to hear about the baby. Standing aside, Marta let Caroline go to Mr. Pierce, where she caressed her husband's face and said, "You are grandpa to a tiny healthy baby boy, my dear." Then kissed him on his cheek. They all laughed, and the men slapped each other on their backs. Caroline offered Marta something to eat, but she declined, saying she was too tired.

Caroline gave Marta a big hug and whispered in her ear, "God bless you, and thank you for all you did for Jenny."

"Posh," said Marta as Jason walked us to the door. "Please tell Jenny congratulations on the birth of her son, and also tell her how sorry I am. I will come back soon to see her."

"I will tell her. We will look forward to seeing you soon."

I took Marta's bag, and we walked down the steps to the buggy, leaving Jason to close the door behind him. I put the bag on the floor of the buggy, helping Marta up to sit on the seat as she wrapped her cloak around her to ward off the chill in the night air. It was going to be a long ride home. I climbed in beside Marta and started the horse moving toward our plantation. We were both quiet, each in our own thoughts, when Marta said in a voice that demanded she be told what was going on in that house. She then showed me the crumpled-up letter she had found on the floor and told me what was written in it.

I sighed and told Marta all that Jason had told me. After I finished telling her, she thought about what I said and thought about what was written in the letter from Jeremy to Jenny. Then Marta asked me, "You weren't fooling around with Jenny, were you, Thomas?"

"Hell, no, I wasn't. How could you even ask me something like that?" I replied.

"I had to ask. You see, the letter sounded like Jeremy blamed you for the way Jenny thought of you," Marta said quietly.

"Marta, you know how I feel about Jenny. I've always treated her like a sister and loved her like one. You know this," I said.

"Yes, I know that is what you have always said and acted like toward Jenny," Marta answered me in an unsure voice.

"I love Celine. I would never betray her or Jeremy. You know this, Marta," I said in a voice that would tolerate any arguments on the subject.

"I know, and I am sorry, Thomas. It's just that I know Jenny loved you—and not like a brother. She always thought it would be you and her together someday. When you came back from England, she knew that you still thought of her like a sister and not a grown lady. So, when she met Jeremy and he asked to call on her, she said yes. She liked him very much and thought she would learn to love him in time. And maybe she did—I don't know," Marta told me.

"I am sorry, I didn't know she felt that way, she acted so indifferent toward me when I got back and she had come home from finishing school. I saw she had grown into a beautiful, confident young woman, but I thought she also just thought of me like a brother. If I had known, maybe things would have been different. I just didn't put two and two together, but I do love Celine, and we are getting married," I said to Marta.

We rode the rest of the way home in silence. When we arrived at the plantation, I stopped the buggy in front of Marta's cabin, got out, and helped her down. I kissed her on her cheek and told her I would see her in the morning. When I woke up the next morning, the sun was already up. I'd had a restless night and had overslept. When I went downstairs, only Marta was in the kitchen. After saying good morning, I grabbed a piece of bread and a peach. Marta handed me a hot cup of coffee, and I headed for the office to speak to Eli about the schedule for today.

When I entered the office, Eli was sitting going over the books. When he looked up and saw me, he said, "You look terrible, man, like something a badger got hold of."

"I feel just that way, too," I replied.

"Momma told me what happened at Pierce's place. How is Jenny doing?" Eli asked.

"I don't know. I didn't get to see her with all that was going on at that place, but I will call on her soon," I said.

"Good. Roslyn has some baby things she would like you to take to her when you go. God willing, we won't be needing them anymore," Eli said, followed by a laugh.

"I am sure she could use them—if you are sure you won't be needing them," I said as I looked at Eli.

Eli looked up at me, rolled his eyes, and handed me the schedule for the day.

Time flew by as I worked in the fields and kept busy working on the house for Celine. Finally, things slowed down, so I decided it was time to call on Jenny to see how she was doing. I arrived at Pierce's place just after lunch. I got down off my horse feeling a little apprehensive, as I hadn't seen Jenny since Jeremy's funeral, and then I did not get to talk to her, as there were so many people that attended it. I decided to wait.

As I climbed the stairs, Jason came around the corner of the house and hollered hello to me. Then he ran up the steps to stand next to me. We shook hands, and Jason opened the door for us to go inside. As we stepped inside, I asked Jason how his sister was doing.

"Why don't you ask me yourself?" Jenny said as she stepped out of the parlor.

She smiled up at me as she held out her hand for me to take. I took hold of her hand and pulled her to me. I gave her a big hug, then held her away from me. "You look beautiful for a new mother," I told her.

Jenny gave me a soft laugh and replied, "If you say so."

Just then, they heard the cry of a baby. Jenny rolled her eyes in mock exasperation. "Sounds like feeding time. If you will excuse me, I'll tend to him and be back soon," Jenny said to me. I watched as she climbed the stairs to her room. I noticed even with her beautiful smile, there was a sadness to her eyes. I shook my head and joined Jason in the parlor.

"How is she really doing?" I asked Jason.

"As good as she can, under the circumstances," he replied. "She is having a hard time coping with all this. I guess she blames herself," Jason added.

"And me?" I asked. Jason studied my face hard, trying to read if anything was there, but the only thing he saw was sadness and concern for his sister. "I swear to you, Jason, I did nothing to bring on these feelings Jenny has for me. In fact, I didn't even know she thought I existed, except as a friend or as a big brother," I said as I held up my hand.

"I know you didn't encourage her, but no one can control how they feel for someone, right?" Jason replied.

"Speaking of which, I heard through the workers' grapevine that you set a date to be married yourself," I said, changing the subject.

"Yes, finally, Emily said yes. After all the running I did after her—and believe me, she led a merry chase"—Jason laughed—"she finally caught me. I also heard through the grapevine that you are getting married and are going to become a father. Is this true?"

"Yes, it is true." I sighed. "I fear if I don't hurry with the wedding, I will become a father first. I don't want to put Celine through that and have her put up with all the gossip."

"I hear you," Jason said. "So, when is the big day?" he asked.

"Next Sunday," I replied.

"Wow, you don't waste any time, do you?" Jason said.

"Can't. No time to wait. The baby is due in a month, I believe," I said. Jason gave a small whistle.

When Jenny returned to the parlor, she was carrying her small son. I stood up and walked over to her. I lifted the blanket and looked down at the tiny bundle in her arms and said to her, "You did real good, Jenny. He's a fine-looking boy."

"Why, thank you, Tommy," she replied.

"What did you name him?" I asked.

"This little guy's name is Jeremy Wesley Benson," Jenny replied, all the while watching my face. I didn't change expressions as I said to her, "And a fine name it is," but you could have knocked me over with a feather upon hearing my middle name.

"I am so happy to see you doing so well, Jenny, and I hope you find happiness in your life again soon," I told her.

"Thank you, Tommy. It's always a pleasure to see you," Jenny replied.

"Well, I'm not getting anything done here, so I had better be going. I just wanted you to know that I am here for you, Jenny, and if you ever need anything—"

Before I could finish, Jenny laid her hand on my arm and said, "I know you are, Tommy."

I said my goodbyes and left for home.

Wednesday, I decided to go to the inn and bring Celine back to the plantation. She could get ready here, as she would have plenty of time before Sunday to do so. When I got to the inn and found Celine, she was surprised to see me, as I wasn't supposed to be there before Saturday.

I told her I didn't want to wait any longer to bring her to my home. She said the dress that was being made for her for the wedding had not arrived and would not be delivered until Saturday morning. I assured Celine that someone would be sent to get the dress in time,

I then bent down and kissed her on the nose. As she looked up at him, Celine's heart was so full of love for Thomas, she could think of nothing but being with him for the rest of her life.

As she smiled up at me, her whole face lit up. Then she said she would go gather up her things, find her uncle, and remind him of the wedding on Sunday. Even though her uncle was not happy about the way things had come together, he loved his niece and liked Thomas. He was also happy that she would be well taken care of.

Celine's things were loaded into the buggy, and her uncle wished them well and said he would see them on Sunday. Celine asked me to please stop by the cabin on our way out. I laughed and told her we would visit the cabin anytime she wanted to. Celine then explained that she wanted to pick up something that belonged to her mother, a small brooch that her mother had given to her when she was small. She wanted to wear it on her wedding day.

When we arrived at the cabin, I got down, went around, and lifted Celine down from the buggy. As she started for the door, in her haste and excitement to retrieve the brooch, she didn't see the root of the tree sticking out of the ground in front of her. As her foot caught the root, she stumbled. She tried to catch herself, but being big and clumsy with the baby she was carrying, she was unable to keep from falling to the ground.

I could see what was about to happen even as I hollered for Celine to watch out for the root. I tried to run to catch her, but it was too late. Everything looked like it was happening a lot slower then it was. Even my body seemed to be moving slower than it should have, and it all happened too quickly to prevent it.

As Celine fell, she wrapped her arms around her stomach, trying to shield her unborn child. When she hit the ground, a pain jolted through her like a hot iron. When I reached Celine, I told her to lie still. She was moaning and still clutching her stomach. When I slowly turned her over, her nose was bleeding, and her lip was split open where her face hit the ground. Celine opened her eyes and looked into mine. She smiled a tiny smile and said, "Do I look that bad?"

"Well, let's just say you're going to have to wear a lot of makeup at our wedding," I replied, attempting to keep things light. I gently lifted her up into my arms, opened the cabin door, and walked over to the bed, where I slowly laid her down, then lit the lantern. Bringing the light closer to her, I looked her over to see where else she might be hurt.

When I moved her, she groaned out loud. Her arms seemed to be all right except for a few scrapes and bruises. But when I looked down toward her feet, I saw the blood seeping through her dress onto the bedding. *Jesus Christ*, I swore to myself. Celine could see all the emotions playing across my face.

She looked me in the eye and said, "What is it, Thomas? What is happening?"

"You are starting to bleed, and I think your water has ruptured," I answered in as calm a voice as I could. About that time, a large pain ripped across Celine's stomach. She cried out and grabbed my hand.

I knew I could not move her to take her in the buggy and the ride would be too bumpy for her. I looked around helplessly. I knew I could not leave her to go for help either. About that time, there was a thump on the window. Looking at the window, to my surprise, I saw a face staring back at me. I ran out the door and around to the side of the cabin, where I caught Lester running toward me.

"What the? Lester, what the hell are you doing out here?" I asked the shaking young man.

"It's a long story, Master Thomas, but now I sees you need help with your Missy Celine," Lester replied. About that time, Celine let out another loud groan. I was beside her in a flash, with Lester right behind me.

I took hold of Celine's hand and told her that everything was going to be all right, that they had help now. Turning to Lester, I told him to take the buggy and go get Marta as fast as he could and bring her back here as I pushed him out the door. Lester ran outside and climbed up into the buggy, grabbed the reins, and slapped the horse on the rump. The horse shot forward, almost throwing Lester out of the buggy. Lester settled himself on the seat and whipped the horse to go faster, praying to the Lord to keep from tipping over.

It took less than two hours for Lester to reach the plantation. When he pulled up to the porch, Marta was just walking to the house when she saw Lester pull the buggy to a halt. Jumping from the buggy, Lester ran over to Marta and was talking so fast Marta could not understand him. Putting up her hand, she told the young man to slow down, take a breath, and tell her why he had the buggy and where Thomas was.

Taking a deep breath, Lester related very slowly what had happened and told Marta she needed to come with him right away. Marta told Lester to go to the stable right now and change horses, as this one was tuckered out and would not make the trip back. Meanwhile, she went into the house to get her things together.

As Marta turned to go back outside, she saw Phillip standing at the bottom of the stairs. Startled, she took a step back. Looking into Phillip's eyes, she thought he looked deranged as he told her to come nearer to him. Marta took a few steps closer to him but not close enough for him to reach out and grab her. Lifting her chin a little, Marta asked in a calm voice, "What is it, Phillip? What do you want? I haven't got time for this. I have to go now."

When Phillip finished telling Marta what he wanted of her, she stepped back. Her face went pale, and she said in a low, horrified voice, "No, I won't do it."

She tried to push past him to get to the door. In doing so, she got too close to him, and he grabbed her arm and pulled her close to him and said in a bitter voice, "If you don't do as I say, I will do it myself, then send you away and see that harm comes to your family and to Thomas." Squeezing her arm hard, Phillip said in a threatening voice, "Do you understand me, Marta?"

"Yes," she said, pulling her arm from his grasp and moving away from him.

Looking into Phillip's eyes, Marta could see he was capable of doing all he had threatened to do. Gripping her bag, Marta went outside to the waiting Lester. The young man helped Marta up into the buggy, then put her bag in the back. When she was settled, she whispered to Lester so no one could hear her. Lester nodded his head and went to fetch Jacob and told him that Marta wanted to see him out front.

Lester then went to the barn and talked to the carpenter, who was repairing a broken wagon. Lester explained what Marta wanted the man to do. He shook his head but said all right. After that, Lester went to see two of the strongest workers and told them to follow him, as Marta needed to see them. When they got to the buggy, Marta told them very quietly to saddle two horses and then follow the buggy from a distance.

When everything was set in motion and the two men were on their horses, they rode away from the plantation with Phillip watching out the window. He knew Marta would do as he ordered. He knew she would do anything to protect her family and Thomas. He smiled a very evil smile.

Lester and Marta rode along rapidly with Marta hanging on the side of the buggy for dear life. She hollered at Lester to slow down, but Lester kept up the speed, whipping the horse to go faster. When Marta was almost thrown out of the buggy going around a turn, she told Lester that if the ride didn't kill them, she was going to kill him. Lester slowed down some, so it took a good two hours to get to the cabin.

When I heard the buggy pull up to the front of the cabin, I was out the door, pulling Marta off the buggy and practically dragging her into the cabin. I told Lester to bring in her bag, then tend to the horse by rubbing it down. As Marta was being ushered into the cabin, she could make out the bed on the far wall and see the young girl lying on it.

She moved quickly over to the bed. The young girl's face clearly showed the pain she was enduring. Celine looked up at Marta and knew she was in good hands as she saw the deep concern in this woman's eyes. Celine told Marta, "Thank you for coming. Thomas has been very worried about me and the baby." Her words were cut off as another pain hit again.

Marta examined Celine and saw she would not be having this baby anytime soon. *Good*, she thought to herself. *It will give me time to plan what must be done.* To keep Thomas busy, Marta sent Thomas to get wood to start a fire and water to start boiling. Marta then started to clean the girl up so she would feel better. Marta removed the clothing that would restrict the birthing process and the top blanket the girl was lying on.

Marta then began to wash the dirt from Celine's face where she had fallen to the ground. When the dirt was washed off, Marta could see the black and blue marks on her cheeks and chin and the split lip. As she rubbed the cloth over Celine's nose, the girl winced. Marta asked if it hurt when she touched her nose, Celine answered, "Yes, it did."

"Well," said Marta, "you have probably broken your nose. I can fix that for you, but I don't think I can do anything for your split lip. I can put medicine on it to help heal it. I don't think it will be noticeable when it heals up."

"Whatever you think," Celine told Marta.

"Okay, then. Thomas, I need your help."

I went over to assist Marta with whatever she needed me to do. Marta told me to hold Celine's face still, and when I had it secured, Marta reached over and, as quick as she could, grabbed Celine's nose and twisted it straight, then packed it with cotton, making Celine cry out in pain. When Marta finished, I wiped the tears from Celine's face and kissed her forehead, telling her how sorry I was.

Marta put a strip of bandage over Celine's nose and told her to not move it if possible. "It's not the prettiest job, but it will keep your nose straight."

Celine gave a slight laugh, telling Marta that Thomas had said she might not be presentable at their wedding. At that statement,

Marta looked away, pretending to look for something in her bag but not before Celine saw the sadness in the older woman's eyes.

Marta got a dry nightgown from her bag and put it on the young girl, then put her under the warm, dry covers. Celine was so exhausted she dozed off. A half hour later another pain hit Celine and she groaned aloud. Marta told Thomas to sit on the bed and rub Celine's back when another one came, she said it would help ease the pain. He moved to the bed and sat down waiting to help Celine, Marta told him she had to go outside and would be back in a minute.

When Marta got outside, she called Lester over to her and told him what she wanted him to do. Lester nodded his head yes, walked over and got on one of the horses and rode away toward town. Marta talked to the two men who had followed her and Lester. She told them what she wanted them to do and when the time came, she would let them know, then she went back inside.

When Marta entered the cabin, she asked Thomas how Celine was doing. He told her the pains were not that close and that she was finally resting. Marta could see how worried and how tired Thomas was. Marta asked him if he remembered a short time ago, when Jenny had given birth to little Jeremy, how long it took for the little rascal to come into this world and, when he did, how it was all worth it.

He sighed and told Marta, "Yes, I do remember. I also remember what Jenny went through, and I don't want Celine to have to go through that pain and suffering." While Marta and Thomas talked, Celine slept, not deeply but enough to rest up for what lay ahead for her. By that night, the pains had gotten closer together. Marta thought to herself that it would not be long now.

Everyone was getting exhausted, so Marta made tea that she had brought along with her in her bag. Marta poured Thomas a cup, and as she did so, she felt the two vials of potion she carried in her apron pocket at all times. Once she felt the one she wanted, she turned her back to Thomas and poured two drops into his cup. Turning to face him, she smiled, handed him a cup of hot tea, and said, "Here. This will perk you right up."

Then, pointing to the big easy chair in the corner by the fireplace, Marta said, "Why don't you sit there and drink your tea and relax while you can. I will let you know when the time is near."

He was a little tired, so he said, "All right, but call me as soon as things change."

He took his cup of tea and sat down. After drinking about a half cup of tea, he felt himself starting to relax. Then his eyelids began to close, and he fell into a deep sleep.

Off and on, the pain began to get closer and closer. When Marta thought they were close enough, she poured Celine a cup of tea and felt for the other vial that contained a mixture of poison that would cause instant death. Marta fingered both of the vials. Finally, she sadly took one out and put a few drops into the cup of tea. Turning toward Celine, Marta gently woke the sleeping girl and told her to drink it. Then Marta poured herself a cup and sat on the bed beside Celine to wait.

When Celine's stomach started to spasm, Marta held Celine's hand, looked sadly into the young girl's eyes, and said to her, "I hope you can forgive me. I did what I had to do." Not understanding, Celine cried out as pain racked her body. After setting the cups aside, with tears blurring her eyes, Marta prayed, "God, please forgive me."

When Thomas finally woke up, he felt disoriented. His head felt heavy, as did his eyelids. He finally opened his eyes and looked around. He was confused. What was he doing in his own room? What was going on? He slowly sat up. Looking around, he called Celine's name. She did not answer. He called again this time louder. Still no answer. He threw back the covers and sat up on the side of the bed. A wave of dizziness hit him like a ton of bricks, and he fell back on the bed. Slowly getting up, he managed to get dressed and sat on the side of the bed.

About that time, the door opened, and Marta came in carrying a tray.

"Oh, good, you're awake," she said.

"Marta, where are Celine and the baby?" he asked her in a panic.

Marta set the tray down and sat down beside him. Averting his gaze, she said in a sad, quiet tone, "Don't you remember what happened, Tommy?"

"No, no, I don't remember. Tell me, Marta. Tell me now," he said, a sense of dread washing over him.

"The baby was breech, and as hard as Celine tried, the little thing would not come out. I could see Celine was exhausted from all the pushing, and she just gave up, so I tried to turn the baby's head down. When I finally did get it turned around, the pain stopped. The baby's heart could not take it anymore. It was too long of a struggle for the little babe. I pushed and pushed on Celine's stomach and finally managed to get the baby expelled, but then I could not stop the bleeding. I tried, Thomas. I really did try. I am so sorry," Marta said.

Thomas tried hard to understand what Marta was telling him, but the droning in his head was too loud. When his head cleared, he said to Marta, "But I heard a baby cry. I heard it cry,"

"No, Thomas, you wanted to hear it cry. You wanted everything to be all right. We all did. But it wasn't," Marta said with tears running down her cheeks.

"What was the baby?" he quietly asked Marta.

"It was a little girl," she said softly, then added, "Celine wanted to name her Elizabeth LeAnn Sanduval, after yours and her mother."

He buried his head in his hands and began to sob. "Please leave Marta. I would like to be alone." Patting him on the shoulder, Marta rose and left the room with a great weight on her shoulders. At this moment, she hated herself. The next morning, when Thomas came downstairs, he asked Marta where Celine's and the baby's bodies were. Marta looked up at him with sadness on her face and said, "We cleaned them, dressed them and buried them, Thomas up on the hill with the rest of our loved ones."

"How could you, Marta?" he spat out. "I didn't get to say goodbye to Celine or kiss my daughter's little head," Thomas said.

"I am sorry, Thomas," Marta said, "but you know we cannot keep a body around for very long in this climate, as it decays things fast. I wasn't sure when you would wake up from your shocked state. If I had known you would come around as fast as you did, maybe we could have waited a day longer, but as it was, we waited as long as I thought we could. We had a quiet burial and thought if you were up to it later on, we would have a memorial."

Before Marta could say anything more, Thomas turned and left the room, ran down the stairs, and left the house. He went to the barn and started to saddle a horse when Eli hobbled into the barn and put his hand on Thomas's shoulder. He said he was sorry for all that had happened and if there was anything, anything at all, that he could do, let him know. Thomas turned toward Eli, pushed his hand away, climbed on the horse, and rode away, not looking back.

Thomas knew Eli was sorry, but he didn't need his pity right now. He didn't need anyone's pity right now. Right now he was angry, angry at what he didn't know. He was just angry and hurt. Thomas rode hard and fast, not knowing or caring where he was going. The wind whipped through his hair and stung his face, but he didn't care. Before he knew it, he was at the inn. Dismounting, he went inside, hoping Ox might be there, wanting to punch something or someone, but Ox wasn't around.

Looking around, he saw Celine's uncle. When the uncle looked up and saw Tommy and the look on his face, he grabbed a bottle of whisky from the shelf and two glasses, walked over to a table, sat down, and motioned for Thomas to join him. He poured them both a drink and said with sadness in his voice, "I am so sorry, Tommy. I found out yesterday what happened to our little girl. I know how much she meant to you. I know how hard it is to accept that she is gone. I loved her too." He raised his glass and said, "Here's to Celine." Thomas raised his glass and then drank his drink.

Celine's uncle refilled the glasses, and this time, they drank to his unborn daughter. A few more drinks, and Thomas said, "I had better go, but will take a bottle with me." On his way home, he stopped by the cabin, slid down off the horse with the bottle, he made his way to the door, and with some effort, managed to get it open. Stumbling in, he went over, found the lantern, and after a few tries, managed to get it lit. Holding it up high, he looked in every corner as if Celine would suddenly appear. She didn't. He set the lantern on the small table by the bed, then went over, got a glass, and sat down in the overstuffed chair in the corner, where he had last seen Celine. He poured the glass full. He poured another after emptying the first. He tried to remember what happened that night, but his mind just kept coming back to Celine. He tried to black out the idea that he would never make love to Celine in this cabin or any other place again. He would never hear her laugh or see the love for him in her beautiful eyes. Shaking his head, he poured the glass full again and drank half of it. He laid his head back against the chair and closed his eyes.

Thomas woke up with a start. Looking around, he was disoriented and could not remember where he was. Closing his eyes, he heard a baby cry and someone's soft laughter. He heard someone quietly saying, "It's a girl."

Thomas' eyes flew open, and he looked in the direction of the bed. He saw no one. Nobody was there. It was all a dream, a damn dream. He looked down where he had let his glass fall when he dozed off and saw the puddle of liquor that had splashed out when the glass dropped to the floor. He rose from the chair, went to the lantern, picked it up, and threw it at the puddle on the floor.

Thomas watched as the flames rose and engulfed the chair, jumped up the wall, and spread across the ceiling to the bed. Thomas watched as the bed burned, tears rolling down his face. He turned away, walked to the door, opened it, and made his way out into the cool night air. Thomas mounted his horse and rode off, never looking back.

Thomas rode home, and when he got there, he rode past the

house to the hill where the graveyard was. He sat on his horse for a while, looking at the fresh-turned earth, where his beloved tiny little daughter lay together under the cold ground. He dismounted, walked up the hill where the two graves were, and knelt down beside them. Thomas whispered a prayer: "May God take you both into his arms and keep you safe until I can join you both."

All the wedding preparations were gone, no sign was left of what was to be a beautiful celebration of love. Thomas worked like a zombie, putting in long hours, going about his routine without feeling, then going to bed and reliving the same dream he'd had in the cabin when he burnt it down. After a while, even the dream began to fade, and Thomas began to live again.

Marta felt guilty about her part in what she'd had to do, and she too was plagued by dreams at night. For a while, Thomas and Marta avoided each other as much as they could, but as time went on, they began to relax around each other and things became normal once again. There was a strong unspoken bond between the two.

When Marta reported to Phillip that the deed was done and over with, it was the last time she set foot in his room or spoke to him. Marta sent Moses in her place when Phillip needed anything. When everyone would get together, the conversations were always about the plantation and what was being done that day or about what Eli's family was doing. Even that topic was kept to a minimum, as they all saw the hurt on Tommy's face at the mention of family.

Thomas loved Eli's children and was always playing with them and carving toys for them to play with and the children all loved him. Thomas would look in on his father every night and could see the old man was getting worse. He would ramble about taking care of business for the sake of the plantation, about committing murder. He made no sense at all, Tommy thought. They sent for the doctor one evening as Phillip was extremely agitated and they could not calm him down.

When the doctor finally arrived, he went up to examine Phillip. When he finished, he went downstairs and gave Marta some medicine that would keep Phillip calm. Then the doctor spoke to Thomas and told him that his father was not doing well and had maybe six months left. He told Thomas that his mind was gone and that he really didn't know where he was. He said that he was sorry but there wasn't any more that he could do. They should just keep Phillip as comfortable as possible and see that he ate and drank something every day.

One afternoon, while Thomas was in the barn helping Jacob shoe some horses, he heard a buggy pull up to the house. When he looked out, he saw Jason, Jenny, and her son, Jeremy. Wiping the sweat from his face, he walked out of the barn toward them. When Jeremy saw Thomas, he tried to get down from the buggy, hollering, "Cincle Ommy, Cincle Ommy." With a big smile on his face, Thomas laughed at the way Jeremy said Uncle Tommy.

When Thomas got to the buggy, he reached over, grabbed Jeremy, and swung him high into the air and back into his arms. Jeremy laughed and put his little arms around Thomas's neck. Thomas felt a pang of sadness, but when he turned and looked into Jenny's eyes, the sadness went away, and he held out his hand to help Jenny down from the buggy. Jason came around the side of the buggy and the two shook hands.

"What brings you three here today?" Thomas asked as he ruffled young Jeremy's hair.

"We never see you enough, Tommy," Jenny spoke up.

"I've been busy trying to get everything done on the plantation before fall," replied Tommy.

"Well," said Jason with a big grin on his face, "not too busy to be the best man at Emily's and my wedding, I hope?"

Hiding his emotions, Thomas said, "Well, it's about time this takes place. I'm surprised Emily agreed to wait this long for you to get over your cold feet," and he laughed. Jason and Jenny both laughed with him. Then they got hold of Jeremy, and they all went into the house to tell Marta and Eli the good news and to ask Eli to be in the wedding too.

Emily and Jason's wedding was held at the Pierce plantation, the first week in the fall. All the neighbors for miles around showed up, and everyone had a great time. Emily looked lovely in her beautiful white wedding gown, and Jason looked handsome in his brown Sunday suit. Thomas thought they made a great pair, both with a quick wit and bubbly personality. Jenny looked exceptionally beautiful as Emily's matron of honor. She wore a deep blue velvet gown with a low neckline, showing her ample bust above the neckline. Her glossy blonde hair was swept up off her neck and shoulders.

The blue gown brought out the blue of Jenny's eyes, and Thomas thought she never looked more enticing. To take his thoughts from the path they were heading, he turned his thoughts to Eli, who also looked handsome in his dark gray Sunday suit, and he didn't even drop the rings he was holding for the bride and groom. He was so nervous that Thomas thought he would.

The music started up, and Mr. Cox, Emily's father, took Emily out onto the dance floor and they began dancing. After they danced around the dance floor a few times, Mr. Cox handed his daughter over to Jason, and they took a couple of turns around before motioning for everyone to join them.

Thomas was standing next to the punch bowl when a young woman came up and asked him, "Do you remember me, Tommy?"

Looking at her, he politely replied, "I don't think so."

"It's me, Annabelle, Annabelle Guiz, silly," she said, as if Thomas should have recognized her. Thomas looked at the woman more closely. Then it dawned on him who she was.

"Oh, yes," he said, "I do remember you."

"I thought you would, Tommy. It was a very memorable evening." Annabelle sighed.

"I don't recall anything happening that night," Thomas said defensively.

"Oh, it didn't, but you were going to call on me, and I waited and waited for nothing," the young woman replied. Thomas stammered, trying to think of an excuse, when Annabelle started to laugh. She had been toying with Thomas for him standing her up. Instead of being mad at him, she thanked Thomas. When he asked her for what, she replied, "Because I met the man I was to marry and I was still intact—if you get my meaning."

Thomas's face was turning red when Jenny decided to let him off the hook. Jenny had been on the other side of the table and had overheard their conversation. Jenny walked up to Thomas and put her arm through his. Smiling at Annabelle, she said sweetly, "Thomas, I believe this is our dance."

"Oh, yes. Please excuse us," he said to Annabelle as they walked away, softly laughing to each other.

On the dance floor, Thomas held Jenny close, so close he could feel every curve of her body. He looked down at her as she looked up at him. He could see the love she had for him plainly in her eyes. It would be so easy to take advantage of her, Thomas thought. He hadn't been with a woman since Celine died. At the thought of Celine, he groaned and stepped away from Jenny. "I'm sorry, Jenny. It's too soon. I can't. I have to go." And with that, he turned and left Jenny standing there.

Jason and Emily took the ferry to New Orleans for a week on their honeymoon. Thomas went back to work and got everything ready for the harvest. When the harvest season came and went, Thomas had too much time on his hands, too much time to think of things, so he worked harder. One day, he went to the house he had been building for Celine and himself. He had not been back there since Celine had passed away.

When he rode up to the house, so many memories came flooding back. He slowly slid off his horse and slowly walked up the front steps onto the porch. He faltered, then stepped into the house where the parlor was going to be. Thomas slowly walked through the whole place, and when he found himself back out on the front porch again, all his grief returned. Thomas walked over to where a bunch of dried leaves were blowing around on the porch. He piled them up against the front of the house. Taking out a match, he lit it and, bending down, put it to the dried leaves. A wind came up and blew out the match. Cursing, he threw down the burnt-out matchstick, covered his face with his hands, sat on the porch steps, and cried until he couldn't cry anymore. He wiped his eyes on his shirt sleeve. He didn't know how long he sat there. The sun had started to set. He looked at the hill of the graveyard, and the next thing he knew, he had led his horse to Celine's grave. He bent down and ran his hand over the grass that had sprung up over time.

Thomas whispered, "Thank you, my darling, for not letting me burn down the last good thing that was ours." He rose, got on his horse, and headed for home.

The rest of the year, he worked on finishing the house. When the house was finally completed, Thomas stepped back and admired how magnificently it had turned out. He loved the place, and someday, he would move into it and start a new life.

The ship had sailed out of the harbor on the midnight tide. It had made good time the day and a half they had been sailing, getting them closer to their destination. The young girl who was lying below on the bunk stirred and stretched out her legs. She heard the sound of water slapping against the side of something. *But what?* she wondered. She felt the slight rocking of the bed and thought she was having a dream, when suddenly, she was wide awake. She sat up and saw she was in a small cabin on a vessel. Then she screamed, "Marta, my baby? Where is she?"

At first, there was no answer, and panic set in.

She cried out again, "Marta." Still nothing. Then from the dark corner came a small scared voice. "She over here, Missy Celine," replied the young black girl. Celine bounded off the bunk and hurried over to the corner. She saw the young girl who spoke to her, cowering in the corner, holding a small still bundle in her arms. Celine held out her arms, and the girl placed the bundle in Celine's arms. "Please don't be angry with me, missy. I only do what I was ordered to do."

"I am not angry, but please tell me what is going on. Where are Thomas and Marta?" Celine asked the girl.

"I don't know. I was just told to go with the men who took us to the ship and left us here. The captain of the ship told me to go below with the baby while they brought you down and put you on the bunk, as you were out. He said I was to take care of you and your baby, and he gave me this piece of paper to give to you when you woke up."

She handed it to Celine. Celine went over and sat on a chair next to the bunk. She unwrapped the sleeping baby and let out a sigh of relief when she saw the baby was sleeping and heard the faintest little snore.

After looking at the baby all over, Celine was satisfied the baby was indeed a perfectly healthy little girl. Celine covered her daughter back up, laid her on her lap, picked up the paper the girl had given to her, and began to read it.

My dearest Celine,

I know you will find this hard to believe, but I am doing what I think is best for both of us and the baby. I thought I could go through with this deception but found I cannot. I do admire you very much, but after the baby was born, I found I do not love you as you deserve to be loved. I am not ready to settle down and take on the responsibilities of a husband or father. You and the baby will be well taken care of—I will see to that.

You are accompanied by a young girl whose name is Emeline. She will help you when you get to San Francisco. The captain has been instructed to give you an envelope and the name of a bank where an account has been set up for you for as long as you will need it. There is also a small trunk containing clothes for you and items for the baby for now. Again, I am sorry, but hope you will find this is best for all of us.

Thomas

For a long time, Celine sat there stunned, with tears running down her cheeks. She could not move or speak. Her heart was so destroyed, she didn't think she would live. The look on Celine's face scared the young girl still cowering in the corner of the room. Finally, she moved from the corner and crawled over to Celine. Her face was so pale, and when Emeline touched her hand, it was so cold.

She asked softly, "Missy, Missy Celine, is you all right? Please, missy, say something. Tell me whats you want me to do."

Celine didn't move. She didn't look at the girl, just sat there in shock for almost an hour. Suddenly, the baby began to move and fuss, then cry. Hearing the cry of the baby, Celine's mind slowly came back to reality, and she shook her head to clear it. Looking down at the crying baby and then over to Emeline, Emeline could tell by the blank look in Celine's eyes that she didn't know what to do with this suddenly annoyed little bundle in her lap.

"She's all right, just a mite hungry, I suspects," the girl said to Celine. Celine looked blankly at Emeline, and it dawned on the girl that Celine really didn't know what to do. "If you will, please let me show you what to do." Celine nodded her head yes and the young girl proceeded. Emeline carefully reached over and undid Celine's gown, then slipped it off her shoulder, exposing a swollen breast. She then picked up the baby, which was now sucking on its fist, and put her up to Celine's full breast, removing her fist from the baby's mouth. The baby proceeded to clamp on to the nipple and began to suck greedily.

Looking at Emeline questioningly, the girl explained that while Celine was out, she'd had to make sure the baby was fed frequently or it would have perished. After a while, Emeline told Celine to change sides so she would relieve both sides of her breasts. While the baby nursed, Celine thought about what Thomas had written to her. She could not believe it, not after all they had meant to each other. He couldn't have meant what he had written. He had promised he would always love her and the baby and would always take care of them, hadn't he? Was it all a lie?

Celine thought, if he hadn't meant it, then what was she doing here with her baby on a ship bound for a faraway place? She shook her head in disbelief and said to herself, *What am I going to do? I have a baby, a young girl, and myself to take care of? How will we all manage?* Celine looked down and saw her daughter had fallen asleep while still sucking on her. Emeline told her to gently move her away and she would be okay.

Emeline took the little girl from Celine and showed her how to pat her on her back, explaining how it gets rid of gas from the baby's tummy. Afterward, she showed Celine how to change the baby and clean her. Celine asked Emeline how she knew all this. Emeline laughed and told her she was the oldest of six children born to her mother. Emeline then showed Celine a large basket that contained blankets, where the baby had been sleeping. Celine handed the baby to Emeline, and the girl laid the baby in the basket.

After putting the baby down, there was a knock on the door. Emeline said, "It is probably the man that brings the food." Celine pulled her nightgown up to cover herself, went to the door, and opened it.

"Oh good, you're awake and up," said the older man standing before her. "I am Captain Hale. Is there anything I can get you?" he asked her.

"No," said Celine sternly, "what you can do is turn this boat around and take us back to Baton Rouge."

"I am afraid I cannot do that, my dear. Your passage has been paid in advance, a hefty sum that I do not intend to return. I have my instructions from a Thomas Sanduvale to deliver you three," he pointed to each one of them, "to San Francisco," he said in a gruff voice, "and that's what I intend to do. Now, if you will kindly step back, I will have my steward bring in your food." Then he stepped aside for the young man to bring in a large tray full of food for the women.

After setting the tray on a small table in the middle of the small room, the captain and steward left, closing the door behind them. *Well*, thought Celine, *that didn't go as planned*. She turned to Emeline and motioned for the girl to join her at the table. As she sat down and smelled the food, Celine found she was famished. She could not remember when she had eaten last. While the two girls ate, Celine asked Emeline to tell her what had happened that night at the cabin.

Emeline told her what she knew, speaking softly. "I was told to accompany two of the men to the cabin and to wait outside in the wagon." Emeline told Celine that she could hear Celine giving birth to her baby. It took hours, but finally, the baby was born. Then she said, "It was very quiet. I could hear nothing more. A little while later, you were brought out wrapped in blankets along with your baby. You were laid gently on blankets in the back of the wagon, as you were out cold."

Emeline continued telling Celine what had happened. "I was given the baby and told to guard her with my life. I was to go with you and stay with you, no matter what. I was told to watch over you and tend the baby until you woke up. We were brought to the wharf and brought aboard this vessel in the dark of night. We were put down here in this cabin, and that's all I know, I swear to you, Missy Celine."

"Did you see Master Thomas at all?" Celine asked the girl.

"No, *maman*, he were nowhere in sight," Emeline replied.

"Well, we will have to make the best of it until we can do otherwise. In the meantime, we will eat and keep our strength up," Celine said with determination in her voice.

One day, Celine and Emeline wrapped the baby in a blanket and went above to the deck to get some fresh air. As they walked around the deck, the men all leered at them and made snide remarks. After that, the two girls stayed down below until they docked.

It took a week and a half for them to reach San Francisco, California. On the morning they docked, Celine and Emeline were both ready to get on any dry land. The captain came below and told them it was time for them to disembark from the ship. They gathered up all their belongings, and then the steward came below, took their things, and escorted them upstairs to the deck.

The captain was waiting for them by the gangplank. He motioned for the steward to take their trunk and other things down to the dock and leave them there. He then turned to the two girls and said, "It was my pleasure escorting you to San Francisco. Enjoy your stay." Then he turned to leave.

Celine said, "Excuse me, but aren't you forgetting something, Captain? I believe you have something for me."

"Oh, yes. Sorry, I forgot."

Reaching in his jacket pocket, he pulled out an envelope and handed it to Celine, then turned and strolled away. Celine took the envelope and put it in her coat pocket, holding her baby tightly. The two went down the gangplank, leaving the vessel behind them. The minute their feet hit solid ground, they both let out a sigh of relief.

Celine looked around at the noisy throng of people, darting here and there, all around the two girls, who were now being bumped about for being in the way. Celine had Emeline hold the baby while she took out the envelope the captain had given her so she could see just how much money they actually had and the name of the bank they needed to go to until they could make arrangements to return to New Orleans.

When Celine opened the envelope, she almost fell over. Emeline caught her by her elbow and asked her what was the matter. Celine pulled out the bundle of blank papers that were inside of the envelope. Her face turned red with anger. She turned to go back up the gangplank to confront the captain. As she put her foot onto the gangplank, two burly men stood in front of her. She recognized them as workers from the ship.

"Pardon me, but I need to see your captain now," said Celine.

"Sorry, girly, but the captain is getting ready to set sail," one of the men told Celine.

"You don't understand. He gave me the wrong envelope. I need to see him now," Celine said again, almost hysterically, to the large man.

The two men started to laugh, and one said, "Oh, I'm sure he gave you the right one. Now be off with you, unless you and your little friend over there would like to join me and my friend here down below for a little get-together, if you know what I mean." He winked at Celine and then leered at her, showing his rotten, yellow-stained teeth.

The two men, laughing, turned and walked up the gangplank, leaving Celine staring after them, looking defeated. She turned and looked at Emeline, her shoulders slumped.

"I don't know what we will do now," Celine said. "We have no money, and I haven't the faintest idea where the bank we were supposed to go to, or even the name of it." Emeline reached into her pocket and withdrew a five-dollar piece, which Marta had given the girl in case of an emergency. *Well*, thought Emeline, *this is an emergency.*

She showed it to Celine and said with a big grin on her face, "We can use this until it runs out."

Emeline carried the baby's basket on her head with one hand, and Celine carried her baby in one arm. Each of them, with their free hand, carried one handle on each side of the trunk. As they walked, people stopped and stared at the two young girls, and even they had to admit, they were a sight to behold. After walking several long blocks and being rejected by too many places advertising rooms for rent, they ended up on a street called Market Street.

The two girls finally found lodging in the back of a saloon. It was only one large room, but it was clean, with two small beds and a small kitchen. There was an outhouse in the back of it, and it was only twenty-five cents a night. They were so tired, they were glad to get it. Once inside, Celine fed her baby, and when she was full, burped, and changed, she put her down for the night and went and lay down on one of the beds. Emeline had gone to use the outhouse. When she came back, she too lay down on the other bed. The three exhausted girls slept until the next morning.

When they awoke that morning, the place was already brimming with the hustle and bustle of people as they went about hawking their wares. They heard wagons and buggies being pulled along by horses. They hurried and did their business, feeding and changing the baby. They cleaned themselves up and went outside. The whole street was buzzing with activity. Looking across the street, they saw a vendor selling hot beef pies and realized they hadn't eaten anything since they left the ship the day before.

Celine hurried across the street and bought two pies for each of them at five cents apiece, then hurried back across to Emeline. The two girls then went back to the room, sat down, and ate every bit of the pies. Celine counted the money they had left. She told Emeline that they had already spent near one half dollar. At this rate, the money they had left would not last long. One or both of them would have to get a job.

They decided to go around the neighborhood and knock on doors to see if one of them could find work. When they met at the room sometime later, Emeline was all smiles. She told Celine she had no luck, until she came back and decided to ask in the saloon. She told Celine the owner of the saloon was a large white woman named Roseanne Burke and that she was very, very nice.

"She hired me to clean up the saloon after the place closes up for the night," Emeline said. "I told missy Burke what had happened to us and why we ended up in San Francisco, so she told me to tell you to come see her also." Celine was very excited about the news, as she'd had no luck at all on her own. Celine told Emeline that one woman had thought about hiring her when she saw that Celine had a baby. The woman wanted Celine as her children's nanny, but when she caught her husband leering at Celine, she changed her mind. Both girls started to laugh at that.

The next day, Celine was up early. After feeding the baby and leaving her with Emeline, she went to meet with Roseanne to apply for a job. When she knocked on Roseanne's office door, Celine heard a low, husky voice say, "Come in."

Celine thought to herself, *Probably from years of being in a smoke-filled saloon.* When she entered the office, she saw a big woman, as Emeline had described, sitting at a desk.

Without looking up, Roseanne told her to take a seat. Celine looked the woman over and saw the woman was big boned but not fat and was nicely filled out. She was a tall woman, probably around five feet, ten inches. She had soft brown hair, and her skin was a smooth, satiny white. When she looked up at Celine, she got a big smile on her face and held out her hand. Celine took her hand and shook it and found she had a firm grip. Looking into her blue-gray eyes, Celine instantly took a liking to the woman. Her eyes were full of wisdom, and she had a motherly quality about her.

Celine introduced herself. "How kind of you to consider me for employment."

"Well, "Roseanne said, "after your servant—"

"Oh, no," Celine interrupted, hurrying to correct the mistake, "Emeline isn't my servant. She's my friend,"

"Ah, okay. After your friend told me of your bad experience with your finances, I knew I could help you out for a while. Do you have any experience serving drinks?" the woman asked Celine.

"Why, yes, I worked in a tavern that my uncle owned," replied Celine.

"Good, then it's settled. You can start tomorrow, if that's okay with you?"

"Yes, that would be wonderful," Celine responded with a big smile.

That evening, before Emeline went to work, the two girls celebrated by going across the street to a small restaurant on the corner and had dinner. Celine suggested that Emeline could watch the baby during the day while she worked and Celine would be home to watch her when Emeline went to work. Emeline agreed it was a good plan. *Yes*, thought Celine, *everything is going to be all right. I will get through this terrible hurt and make a good life for the three of us.*

When they finished eating and returned to their room, Emeline said, "Missy Celine."

Interrupting Emeline, Celine said, "Please, Emeline, call me Celine. Not Missy. We are the same, you and I, and we're friends, aren't we?"

"Yes, mis—I mean, Celine, we are friends."

"Good, now what was it you were saying?"

"I just wanted to know, what is your baby's name? We can't go around calling her 'baby,' can we?"

Celine didn't know what to say. She never gave it a thought until now.

She thought about the night she had told Thomas that if they had a girl, she wanted to name her after both of their mothers. Emeline saw Celine's features change from happiness to extreme sadness and said, "I am sorry. I didn't mean to make you sad."

"You didn't, not really," Celine replied.

She thought about her mother, LeAnn, and a tear slipped down her cheek. Wiping it away, she decided to call her daughter Elizabeth LeeAnn Sanduvale. Thinking back, Celine recalled having this same conversation with Marta the night she gave birth.

Smiling, she told Emeline the name she had chosen. Emeline said, "It's a beautiful name for a beautiful baby girl but a very big name for such a little bitty thing." Between them, they decided to call her Lizzie for short. After that was settled, the two girls talked about things in their past and got to know each other better.

Celine went to work the next morning after feeding Lizzie and getting her back to sleep so Emeline could sleep in some more, as she worked late into the night. When Celine walked into the saloon, a friendly older man told Celine the saloon would not be open for another two hours. He said she would have to come back. Celine informed the man that she was to start work here today and had come early so she could be shown what it was she was to do.

The man looked surprised and told her to wait there. Then he disappeared. When he came back, he was accompanied by Roseanne.

"Ah, good, you're early. Did you bring your dress to change into?" she asked Celine.

Puzzled, Celine replied, "My dress to change into? This is the only good dress I have."

"I see. No matter. Come with me. We will get you fixed up in no time," said Roseanne.

Roseanne took Celine around a corner and up some stairs to the second floor. There were a lot of rooms up there. They entered one at the end of the hall, and when they walked in, Celine sucked in her breath. It was big and spacious, with a huge four-poster bed next to a large window. Through the window, she could see a balcony outside. On one wall, there was a large mirror above a vanity with a bench in which to sit. And on the vanity were jars of makeup, brushes and combs, and jewelry of all sorts. On the other wall, there was a large wardrobe. When Roseanne opened it, she saw that it was filled with rows of beautiful gowns.

"None of these will do, as none will fit you. Way too big," Roseanne said, talking out loud to herself. She shut the wardrobe door and went across the room to the door. Opening the door, Roseanne stepped into the hallway and hollered down the corridor, "Celeste, Celeste, come here, please." She then stepped back into her room.

A few minutes later, a young woman, a little older than Celine, came rushing into the room. "What is it?" she asked Roseanne.

"I need you to take this girl and fit her with one of your gowns for today, as you are almost the same size."

"Okay," Celeste said, looking Celine over. She decided that she and this girl were about the same size. "All right, come with me and l we'll see what I can do," Celeste said with a slight French accent.

Bewildered, Celine followed Celeste back to her room, after giving Roseanne a curious look. "I will see you in a minute, when you have been properly dressed," Roseanne said. Then she went back inside her own room, closing the door behind her. When the two girls got to the room at the other end of the hall, Celeste opened the door and motioned for Celine to enter. When they were inside, Celeste went to her wardrobe and opened the door to it. She started sorting through her gowns, looking for just the right one.

While waiting, Celine looked around the room. She was surprised, as it was just like Roseanne's room, only smaller, even to the balcony outside the windows.

"Ah ha, this one will do, I think," said Celeste, bringing Celine back to why she was here. Celeste pulled a dark-blue low-cut gown from the wardrobe and walked over to Celine, telling her to remove her dress.

Turning red, Celine undid her dress and stepped out of it and into the beautiful blue dress Celeste held up for her. After Celeste buttoned up the back, she turned Celine around, and Celeste's face broke into a big smile. "*Mon Dieu*, it is just perfect. It is, how you say it, fits like the glove." Celeste turned Celine toward the full-length mirror so she could see for herself.

At first glance, Celine didn't recognize herself. The gown had short sleeves coming off the shoulders, and the low-cut dress had a small row of lace that just covered the dark pink nipples of her breasts, which jutted above the bodice. It was form-fitting all the way to the bottom, where it flared out around her ankles.

"Oh, I can't wear this," she said out loud.

"Why not?" asked Celeste. "It is what we all wear when we are working."

"Why? Because it shows too much," said Celine.

"Oh, posh. It shows just enough to get the men to buy you a drink," replied Celeste.

About that time, Roseanne came into the room to see how everything was going. When she opened the door, she smiled and thought to herself, *I was right. I thought she was extremely pretty, but she is downright beautiful.* She walked around Celine and told Celeste the dress was perfect. "As soon as we do her hair and face, she will be ready to go to work." Celine started to protest, but the other two pushed her over to a smaller mirror on top of a table that also held combs, brushes, and makeup.

They sat Celine down and went to work on her. When they had finished, they had Celine look at herself in the mirror. Celine could not believe she was looking at herself. The women had swept her long, curly hair on top of her head, with a few short curls framing her face and some longer ones hanging over one bare shoulder. They had put a light rouge on her cheeks and covered her lips with a light pink. They also put dark mascara on her golden eyelashes to bring out the unusual color of her eyes.

"Magnificent," said Roseanne out loud. Before Celine could protest any more, the two ushered her out the door and down the stairs to the saloon. The older man that let her in that morning stepped out from behind the bar. They took one look at Celine and whistled, making Celine turn red.

"Better get used to that, young lady. You're going to get a lot of it around here."

Roseanne laughed and introduced him to Celine. "Charlie, this here is our new girl, Celine. Celine, this is Charlie Stokes, our best bartender," Roseanne said with pride. Celine could not help but notice the look that passed between them.

"Nice to meet you, ma'am," Charlie said while shaking Celine's dainty little hand.

"Likewise, Mr. Stokes," said Celine.

"No, no. Now, little lady, it's just plain Charlie."

"All right, Charlie it is—if you call me Celine."

"It's a deal, Celine," Charlie replied, laughing.

"Charlie takes care of you and the rest of the girls while you are working, so if you get anyone that gives you trouble, just let him know and he will take care of it."

Celine nodded her head all right. As Charlie went back behind the bar, Roseanne said, "Celeste will show you around and how to do your job and introduce you to the other ladies that work this shift when they come down. If you need anything, you know where to find me. I'll be in my office," and she turned and left.

As the other girls that worked for Roseanne came down. Celeste introduced them to Celine. The first one to show up was Dixie, a buxom redhead in her early thirties with a great bubbly smile. The second one was Claudine, a black-haired beauty. She was tall and very shapely and was in her twenties. The next one, who was always late, was Willy, short for Wilhelmina. She was the oldest of all the girls and had worked the longest for Roseanne. She had blonde hair and a round face. She was friendly and motherly to all the girls. Willy was almost forty.

That made five girls working the shift from eleven to seven o'clock. Then the next five would come and work from seven to closing time, as they were the youngest of the lot, all except for Celine, who was the youngest of all of them, but Roseanne gave her the early shift so she could go and tend to her baby and let Emeline have time before she had to go to work.

Celine liked all the girls. They all gave her a warm welcome and told her if she ever needed anything, just to ask. The saloon opened promptly at eleven in the morning, and no sooner did the doors open than the saloon filled up with men. Celeste, seeing the scared look on Celine's face, told her, "Follow my lead. Do what I do and you will be fine. All you have to do is have a drink with them if they ask you and listen to what they have to say. Nothing else, unless you want to," added Celeste with a smile and a wink at Celine.

Celine followed Celeste to the bar and watched as Celeste backed up to the bar and put her elbows on top of the bar, making her breasts push upward. Upon doing this, three men rushed over to her and clambered to buy Celeste a drink. Celine watched Celeste in fascination at how easy she made it look. She thought to herself, *I can do this*. Celine backed up to the bar. Because she was shorter than Celeste, it was difficult for her to put her elbows on the bar without standing on her tiptoes, but she managed to do it.

Not quite getting her elbows completely on the bar top, Celine started to fall forward when all of a sudden she felt two strong hands around her waist and was pulled up against a hard body. When she glanced up, she found herself looking into laughing clear blue eyes. The way they were dancing with amusement at her dilemma brought Celine's temper to the surface as she turned red with embarrassment. She looked over at Celeste, who was busy with her three gentlemen. No help there, Celine thought, so in her most sophisticated voice, she said to the stranger, "Kindly let go of me."

"Only if you think you can stand up on your own," the stranger said with laughter in his voice.

"I think I can manage," Celine replied irritability. The man let her go, and Celine stepped back away from him. From this view, she got a better look at him. As irritated as she was, she had to admit he was very handsome. His sandy brown hair was thick and slightly wavy. His jaw was square, and his chin had a small dimple in it. But it was those clear blue eyes, fringed in long, dark eyelashes, that held her spellbound.

Celine realized she was staring at him and turned a deeper red. Seeing her embarrassment, he asked her if she would like to sit at a table and have a drink with him. At first, Celine was going to refuse him, but then she remembered it was her job to get men to buy drinks for her and them. So she nodded her head yes, and they walked over to a table. The man pulled out her chair for her to sit down.

"You're quite the gentleman," said Celine haughtily, unable to stop herself. There was something about the man that caused her to be rude.

"My mother taught me. She always said to treat a lady like a lady."

"Humph," replied Celine, saying to herself, *He's doing it again, trying to best me and make me feel like a fool.* She looked away, avoiding his eyes. The stranger held up two fingers, and Charlie nodded his head in understanding. A few minutes later, Charlie brought over a drink for Celine and a cup of coffee for the man. When Celine looked at him with a puzzled look, he smiled and said, "I'm on duty, so I only drink coffee," and pulled his vest aside to expose a sheriff's badge. "Allow me to introduce myself. Sheriff Bradley Taylor, at your service, but please call me Brad," he said as he extended his large hand out to her.

Taken aback, she replied, "I am Celine LeeAnn Sanduvale," and she took his hand and shook it. She thought his grip was firm and sturdy, that he was a man she could trust.

Celine picked up her drink and took a small sip of it. She almost choked when she tasted the cold tea instead of the hard liquor she was expecting. With a big smile on his face, Brad explained to her that the girls were served only cold tea to drink so they could keep their wits about them, but the gents were charged for hard liquor. "Oh," said Celine, "sounds a bit dishonest to me."

"No, not really," Brad told her. "The place advertises the price of drinks at a certain price, not what the drinks are made of." He went on to explain, "The men who come in are usually drifters, cow punchers, or just lonely men in need of companionship—you know, someone to talk to and keep them company for a few hours. It's good business and keeps down trouble."

At that moment, Roseanne walked over to their table and said, "I see you have met our local lawman."

"Yes, I have," replied Celine.

After a short time, Brad excused himself, saying, "I have to make my rounds."

Looking directly at Celine, he said, "Maybe I'll see you later this afternoon." Tipping his hat at the two ladies, he turned and left the saloon.

Roseanne got up to leave, but before she did, she told Celine, "Watch out for that one. Every girl and woman in town is after him."

Celine got through the day fine, but she thought if she never saw another glass of tea, it would be all right with her. At the end of her shift, Roseanne told Celine that she had been very well for her first day. Most of the men who came in wanted to buy the pretty new girl a drink.

Celine went outside and down the alley to the room she shared with Emeline. When she walked in, Emeline was sitting in a rocking chair, singing a soft lullaby to Lizzy. *She has a beautiful voice*, thought Celine. Emeline stopped in the middle of a verse when she saw Celine standing there. "Please, don't stop singing, Emeline. You have a beautiful voice."

"Why, thank you, missy—I mean, Celine. I sang in church every Sunday back home," Emeline said with a little sadness in her voice.

"I am so sorry about this mess I got you into, Emeline. Someday, I will get us back home," Celine said.

"Don't you fret none. I know everything's gonna be all right," replied Emeline with confidence. Then she handed Celine the baby, saying, "She's mighty hungry."

While Celine fed Lizzy, Emeline set two dishes out for them to eat the stew she had made earlier. After feeding and changing the baby, Celine placed Lizzy in the basket she slept in.

Celine slipped off the dress she wore to work and carefully hung it up, then went over to the basin and washed the makeup off her face. She put on a robe, went over, and sat down to eat with Emeline. While eating, the girls told each other about their work. Emeline said her work consisted of washing all the glasses and dishes that were used that day, sweeping the floors, and wiping clean all the tables and chairs. Celine said it sounded like hard work, but Emeline waved her hand and said she had perks while she worked. Interested, Celine asked her what she meant by perks. "Well," said Emeline, "I don't work alone."

"No, who works with you?" asked Celine.

"His name is Jesse Baxter. He's a young black man in his early twenties. He's tall and very strong," Emeline replied dreamily.

"Sounds like you might have a crush on this guy," Celine said, laughing.

"I could easily if I let myself. He's good looking, but I don't know anything about him. But enough about my work. Tell me about your work," Emeline said.

"Mine? Oh, it was a very educational experience," Celine said, laughing and rolling her eyes toward the ceiling. Celine told her friend about meeting Brad Taylor, the town sheriff. As Celine told her story, the two girls laughed, and before they knew it, it was time for Emeline to go to work. Celine watched as Emeline took special care to look her best and said, "Get to know this guy real good before you let your guard down. You can't really trust them you know." Emeline shook her head in understanding and left for work.

Celine checked on her baby and found her sleeping peacefully. Bending down, she kissed her baby's forehead and whispered, "You're the only good thing out of this whole mess." Celine went to bed and slept fitfully, having the same dream she had every night. She dreamt Thomas was there standing over her. He would slowly lower his naked body on top of her. She could feel his muscles rippling as she reached for him to bring his warm body closer to hers. But he would pull back from her with a terrible grin on his contorted face and would fade away, laughing.

Celine would cry out his name and wake herself up, sweating and breathing hard, tears rolling down her cheeks. She sat up and swore, vowing to forget about Thomas. He would be gone from her life for good. She had written him a dozen letters without a single letter back from him. It hurt to think she met so little to him. She would not write to him again.

When morning came, Celine jumped from the bed as Lizzy was starting to fuss for her breakfast and she did not want her to wake Emeline. Celine looked over and saw that Emeline was soundly sleeping. She reached Lizzy just as she was about to let out a loud howl. Picking her baby up, she sat in the rocking chair, undid her top, and placed the babe to her breast, where she ate greedily. Celine thought her daughter made funny noises while she ate and smiled to herself.

Celine washed Lizzy all over, dried her, and put all clean clothes on her. When Celine was done, she laid the baby back down in the basket, where she immediately fell asleep. Celine made coffee, and after drinking a cup, she cleaned herself up, and got herself dressed in the only other dress she had. She then brushed her hair until it shined, pinching her cheeks for color.

She moved the baby's basket over close to Emeline so the girl would not have to get up to tend to Lizzy if she woke up. Celine then undid her dress and proceeded to milk each breast, to put in bottles for her baby, until she returned from work. When she was finished, Celine did up her dress, checked to see if everything was all right, and then quietly left the room and went straight to Roseanne's office.

Roseanne was glad to see her and told her to sit down for a minute while she finished up her books. Celine sat down and watched as Roseanne worked on her ledger. Watching, Celine realized that Roseanne was a woman not to be taken lightly. She was smart and savvy, which is why she owned this saloon—a feat very few women ever accomplished, never having to depend on any man, thought Celine bitterly. Celine admired Roseanne and hoped someday she could be like her.

"Well, now," said Roseanne, breaking into Celine's thoughts. "Today we will take off and visit a dressmaker to get you some suitable dresses for you to work in."

"But" protested Celine, "I don't have any money."

"Don't worry, I will lend you some and you can pay me back a little at a time," replied Roseanne. "After the money you brought in yesterday, I am sure you will be debt-free in no time." Roseanne left the office with Celine following after her, carrying the dress she had borrowed from Celeste the night before. Celine hurried up the stairs and returned the dress while Roseanne found Charlie and gave him instructions for the day.

As the two crossed the busy street, Roseanne pointed out that a person had to be very careful crossing, as Market Street was one of the busiest streets in town and some of the wagon drivers were not careful. After crossing, they turned and headed away from the saloon for several blocks. They came to a small building with large windows in the front of it.

In the windows were a variety of dresses. Celine stood for a moment and admired them, then followed Roseanne into the dress shop. A small gray-haired woman came from the back of the store to greet them. When she saw Roseanne, her face lit up, and her smile was contagious. Celine caught herself smiling back at the woman. "Celine, this is Madame LeNore, the best seamstress in all of San Francisco."

"Of course you say that, my dear. You are my best customer, and there are only three more dressmakers here in town," replied the woman, laughing.

"I am pleased to meet you," said Celine, holding out her hand. "I am Celine."

The woman took Celine's hand, and Celine noticed not only how small it was but how strong it felt in her own hand. *Probably from years of sewing*, thought Celine to herself.

"So, this is the young lady you want Madame LeNore to make dresses for?" she said, checking out the young girl's figure as she walked around Celine. "Yes, yes you are exquisite, my dear. Your form is almost perfect. Your breasts are overly large, but the rest of you is perfect," Madame LeNore stated matter-of-factly, making Celine blush.

She quickly replied, "It is because I just had a baby a little over three weeks ago."

"Ah, that explains everything." She waved her hand dismissively. Roseanne and Celine spent most of the morning picking out material for the dresses to be made, and Celine stood for an hour while Madame LeNore took her measurements. It was shortly before noon when they finally finished. Roseanne thanked Madame LeNore for taking her time for them, as she knew how busy this woman was. Madame LeNore told them that she would have the first two dresses ready in one week. Thanking her again, the two left the shop.

Roseanne asked Celine if she was hungry. Nodding her head yes, Celine rubbed her stomach, making Roseanne laugh. "Come on. I will treat you to a lunch I know you will enjoy," said Roseanne. The two women walked for about ten minutes and finally came to a part of San Francisco that surprised and delighted Celine all at once. Roseanne smiled and explained to Celine that this area was called China Town, as it was inhabited by Chinese people. They came to a restaurant called Ling Chow's, and when the women walked in, the owner, a small man dressed in bright-colored traditional Chinese clothing, came up to them and bowed. Roseanne bowed her head in acknowledgment and said, "How have you been, Ling?"

The man replied in broken English, "Ling has been very well, Missy Rosie," and led the two to a table, where they dined on a most delicious meal.

After lunch, they slowly walked back to the saloon, each savoring the meal and enjoying the day. When they reached the saloon, Roseanne told Celine to take the rest of the day off, as it was late in the day. Celine thanked her and went down the alley to their room. She quietly opened the door so as not to disturb Emeline, but she was already up, while Lizzy was still sound asleep. Emeline asked Celine, "What are you doing here and not at work? Is everything all right?" Then, looking horrified, she asked, "You didn't get fired, did you?"

Smiling at the baffled girl, Celine said, "No, I didn't get fired," and then she told her all about her day with Roseanne.

After talking a while, Lizzy woke up, so Celine busied herself taking care of the baby while Emeline took care of a few chores. Celine was glad her daughter had woken, as her breasts were full and she had to relive them, which Lizzy did gladly. Around dinnertime, Celine was about to warm up some of the leftover stew for the third day in a row when she heard someone knocking on their door. Emeline went to the door and opened it. There, in the doorway, stood a tall, handsome young man.

He had a beautiful smile, and when he saw Emeline, he removed his large cowboy hat. He spoke in a pleasant voice, "Hello, ma'am. Is Celine here?"

"Yes, she is," Emeline replied, and she stepped aside for him to enter the room.

Celine was surprised when she saw the sheriff had stepped into the room but caught herself and said, "Nice to see you again, Sheriff Taylor." He walked over to Celine, and she felt her pulse quicken.

The sheriff said, "I didn't see you in Rosie's this morning when I made my rounds. I thought maybe you had quit already."

"Now, why would I do that?" Celine asked him a little sharply. The man had a way of raising her hackles, she thought to herself.

"Well, an inexperienced girl like you—it might be too much to take on," he answered her with laughter in his eyes.

"Did you want something, Sheriff?" Celine asked him.

"Oh, I almost forgot. I brought some chicken from the restaurant across the street. I thought we might sit down and eat together," he said, looking from Celine to Emeline.

Looking at the tilt of Celine's chin, Emeline said, "We would love to," before Celine could say, "No, thank you" to this angel in disguise. Emeline did not want stew tonight, not after smelling the chicken the man had brought. She rushed around and put three dishes on the table, moving one chair next to the other one on one side of the table. Then Emeline moved a wooden box on the other side and sat down on it. Looking up at the two people standing there looking back at her, Emeline said, "Well, aren't you two going to sit down so's we can eat?"

Pulling the chair out for Celine, Brad motioned for her to be seated. Hesitating for a moment, Celine finally sat down after she saw the pleading look on Emeline's face. Saying a quick prayer of thanks, Emeline lifted the lid off the box of chicken and helped herself to a piece and began to slowly savor it. Brad took a piece and put it in Celine's plate, then took a piece for himself. Before taking the first bite, Brad stuck his hand in front of Emeline and said, "By the way, my name is Bradley Taylor. But please call me Brad."

Embarrassed at her manners, Celine choked on the bite of chicken she had taken. Patting her on her back, Brad asked if she was all right. Nodding her head yes, she said, "I am sorry. This is my friend Emeline."

"Pleased to meet you, ma'am," he replied.

With her mouth full of chicken, Emeline said, "Me too, but please, call me Emeline."

While they ate, they talked and Celine relaxed. Celine found when she relaxed, she enjoyed Brad's company. He was fairly intelligent in all matters and well versed in conversation, and she found herself comparing him to Thomas and berated herself for doing so. All too soon, it was time for Emeline to go to work. She stood up, and as she did, so did Brad. When she reached for her coat, Brad took it and helped her into it. Emeline thanked Brad for the help and for the chicken and left for work.

When Emeline shut the door, it woke up Lizzy, and she started to fuss. Celine hurried over to the basket and picked her up before she could let out her full-blown cry. Walking back over to Brad, Celine introduced Brad to Lizzy. Brad asked, "Mind if I hold this little tyke?" Seeing the surprised look on Celine's face, he explained to her, "My sister has two of her own, and I miss holding them something awful, as they are older now and don't care to be held." At first, Celine was apprehensive about letting this stranger hold her baby, but she noticed as he looked at Lizzy his face took on a soft, joyous look. She relented and handed him the baby.

Brad took Lizzy and started talking to her in a soft voice. Shortly after, Lizzy started cooing back at Brad and smiling at him. Celine decided that if her daughter trusted him, then so could she. Brad played with the baby until Lizzy decided it was time to eat and began to get fussy. Handing the baby back to Celine, Brad said, "It's getting late, and I have rounds to make before I can call it a night." He picked up his hat and headed for the door. At the door, he turned and said, "It was fun tonight. Maybe we can do it again soon."

"I guess so. Sure, why not?" replied Celine with a smile on her face.

"Good," Brad said, "I'll see you on my rounds in the morning," and he left.

Celine sighed, then set about feeding and changing Lizzy, getting her ready for bed. After putting her baby down for the night, Celine changed into her nightgown, washed her face and hands, and brushed her hair. She cleaned up the table, did the dishes, and put things away. When she was through, she went to bed, and when she slept, she did not have the bad dream that had been plaguing her every night.

The next day, and every day after that, it became a routine for Sheriff Taylor to stop in and have his coffee with Celine at the saloon. And once a week, he would pick up something from the restaurant and share it with Celine and Emeline for dinner in their room. They all would tell funny stories, laughing while they ate. He became attached to Lizzy and played with her by the hour. Madame LeNore finished all Celine's dresses, and when she tried them on, they fit like a glove, and she looked exquisite in them.

Celine wrote one last letter to Thomas, asking him to please explain to her why all this had happened. She wrote about Lizzy, how much she looked like him and what she had named her, and she asked him how he could give up his daughter. She wanted to know why he had broken his promise to take care of them. She would not write again, she vowed. She would get on with her life, for her daughter's sake. Celine had confided in Roseanne all that had happened between Thomas and her. Roseanne could not understand how a man could be so callous and dishonorable. She disliked Thomas immensely and was glad when Celine finally decided to forget him and move on. Celine never received an answer to her letter.

What Celine did not know was her letters had been intercepted and Thomas never received them. Marta felt terrible about the letters, but she could not take a chance on him seeing them, because if he did, he would know that Celine and his daughter were alive. He would hate her for her part in the deception and she would most likely never see him again. No, better to keep them hidden away, and besides, Thomas was starting to see Jenny and get on with his life.

Thomas had called on Jenny a couple of times. He had taken Jenny and her son, Jeremy, on a picnic, and they'd had a great time. Thomas enjoyed Jenny's company, always had, even when they were kids, they had gotten along great and were good friends. Now, most of all, Thomas needed a distraction. He found that Jenny and Jeremy gave him that.

Thomas found that when he was with them, he didn't think of Celine or his little baby girl as much. The hurt wasn't as bad with them around. He loved little Jeremy and the funny little things he did to make them all laugh. He thought maybe he could begin a new life for himself.

The next year came and went. It seemed to Celine that time just slipped by. One evening, Roseanne went to the room in the back to see Celine and heard a voice that sounded like an angel singing. When Roseanne knocked on the door, Celine answered it and motioned for the woman to come in. To Roseanne's surprise, it was Emeline, singing a soft lullaby to Lizzy. When Emeline saw Roseanne, she stopped singing, to Roseanne's dismay. The woman said, "No, no, please don't stop singing. Do continue." Emeline finished the song and laid Lizzy in her basket, as she had fallen fast asleep.

Roseanne asked Emeline, "Where did you learn to sing like that?"

The girl replied, "In my mother's church choir back home, in New Orleans."

"You wouldn't consider singing at the saloon one hour a night, would you?" asked Roseanne.

"Daisy went and got herself pregnant, and the father of the baby asked her to marry him and move to Sacramento with him. The silly girl said yes, so I am in desperate need of a singer."

"I don't know. I have my other chores to do after the saloon closes," Emeline answered her.

"I am sure Jesse will be glad to help you out so you don't fall behind. I saw the way that boy looks at you—and how you look at him," Roseanne said with laughter in her voice, making Emeline blush. "Just give it some thought, all right?"

"I will consider it and let you know," Emeline said. Emeline and Jesse had gotten very close since working together every night for over two years now. Emeline wasn't sure Jesse would approve of her singing in the saloon, in front of all those men, but she would speak to him about it.

Roseanne had said it would mean more money, as she would pay her extra. Emeline really would like to earn extra money, as she was trying to save up so she could open her own store, fulfilling her dream of making women's hats. She had made Roseanne and all the girls who worked there big, beautiful hats, with lots of flowers and feathers on them, to wear on their days off. The girls all told Emeline that when they wore their hats when they went out on their days off, all the woman stopped them on the street and asked them where they had gotten them made. That night, when Emeline went to work, she explained to Jesse the proposition Roseanne had presented to her and asked him if he would mind. Jesse loved Emeline and really didn't want all those drunks lusting after her, but he said if that's what she wanted, he would help her keep up on her chores so she wouldn't fall behind. Emeline stood on her toes and placed a kiss on his cheek to thank him.

Jesse put his arms around her waist and looked into her eyes, showing all the love he had for her. He bent down and slowly kissed her lightly on her full mouth. Emeline felt as if she had been drugged, as his kiss was so intoxicating. When Jesse finally pulled away, Emeline stood rooted to the spot. Her eyes were shut, and her lips were still puckered up, as if she were still being kissed.

Jesse chuckled, and Emeline's eyes flew open. She turned a deep crimson.

"That the first time those lips ever been kissed?" Jesse asked her, with a smile on his face.

"Of course not, you fool. I have been kissed a lot of times," Emeline answered him.

"By who, your mama?" Jesse laughed.

Emeline turned abruptly to leave, but Jesse caught her hand and pulled her close to him. She struggled to get away, but he held her tightly until she stopped moving against him.

Jesse was glad when she finally stopped moving, as she was beginning to stir things up in him. "I'm sorry, Emeline. I was just having some fun with you. I loved your kiss and would love to kiss you again if you let me." His hold on her slackened, so she took that opportunity to jerk away from him and take a few steps back.

It was her turn to smile as she said, "I'll think about it and let you know. "Then she turned and walked away, leaving him standing there slack-jawed.

That night, Emeline dressed in one of Celine's beautiful dresses, piled her hair on top of her head, and nervously went out on the stage to sing. When the curtain opened, a few of the men looked up, expecting to see Daisey standing there but were surprised to see a pretty young black girl instead, nervously staring out at them with big black eyes. When the piano music started to play, Emeline started to sing. The men looked up and started to holler. One of them said, "Who the heck is this and where is Daisey? Get off the stage, little girl, so's a real singer can perform."

Charlie reached for his shotgun from under the bar and fired off a shot toward the ceiling, getting everyone's attention. When everyone looked in his direction, Charlie told all the men to shut up and sit down and listen to the girl sing. All of them did as they were told, grumbling to each other. When the piano man started again, Emeline began to sing. One by one the men stopped their grumbling and sat quietly, listening to Emeline sing. When she finished, the men jumped up clapping their hands, whistling hooting and hollering for more.

Roseanne stepped up to the bar, and Charlie handed her a drink. With a huge smile on her face, she said, "Yes, sir, Charlie. The day those two girls came into my life was the luckiest day ever," and she swallowed her drink.

Everything was going along great. Jenny, Jeremy, and Thomas were all having dinner with Jason and Emma. Jason and Thomas were talking about what they were going to plant in the spring while Emma and Jenny were laughing about three-year-old Jeremy's silly antics, when Emma suddenly asked Jenny, "When are you and Tommy going to quit fooling around, get serious, and set a date to be married? After all, it's been three years since that tragic day."

"I don't know," replied Jenny. "He loves me, I am sure, but something is holding him back.

"Well, you're both not getting any younger, and Jeremy is already three. He needs a playmate—besides my two young'uns," said Emma.

"I agree," Jenny said, laughing. Then, getting serious, she said, "Maybe I will ask him to marry me." Both women laughed.

A week later, when Marta went to check on Phillip, she found him staring off into space. "Very quiet," she said out loud to herself. "Not like him to be so quiet." She went over to pull the curtain back to let in some light. She then walked over to the bed and stared down at Phillip, who had become a broken-down shell of his former self. She thought about how she had admired this man when she was a young girl of fifteen and he had bought her and her son from an auction on the insistence of his wife, Elizabeth, who had become her very dearest friend and was long gone from their lives.

Looking at Phillip now, she wondered how she could have betrayed her friend with this man and felt a pang of sorrow for doing so. She recalled how after Elizabeth had died. She would not go to Phillip's bed again, so he satisfied his needs with other slave women, making sure he never fathered a child with any of them. That was fine with Marta, as she had her hands full taking care of her son, Eli, and as well as Thomas, Phillip's small son.

Staring down at Phillip, at the man he had become, all the hatred she ever felt for him came bubbling to the surface. While Marta stared at him, she became aware that he was staring back at her. She quickly took a couple of steps away from the bed as she saw the loathing for her in his eyes.

"You made my life a living hell," Phillip said to her. "You knew I cared deeply for you. You also knew I didn't want a bastard child born from a slave, and you knew I couldn't marry you, as it would have been scandalous to me."

Trying to keep her anger under control, Marta replied, "You have that backward. Don't you mean you made my life a living hell? You moved me into your house to raise Thomas for you, knowing how much I loved him. You used him to get me to do your bidding." Marta continued, "You knew and you used him to get me to do your dirty work."

Softening his tone, Phillip said, "I didn't think it would bother me."

"But it did bother you, so much so that you couldn't be a real father to him," replied Marta.

"Yes, it did bother me, and it's something I truly regret," Phillip replied. Standing there, Marta thought back to when Elizabeth became pregnant and how happy she was for Elizabeth and Phillip.

"Are you really sorry, Phillip, that you hurt your son by denying him his one true love and his daughter, your granddaughter."

"I had to, don't you see? I couldn't take the chance with that one either," Phillip answered.

Shaking her head in disgust, Marta turned to leave the room when Phillip stopped her. "Please, Marta. I can't sleep at night, and I don't feel well. I know you carry a potion with you for sleeping. Please, leave me some," Phillip begged her. Stopping, Marta turned and looked at him. Then, sighing, she felt for the two bottles she kept with her at all times in her apron pocket. She removed one and walked over and placed it on his nightstand next to his bed. "This should help you sleep," Marta said, then turned and left the room, closing the door.

Very early the next morning, before daybreak, before anyone else was up, a lone figure crept upstairs, entered Phillip's room, and removed the empty bottle from the nightstand. When Moses went up that morning to tend to Phillip, he thought he was sleeping peacefully, until he gently shook him and he didn't respond.

The funeral for Phillip was a grand affair. Everyone for miles around came to pay their respects and let Thomas know how sorry they were for his loss. Thomas stood and shook everyone's hand and accepted their condolences, but in his mind, he celebrated his father's life and remembered only the good times he had with him, as he had done with his friend Sean in Ireland. Phillip was buried in between Elizabeth and an unmarked grave on the hill.

As Marta stood and listened to what people had to say about Phillip being a good man, she sadly thought to herself, *Yes, at one time, Phillip had been a very good man.* Looking over at Thomas standing next to Eli and Jacob, Marta smiled and said to herself that Thomas was the best thing Phillip had ever done.

Life on the plantation went on, and soon, everything returned to normal. Thomas and Jenny began spending more time with each other, enjoying each other's company, laughing, talking, and sometimes just taking quiet walks without saying much of anything.

Thomas and Jeremy got along and had fun being together, and little Jeremy loved Thomas like a father. Jenny had offers from other suitors but held out on the hopes of Thomas asking for her hand.

Celine was headed across the street to visit with Emeline at the shop. Emeline had purchased it to make her hats in almost six months earlier. With the help of Celine, Jesse, Roseanne, and Brad, they got it painted inside and out, put up shelves in the back for all the supplies she needed for making her hats, and added shelves in the front to display all of them. Jesse had painted across the top of the building in big bold lettering, "Emeline's Hat Boutique."

While Celine worked at the saloon during the day, Emeline would watch Lizzy in the store until Celine got off work. This gave Emeline time to get things done and still have time to eat with Celine before going to the saloon to sing, which she enjoyed doing very much, and she still did it even though she opened her store. Emeline no longer worked in the saloon after closing, as it became too much for her to run her hat shop and work at nights at the saloon.

Jesse and Emeline set a date to be married, and that spring, they had a beautiful wedding and celebrated in style at Roseanne's place. Roseanne gave them a grand party as Roseanne treated Emeline and Celine like her daughter's. When Lizzy wasn't staying at Emeline's, the girls upstairs kept care of her as everyone loved Celine and Lizzy. Celine was always helping anyone that needed help, and Lizzy kept everyone laughing at the funny things she did and said.

As time went by everything ran smoothly, until the day Celine started across the street to see how Emeline was feeling, as she was eight months pregnant and had not been feeling well. As Celine neared the center of the street, Lizzy called her mother from the balcony of Celeste's room. Celine turned at the sound of her daughter's voice calling out, "Look at me, Momma. Look at me." Looking up, she saw Lizzy waving her hand at her. Celine waved back at the little girl, not seeing the large wagon carrying a load of barrels bearing down on her. Emeline, however, who had been watching the exchange between Lizzy and her mother through the shop's window, did see it. She hurried to the door and threw it open and screamed at Celine to look out, but there was too much noise for Celine to hear her. The girls on the balcony also saw what was about to happen and started to holler at Celine to look out, but to no avail.

The driver of the wagon tried to stop, but the horses were going too fast and couldn't stop in time to keep from hitting the young woman, so he pulled the reins to make the horses go around this foolish young woman who had stopped in the middle of this busy street. Celine stopped waving at her daughter, turned, and saw the wagon coming straight for her. Confused at what to do, as the wagon veered away from her, she stepped right into the side of it.

Celine was knocked down, and the back wheel of the wagon ran over her right leg. Celine screamed and then was silent. Emeline screamed and fainted. Lizzy was crying hysterically and trying to climb over the balcony. Everyone was stunned. Then everything started to happen all at once. The wagon was finally brought to a halt a little way down the street, and the driver jumped down from his seat and ran over to Celine. The ladies in Emeline's store tried to revive Emeline by patting her hands and fanning her face. They sent someone for Doc Jones up the street.

Roseanne was out the door and over to Celine quicker than a jackrabbit. Bending down, she felt for a pulse and let out the breath she was holding when she found one. Looking down at her leg, she saw how badly it was twisted and all the blood on the ground. Lifting her dress a little, she saw the bone sticking out and almost passed out herself. Roseanne shouted for someone to fetch the doc and was told that he was on his way. Sheriff Brad came running from his office after a passerby told him of the accident. When he got there and saw it was Celine, he turned white but kept himself calm and asked what had happened.

A dozen people started to talk all at once, the sheriff stood up and told someone to get something to fashion a stretcher. Some men ran to the saloon but found nothing big enough. Some of the women on the balcony threw down some blankets and clean towels.

The doctor finally arrived. He bent down and examined Celine's head, neck, arms, and back, finding nothing wrong with anything there but a few cuts and bruises. He examined her leg. He reached for a clean towel and asked Roseanne to hold it tight on the cut just above her knee to stop the flow of blood. The doc looked at the bone protruding through the young woman's flesh just above the knee. Then he noticed her starting to shake and said, "She's going into shock. Find something quick to lay her on and take her to my office so I can get to work on her."

Brad and two other men went to Emeline's shop and removed the front door. Then they went over to where Celine was lying on the street and, with help from the doc, the four men gently lifted Celine and carefully placed her on the door. Celine was in and out of consciousness, but when she was lifted up, the pain was so intense, she screamed and fainted. Roseanne quickly covered her with a blanket, and they all moved down to the doc's office, where they placed Celine on a long, wide table. The two men, following the sheriff's orders, then took the door back to Emeline's shop and replaced it.

The women at the shop had placed smelling salts under Emeline's nose and had managed to revive her. In the meantime, Jesse had been told about the accident and had made his way through the crowd and into the shop, where he found his wife still lying on the floor. With deep concern, he rushed over, bent down, and asked Emeline if she was all right. Just as she was about to assure him that she was all right, severe pain shot across her lower back, and she cried out.

Lifting her in his arms, Jesse looked down and saw the water on the floor, as did the two women.

"Oh my. It looks as if your wife's going into labor. It must have been the shock of seeing the accident that brought it on," one of them said.

Without waiting for the women to say more, Jesse turned, went out the door, and headed for doc's office down the street.

When Jesse arrived a few minutes later, he kicked open the door, took Emeline into the office, and laid her on a small bed, asking the doc, "Please, look at my wife. I think she's gone into labor."

Doc Jones, without even looking their way, said, "Can't right now, Jesse. Have to concentrate on Celine, but will see to Emeline in a while. In the meantime, sit with your wife, and both of you just stay calm."

Emeline tried to set up to see Celine, but Jesse held her down and explained to her how bad Celine was. "Oh God, Jesse, please. She cannot die. She's my sister. She has to be all right," said Emeline through her tears.

"She will be, girl, but you have got to lie still. Your water broke, and you're going into labor."

Doc Jones sent someone to fetch the midwife to tend to Emeline so he could try to repair the damage to Celine's leg. He made everyone leave his office—that is, everyone but Roseanne, who refused to budge, so he said she could stay and help him with the two girls. Brad and Jesse tried to stay also, but doc put his foot down and said, "No. Go to Roseanne's and have a drink. When I am done here, I will send word to you and you can visit then." Reluctantly, the two men left and went to the saloon to wait.

Doc washed up and put on an apron and had Roseanne do the same while he cut away Celine's clothing. Then he had Roseanne get hot water and gently wash away any dirt or gravel that might be around the wounds. After he had Roseanne pour an antiseptic all up and down her leg, which made Celine try to move away from whatever was making her leg sting and burn. Doc then covered her from her neck down, leaving her right leg exposed.

He told Roseanne to get a bottle from his top shelf and pour a little at a time onto a cloth covering Celine's mouth and nose. When Roseanne asked why she would do that, he answered, saying it was called ether, and it would keep her asleep until they were through with what had to be done. Reading from a thick book the doc had on his desk, he took several instruments from an airtight container and laid them out on a clean white cloth close to where Celine lay.

After a minute of dropping a small amount of ether onto the cloth, Celine was sleeping like a baby. Doc Jones instructed Roseanne to hold Celine down if she began to move at all. Then Doc Jones began to repair Celine. First, he stitched a small cut on her forehead and another one on her shoulder. Celine moaned but did not wake up or move about. As he had started to sweat some, Roseanne blotted the doc's forehead with a clean cloth. When the doc started to work on Celine's leg, he told Roseanne to be ready to hold Celine down tight as he was going to have to hurt her to fix her leg.

At that, Doc lifted the leg and pulled to straighten it. It took all his strength to pull hard enough and turn it to get it in the right place so Celine would not end up with a bad limp. Doc jerked and turned it until he felt it going into position, and when he did that, Celine screamed and tried to sit up—and would have if Roseanne had not been lying over her to hold her down.

Doc stepped back and wiped the sweat from his forehead onto his rolled-up sleeves. He told Roseanne, "Good job. Now give her a little more ether while I stitch up the leg." Roseanne poured a few drops more ether onto the cloth and placed it over Celine's nose and mouth. The doc said, "Be careful not to breathe any of that, or you will end up on the table with your friend."

It took a long time to stitch Celine's leg, as it was a large shaggy cut where the bone had protruded through and he wanted it to be a neat sewing job to prevent a horrific scar.

After he was through, Doc Jones went to the back of the building and brought back two thin slats. He had Roseanne hold them in place on the leg while he wrapped strips of cloth around the slats from her ankle almost to the thigh. He told Roseanne it was to keep her from walking on the leg until it healed up.

Emeline was having pains in her stomach and her back, but she kept silent, as she knew Celine needed the doc more than she did right now. The midwife had come and examined Emeline and had told her she had quite a while before she would give birth. She should try to rest as much as she could, she said. The doc would be through before she was ready to give birth, so she would leave for a while and would come to check on her in a couple of hours.

Jesse came back to the doc's office to check on his wife. Roseanne was just leaving to go to the saloon to give everyone the report on Celine. She told Jesse that Celine was going to be fine and that Emeline was waiting for him, so Jesse went on in. Doc was just cleaning up and getting ready to head for the saloon for a drink when he saw Jesse. He told him to go back and visit with his wife, as it would be a while, maybe not before morning. Doc asked if he would keep an eye on Celine for him. He would be back in a jiffy. Jesse said he would be glad to.

When Doc Jones entered the saloon, everyone cheered and patted him on the back. He thanked them and told them how Celine was doing, as he knew how everyone felt about Roseanna's two girls. They were both well loved, as neither one had a mean bone in her body. Sheriff Taylor walked over and offered to buy the doc a drink. He accepted and thanked him. Brad asked the doc how Celine was doing, and Doc could tell by the concerned tone of his voice how deeply he cared for this young lady. Replying, Doc said she was doing well, but it was going to be a long recovery, and she would need someone to help keep her spirits up.

Brad asked, "When can I see her, Doc?"

"Probably in the morning. She is sleeping now and will be all through the night. I'll see to that," said Doc as he lifted his glass and swallowed his drink.

The next morning, Roseanne came by and told Doc that when Celine could be moved, she would like her to be moved upstairs, over the saloon. That way, she explained, she and the girls could watch her and Lizzy while Celine was recuperating. She wanted her to be put in Daisy's room as Daisy was no longer there. Doc agreed to do that when Celine could be moved. Roseanne then popped her head through the curtain at the back of the office to see how Emeline was doing. Jesse said, "doc said it could be any minute, all we can do is wait."

"All right," said Roseanne, "send someone if you need me, "and she left.

Sheriff Taylor kept popping in to see how the two girls were doing. Celine slept most of the time, but Doc Jones assured him that she was fine. Just before the noon hour, Brad came back to check for the hundredth time (or at least it seemed so to Doc Jones). The doc told the sheriff he would send word if there were any changes, but just about that time, Jesse came out from behind the curtain and told Doc that his wife had told him to get out; if he came back in, she would fix him good. Laughing, Doc told Jesse that it was common for women to get mad at their husbands in these circumstances. He went in to see how Emeline was doing, and a half hour later, Jesse heard the sound of a baby crying.

Now crying himself, Jesse peeked through the curtain and saw doc hand a small bundle to his wife, saying, "Congratulations, you have a very handsome son." Jesse went all the way in and knelt beside the bed with tears of joy streaming down his cheeks. He bent and kissed his wife and then kissed his firstborn son on the head. Sheriff Brad, hearing the exchange between the two behind the curtain, was very happy for them.

Seeing Celine was still sleeping, Brad was about to leave when Roseanne came through the door. "Oh, Brad, how are all the patients doing today?" she asked as she looked over at Celine. Brad told her that Emeline had just given birth to a son and that Celine was still sleeping. "Wonderful," replied Roseanne. "I will quickly peek in and see." As Brad opened the door, Celine stirred and woke up. Seeing Brad standing there, she reached out her hand to him, and he reached to take hers. He longed to take her in his arms. She looked so helpless, but in her groggy state of mind, she was taken back in time to when she was giving birth and thought he was Thomas. She said, "Thomas, thank God you made it. You're here." Roseanne, reentering the room, heard what Celine had said to Brad.

Roseanne watched as Brad dropped his hand and saw his jaw clench and unclench. Roseanne went over to him and put her hand on his arm. She said, "It's all right. It's just the pain medicine talking."

"No, I don't think so. Just who is this Thomas, and what does he mean to Celine?"

Doc Jones came in, interrupting the two deep in conversation. "Ah, you're awake. Good. How are you feeling, my dear?"

"I, I don't know what happened?"

He motioned for Brad and Roseanne to step outside while he explained to Celine what had happened to her and then wanted to examine her.

After they had retreated outside, Roseanne explained to Brad all about Thomas and what had happened between them. Again, Roseanne watched Brad's jaw and his fists clench. She could see he was angry. Then Brad spoke up. "She didn't tell me, but I knew something was really off, as she wouldn't let me get too close to her, to get to know her. Hell, Roseanne, she should have told me. I would have understood. I would have helped her forget the bastard if only she would have let me."

"I know you would have, Brad. Just be there for her and give her some time. She'll come around," replied Roseanne.

Doc opened the door and told the two to go home, get some rest, and come back tomorrow; the girls were doing fine. Putting her arm through Brad's arm, Roseanne said, "You're right, Doc. Thank you for all you did for my girls. Come on over later and I'll buy you a drink. You earned one."

"Sounds good. Just might take you up on that," Doc stated. He shut the door.

"How about you, Brad? Can I buy you one?" Roseanne asked as the two walked down the street to her saloon.

"No, I think I will take another stroll around and then turn in, but I will take a raincheck on that drink," Brad answered as he

239

walked away. Roseanne went into the saloon and went upstairs to tell Lizzy that her momma was going to be all right.

When Celine could be moved, she was brought upstairs as Roseanne had requested. She had all Celine's things along with Lizzy's items, as Roseanne knew it would take a long time for Celine to heal; in the meantime, she and Lizzy would be well cared for. Jesse, Emeline, and their new son moved from the back of the hat shop to the room in the back of the saloon.

It took weeks, then months, for Celine to get better, but with everyone's help, she did. The girls took turns exercising her leg, making it stronger by raising it up and down as Doc said to do and massaging the muscles to keep them firm and strong. At first, Celine fought all of them—it hurt too much, and she just wanted to be left alone—but none of them would let her wallow in her self-pity, making her mad, making her fight to get better.

Brad would come by several times a day, heckling her and telling her she was weak and frail and didn't have it in her to fight harder. This made her angry, motivating her to reach deep inside herself to find the strength to prove him wrong. At times, she would tell Brad to get out and not come back, but the next day, he would be there, and if he was late, Celine would worry that he wasn't coming, and when he would walk in, she would ask him what he was doing there, as she had told him to stay away. Ignoring her, Brad would start the heckling all over again.

This went on until Brad could see the much-needed improvement in Celine. The first time they got her up to walk. Brad was there to study her and catch her if she started to fall. This went on for about a month. Then, one day, when Brad opened the door, Celine was standing up next to the bed with no one near her. He started to rush forward in case she fell, but Celine put up her hand and said, "Stop. Stay where you are." Confused, Brad stopped in his tracks and watched as Celine slowly walked the distance from the bed to him without any aid from the girls standing on the other side of the room.

When she reached Brad, she put her arms around his waist and hugged him tight. Everyone cheered, some with tears in their eyes. Brad held Celine at arm's length and looked at her with a big smile on his face. Looking up at Brad, he saw the gratitude in her eyes as she mouthed the words, "Thank you very much." It wasn't gratitude Brad wanted to see in Celine's eyes. He wanted to see love for him, love like he had for her. Brad vowed that he would see that love if it was the last thing he ever saw.

Stepping away from Brad, she turned and started back to the bed. Celine did see the love in Brad's eyes but knew she couldn't return it—not just yet. She had to rid herself of her past. As she got closer to the bed, her leg gave out and she started to fall. Brad was the first to reach her as he scooped her up and carried her to the bed and sat her down on it. Just feeling the heat from her body made him want to lay her down, slowly undress her, and make passionate love to her, to make her want him as much as he wanted her. Smiling at Celine, Brad rose and said, "Well, I think that is enough of a surprise for today, ladies." Tipping his hat, he left the room.

After all the girls left with Lizzy, Roseanne sat in a chair in the corner, watching Celine fidget with the fringe on the bedspread. Celine was well aware that Roseanne was studying her. Roseanne knew her well, better than she knew herself.

"Well," Roseanne finally spoke up.

"Well, what?" replied Celine.

"You know perfectly well what," said Roseanne, thoroughly exasperated at the girl. "How could you let him go on like this, knowing all too well how he feels about you? Why don't you tell him how you feel about him?"

"Because I don't know how I feel about him, Rose—that's why. I like him a lot, but do I love him enough to marry him? I just don't know."

"Well," said Roseanne, "good things don't come along that often. He's liable to give up and move on if you don't find out soon." At that, Roseanne got up, went over, and patted Celine on the shoulder, then left her to ponder over what she had just told her.

After Roseanne left, Celine lay down. Closing her eyes, she tried to think of Thomas, of the powerful love they had shared, but it was becoming harder and harder to think of him at all. Sometimes, when she did think of him and saw his face, his face changed to that of Brad. She knew Brad loved her, and most importantly, he loved Lizzy and Lizzy loved him also, so what was holding her back? She said out loud, "I will try to love Brad. I swear, I will."

Over the next month, Brad brought flowers and candy to Celine and Lizzy. He would come and walk with her every day from her room down to the other end of the hallway. She was walking pretty well on her own and had a slight limp that was noticeable only if she tried to walk too fast. Celine's feelings started to change for Brad, growing even deeper for the way he treated Lizzy. Brad would call on the two and take them on long buggy rides around the city. He would take them on picnics to the outskirts of town, where they got fresh air and lots of sunshine.

One day, he took them to the beach for a day in the sun and surf. Lizzy was so excited, she could hardly sit still for the ride there. When they finally got to the shore, it took Celine and Lizzy's breath away. The sky was so blue, as was the water, and the sand sparkled like gold. Brad told them to take off their shoes and stockings or they would get full of sand and be uncomfortable to walk in. Lizzy was the first to remove her shoes and stockings, running out onto the sand, laughing at how it went between her toes and how warm it was.

When Brad and Celine had removed their shoes and stockings, Brad got the blanket from the buggy and handed it to Celine to carry while he carried the basket of food they brought with them. After getting settled on the blanket next to Celine, who was keeping an eye on Lizzy picking up seashells near the water, Brad asked, "I gather you've never seen the beach before?"

"No. I have crossed a large river, but when we were brought to

San Francisco, we went on deck only once, as the men frightened us, so we did not get to view the ocean."

Seeing how Celine's mood was changing, he said, "Well, now you can see it all you want to. You can even play in it if you want."

This brought a smile to Celine's face. "No thank you," she said. "I'll take your word for it."

The three of them had a great time. They laughed while eating lunch, as Lizzy couldn't keep sand from her hands and ate more sand than food. After attempting to eat, Lizzy decided she would collect more shells to take to the girls at the saloon. When she found a shell, she would run to the blanket to show her momma, then run back to look for more. Brad told Lizzy to set down for a minute as he wanted to talk to her and her momma, so she reluctantly sat next to her mother.

Brad got down on one knee, and holding a small ring in his hand, looking at Celine but talking to both of them, said, "Will you girls marry me? I promise I will be a good husband and a good father."

Celine just stared at him, but Lizzy jumped up, throwing her little arms around his neck, saying, "Can we, Momma? Can we?"

Brad looked at her with puppy-dog eyes and said, "Can we, Momma? Can we?"

The silly look on his face and her daughter's chokehold on him made Celine bust out laughing, and she said, "Yes, yes, we can."

Thomas had made up his mind that he would ask Jenny to marry him. He thought it was time. Jenny had been patient long enough with him. He would ask her tonight, when she and Jeremy came for dinner. Thomas knew he loved her. It was not like the love he had had with Celine, but he knew the friendship he and Jenny shared had turned into a love that ran deep and would last a lifetime. He knew Jenny loved him, as did little Jeremy. Thomas didn't know when their friendship had turned to love, but it had, and the pain he carried in his heart for so long was almost gone thanks to Jenny and her son.

That night, after dinner, Thomas asked Jenny if she would like to go for a ride. He wanted to show her something. Jeremy said, "Me too go for ride."

"Not this time, pal. Just your mom and I," replied Thomas.

A look of disappointment crossed over the little boy's face so Marta spoke up and said, "Why don't you stay and play with Eli's boy, Isaac? You'll have fun."

"Yeah," said Isaac. "We'll play cowboys and Indians,"

"Can I be the Indian?" asked Jeremy.

"Sure you can," replied Issac, and they ran outside onto the porch to play.

Thomas had the buggy brought around and helped Jenny into the buggy, then climbed in beside her, and they started off. It was a beautiful evening, the air warm and fragrant with all the magnolias in bloom. They rode in silence, admiring the surroundings and each other's company. After several miles, Thomas spoke up.

"I wanted to show you the house I built. I finished it and needed your advice on how to decorate it."

"Oh, all right. I'll be glad to help you however I can. You know that Tommy," Jenny said, a little disappointed, as she was hoping Tommy was going to ask her to marry him, not ask for advice on how to decorate something.

When Thomas pulled the buggy to a stop in front of the big house, the sun was just setting, and the place took her breath away. It was beautiful. The house was painted all white, with green shutters and doors, and the porch surrounding the house was painted all green, along with the many steps leading up to the porch. The trees around the house were all in bloom, as were all the flowers of so many different colors. The grass around the house and yard was a brilliant green, making the white house stand out even more.

Jenny, standing up in the buggy, exclaimed, "Oh, Tommy, it is outstanding, simply outstanding."

Thomas's chest swelled with pride, so pleased was he with her reaction. Jumping down from the buggy, he went around and helped Jenny down. Then they walked up the walkway to the front porch. When they reached the top and stood on the porch, Jenny caught her breath again as she took in the view from the porch of the sunset, the hills, and the flat ground all around them.

"I don't know what to say, Tommy. It's absolutely magnificent," Jenny told him. When she turned to look at him, he had a huge grin on his face. "Don't get too cocky. You did a great job, but don't let your head swell up," she teased him.

Thomas laughed. "You used to tell me that a lot when we were kids."

"Yes, well, you did used to think you were the best, right?" she replied.

"Yes, I guess I did," he answered her.

As they went through each room, Thomas explained to Jenny what he had made each room for. Jenny agreed with all his decisions, thinking to herself that he had planned it out very well. When they reached the back of the house, he opened the door, and they stepped out into a big backyard. Thomas said it was big enough to hang the laundry on wash days, raise a garden, and have plenty of room for lots of kids to play in.

The sun had gone down. The moon had risen and was shining down on them when they turned toward each other. Thomas could see the love in Jenny's eyes for him, and his heart swelled with love for her. He placed his hand on her cheek and softly stroked it. Her skin was silky soft and smooth. In the moonlight, her hair looked like spun gold hanging down her back and over her shoulders. Her lips were parted and looked so inviting. Without hesitation, he bent down and kissed her mouth. He pulled her close to him and could feel her heart beating through the thin material of her dress. Without waiting, she put her arms around his neck and kissed him back, hard and demanding.

Thomas's pulse began to beat faster. He deepened the kiss, and he felt her tongue slide across his lips. Moaning, he thrust his tongue in, and she fenced back and forth with his tongue. Thomas picked Jenny up and walked down the steps to the soft cool grass. Standing her up beside him, he slowly undressed her, and when she was completely naked, he marveled at how truly beautiful she was. He removed his coat and laid it on the ground. Without taking her eyes off him, Jenny slowly undressed him, and when he was naked, she moved closer to him, feeling his manhood against her leg. She reached down and gently fondled him.

Thomas cried out and reached for her. Laying her down on his coat, he lay down beside her. He kissed her eyes, her lips, her mouth, and her neck. He worked his way down to her soft, full white breasts and paid tribute to both of them, kissing one, then the other. Jenny was trembling with desire, and she could feel Thomas's desire pulsating in his manhood lying next to her hip.

Jenny groaned and Thomas climbed on top of her. Spreading her legs apart, he reached to touch the very core of her, and he knew she was ready for him. He slid into her and started to move very slowly. He wanted it to last as long as possible, for her and for him. Jenny couldn't wait any longer. She started to move with Thomas, and they both picked up the tempo, moving faster and faster until they both cried out, reaching their release together.

When Jenny reached up and gently touched his cheek, Thomas rolled off to one side and drew her up close to him to keep her warm, pulling his coat around her. He felt the tears fall on his shoulder and raised up on his shoulder to look at her in the moonlight.

"Did I hurt you, Jenny?" he asked her softly.

"No," she replied. "It's just that I have waited so long for us to be together like this. I can't control how happy you have made me. That's all, Tommy."

"I know," he said. "I feel the same way you do—and I want you to marry me." Then he bent down and gave her a long, slow kiss.

"Are you sure, Tommy?" she asked him.

"Yes, I am sure. I want you to marry me. I want you to be my wife. That's why I brought you here tonight—to show you the house, our house. Will you marry me, Jenny?" he asked.

Jenny looked him in his eyes for what seemed a long time, then answered him, "Yes, yes, I will marry you."

They lay on the cool grass, unclothed, holding each other and talking. They made love again, slowly, taking their time, savoring each other. When they were through, they helped each other dress, touching and kissing one another, unable to get enough of each other.

They traveled slowly back to the house, and when they got there, Thomas helped Jenny from the buggy, letting her slide down the length of him and kissing her deeply. Jenny sighed and whispered, "I love you," in his ear.

"Ahem," came the sound from the dark porch.

"Who's there?" asked Thomas.

"It's just me," replied Eli.

"What are you doing sitting out here in the dark by yourself?" Thomas asked him, a little sterner than he had intended to after being caught by Eli.

"Oh, just takin' in the sights," Eli said, laughing, "and what a sight I seed," he added, getting up and hobbling to the porch rail.

"What's all the ruckus out here?" asked Marta as she stepped through the doorway onto the porch. "Oh, you're home. Where you two been? It's getting late. I had to put little Jeremy down. Plumb tuckered out that boy was."

"I'm sorry, Marta," said Jenny. "It's my fault we're late."

"No, it's my fault," said Thomas.

"Looks to me like it's both your fault—from the looks of both of you," Eli said, trying to keep from laughing.

"Eli, behave yourself," scolded Marta, smiling to herself.

"Is Jacob in bed?" asked Thomas.

"No, he's inside," said Marta.

"Would you ask him to come out here for a minute?" Thomas asked her.

Marta opened the door and hollered for Jacob to come outside. "What's all the yelling about?" asked Jacob as he came through the doorway.

"Thomas wants to tell us something," replied Marta.

"Is that so? And I supposed it couldn't wait 'til morning" said Jacob, eyeing Thomas suspiciously.

Thomas reached over and took Jenny's hand. Standing side by side with her, looking up at the gathering on the porch.

"Well, out with it," snapped Jacob. "I ain't getting any younger standing out here." Thomas smiled, and at the same time, he and Jenny said, "We're getting married."

"Damn, it's about time," Eli said.

"Praise the Lord," replied Marta.

"Is that what this fuss was all about?" asked Jacob with a smile on his face. Everyone went into the house and congratulated the young couple, celebrating with a glass of wine. Afterward, Thomas took Jenny and Jeremy home. They set a date for that fall, after Jeremy's fifth birthday so he could have his day and they could have theirs.

Roseanne couldn't wait to plan Celine and Brad's wedding. She had known Brad since he was a young boy and knew he would be good for Celine and for Lizzy. Roseanne and all the girls would help with the wedding preparations and would all take part in the ceremony. They set the date for late summer so the weather would be nice. Emeline would be her matron of honor, Lizzy would be her flower girl, and all nine of Roseanne's girls would be bridesmaids. Roseanne would do the honor of giving Celine away. It would be an open affair for the whole community, as they all knew Celine and loved her.

One day, while Celine was working her shift, an old prospector came into the saloon for a drink. As he entered the saloon, the old man stumbled and almost fell. Celine, being the nearest to him, reached over and caught him by the arm, preventing him from falling. She asked the old man if he was all right. He said he needed a drink, so Cline motioned for Charlie to bring him one and helped the old man to a chair. Sitting down, the old man looked up at Celine to thank her for her kindness. This was followed by a coughing spell. Spit from the old man's mouth hit Celine on her face, with some landing on her lips. Charlie, coming over with the man's drink, saw what had happened. After handing Celine the towel he always carried in case of a spilt drink, Celine wiped her face. Looking down at her dress she saw sputum on her bodice and noticed it was tinged with blood.

Celine again asked the old man if he was all right or if maybe he should see the doctor who was right up the street. The old man waved her off with his hand, picked up his drink, and swallowed it in one gulp. He then took out his handkerchief to wipe his mouth. That's when Celine saw it was covered in blood. Before she could say anything to the man, he got up, threw down a coin, and left the saloon.

"Well," said Charlie, "what do you suppose that's all about? He shook his head and went back behind the bar after picking up the glass and wiping off the table.

Celine stood there watching the old man's retreating back and said to no one in particular, "I don't know, but I hope he's all right."

One week later, Sheriff Taylor came riding into town leading a mule with a body slung over it. The body was covered with a blanket. Celeste, looking out from over her balcony, saw the body and called to the other girls to come see. They all ran out onto the balcony, including Celine, who was curious to get a look and wondered who it was under the blanket. The sheriff stopped his horse in front of Doc Jones' office, slid off the mule and pulled it by the reins, and tied it to the hitching post. Leaving the body on the mule, he went inside. A few minutes later, he came out with the doc.

Doc Jones went over, lifted the blanket off the dead man's head, and then covered him again. Celine, watching the transaction, sucked in her breath.

"That's the old man that was in here not too long ago," she told the girls. "I knew he was sick. I should have sent for the Doc. Then maybe he would still be alive," Celine said.

"You don't know that," said Willy, the oldest of the women. "Can't blame yourself for everything that happens to people."

"That's true," they all agreed. They all headed back to their rooms, some to get ready for work and some just going to bed.

When Brad came to call on Celine, she asked him about the dead prospector, about what had happened to him. Brad told her that early that morning Gill Morgan had ridden in from the range and spotted the mule. When he got closer, he saw the mule was standing next to a man lying on the ground. When he dismounted to check on the man, he saw he was dead and had been for a while. Celine told him about the old man being in the saloon and felt that he was sick, but she hadn't sent for the doctor.

Brad took hold of Celine and brought her close to him. He kissed her forehead and told her, "You can't take care of everybody that walks through those saloon doors, and pretty soon, you'll have your hands full just taking care of me."

Lifting her chin up, he kissed her soundly and passionately on her mouth, making her forget all about the old man.

A week later, Doc was at the saloon, deep in conversation with Roseanne and Charlie. He was asking for all the names of the people who had come into contact with the man Gill Morgan had found out on the range. When Roseanne asked Doc why, he said he needed them, as he just got the results back from the samples belonging to the old man. He had sent to Sacramento, to the big hospital there.

"It's just as I feared. It's a new disease just discovered. It affects the lungs, kidneys, and spine. I have been reading about it in a medical book I had sent to me from that same hospital in Sacramento," Doc said.

Doc went on to explain to the two how he had sent a sample of the man's tissue to the hospital in Sacramento. Upon their examination, they sent a telegram to me this morning confirming what he suspected: something called tuberculosis. "It affects the lungs, so eventually, you can't breathe."

"How do you catch it?" asked Charlie.

"Close contact with the infected party or fluids from them," replied Doc, "so that's why I need the names of anybody that was close to him."

"We had just opened up when he came in, Doc. It was just me, Celine, and Willy," Charlie replied.

"Well were any of you near him?" Doc asked.

"I brought him a drink. Celine helped him to a chair, but Willy was on the other end of the saloon by the back door, putting the cat out."

"How close was Celine to the man?" Doc asked anxiously.

"I don't recollect, but I think close. As I recall, I handed her my towel when the man coughed on her."

"What?" Doc said, getting excited.

Just about that time, the girls started coming down to work. The three at the bar watched, transfixed on the girls, as, one by one, as one they made their way downstairs. When the fourth came down, Roseanne asked her where Celine was. Celeste spoke up and said that Celine wasn't feeling well this morning. "She said to tell you she thought she was coming down with something."

Growing frantic, Roseanne started for the stairs. Doc stopped her and said, "No, Roseanne. Better let me go. That way, I can examine her to be sure."

As Doc made his way upstairs, his heart started beating at a fast rate. As he recalled the symptoms of the disease and hoped Celine didn't have any of them. When he reached Celine's room, Doc knocked on the door and entered the room. It was dark, and he could hear the girl's breathing. It didn't sound to him as if it was labored. Going over to the window, he drew back the curtains and opened the window to let in some fresh air.

Going over to the bed, Doc pulled out his handkerchief and tied it around his nose and mouth in case Celine started to cough.

Feeling her forehead, he determined she had a slight fever. When he removed his hand, Celine stirred. Looking up, she asked, "Doc, is that you?"

"Yes," he replied, and he explained what was going on.

"That can't be. It must be a mistake," she said when he was through.

"To be sure. Do you mind if I take a blood sample from you this morning?" Doc asked her if she felt achy or if she had lost any weight, whether she had coughed up any blood. She answered no to coughing any blood but said she had lost a little weight.

When Doc got downstairs, the look on his face told everyone it looked bad for Celine. He told them he was going to take a blood sample and compare it to the sample of blood he still had in the icebox at the office from the old man. If it was a match, he would go from there. When he returned to Celine's room with the supplies he needed, the girls were gathered outside her door. He told them not to enter that room until he said it was all right and to keep Lizzy away from her mother for now.

After getting a sample of her blood from her finger, Doc put it between two sterilized pieces of glass and placed it under his microscope in his office, alongside the old man's sample. He studied it for an hour, over and over, and found it was a match. Sick to his stomach, Doc brought out the bottle of whiskey he kept in his drawer, poured a glass, and drank it, then poured another and sipped it slowly, unwilling to break the news to everyone.

Unable to wait any longer, Roseanne walked up the street to Doc's office. When she opened the door, she knew without asking by the look on the doc's face.

"No, no, no. Tell me, Doc. It can't be. Not now, when she has finally found love again and is getting on with her life."

"I'm sorry, Rosie. If I could change the results, I would."

Spying the bottle of whiskey Doc had been drinking, Roseanne reached for his glass and poured herself a glassful. She sat down and began drinking it.

"I just don't know how to tell her that within a year or less, she will probably die from this awful thing. She is so young, not even twenty-two yet, and what will Lizzy do without her?" Doc said as an afterthought.

"You are sure there is no cure for it?" asked Roseanne, finishing her drink.

"No known cure. It's rather new, and we don't know much about it, but there's always hope," Doc replied.

"And prayer," Roseanne responded. "If anything will make us go to church, this is it."

Roseanne rose and patted Doc on the shoulder. "I'll tell her if you like, Doc," Roseanne said as she headed for the door.

"No, she will probably have questions you can't answer, Rosie. Best I tell her,"

"Okay, doc, but just when are you going to tell her so I can be nearby?"

"Just as soon as I finish this drink I'm pouring."

Doc slowly went up the stairs to Celine's room and knocked on the door. Celine said, "Come in." Doc opened the door and entered the room, carrying his bag, and was surprised to see Celine dressed and sitting on her bed.

"You're up," he said. "How are you feeling?"

"Much better, thank you. I must have caught a cold when we went to the beach the other day," she answered him.

"I'm afraid it's a little more serious than that, my dear."

Looking a little startled, Celine, trying to joke, said, "Now, don't go telling me I have what that old man had."

"I wish I didn't have to tell you that—" Doc began, but Celine interrupted him.

"Then don't tell me."

"You have to know what you're in store for, to know what you can and can't do," Doc said.

"Just tell me there's a cure for it, Doc, that it will go away."

"I can't tell you that, either. I can tell you that if you are careful and don't catch a cold, maybe do some breathing exercises and take care of yourself, you may buy yourself more time," he said, trying to sound positive for her.

"How much time are we talking about?" she asked him.

"Maybe up to a year or more—if they find medicine to help you. I understand they are working on something, but how long it takes them is the question," Doc replied.

"I see," she said. "And if they don't?"

"Let's not get ahead of ourselves, Celine. Let's do one day at a time. In the meantime, I will telegraph the big clinic in New York for more information and keep you posted. But for now, I would like to listen to your chest and heart."

After, Doc told her that her heart was very strong, and that was a good thing, as it meant she was in good health otherwise.

"I want to find out all I can about this disease and what you can take to make it easier on you. I will keep you informed. In the meantime, try to always cover your mouth if you cough. Don't share food or drink with anybody. We don't want to spread this around. I am very sorry this happened, Celine, but together, we will help you get through this," Doc said as he got up to go.

"Thanks, Doc. Please don't say anything to Brad or Lizzy about this. I will tell them," Celine said.

Celine went downstairs to the bar, where Roseanne and Charlie were in deep conversation. She asked Charlie to pour her a drink. Looking from Celine to Roseanne, Roseanne nodded her head, and Charlie poured the drink and handed it to Celine. Charlie then went to the other end of the bar and pretended to wipe down the top. Roseanne told Celine to sit at a table, and she joined her.

"I'm so sorry, my dear. You know I'm here for you, as is everyone else. So what can I do to help?"

"I don't know, Rosie. I'm numb. I guess it hasn't really hit me yet. I have to talk to Brad and to Lizzy and somehow convince them that everything is going to be all right," Celine replied. Leaving her drink untouched, Celine got up, turned to Roseanne, and said, "Thank you so much, Rosie, for being here for me."

Roseanne got up and took Celine in her arms and hugged her tightly for a minute, then whispered, "I love you. You're like the daughter I never had."

Celine, looking up through tears in her eyes, saw the tears running down Roseanne's cheeks. She squeezed the older woman's hand, turned, and started for the stairs. As she passed by Charlie, she saw the moisture gather in his eyes, so Celine gave him a smile as best she could. Roseanne stood and watched her climb the stairs with her shoulders slumped in defeat. She reached down, took the drink from the table, and gulped it down. When Celine reached the top of the stairs, the girls were all standing in the hallway. One by one, they hugged Celine, silently crying to themselves. Celine hugged them back; she thought of them all as her sisters. *Oh, I forgot,* Celine thought to herself. *I have to see Emeline and talk to her as well.*

She found Lizzy playing in Willy's room and asked the little girl what she was doing. Lizzy looked up at her mother and said, "Waiting for you, Momma. Why are you crying?"

"Because I have the most beautiful little girl in the whole wide world," Celine replied.

"But that should make you happy," Lizzy said as she grinned back at her mother, making her mother smile back at her. Lizzie had lost her front tooth a week ago, and it had left a big gap. Sitting down beside her daughter on the floor, she reached over, picked her up, and sat the little girl on her lap, making sure to breathe and talk away from her daughter's face.

Brushing the riot of curly hair away from Lizzie's face, Celine told her, "I am happy. You make me happy, and I love you so much. Never forget that."

Laughing, Lizzy replied, "I can't forget. You tell me every day, Momma,"

"I know, but if I'm not around to tell you, I just want you to remember, okay?" Reaching down, she picked up a toy to play with and nodded her head yes.

That evening, Celine had dinner with Brad. She asked him if he had heard. He said he had heard something but needed her to tell him exactly what was going on. Putting her fork down, Celine told Brad what the doctor had told her, ending by saying that doc would keep her informed. Looking into his eyes, Celine said, "If you want to call off the wedding, I will understand." She watched as the emotions played across his face.

"Celine," Brad said sharply, "do you think so little of me that I would do something like that to you? I am not that Thomas fella. You should know that by now."

Letting her breath out, she softly said, "I do know that. I also know that you are a gentleman and a man of your word and would not go back on it, no matter what."

Starting to get angry, Brad snapped, "Do you think that is what I'm doing, keeping my word? I love you, Celine, no matter what. It boils down to just that: I love you and want to be with you for as long as I can. No matter if it's just a day or a lifetime, I want to have that time with you."

"I'm not sure how long of a future I have. I'd like to think of some things I have to do before I"—Celine cut off her own words—"I would like to postpone the wedding." Seeing the hurt look on Brad's face, she hurried on to say, "Just for a little while. Please say you understand."

Looking into her eyes, he saw the pleading in them and gave into her, but he said, "We won't wait too long Celine, agreed?"

The next day, Celine went to visit Emeline out back, as it was Sunday and her shop was closed. She knocked on the door, and when Emeline opened the door, Celine saw she had been crying. Before she could ask what was the matter, Emeline grabbed her, held her close to her, and started to cry again. Celine pulled her away and said, "Who told you?"

"No one. They all prayed for you in church this morning. Why didn't you tell me?" Emeline said in a hurt tone.

"I tried to tell you several times but didn't know how. I didn't know the words to tell you. You're my sister, and I didn't want to say things that might upset you," replied Celine. "Please forgive me."

"Of course I forgive you. I can't stay mad at you. I love you," responded Emeline, pulling Celine into the room. Jesse had put up curtains to partition off part of the large room to make a private bedroom for them and the three children they now had.

"What's you going to do now Celine? Who's going to watch over Lizzy when it's all done with?"

"I don't know. Brad wants to marry right away and adopt Lizzy, but I don't know if I can do it to him. He's still young and has his whole life ahead of him. Roseanne wants to take her, but she's not young anymore. It wouldn't be fair to her either. I'm of a mind to write another letter to Thomas telling him about my situation."

Before Celine could finish, Emeline said loudly, "What are you, out of your mind? After what he did to you, how could you even think of him?"

The truth be known, Celine had never stopped thinking of Thomas. Something kept pulling the memories up to the surface of her mind, and she kept burying them back—but never too deeply.

After a while, things went back to normal—or as normal as could be. Celine felt good except for being tired a lot more. She developed a slight cough and kept a regular appointment with the doc, once a month, unless something more severe came along. And she kept postponing the wedding.

Celine worked only a few hours a day now, as she would become extremely tired as the afternoon approached. She could feel her strength slipping away, and her cough had gotten worse. Doc kept a close eye on her. He could see she was losing weight and how tired she was, despite putting up a good front. He had contacted most all the major hospitals he could think of, and they all said the same: no cure at this time.

One day, when Celine didn't come down, Roseanne went to check on her. When she entered her room, she found her sitting at the window, looking out. Celine heard her enter and wiped away the tears that were forming in her eyes and running down her cheeks.

"What are you doing at the window?" Roseanne asked her.

"Just thinking," Celine answered her.

"About what?" Roseanne said.

"Things I need to take care of," Celine said matter-of-factly, and she turned and gave Roseanne a faint smile.

It broke Roseanne's heart to see Celine so downhearted and knowing she could do nothing about it. She went over and gave Celine a big hug and said, "What can I do to help you? Is there anyone I can contact for you? Anything at all, just tell me, and if it's within my power, I will do it."

Looking at the older woman, Celine said, "Yes, there is something you can do, but you won't like it, Rosie."

"Just tell me what it is and let me decide for myself," responded Roseanne.

Thinking on it for a few minutes, Celine said, "I would like you to send a telegram to Thomas telling him of my situation."

Stunned, Roseanne asked, "Why, after all this time and after all he did, why would you do this?"

"Because he is Lizzy's father and has a right to know that I am giving her to another man to raise. If he does not respond, my conscience will be clear," Celine answered her. Then she thought to herself, *And because I need to see him again.*

"What about Brad? He loves that little girl like she was his own, and he loves you—you know this," said Roseanne.

"I know Rosie, and I am grateful for all Brad has done for Lizzy and for me, but if the shoe were on the other foot, Brad would want to know," Celine replied.

Roseanne could not argue with that logic. She didn't like it, but it wasn't her choice; it was Celine's. Celine saw the raw emotions playing across Roseanne's face and said in a low voice, "Besides, he may not even come. In that case, I will marry Brad and make arrangements for Brad to adopt Lizzy."

When Roseanne saw the toll this was taking on Celine, she sighed and said, "I will send the telegram in the morning. Now, please, get into bed and rest. I will come up later and bring you and Lizzy some food for dinner." Then she reached over and hugged Celine and said, "Don't worry. Everything will be all right," and she left the room, leaving Celine to wonder if she was doing the right thing for her daughter or if she was being selfish and doing it for herself.

The next morning, Roseanne was up and at the telegraph office when it opened. She sent off a telegram to Thomas, as she had promised Celine. At first, she was going to ignore her promise and forget about sending it, but after she had left Celine and went downstairs for a drink, she told Charlie about their conversation and what she planned to do. Charlie reminded her that it was not her choice but Celine's and that Roseanne would regret not doing it.

Marta was just leaving to go see her grandchildren in their cabin a few doors down from hers when a young man rode into the yard and stopped in front of Marta, asking if a Thomas Sanduvale lived there, and if so, was he at home?

Marta answered, "Yes, he lives here, and no, he isn't at home. He is in the field and will be home a little later. Can I do something for you?"

"Yes, I have a telegram from San Francisco marked urgent for him."

Upon hearing this, Marta took a step back as her knees almost buckled out from under her. Catching herself, she responded, "I can take it and give it to him when he gets home."

"That would be great," he replied, and then he handed the telegram to Marta, turned his horse around, and galloped away. Marta turned around and headed back to her cabin.

When Marta got to her cabin, she opened the door and went

inside, shutting the door behind her. With trembling fingers, she carefully opened the telegram. It was not from Celine, as she had feared. It was from someone named Roseanne Burke. It read,

> Celine is ill. Daughter needs you to come now. Address Rosie's Saloon, Market Street, San Francisco. Signed, Roseanne Burke.

Marta sat down, still holding the telegram. She sat for some time, trying to decide what to do. If she gave the telegram to Thomas, it would end their relationship for good. But if she didn't and something awful happened to Celine and their child, she knew for certain if he ever found out, he would never forgive her. Either way, he would never forgive her for her part in the whole sordid mess. In the end, Marta decided to do the right thing and give Thomas the telegram.

All day Marta walked around on pins and needles, every time a door would open or close, Marta would jump, thinking it was Thomas. When Jacob came in from the barn and went to the kitchen, Marta, doing the breakfast dishes, hearing the door, dropped a cup, breaking it to pieces. Jacob, seeing the expression on her face and the broken cup on the floor, knew something was wrong. He asked her what was the matter.

At first, Marta was going to tell Jacob that nothing was wrong, but seeing the concern on his face was her undoing, and she broke down and started to cry. Jacob rushed around and helped Marta to a chair, then said to her, "It's just a cup. Nothing to get so upset over."

Looking up at Jacob exasperated, Marta replied, "It's not the cup, you old fool," and then she reached into her apron pocket and pulled out the telegram, handed it to him, and resumed crying.

Bewildered, Jacob took the telegram and read it. When he finished reading it, he handed it back to Marta, saying, "What you gonna do now, girl?"

"I'm going to give it to Thomas when he gets home this evening and hope and pray he don't throw me and Eli out on our ear."

"Hold on, girl. When Thomas hears why you done what you done, I'm sure he'll understand."

"I'm not so sure, Jacob. That was the love of his life, and I kept it a secret for five years. I just hope he can forgive me."

That evening, when Thomas finally did arrive home, he could sense something was wrong. Marta was alone, standing in front of the stove, and when she turned to face him, he could see her eyes were swollen from crying. Thomas asked, "What's wrong? Where's Jacob? Did something happen to him?" Jacob was always in the kitchen with Marta this time of the night, waiting to eat. Thomas started toward her, but she held up her hand, stopping him.

Perplexed, Thomas stopped. Marta held up an envelope and motioned for him to take it. When he did, Marta turned back toward the stove. Thomas asked, "What's this?" When she didn't reply, he took the telegram from the envelope and read it, then reread it. Marta felt his big hand on her shoulder as he turned her to face him. In a calm voice, he asked her to please explain this cruel joke to him. When she didn't look up at him, he said in a louder tone with a hint of warning in it, "Marta, who is this woman, and what is she talking about? And how does she know Celine's name?"

Marta reluctantly reached into her other pocket and withdrew a small packet of letters, tied together with a piece of twine. Slumping down into a chair and without looking at Thomas, she held the letters out for him to take. Taking the letters from Marta, Thomas asked, "What is this? I think you had better start explaining to me what is going on here, starting with the telegram and these letters."

In a very low voice, Marta asked Thomas to please sit down and she would explain everything to him, starting at the beginning. Thomas sighed heavily and sat down, growing impatient with this woman. Marta told Thomas everything, starting with being bought as a slave along with Eli by his father, on Elizabeth's request. She told him how Elizabeth had died and how the baby had been saved. At that piece of news, Thomas's face turned white. She told him how his father had changed after that, how he had become detached from everything and everybody around him.

Marta told him how his father used to be kind to the people who worked for him, but after that terrible thing happened, he hardly acknowledged them, including Marta, of whom he had been very fond.

Thomas interrupted Marta, "What has that got to do with this woman and these letters?"

"Read the letters, Thomas. They well explain most of it, and then I will fill in the blank parts so you will understand."

Looking at the letters in his shaking hand, Thomas opened the first one and read it. As he read, Marta could see his jaw clench and unclench. When he finished the first one, he looked up at Marta with blazing eyes. Marta looked away, and Thomas began reading the rest of the letters Celine had written to him but that he had never received. When he finished, Thomas's demeanor changed. He was sad and angry at the same time. Thomas looked over at Marta and saw the tears streaming down her face.

"Why, Marta? Why would you do such a thing to me?"

Stammering, Marta said, "I am so sorry, Tommy. I would never hurt you. If I could have prevented it, I would have."

She reached up to touch his face, but he slapped her hand away.

Jacob, who had been standing outside the kitchen, heard the slap and rushed into the room.

"Now, just a minute, young man," Jacob said, looking from Thomas to Marta. "There'll be no hitting while I'm here."

Thomas, taken by surprise, with a hurt sound in his voice, said, "You too, Jacob. Are you in on this terrible deception? You, whom I held in higher esteem than my father, how could you, how could either one of you do this to me?"

"You just wait a minute, boy. You don't know the whole story."

"Then why don't you enlighten me," Thomas said with a look that made his eyes look like deep black pools, void of all expression except hatred and loathing directed at the two standing in front of him, making them back up a bit.

"Thomas, let me explain," Marta said, "so you will understand why I did what I did."

"Go ahead, but whatever you say won't make any difference to how I feel right now about the two of you."

Feeling that she had lost him already, Marta sat down with Jacob standing protectively behind her. Marta, not knowing where to begin, started with the loss of Phillip and Elizabeth's child, glancing at Thomas under her eyelashes and seeing the look of confusion on his face. She continued to explain how that child died one week after they buried its mother.

"You mean my mother," Thomas spoke up.

Marta continued, "No, Thomas. Elizabeth was not your mother. What I didn't tell you about what happened after Elizabeth was killed was what happened to the baby we delivered. It was a very sickly baby, and within the week, it too passed away, and we buried it on the hill between Elizabeth and Sam in an unmarked grave so's no one would ever find out."

"Then who is my mother?" Thomas asked her.

Without looking up at him, Marta said, "Let me finish my story, and you will understand everything. When Elizabeth got with child, she was deathly sick and could not be a wife to your father, so he took me to his bed to satisfy his needs, with the approval of his wife, unbeknownst to him. In the months I slept with him, I became pregnant. Elizabeth and I kept it a secret, as Phillip would have demanded I get rid of the child. With Elizabeth and the baby gone, Phillip became lonely and came to my cabin to fetch me once again to his bed."

Sighing, Marta went on in a barely audible whisper, "When he opened the door, He found me giving birth to you. Needless to say, he was furious and yelled that I deceived him into having a bastard slave baby and said I was to get out and take you with me. Then you came out into the world—a beautiful, healthy boy, that didn't show he was from a black slave. He looked you over and told the midwife, who was helping me, to clean us both up and move us into the big house as soon as possible, where you would be raised as the baby that died and was raised by me, as your servant.

"The midwife was told to keep quiet or she would be sent away while her family stayed behind. I was told that if I ever told a soul, I also would be sent away while you and Eli would stay behind, as he had bought Eli therefore owned him. So I never told a soul except for Jacob, who I swore to silence."

Looking up at Thomas, Marta could see the turmoil going through her son's features. He looked from Jacob to Marta, trying to comprehend what he had just heard. Finally, Thomas said in a tired voice, "It's all starting to make sense, now that I think about it—the way you mothered me and treated me the same as you did Eli. I should have guessed just from those signs."

"Don't talk that way. There was no way you could have known. No, I'm to blame. I should have told you years ago, and maybe all this could have been prevented," Marta responded.

"What I want to know is how this all came about with Celine," Thomas said.

"When your father overheard your conversation with Jacob and me in the kitchen that night, he formed a plan to keep you apart so you wouldn't get involved with her, as he knew of her and knew she was part black and couldn't stand the thought of you marrying and having children. Your father was a vain man and couldn't take the chance of being exposed as having fathered a black child."

"But," Thomas said, "Celine told me about her mother and father. It didn't matter to me. I loved her. I need to know how she ended up in San Francisco," he said to Marta.

She did not wish to relive it, but knew she had to tell him, so Marta related everything she had done. She described how his father wanted Celine dead. "I could not do what he asked of me, so I made a plan of my own and made arrangements for the passage of Celine, your daughter, and a young girl named Emeline to go to

San Francisco, far enough away but not far enough that she couldn't come back, as I gave her money and access to a bank account."

"Then why didn't she come home?" Thomas asked.

"I can't answer that," Marta replied. Continuing with her account, Marta said, "I drugged you and Celine so I could carry out my plan to save her life. After Celine was safely on her way to the ship, I had you taken home and placed into your bed, where I kept you drugged for two days while I had the men make caskets and bury them so your father would believe I did want he told me to do. I am so sorry, my son. I did what I thought I had to do to protect my family and Celine."

Brushing her apology aside, Thomas sat down. He felt lightheaded and thought his legs were going to give out from under him. It was a lot to process. Marta started to ask him if he were all right, but Jacob put his hands on her shoulder and squeezed it to silence her. Looking around and up at Jacob, he mouthed the words, *Not now.*

A few minutes later, Thomas got up and announced, "I am going to my room. I have a lot to think about and some decisions to make. Please do not bother me." He turned and left the room, going upstairs. Marta, with tears in her eyes, turned to Jacob for comfort.

When Thomas reached his room, he went inside and shut the door. Going over to the bed, he sat down and started to read Celine's letters again. He read each word to understand why she didn't try to come home. She just kept asking why he had cast her and their daughter aside after all she thought they meant to each other and the promise he broke to keep them safe. Thinking of all Marta had told him, Thomas berated himself for not seeing what was going on around him at the plantation. He was so caught up in his love for Celine, he thought of nothing else.

Thomas went back downstairs and into the kitchen, where the two older people were still sitting at the table. He watched as Jacob tenderly comforted Marta. He could see the love they had with each other—another thing he had missed by being so caught up in his own life. Hearing Thomas enter the kitchen, Marta turned to look up at him with tears streaming down her cheeks. Looking down at Marta, at how frail and old she had become, he could see she was holding her breath, afraid to move.

Thomas went around the table and drew her up into his arms. Marta sank against his chest and wept her heart out. She knew he wasn't mad, just heartbroken. When Marta quit crying, she pushed away from him and looked up into his eyes.

"I'm sorry, my son. I didn't know how else to save them. I did what I thought I had to do. I wanted to tell you the truth so many times, but when you were a slave as long as I was, you do what you're told and don't ask no questions."

"But I gave you your freedom a long time ago," Thomas responded to her.

"Yes, you did, but not from your father," she said.

"Why didn't you tell me when he passed away?" he asked her.

"Because I thought to much time had passed by and you seemed to have gotten over Celine and had moved on with your life with Jenny." At the mention of Jenny's name, Thomas groaned and said, "Oh, my God. Jenny. How am I going to tell her?"

Jacob spoke up. "The question is, what's you going to do now with the whole situation?"

"First thing I am going to do," Thomas said to no one in particular, "is to make arrangements to get to San Francisco as quickly as possible. Then I am going to see Jenny and explain everything to her and hope to God she understands." Kissing Marta on the forehead, Thomas said, "Everything is going to be all right—you'll see—just as soon as I can get to Celine and my daughter." He turned and left, saying, "I'm going into town now to make arrangements. I will be back late, so I will talk to you in the morning."

Thomas left the house and on his way to the stables. He saw Eli sitting out on his front porch.

"Nice evening, huh, Tommy," Eli said.

"Guess so," replied Thomas.

"Where are you off to this late in the evening? Are you going to see Jenny?" Eli asked with a grin on his face.

"No," Thomas answered grimly, "into town. I have some business to attend to."

"This late?" replied Eli, curious.

"Marta will explain everything to you," Thomas said. He walked over to the stables, saddled his horse, and rode away, leaving Eli wondering what was going on.

The next morning, he told Marta and Jacob he had made arrangements to go to San Francisco by train, as the man at the docks said it was the fastest way to get there. Jacob asked Thomas why he was going to San Francisco. Marta said, "I'll explain after Eli gets here so I don't have to repeat myself." Jacob shrugged his shoulders, poured a cup of coffee, then sat down and told Thomas to have a good trip.

Thomas went upstairs and packed his bags. He put them in the buggy the boy had brought around to the house. Thomas went back in, took hold of Marta, and kissed the top of her head, then hugged her tightly to reassure her that everything was all right between them. He told Jacob goodbye and told them he didn't know when he would be back but would see them when he returned.

Marta said, "Please return to us with your family, and be safe." Thomas replied he would and left the house, climbed onto the buggy, and rode out just as Eli was coming across to the big house. He stopped and watched as Thomas disappeared out of sight, then continued on into the house to find out what was going on.

As Thomas traveled along, he thought about how to tell Jenny about Celine. He loved Jenny with all his heart, but he had also loved Celine deeply. Jenny had helped him renew his life, as she helped him through the really bad times, when he thought he had lost Celine and his daughter. And he had helped Jenny when she lost her husband, Jeremy. Jenny and Thomas had a deep-seated-love for each other, but he still loved Celine and always would. She was part of his soul as well, and he would always have a place in his heart for her. He knew this and hoped he could make Jenny understand.

A few hours later, he arrived at the Pierces' place. Jason was out by the barn, instructing some of his men on the day's work agenda, when he saw Thomas riding in. He finished and walked over to where Thomas had stopped the buggy.

"Pretty early to be calling on Jenny," he said with a grin. Then, looking at the back of the buggy, Jason saw the luggage. He looked back at Thomas and saw the sad look in his friend's eyes. "What's going on?" he asked. "Taking a trip somewhere?"

"I have to talk to Jenny. Is she inside?" Thomas asked.

"No, she and Jeremy are over at the chicken coop, gathering eggs," Jason told him.

"What's happened, Tommy? Something wrong?" Jason asked.

"Yes and no," Thomas replied. He then described the events that had unfolded the night before. Jason whistled through his teeth, shaking his head in disbelief. He said, "Oh, Tommy, that's a bad situation to be in. I am sorry."

About that time Jenny and Jeremy's laughter drifted over to the two men as Jenny and her son came around the corner.

When Jenny saw Thomas, her eyes lit up and her smile was as bright as the sunrise. Looking at her, Thomas caught his breath and thought she was so beautiful even this early in the morning. The sunlight was dancing off her hair, turning it to spun gold, and her eyes were as blue as the clear blue sky. Jeremy hurried over to the two men, and in his excitement at seeing Thomas, he almost spilled the basket of eggs he was carrying.

"Good morning," he said to Thomas in his cheery little voice with a smile like his mother's, holding up his basket to show the men the eggs.

"Good morning, you two. You're up early," Thomas replied.

Jason walked over to Jeremy and said he would help him take the basket of eggs into the house, and when he saw Jeremy was going to protest, he added, "Then we will go see the newborn kittens if you like." Jeremy squealed in delight and told Thomas he would see him later. Thomas watched as Jeremy skipped along with Jason and laughed as he stumbled in his excitement, as Jason grabbed the back of the boy's shirt to keep him from falling. Thomas climbed down from the buggy and over to Jenny. Taking her in his arms, he kissed her deeply, wanting it to last forever, but finally, he pulled away from her.

Jenny, sensing something different in him, looked up into his eyes and saw the sadness there. She asked, "Tommy, what is it? What's wrong?" Thomas told her to walk with him while he explained everything. An hour later, they were sitting under a tree by a pond, Jenny holding her stomach as she felt sick upon hearing about Celine. She told Thomas how sorry she was to hear of her being sick and everything that had happened, but why did he have to go to San Francisco? Couldn't he just send for Celine and his daughter?

Jenny remembered how much Thomas loved Celine and how hard it was for him to accept her and his daughter's death. She was afraid to let him go, afraid he would not come back to her. But she did not tell Thomas all this. Instead, she simply said, "Of course you must go and take care of Celine and your daughter. The sooner you go, the sooner you will come home to me," and all the while praying this would prove true.

Thomas reached over and pulled her close to him, kissing her long and hard, whispering in her ear, "I knew you would understand. I love you. You know that." They walked back to the buggy. Thomas kissed her again and climbed in, settling himself on the seat. He told Jenny to tell Jason and Jeremy he would see them when he returned, then said, "I love you," and rode away, not looking back in fear that he wouldn't go.

Jenny stood and watched him leave, tears running down her cheeks. Jason walked quietly up behind her, wrapped his arms around his sister, gave her a reassuring hug and said, "He'll be back."

"I hope so," Jenny replied.

Thomas made it to the train station in plenty of time to board the horse and buggy for Jacob and Moses to come get them and take them home. As the conductor loaded his bags, Thomas also boarded the train, and when all the passengers were aboard, the conductor signaled the engineer to start up the train, and they were on their way.

Thomas had never been on a train before, and what should have been a great adventure for him was not, as he could not get Celine out of his mind. He kept wondering how sick she was and prayed it was not bad. All in all, it was a long slow trip but faster than if he had taken it to the ocean. The train arrived in San Francisco on the eve of the third day, tired and covered in the soot that blew in on the passengers from the coal used to power the engine.

Thomas stepped off the train, picked up his luggage, and hired a Chinese man pulling a small carriage called a rickshaw to take him to his hotel. The man loaded his luggage onto the back of the rig and helped Thomas in. As soon as Thomas was settled, the man started to run, pulling the rig behind him. Thomas marveled at how fast the man could run, weaving in and out of heavy traffic. When they reached the hotel, Thomas looked up and saw what a magnificent building it was. He got out of the rickshaw while the man unloaded his luggage and set them on the ground. He flipped a coin to the man, who bowed to Thomas, turned, and picked up the rickshaw and was on his way. As Thomas watched, the man ran a couple of blocks, picked up another fare, and began running again.

Shaking his head at the man's stamina, he turned back to the hotel, where a man dressed in a uniform was carrying his bags into the hotel. After checking in, Thomas cleaned himself up, went down to the dining room, and ate some dinner. He asked the young lady waiting on him how to get to Rosie's Saloon. She gave him directions, saying, "Go down this street to the end, turn right, go two blocks, and turn left. You will be on Market Street. In the middle of the block is Rosie's. You can't miss it." Thomas thanked her, paid for his meal and made his way to Rosie's.

When he got to Market Street, he looked down it and could just make out in the lamplights the sheriff's office, a lawyer's office, a doctor's office, and a restaurant. Next to the restaurant was a hat shop. In the middle of the block, across the street, was a big white two-story building, lit up like a Christmas tree. Walking down the block, he stopped and stared at the place. It had a big sign painted bright red that read, "Rosie's Saloon." Just below the balconies were two large swinging doors that would swing open as men went in and out. He could hear the loud music and laughter coming from inside from where he was standing.

My God, Thomas thought, *what is Celine doing in a place like this? How is she making a living there?* He got a lump in his throat and a tightening in his chest from the pictures forming in his mind. Shaking his head to remove the images of Celine with other men, he cursed himself for even thinking that was her way of life. He knew better—he knew Celine—but that was five years ago, and he knew she would survive any way she could. Not knowing how to face Celine, Thomas chickened out and started to turn around and go back to the hotel.

In his haste to leave, he got turned around and instead of going back up the hill, he went down. When he got in front of the hat shop, he almost ran over a young black woman just closing up for the night. When she turned to face him, the look on her face was one of surprise and warmth.

"Mr. Sanduval," she exclaimed.

That the young woman knew his name took Thomas also by surprise, and he asked her, "Do I know you, young lady?"

"It's me, Emeline Jenkins—I mean Baxter. My father worked for you when I was young, back in New Orleans."

Upon closer examination, Thomas did recognize her and said, "Oh, yes, I do remember you as a very young girl, but now you're all grown up."

"Yes," Emeline responded, "I am married with three young babies. But what are you doing here?"

"The question is, what are you doing here?" Thomas asked.

"I was sent to help Celine and your daughter," Emeline responded a little bitterly.

"Oh, you're the one Marta sent with them," Thomas said very lowly.

"Yes," she said accusingly.

Thomas started to say he could explain when Jesse, with two little children tagging after him and him carrying one, came across the street and approached Thomas.

"Is everything all right?" he asked, looking at Emeline with affection but standing between her and Thomas.

"Yes, I guess so." Then Emeline said, "Jesse, this here's Thomas Sanduval, and this here's my husband, Jesse Baxter."

"Pleased to meet you, Jesse," Thomas said as he held out his hand to the man. Jesse turned to Emeline and, ignoring Thomas, said, "I has to go to work in a little while, and it's time to get the little ones feed and into bed, shall we?" He took hold of Emeline's arm and led her and the children across the street.

Emeline turned and gave Thomas a sad look. He watched as they disappeared down an alley to the back of the saloon. Thomas quickly crossed the street to the double doors of the saloon, pushed them open, and entered the place. The place was crowded with men drinking, playing cards, and picking up on the women that worked there. As he started toward the bar to speak to the bartender, a pretty young blonde strolled up to him and asked, "Buy me a drink, stranger?" looking at him with laughing blue eyes.

"Not tonight. I'm looking for Rosie," Thomas replied. The young girl looked disappointed but pointed to a table where a nice-looking woman sat.

"She's over there talking to Sheriff Taylor," she said as she turned her attention to a young cowhand just walking in.

Thomas thanked her and headed over to the table the girl had pointed to. As Roseanne looked up, she spotted the handsome man walking toward her. She instantly knew it was Thomas. Celine had described him to a tee. Roseanne rose gracefully from her chair, excusing herself from the sheriff, as she did not want the two men to meet just yet. She walked quickly over to Thomas, held out her hand, and said, "You must be Thomas Sanduval?"

Taking her hand in his and firmly shaking it, he said in his Louisiana drawl, "At your service, *maman*." Roseanne could see how Celine had fallen for this young man. Tall, handsome and with manners, he would have been the object of desire of any woman. Hell, if she were younger, she herself would have tried to have him.

"Please follow me, Mr. Sanduval," Roseanne said.

"All right, but please call me Tommy. That's what all my friends call me," he said.

"I'm not sure you're my friend," she replied. Once they reached her office, Roseanne ushered him inside and told him to please be seated. Thomas sat down and watched her as she went around her desk and sat down.

"Now, Thomas, what can I do for you?" Roseanne asked him.

Never taking his eyes from hers, Thomas replied, "I think you know. You sent me the telegram. I came to see Celine and my daughter and to take them home with me," he stated definitively.

"I am not sure she will want to see you after all she's been through," Roseanne countered.

"I'm not sure I follow you. Just what, exactly, has she been through," he asked apprehensively. Roseanne began to relate all that had happened to Celine since she had met the girl. She told him about the two scared girls with the baby to take care of and about the captain of the ship leaving them with nothing, all the while watching the emotions play across his face, even though he tried to hide them.

Without letting up, Roseanne went on to tell him about the accident and how hard it was on Celine. She spared no details on how bad the leg was broken and how long and hard her recuperation had been. She talked about everyone's help and support for Celine, including Sheriff Taylor's participation in it. Then, watching Thomas's face very close, Roseanne went on to tell him how much

273

Sheriff Taylor loved Celine and his daughter, Lizzy. Thomas looked perplexed. Roseanne continued. She said the sheriff had asked her to marry him and that Celine had accepted.

When she finished, Roseanne sat there, never taking her eyes off his face. Stunned and staring straight ahead, Thomas, trying to mask his feelings about what he had heard this woman saying to him, could not keep the pain of her words from his eyes, even though he kept his face blank. Roseanne, adept at reading what a person was feeling, saw the raw pain and knew this man loved Celine very much and knew this was going to cause quite a problem.

Finally, Thomas spoke in a soft low voice. "I would like to speak to Celine. If she tells me she loves this man, I will step aside. I will not interfere in her happiness."

Letting out a sigh, Roseanne said, "Do you still think Celine wants to see you?"

Without blinking an eye, Thomas said in a determined voice, "Whether she wants to or not, I must see her and tell her my side of the story. She can then decide for herself if she wants to stay and have a life here or come home with me and start our life together, as it should have been. If she doesn't see me, she will never have the chance to choose."

After studying him for a while, Roseanne said, "All right. I'll give you the chance to explain everything to her, but there's something I didn't tell you."

"Yes, what is it?"

"Before I tell you, you have to promise to still see Celine and let her know why you abandoned her and your daughter, in case you decide you no longer want her."

"Nothing you can say will keep me from seeing Celine and putting things right between us," Thomas replied, starting to lose patience.

Roseanne took out two glasses and a bottle of whiskey from the drawer in her desk. She poured one drink and handed it to Thomas, then poured one for herself. After they both took a sip of their drinks, Roseanne said, "I didn't tell you the part about Celine catching a disease a few months back. It's called tuberculosis, and she is gravely ill right now. The doc said there is no known cure and she may have only a few months left." Roseanne watched as the blood drained from Thomas's face. He sat staring at her as if willing her to take back what she had just told him.

After a minute, Roseanne asked him, "Are you all right?"

"No, goddamn it, I'm not all right," Thomas shouted, jumping up and knocking over the chair he was sitting in, making a loud noise. "I just found Celine, and now you're telling me I am going to lose her again."

Just then, the door flew open, and standing in the doorway was Charlie, holding his shotgun on Thomas. Charlie asked Roseanne if everything was all right.

"Yes, Charlie, everything is all right," Roseanne replied.

About that time, Sheriff Taylor came up behind Charlie and asked, "What's going on in here? You okay, Rosie?"

Letting out a huge sigh, Roseanne said, "Yes, I'm all right. Everything is fine. I'll explain everything to the both of you later, but now, I would like to introduce you to Mr. Thomas Sanduval."

The room became deathly quiet. You could have knocked over the two men with a feather. When Roseanne pointed to Thomas, Sheriff Taylor's face became distorted with emotions, and Charlie said, "What's he doing here?"

"Easy, Charlie. I sent for him."

"Why?" asked Sheriff Taylor.

"I am sorry, Brad, but Celine has a right to know, especially now, and a right to feel at ease concerning Lizzy. You understand, don't you, Brad?" Roseanne said pleadingly to him.

Brad turned, and without saying a word, he walked out and over to the bar. Over his shoulder, he shouted, "Charlie, get over here and get me a drink."

After Charlie left, Roseanne turned to Thomas and said, "I hope after all this you don't let me down and prove to them I wasn't wrong in sending for you. Celine and Emeline are like my own daughters, and Lizzy is like my granddaughter. I love them with all my heart." Tears started to run down her cheeks. Roseanne went on to say, "If you hurt Celine, I swear I will put a bullet in your heart myself."

"I believe you, Roseanne," Thomas said. Then he crossed the room, took the older woman in his arms, and held her while she cried. When she finished, she stepped away from him and said, "Thank you. I haven't been able to do that until now." Looking at Thomas, Roseanne could tell he was a decent and kind person, so what, she wondered, could have made him give them up? She guessed she would find out soon enough.

Roseanne sat very still in the dark corner of the room. That was just enough light coming from the streetlamp outside the window to see the faces of the two people. Roseanne was only there to make sure Celine would not get upset. She watched as Thomas gently took hold of Celine's frail little hand and brought it to his lips. Kissing it ever so lightly, he said in almost a whisper, "It's time to wake up, my darling. I'm here, longing to take you in my arms and never let you away from me again."

Celine opened her eyes and looked at Thomas a little confused. Then, with a smile on her face, she said, "You came, my love. Thank you."

"I would have been here sooner, but I didn't know where you were until I received the telegram your friend sent to me."

"How could you not know? I wrote you letters asking why you sent us away, why you stopped loving me, and why you didn't want your daughter." This said with bitterness. Burying his head on her shoulder, so Celine could not see the tears forming in his eyes. He lifted his head just enough for her to hear him, but he couldn't mask the sound of hurt and pain Roseanne heard in his voice.

"Please, "he said pleadingly, "let me explain what I myself just learned after receiving the telegram."

He started telling the whole story, not stopping until it all came out. He omitted the part about Jenny and him, as he didn't want to upset her, and when he finished telling her, she asked, "But why? Why would your father do this to us?"

"I guess because he was a sick man and very vain and did not want anyone to know that he fathered a son from a black slave. I am so sorry, Celine. I should have insisted on seeing your bodies. I should have had them dug up, but I was so overcome with grief, I could not bear to see you or our daughter in a pine box, to be buried under the cold, dark ground."

"I loved you so much, Celine. You have to believe me that a day didn't go by that I didn't suffer the loss of you and our baby."

Tears were flowing down his cheeks now. Celine said, "But I sent you letters letting you know I was very much alive," not wanting to believe him, not now.

"Marta kept the letters from me, as I have already told you."

"Why would she do such a thing?" Celine asked, not wanting to believe a person could do such a thing as she began to cry herself.

"Because my father wanted Marta to do away with you and the baby, and if she didn't, he would send her away from Eli and me, her two sons. And she would never see either one of us again. It was the only way to protect you and the baby from him—by pretending you both were dead and by not letting me know you were alive and well."

Roseanne silently listened to the conversion of the two people in front of her. Her eyes filled with tears at the cruel hand life had dealt them, tearing them apart, and now that they had been brought together, it would soon tear them apart again. She wondered how anyone could do something so cruel to other human beings. She could tell that these two surely were soulmates and belonged together, no matter how much time they had left.

As Thomas laid his head back down on her thin shoulder, Celine reached up and smoothed the hair from his forehead, thinking of the love they once shared, taking her back in time. It was as if nothing had kept them apart. She felt his love as strong as ever and knew she belonged to him and him only.

Thomas longed to take her in his arms and show the love he

still had for her, but knew he could not. He could feel the toll this meeting had taken on her. His only thought was to take her home and nurse her back to health, to be together, and she would be all right. Then, he would show her. Just then, the door swung open, and the light from the hallway outlined a small figure with curly hair. With her hands on her hips, Lizzy yelled, "Get away from my momma," in a small voice that said she meant it.

Startled at first, Thomas turned around. The little face he stared at was a combination of himself and Celine. He marveled at the confidence she projected as she stood her ground. Celine gently told her to come over to the bed. Cautiously and slowly, she stepped around Thomas and crawled up beside her mother, getting in between Thomas and her mother in a protective manner.

Celine said softly, "Dear, I want you to meet your father."

Thomas put his hand out and said, "It's nice to meet you."

Lizzy put her little hands over her eyes and shouted, "No, no, he isn't my father. Brad is my father. My real father is gone—you said so."

Her eyes filled with tears. Thomas gently took hold of the little girl and said in a calm, quiet voice, "Elizabeth."

"Don't call me that. My name is Lizzy," she said.

"All right, Lizzy it is. I am your father. I thought you and your mother were gone as well." At that, Lizzy blinked, and the tears rolled down her cheeks. Thomas gently wiped them away with his thumb, then continued, "But when I found out you weren't gone, I rushed here to be with both of you. I really am your father, and I would like to take you and your mother home to Louisiana, where I built a house for all of us to live in, if it's all right with you" and looking at Celine, he said, "and your mother." Lizzy looked at her mother then back at Thomas. He could see the doubt on his little girl's face as she decided what to do. After a few minutes, the little girl's shoulders slumped forward. She patted her mother's face with her small hand. Looking into her mother's eyes, Lizzy finally said, "If you want to, Momma, then I do too." Thomas slowly let out the breath he had been holding, as he was afraid this little girl would not give him the chance to show how much he loved her and her mother.

Roseanne rose from her chair and walked over to where the three of them were. She said to Lizzy, "Why don't you and I go to Willy's room and I'll read you a story."

Looking from Celine to Thomas, she started to say, "I don't think so," when her mother interrupted her and said, "Please, dear, go with Rosie, and in a little while, you can come back and get ready for bed. You can sleep next to me tonight, okay?"

With a doubtful look on her little face, she kissed her mother's cheek and said, "Okay." Looking Thomas straight in the eye, she said, "But I will be back right away."

After they left, Thomas turned back to Celine and said in a voice filled with emotion, "I'm so sorry we lost all these years, but I swear, if you and Lizzy come home with me, I will make it up to you every single day of our lives."

Reaching up and running her fingers down the side of his face, Celine asked, "What if I don't have that much time left?"

"Then we will make whatever time we do have count that much more, my darling. If it is only one day, it's more time than we had. I love you," he replied.

"I love you too. I never stopped loving you, even when I thought you didn't love me," she answered.

Standing outside the open doorway of Celine's room was Brad, listening to the conversation between the two inside. He stood alone in silence, twisting his hat in his hands. Turning away from the room, he put his hat back on his head and headed for the stairs. Just as he put his foot on the first step, the door to Willy's room opened, and ran Lizzy out. When she saw Brad, she skidded to a halt.

"Brad, Brad," she called to him, and as he turned toward her, she ran and jumped into his arms. Lizzy threw her arms around him and hugged him tightly around his neck.

"Whoa, little girl. You want us both to fall down this flight of stairs?" Brad asked her. Roseanne stood in the hallway watching them interact with a lump in her throat. Brad looked past Lizzy to Roseanne with such a sad look, it broke Roseanne's heart and made her feel guilty for sending the telegram, but she knew she had made the right choice when she saw the look in Celine's eyes when the girl looked at Thomas.

Lizzy said with excitement in her voice, "Guess where Momma and I are going?"

Before Brad could even answer her, she exclaimed, "We're going to a place called Loosyana, and maybe you could come with us."

Trying to keep his voice from cracking, Brad replied, "Well, that sounds tempting, baby girl. Maybe someday I could come visit you and your momma, but right now, I have to go make my rounds, and you," putting his finger on her small nose, "have to get ready for bed."

Celine and Thomas talked about the best way for them to travel back to Louisiana. Thomas had wanted to make arrangements to take the train, as he thought it would be faster and easier on Celine, but Celine wanted to travel by sea, saying the sea air would be better than breathing in the dust and soot from the train, even if the trip was shorter. In the end, Thomas gave in and booked passage on a ship going to New Orleans. They would leave the day after. All the girls came by to say their goodbyes to Celine and Lizzy, and they all had a good cry. Charlie came to see them as well, and in his gruff voice, he told them he would miss them both very much.

The day they were to board the ship, Doc came by to check on Celine and to give her a supply of pills containing ingredients that would help her breathe better. He said, "It will not cure you, but it may help to relieve the discomfort you feel in your chest. I hope it will help make the trip easier for you."

Doc told her to take care of herself and that it was a pleasure to know her. He blew his nose and swiped at his eyes.

On the day before they were to depart, she did not see Brad. She was told he had written to a ranch outside of town to check on some cattle that had been stolen. She had wanted to see him in person to explain her actions to him, to let him know she did love him but not in the same way she loved Thomas, and she thought it would not be fair for him if she stayed and married him. So she wrote it all in a long letter and asked Roseanne to see that he got it.

Emeline, Jesse, and their three children, along with Roseanne, all went to the dock to see them off. Celine hugged Emeline and asked her for the hundredth time if she and her family didn't want to come home too. Emeline, holding back the tears, told her no, her place was here in San Francisco, where she had made a good life with Jesse, her kids, and Rosie. Holding tight to Celine, Emeline whispered in her ear, "I love you, sister. You and I will meet again."

Stepping back away from Emeline, Celine whispered back to her, "Yes, we will, my dear sister."

Roseanne stepped up to Celine and gently took her in her arms, hugging her a long time. Softly crying, she said to Celine, "Thank you for bringing so much joy to my life, giving me the daughter and granddaughter I would never have had. I love you very much, and if you ever need anything, just let me know."

Celine replied, "You know I feel the same about you. You are the mother I lost. I love you too." Then, bending down, Roseanne hugged little Lizzy, telling her to watch over her mother and be good. Lizzy said she would, then reached up and kissed Roseanne on the cheek, gave her a big hug, stepped back, and took her mother's hand.

Finally, Roseanne went over to Thomas and said, "Take good care of my girls. Watch over them and treat them right." Taking Roseanne by surprise, Thomas took hold of her and gave her a big hug, saying, "Thank you so much for sending that telegram. I am forever indebted to you. I know I can never repay you for all you've done for Celine and Lizzy, but I will always be grateful." When it was time for them to board, Thomas picked up Celine and carried her up the gangplank, with Lizzy following them.

When the three reached the deck, they turned around to wave goodbye to the people below. Celine scanned the wharf below her for any sign of Brad. She had been sure he would come and say goodbye—if not to her, then to Lizzy. When she saw no sign of him, she felt a pang of pain in her heart. Brad had been so good to her and Lizzy, always there for them. She knew if she hadn't gotten sick, she would have married him. But now, it was time to lay the past to rest and start a new life.

Lizzy also was looking for Brad in the crowd of people. She just knew he would come, but when she didn't see him, she got angry at him. What neither of them knew was that the lone figure standing in the shadows of the tall stack of cotton bales the ship had unloaded earlier that morning was Brad. He had come early to find a place he couldn't be seen. He could not bear to say goodbye to Celine or Lizzy; he loved them both so much. As the ship pulled away from the dock, a lone tear slipped out of the corner of his eye and down his cheek, and he mouthed the word goodbye as he watched the two he loved sail out of his life.

The cabin they were assigned to was a fairly large room. It had a sitting room with a table and chairs along with a lounge for Celine to rest on when she felt like getting out of bed. There was one large bedroom and one small bedroom. Each one had a commode behind a screen and a wash basin for them to wash up when needed. All in all, Thomas thought the three of them would be comfortable while making the journey home.

Carrying Celine into their cabin, he said he would take the smaller room. She and Lizzy could share the larger room, and that way, it would not upset Lizzy seeing a stranger sharing her mother's bed, until they got home.

"No, Thomas, we will share a bed together. Even if we do not join our bodies together, I need you next to me, to hold me. Please," she implored him.

"All right, then it's settled. I will stay here with you if you're sure it's what you want," Thomas said.

"Yes, I'm sure," she responded.

Thomas laid Celine on the bed and told her to rest. He could see how all this excitement was beginning to affect her. She had dark circles under her beautiful eyes, and her breathing was becoming labored. It broke his heart to see her like this, a far cry from the girl that she once was, so full of life, with so much to live for. Shaking his head to stop this train of thought, he smiled at her and said, "Just rest, and I will go take care of everything." Helping Celine undress and putting on her nightgown, he laid her down on a few pillows and covered her up. As he kissed her forehead, she was so exhausted, she fell asleep immediately.

Thomas stood for a minute, watching her, fighting himself to keep from gathering her up in his arms to keep her safe. When he heard Lizzy calling to her mother, it brought him back to his present state of mind. Thomas turned and quietly left the room to attend to his daughter's needs. Entering the sitting room, he found Lizzy standing in the middle of the room. Her eyes were big and full of fright. She looked so little and so lost, his heart went out to her. Thomas said in a light tone of voice, "So, there you are—and here I thought I had lost you."

"Oh, no," Lizzy answered him, her eyes still big and filling with tears. "You can't lose me. I am right here."

"Good. Do you think you can help me with a few things?" Thomas asked.

Lizzy's eyes still looked big as she looked at Thomas and replied with pride in her little but strong voice, "Yes, my momma said I am a big help."

"Good," he said, taking her by her tiny hand. They went outside the cabin and up onto the deck, where he found the captain of the ship.

"Ah, Mr. Sanduval, what can I do for you?" the captain asked.

"We will be eating in the cabin the whole trip. As the young lady is not feeling well, if you could arrange for our meals to be brought to our cabin, we would be very grateful," answered Thomas.

"Yes, that can be arranged. Any other requests?" he asked Thomas.

"Yes, your ship's doctor, if he could come check on Miss Celine once a day, I would appreciate it."

"Of course. I will inform him at once," the captain assured Thomas.

Thomas led Lizzy over to the rail, picking her up so she could see better and he could keep a good hold of her. The two stood for a while, looking at the ocean. Lizzy got excited when the seagulls started flying overhead and marveled at how the ship sailed over the waves. Thomas watched as the wonder of it all passed over his daughter's small features. He felt a pang of sadness flow through him as he thought of all the time he didn't have with Celine and Lizzy, at all he had missed. He vowed he would make it up to them.

When they returned to the cabin, Thomas could hear the awful sound of Celine coughing from her room. He told Lizzy to go wash up, as it would soon be time for lunch to arrive and they would eat. As the little girl disappeared into the other room, Thomas hurried into Celine's room. She was sitting on the side of the bed, holding a handkerchief over her mouth. She coughed again, and Thomas was grieved at the pain that racked her small frame.

Thomas hurried to her side, kneeling down and looking into her eyes. His worst fears came to the surface, and he asked, "Celine, what can I do? Tell me what I can get for you to help ease your pain."

As she looked at him, she smiled a tiny smile and said in a whisper, "Just be with me, my love. It will help."

"I am here. I won't leave you. I promise."

She removed the handkerchief, and Thomas saw the red stain on the stark white material. Looking up at Celine with alarm on his face, Celine reached out and touched his cheek, saying, "The doctor just left, and everything is going to be all right."

Thomas knew she was being brave for his sake and hoped he could be just as brave for her. Celine knew she didn't have much time left when she agreed to return to Louisiana. Doc told her the night he examined her, she could have taken the train, as it would have been much quicker, but she wanted the extra time with Thomas and wanted him and Lizzy to get to know each other before Lizzy was surrounded by the rest of Thomas's family.

Thomas could see Celine was tired and told her she should stay in bed. Then he would get her up this evening and would carry her in to eat dinner with Lizzy and him, like a family—if she was up to it. He saw a little sparkle come into her eyes as she lay down and he covered her up. She said, "Thank you, Thomas. I would like that."

Thomas went into the other room, where he found his daughter waiting for him. He picked her up and asked if she would like to lay on the bed with her mother until their lunch arrived.

Lizzy put her hands on each side of his face, and with a smile that lit up the room, she shook her head yes so hard, the curls flew around both their faces. Very quietly, Thomas took the little girl into her mother and laid her on the bed next to Celine, with their backs to each other. He then whispered, "I'll come get you when our lunch gets here," and left the room.

After Thomas and Lizzy had eaten, she asked if they could go back on deck. Checking on Celine and seeing she was resting peacefully, he agreed, and they went topside to the deck. They walked around the ship, and Thomas told her stories about going all the way to England on a ship and had her laughing at the silly way he told the stories.

Halfway through their walk, they ran into the ship's doctor. The doctor introduced himself to Thomas and Lizzy.

"Hello," he said, "my name is George Adams," and he asked Thomas how Celine was feeling now.

Thomas said she seemed to be resting more comfortably after his visit. The doctor said he had given her a small amount of morphine to help with the pain in her chest. He wished there were more he could do for her, but unfortunately, there was no more to be done. He was surprised, he said, that she was able to make this trip at all. He breathing was very shallow, and her heartbeat was irregular.

The doctor went on to say Celine had told him that her doctor in San Francisco had given her medicine for her cough. If it helped, she should keep taking it. Thomas thanked him. The doctor said he would see her tomorrow, then turned and walked away. Lizzy, taking hold of Thomas's hand, asked him if the doctor was talking about her momma. Thomas, looking down at eyes that understood too much for a five-year-old, simply answered, "Yes, darling, he was."

With her head held high but her little chin quivering, she said, "I think I want to go back to my momma now."

Celine, Lizzy, and Thomas were all lying on the bed, talking about the seagulls Lizzy had seen that morning, when the steward brought their food for dinner. Lizzy jumped down off the bed to answer the knock on the cabin door. Opening the door, she pointed to the table and told him to set the food there, because her momma was going to eat dinner with her tonight. The young steward smiled at the excited little girl, set the food down, turned, and left the room, closing the door behind him.

As he hurried to set the three plates around the table, some of the food fell off of one plate. Lizzy quickly picked it up and put it back. Licking her fingers clean, she waited for her mother to come for dinner. Thomas carried Celine out to the table and sat her in the chair closest to her daughter, whose face was beaming with delight. Thomas sat on the other side of Celine in case she needed help. Celine asked Lizzy if she would like to say a prayer for this dinner.

"Can I?" replied Lizzy as she closed her eyes and folded her hands together.

Her mother answered, "Yes, dear, you may."

In her soft little voice, she said, "Thank you, Lord, for this food, and please let the doctor be wrong about Momma. Amen. Oh, yes. I'm sorry I dropped some food and gave Thomas the plate I put the food in. Amen." Looking at her mother for approval for the prayer, Celine, hiding a smile, nodded her approval, then looked over at Thomas to see his reaction. Looking at his plate, then at Celine, she saw the hidden laughter in his eyes as they began to eat. Thomas watched with anguish as Celine tried to eat her food, and when he went to help her, she waved him off.

With Lizzy watching them, Thomas went about eating but found he could not swallow his food very easily. He served Lizzy some bread with a big spoon of jam on it. When he looked over at Celine, he saw her smile at him and move her lips, saying, "Thank you." He could see Celine was beginning to tire and could not sit any longer. He told Lizzy he was going to take her mother back to her bed to rest some more and he would be right back to finish eating with her. With jam all over her face, Lizzy nodded her head okay.

After dinner, Thomas told Lizzy to go wash up in a few minutes and get ready for bed, as it had been a long day for all of them. She nodded her head yes. Thomas asked if she needed his help. "No, no," she answered him. "I can do it myself." Then, jumping off the chair, Lizzy ran into the room to wash herself. After a few minutes, Thomas went to the door and asked his daughter if everything was all right.

In a muffled voice, Lizzy said, "No, my head is stuck, and I can't get it out."

Becoming alarmed, Thomas pushed open the door and looked in. He found Lizzy standing in the middle of the room with her dress stuck around her head where she hadn't unbuttoned her dress. Keeping a straight face and his laughter under control, Thomas moved forward and undid the buttons, pulling the dress off.

"Whew, that was harder than I thought," Lizzy exclaimed, licking at the jam she still had around her mouth.

After Thomas got his daughter cleaned up and into her nightgown, he lifted her and carried her into her mother's room to say goodnight.

"Look, Momma, I helped Thomas get me ready for bed," she said proudly.

"So I see," Celine said with a weak smile.

"Can you read me a story, Momma?" Lizzy asked her mother.

"Not tonight, dear," she said. Seeing the disappointment on her little face, Celine quickly added, "but if you get your book and ask nicely, I bet Thomas would read to you."

"Oh, would you, Thomas?" she said while trying to get down to go get her book.

Running back into Thomas with a book and looking up at him with a pleading look in her eyes, he laughed and said, "With a look like that, how can I refuse?" Pulling a chair close to the bed, he picked Lizzy up and sat her on the edge of the bed near her mother. Taking the book, he began to read, making funny faces and changing his voice to match the characters in the book. Both his girls had smiles on their faces. Soon, Lizzy began to yawn, so Thomas finished the book. He reached over and picked Lizzy up, threw her up into the air, and caught her firmly in her arms, making her squeal with delight.

"All right, little princess. It's time for bed. Give your momma a kiss on her cheek goodnight."

Thomas got up and carried Lizzy to her bed. Laying her down, he covered her up, placed a kiss on her forehead, and turned to leave when he heard his daughter softly say, "Thank you, Daddy." As he looked down at this beautiful little girl who was his, his eyes filled with tears.

Leaving the room and closing the door, Thomas swiped at his eyes, getting himself under control. He returned to Celine's room. Celine had seen Lizzy laughing at Thomas and his silly antics and was finally able to relax as she recognized her daughter's slow acceptance of Thomas as her father.

Blowing out the lantern on the wall next to the bed, Thomas undressed in the dark. Trying not to disturb Celine, he crawled into bed beside her. He felt her hand reach over and touch him, sending a quiver through his whole body. Celine softly said, "I'm sorry. It's just, I had to touch you to make sure I wasn't dreaming again, that you are really here with me." Thomas rolled over and gathered her in his arms. Her back to his chest, he held her close to him, savoring her warmth and closeness. He held her firmly but not too tightly, afraid to let her go, afraid for her.

"Thank you for coming for us and bringing us home," Celine said.

With a lump in his throat, Thomas replied, "I thank Roseanne for sending that telegram and sending for me. I would have always thought you and Lizzy were lost to me."

She placed her finger on his lips to quiet him, then said in a pleading tone, "Thomas, I only ask one favor of you."

"Anything, anything at all that I can do, I will," he answered her.

"Please, before it's too late, please, marry me. I want our daughter to be able to walk around with her head held high and not be called a bastard because she is illegitimate."

Thomas was taken aback some. He thought of Jenny and Jeremy and thought of the hurt look that would be on Jenny's face. He loved Celine—he always had—but he also had fallen deeply in love with Jenny, albeit in a different way. It grew out of friendship, of knowing each other for years and finally giving in to a deep love. But without further thought, Thomas answered, "Yes, of course I will marry you and make our daughter a true Sanduval."

"Thank you. Thank you so much, Thomas. You don't know what that means to me," Celine said.

They talked for a while longer, and with the weight of her daughter's future off her mind, the two fell asleep, with Celine sleeping more peacefully in Thomas's arms than she had in some time.

The next morning after breakfast, the doctor came to check on Celine. He found her cough was getting worse and her breathing was getting shallower. He asked if her chest hurt, and she replied that it did somewhat more than it had before. He then asked her if she was coughing up blood. She reached into her pocket, took out her handkerchief, and showed him the dark bloodstain on it. Looking into the doctor's eyes, Celine knew her time was limited.

"Please don't speak of this to anyone," she asked him. "Tonight I am going to be married by the captain, and I would like you to be a witness at my wedding."

"I would be honored to witness your wedding. I look forward to tonight."

The doctor picked up his medical bag, nodded his head at

Celine, and left the room. On his way out of the cabin, the doctor found Thomas and Lizzy. He motioned that he would like to talk to him alone. Looking over at his little girl, Thomas said, "I think you can visit your mother now if you like." Without replying, Lizzy jumped up and ran into her mother's room, leaving the two men smiling after her.

With Lizzy out of hearing range, the doctor told Thomas the prognosis for Celine. He said she should take it easy and not get overly excited or stressed. Nodding his head that he understood, Thomas could not bring himself to say anything. Reaching for the door, the doctor turned and said, "Congratulations on tonight. I'll see you there." Thanking the doctor, Thomas went to where his two girls were.

That evening, Thomas helped Celine get dressed in her finest gown and brushed her hair until it shined. Because it was a little chilly out, Thomas had her wear a warm cape to ward off the night air. Thomas put on his good suit and helped Lizzy put on her favorite dress, telling her she would be her momma's best maid of honor. Lizzy was so excited, she squealed in delight and hugged Thomas around his legs, even though she didn't know what a maid of honor was.

When it was time, Thomas carried Celine up to the deck, where the captain had arranged a nice place out of the wind to perform the ceremony. Thomas sat Celine on a chair that had been placed there for her, but she insisted on standing up for the ceremony. When everyone was present, the captain read the marriage vows from his book and then nodded to Celine, who had asked to say something.

Celine began in a soft but determined voice, "My darling Thomas, I know we were separated for five long years, but now we are back together once again. For how long, I don't know, but for however long it is, I am forever grateful. I never stopped loving you and will love you for all eternity."

When the captain saw that she was finished, he looked over at Thomas and nodded his head. Thomas, speaking in a clear voice and looking directly into Celine's eyes, said, "My darling Celine, finding you again is like time standing still. My love for you never changed. You are my soulmate, and I am yours and always will be, until the end of time."

The captain said, "I now pronounce you man and wife. You may now kiss your bride." As he did so, the other passengers clapped and cheered them on. Holding Celine close to him, he could feel her tremble as her legs grew weak. Picking her up, he started for the cabin, but Celine said, "No. Please, Thomas, let's stay here for a while and enjoy the festivities and celebrate our marriage."

Agreeing, Thomas sat down still holding Celine in his arms. He placed her on his lap and covered her in a blanket the doctor handed him.

A few passengers, along with the captain, his steward, and the doctor, all came by, slapping Thomas on his back and congratulating him and Celine. Lizzy stood by her mother with a big smile on her face, and when the ship's cook came over with a big cake, her eyes got big, and she started to lick her lips, making her mother laugh. Watching Celine and his daughter made his heart swell with joy and sorrow.

After a while, everybody started to leave. The doctor and his wife came over to once again congratulate the couple. The doctor, seeing how tired Celine looked, bent down and whispered in Thomas's ear not to let Celine overexert herself. Then he and his wife left. Thomas stood up and started to go below. Celine protested, but Thomas told her that Lizzy was starting to nod off and needed to be put to bed. Celine conceded, and the three of them went below.

Once he got below and into their cabin, Thomas told Lizzy to go to her room and he would be in to tuck her into bed, kissing her mother goodnight. Celine held on to her daughter and whispered in her ear, "I love you. Never forget that."

Lizzy, yawning, said, "I love you too, Momma," and went to her room. Thomas carried Celine to her room and placed her on the bed. He undressed her, put on her nightgown, and laid her down, covering her up and kissing her on her forehead. He went back to Lizzy's room to tuck her in.

Lizzy had managed to undress herself, put on her nightgown, and crawl into bed and was almost asleep when Thomas got back. He bent down and kissed his daughter's forehead and told her she had done real good tonight. With a smile, she whispered, "Thank you. Goodnight, Daddy," and closed her eyes. Thomas stood up, looking down at his little girl. He watched her drift off to sleep. He thought how every day, she was beginning to look more and more like her mother and that he was the luckiest man alive.

Thomas went back to his and Celine's room and silently lay on the bed, so as not to wake Celine, but she was not asleep. They talked for a while, and Thomas told Celine the captain had said they would be docking in Baton Rouge the day after tomorrow.

"That will be good," she said. Then Celine asked Thomas to wrap her in a blanket and take her backup on deck. She said she felt like she needed some fresh air. Thomas got up, put on his jacket, and picked up a warm, thick quilt. He wrapped her in it and carried her up on deck.

On deck, Thomas found a place out of the wind, next to a chair. He sat down, holding Celine on his lap, close to him for warmth. It was dark. Only the light from the moon shone on the two people. They could hear the waves lapping against the side of the ship as it slowly glided across the water. When Celine looked up, she saw what looked like millions of diamonds shining down on them.

Thomas spoke very softly, saying, "I'm so sorry. I know this is not how we planned our wedding day—"

"Shhh," Celine interrupted him, placing her fingers on his lips. "It was a beautiful ceremony, Thomas. I am very happy right now and hope you are too?"

"Yes, I couldn't be happier, my love," he replied, but he thought to himself, *If only you were well.* They sat like that for a long time, content to be with each other. Thomas felt Celine quiver and asked if she was cold. Very softly, she answered him, "No." Thomas could hear Celine's every breath, labored at first, then very calm.

Two days later, the ship was docking at Baton Rouge. Thomas had sent a telegram to Marta and Jacob when they left San Francisco, telling them to meet him at the dock in Baton Rouge on this day and to bring the buckboard wagon to transport them and their luggage home. Marta and Jacob were there waiting for Thomas and his family when the ship docked. Waiting below, they could see Thomas standing on the deck by the railing with a little girl by his side.

When the gangplank was lowered, Thomas, holding tight to Lizzy's hand, walked slowly down toward a smiling Marta. Marta could tell even from where she was standing that the little girl was his and Celine's, as she looked just like her mother. As she looked at the little face, a pang of regret crossed over Marta's face, and a tear slipped down her cheek. Jacob squeezed her arm and gave her a reassuring look. When they reached the bottom of the gangplank, Marta ran over and gave Thomas a hug. He introduced Lizzy to her grandmother, who in turn bent down and gave the shy little girl, who was holding onto her father's leg, a hug.

Looking up into his face, she asked Thomas, "Where is Celine?"

With a sadness in his voice, he answered, "They're bringing her down now."

Looking up, Marta saw the four men coming down the gangplank carrying the pine box. Marta almost collapsed, and Jacob caught her to keep her from falling to the ground. Without speaking, the four people sat on the two seats up front, with the luggage and pine box riding in the back of the buckboard.

Marta sat next to Lizzy in the back while Thomas sat next to Jacob, who was tending the horses. When they got to the inn, Thomas had Jacob stop. He went inside to see Celine's uncle, explaining as much as he could in a short time. He told her uncle about Celine's illness and how she had passed away on the trip here. Thomas said they would bury Celine at his plantation, and this time, it would be for real.

Thomas then took the uncle outside and introduced him to his grandniece. Wiping his eyes on his sleeve, her uncle gave the little girl a soft hug, told her he was pleased to meet her, and said he would see her in a few days. He then went to the back of the wagon, placed his hand on the pine box, and made the sign of the cross, saying, "Welcome home, little girl." With his shoulders slumped, he turned and went back inside. Continuing on, they rode past Celine's burned-down cabin. No one but Lizzy looked at it, and no one mentioned it aloud.

The day of Celine's funeral was dreary. Thomas had sent word to Jenny and her family that Celine would be buried here at the family cemetery. Thomas didn't expect Jenny to come, but she did, along with Jason, his family, and Mr. and Mrs. Pierce. When he saw Jenny, Jeremy, and the rest of the family pull up, he was anxious at seeing them and wondered how they would react to all this.

Thomas knew he had to talk to Jenny, to explain everything to her, and he hoped she would understand he did what he had to do. Jason helped his wife, his mother, and Jenny down from their carriage. All the women went into the house. Jason and his father went over to give Thomas their condolences, and after Mr. Pierce went into the house, Thomas and Jason walked to the barn. On the way, Thomas explained what had happened when he had arrived in San Francisco. After he finished telling Jason, Thomas turned and looked him in the eye.

"Do you think Jenny will understand?" he asked.

Jason said, "I don't know, Tommy. All I can say is tell her the truth and trust her. She loves you. Just tell her and go from there."

"You're right, of course, as usual. I'll tell her and hope for the best," Thomas replied.

After the services, when everyone went their own way, Thomas took Lizzy and went over to talk to Jenny. When he got close to her, he caught his breath. She was so beautiful, and when she looked up at him, her eyes were so blue and so full of love for him, he stared at her in wonder.

He didn't remember her looking as radiant and glowing as she did today. Lizzy, getting impatient, started pulling on Thomas's hand, wanting to go play with Eli's children and with Jeremy. Thomas pulled his eyes away from Jenny and said, "Jenny, I would like you to meet my daughter, Elizabeth. Lizzy, this is Jenny."

Jenny smiled down at Lizzy and said, "Yes, I know. Lizzy and I have already met."

"Oh, I see, and did you get to know each other a little?" Thomas asked, looking from one to the other with a hopeful look on his face. Jenny smiled an even bigger smile and decided to let him off the hook regarding their meeting.

"Yes, we did. We got along very well," she said. "So did Lizzy and Jeremy."

"I see," Thomas said. "Lizzy, why don't you run and play with the other children so Jenny and I can talk."

Even before he finished his sentence, Lizzy turned and hugged his leg, let go, and ran off toward the others. Jenny said, "She's a beautiful little girl, Thomas, and I'm glad you have brought her home."

Thomas said, "Thank you."

Thomas took hold of Jenny's arm and asked if they could go for a walk, as he wanted to tell her what had taken place between himself and Celine and why. Jenny nodded her head. They walked in silence for a while. Then Thomas told Jenny everything he had told Jason. After he was finished, he stopped and turned Jenny around to face him. Looking into Thomas's eyes and studying him for a few minutes, Jenny knew he loved her. She saw it written all over his face.

Finally breaking the silence between them, Jenny said, "I am so sorry, Tommy. I know what it's like to lose someone you care for. I can only say for the sake of your daughter that under the circumstances, you did the right thing." Then she said, "You know I love you. How could you even doubt I wouldn't understand?"

Thomas, overcome with emotions from the last few weeks, gently took Jenny in his arms and just held her. Then he softly whispered in her ear, "I love you so much, it makes it hard for me to breathe when I'm around you." Looking into her eyes, he added, "Let's set a date to be married as soon as we can."

"I was hoping you would say that," Jenny replied.

Placing his hands on Jenny's waist to pull her closer to him, Thomas was taken aback as he felt the small bulge on Jenny's stomach. In a questioning tone, he asked, "When, Jenny?"

"The night you showed me the house you had built, in the backyard, under the stars," she answered. He thought back to that night. The moon was so bright, and all those stars were shining down on them.

"Jenny, why didn't you tell me?" he asked.

"Because I wanted to be sure I was pregnant, and when I was sure, I was going to tell you, but then all this came up, and I didn't want the pregnancy to influence your decision to go to Celine. There was no need to tell you until now."

Thomas bent down and gently kissed her. Then, to her surprise, he picked her up and swung her around. Jenny laughed with delight and hugged him tightly around his neck.

A month later, they were married, with just the family in attendance. Thomas had Marta, Eli, and Eli's family move into the big house with Jacob, as Jacob had asked Marta to marry him and she had accepted after telling him, "It's about time you asked me, you old fool."

Thomas, along with his new family, moved into the house he built.

Sitting on the front porch, watching the sunset, he looked out over the hill where the family cemetery was. Thomas could just make out all the flowers he and Lizzy had planted there together. The flowers were all in bloom, in an array of beautiful colors. He thought of Celine and of the promise he made to her—to always take care of and see that Lizzy would always be happy. He looked out into the front yard to where Lizzy, Jeremy, and Eli's children were running around laughing while chasing after fireflies as it got dark.

Yes, Thomas thought, he had fulfilled the promise he had made, and Celine would be happy and could now rest in peace.

About the Author

Patty Dinelli raises cattle with her husband, Reno. She has four grown children, nine grandchildren, and five beautiful great-grandchildren, and lives in a small town along the California coast where she enjoys sewing, reading, and writing. *A Promise Fulfilled* is her debut novel.

CPSIA information can be obtained
at www.ICGtesting.com
Printed in the USA
LVHW040825160621
690355LV00002B/54